resonance

Also by Erica O'Rourke

Dissonance series

Dissonance

Torn trilogy

Torn

Tangled

Bound

A Dissonance
novel

resonance

Erica O'Rourke

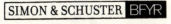
SIMON & SCHUSTER BFYR

NEW YORK • LONDON • TORONTO • SYDNEY • NEW DELHI

SIMON & SCHUSTER BFYR

An imprint of Simon & Schuster Children's Publishing Division
1230 Avenue of the Americas, New York, New York 10020

For information about special discounts for bulk purchases, please contact Simon & Schuster Special Sales at 1-866-506-1949 or business@simonandschuster.com.
The Simon & Schuster Speakers Bureau can bring authors to your live event. For more information or to book an event, contact the Simon & Schuster Speakers Bureau at 1-866-248-3049 or visit our website at www.simonspeakers.com.
Jacket design by Lizzy Bromley
Interior design by Hilary Zarycky
The text for this book is set in Granjon.
Manufactured in the United States of America
2 4 6 8 10 9 7 5 3 1
Library of Congress Cataloging-in-Publication Data
O'Rourke, Erica.
Resonance / Erica O'Rourke. — First edition.
pages cm. — (Dissonance ; [2])
Summary: "The Free Walkers make Del the ultimate promise: if Del joins their fight, she will be reunited with Simon. The fate of the multiverse depends on her choice"— Provided by publisher.
ISBN 978-1-4424-6027-0 (hardcover) — ISBN 978-1-4424-6029-4 (eBook)
[1. Choice—Fiction. 2. Love—Fiction. 3. Science fiction.] I. Title.
PZ7.O649Re 2015
[Fic]—dc23
2014038589

FIRST EDITION

To Danny: best and truest in all the world.
And to my girls: every day an adventure, every day a gift.

ACKNOWLEDGMENTS

First of all, a huge thank-you to the readers, bloggers, librarians, and booksellers who have supported Del's story. Bookish people are my people, and your kindness and enthusiasm means the world. Thanks for taking this journey with me.

Joanna Volpe has been in my corner from the very beginning. She has grit, heart, imagination, and intelligence in vast quantities, and I am so thankful to be working with her. I'm equally grateful to Kathleen Ortiz, Danielle Barthel, Jaida Temperly, and the rest of the team at New Leaf Literary for making this book, and my life, infinitely better.

Zareen Jaffery's brilliant insights ranged from physics to family dynamics, and she made the process of writing this book a genuine pleasure. I am so thankful for the opportunity to work with her. Thanks as well to the rest of the S&S family, who have made me feel so welcome and taken such good care of this book, especially Justin Chanda, Mekisha Telfer, Jenica Nasworthy, Brian Luster, Siena Koncsol, Lizzy Bromley, and Kristin Ostby, secret origami artist.

Writer friends are essential for brainstorming, procrastination, and whip-cracking depending on the situation, and I have the best of the bunch: the women of Chicago-North RWA, particularly Erin Brambilla, Ryann Murphy, and Melanie Bruce. I'm also grateful to farther-flung friends: Dana Kaye, Susan Dennard, Erin Bowman, Sarah J. Maas, Veronica Roth, Lori Lee, Leigh Bardugo, and Stacey Kade, for their kindness, support, and general shenanigans.

Pamala Knight and Thomas Purnell handled inane research questions with speed and good humor. Paula Forman, Judy Bergman, Lisa

Tonkery, Lisa McKernan, and Lexie Craig dragged me out of my office and back into the real world. I thank you, and so does my family.

This book wouldn't exist without my Portland Midwest compatriots, Clara Kensie and Melonie Johnson—and especially Lynne Hartzer, who solves plot problems and supplies popcorn, often at the same time.

Hanna Martine and Loretta Nyhan are dear, wise, wonderful women, generous with their time and talent and compassion. It's a privilege to call you my friends.

Eliza Evans, best friend and partner in crime: I'm grateful every single day that I made that phone call. (You know the one.) Thank you for always knowing the perfect thing to say or do.

A thousand thanks to my sister, for cheering me on—and for explaining the mechanics of IV insertion eleventy billion times. And *two* thousand thanks to my parents, for believing in me and for always making room in the budget for books.

Being a writer has always been a dream of mine—but being the mom of three brave, smart, funny, talented, amazing girls is a far greater dream, and one I get to live every day. Thank you, my sweethearts, for being you.

And most of all, thank you to Danny—for his patience, his encouragement, his kindness, his humor, and his heart. For everything, forever. I love you.

Entropy's a bitch.

Fate is cruel, luck is fickle, love is strange. Entropy is all those and more. Pitiless and brutal and jagged as the rocks that break the tide.

You can clutch to your chest all the things you love most, and entropy will scatter them with a breath. It will leave you cold and alone in the middle of chaos, the eye of your own personal hurricane.

I was born to fight entropy.

I lost.

I am not done fighting.

—Journal of Delancey Sullivan

resonance

BEGIN
FIRST
MOVEMENT

CHAPTER ONE

Days until Tacet: 25

WHEN I WAS LITTLE, MY GRANDFATHER TOLD me nothing was impossible. Given enough time and the right choices, anything could happen. I believed him.

Then I grew up. I stopped believing.

Turns out, he was right.

Walking between worlds turns you invisible. Echoes don't notice you until you touch one of them, so people are forever looking past you. You're a vague impression, more sensed than seen, a flicker in their peripheral vision.

Invisibility suited me fine. Coming here was a risk; I wasn't allowed to Walk unaccompanied, and there was always a chance an Original would spot me crossing. But some things you need to see—or hear—to believe.

I hovered like a ghost at the edge of the crowded hallway. But when Simon Lane came around the corner, dark hair falling into blue eyes, jaw square and stubborn, smile full of trouble . . .

I knew I was the one being haunted.

Pain roared through me, hungry as a wildfire. Not my Simon, though the pitch of this world was sharp and familiar. An Echo of him, and one I knew well: the shape of his hands fitted with mine; the feel of his mouth against my throat; the lazy, prowling movements that made my knees go weak. Doughnut Simon—as vibrant and magnetic as his Original—should no longer exist.

The sound of him reached me clearly, despite the distance and bodies between us. The same frequency as the rest of the Echo, but stronger, as if his volume was turned up to eleven when everyone else was a ten.

He should have been silent. A terminal Echo, one whose Original had died. A little more than a week ago, his Original had trapped himself in a world unraveling to nothingness to save me and the rest of the multiverse. His death in the cleaving should have unraveled his Echoes, robbing them of their frequency and their lives.

This Simon should have been silent, but his pitch was true as ever.

The only explanation was that *my* Simon had survived the cleaving. He'd escaped, somehow, into the vastness of the multiverse.

Impossible.

Hope beat in my chest, the faintest of wings. I tried to smother it, but hope feeds on the impossible as surely as grief feeds on memory.

Simon's voice reached me first, a baritone resonating warmly through my bones.

One touch.

One touch, to be certain, and I would leave. He might not remember me. Echoes didn't, usually. A few minutes, or hours, or days after a Walker left a world, her impression faded from the minds of Echoes like a mirage in the desert. This Simon might forget we'd ever met. I didn't know if the thought relieved me or broke me anew.

He swaggered through the hallway, surrounded by friends, all of them in similar layers of leather and flannel and denim, Simon in the center like a sun amid planets. I readied myself, muscles tense and ears attuned. Time slowed as he drew even with me, and my feet moved of their own accord.

He turned, laughing offhandedly at some inane comment, and caught sight of me.

His eyes met mine.

He stopped laughing.

I froze. He'd seen me. He *remembered* me. Before I could react, he broke away from his friends and grabbed me. The shock of his frequency made me go limp with relief.

My Simon was alive.

This Simon, though, was pissed.

"Del," he growled, waving his friends along and yanking me to the side of the hall. "Where the hell have you been?"

"I'm not supposed to be here," I said. His hand was like iron around my arm. "You're hurting me."

He let go and I breathed him in, leather and rain.

"What do you want?" His palms slammed against the wall

on either side of me, boxing me in. "Why are you here?"

"I needed to know if you were okay." I tore my gaze away from the silver railroad spike flashing at his wrist.

"I'm fucking awesome." The bitterness in his laugh made me flinch. "Until now. What do you *want*?"

I curled my fingers into fists, fighting the urge to reach for him. This close, he looked the same, right down to the scar at the corner of his mouth. He wasn't mine, but he was proof the real Simon was waiting for me, somewhere in the multiverse.

He reached for his wallet and pulled out the origami star I'd given him the night we first kissed. The Key World's frequency drifted from the dark green paper, strengthening as I took it from him. "You said you weren't coming back."

I'd broken off our relationship—which wasn't really a relationship at all, just a series of brain-melting hookups—to be with my Simon. But like every other time I'd messed around with the multiverse, my plan went sideways. The Original Simon had seen the breakup. He'd seen *everything*. Half-Walker himself, he saw through his Echoes' eyes any time they interacted with a Walker. All the times I'd kissed this Simon, the real one had experienced it as a dream; when he found out, I'd nearly lost him.

Now, maybe I could use it to find him.

"Simon." I laced my fingers with his, star pressed between our palms. "I need you to wait for me."

"I'm done waiting," he snapped.

I ignored the words and focused on his eyes, a darkly gleaming blue. "Hang on a little bit longer. Wherever you are, whatever you're doing, keep doing it."

"I'm right here," he said, confusion softening his expression.

"Listen to me. *I will find you.* I'll figure it out, but you need to leave me some breadcrumbs."

Tears gathered on my lashes, and he used his free hand to sweep them away. "Del . . ."

"I'm coming, I swear. I will find you, and we'll fix this, and we'll be good."

"You're crazy," he said, but his fingers stayed twined with mine.

Was I? We'd done so much damage to the multiverse, his signal disrupting world after world . . . could my message get through?

I held his gaze, searching for some flicker of understanding, some sign he'd heard me. Nothing. I'd just have to believe.

We both would.

He slid his hand along my neck, drew me closer until our foreheads touched. "Tell me how to help."

"Listen," I said, dizzy from his nearness. "I'm not kissing him. I'm kissing *you*."

I touched my lips to Echo Simon's for the briefest moment—a promise more than a kiss, and my heart began to crack, a million tiny fault lines threatening to break wide open. And then, because I couldn't bear to say good-bye, I ran.

Losing Simon had turned the music of the multiverse muted and flat. As I raced up the stairs, reality came rushing back. I'd

Walked the Echoes since I was a kid, and no matter how change-able the ground under my feet, I'd always found a way forward. Now I had a destination: Simon, wherever he might be.

I skidded to a halt outside the library and slipped inside, heading for the stacks. Tucked amid the biographies stood the pivot I'd arrived through. The air shivered and hummed where the skin of the world had split. I reached for the rift, felt it widen as my fingers hooked along the edge.

The library doors banged open. "Del!" Simon shouted, only to be shushed by the librarian. Through a gap in the shelves I caught a glimpse of him, raking his hands through his hair in frustration. His gaze swept the room.

Time to go.

I lunged for the Key World's frequency, and the pivot closed around me, the familiar sensation of too-weighty air pressing against my skin and filling my lungs.

An instant later I was home—same library, different books, and no Simon. For the first time in weeks, his absence didn't fill me with despair.

I'd find him soon enough.

CHAPTER TWO

THE TRANSFORMATION FROM ANONYMOUS TO notorious is a surprisingly quick process.

Before I'd starting dating Simon, no one in my school cared who I was or what I did. I was marking time while my teachers marked me tardy, and the rest of the student body didn't mark me at all.

These days, everyone knew who I was and what I'd done: the last girl to kiss Simon Lane, the one who'd driven him out of town.

They were right about the kissing, anyway.

The truth of Simon's disappearance was as far beyond them as he was from me, so I let them believe the whole story and kept the truth buried alongside my grief.

Truth and grief and love, three cold, furious stars that set my course and sent me searching.

The problem was, I wasn't the only one.

I kept my eyes down on the way to the music wing. Reminders of Simon lingered in every corner. Phantom voices, memories clinging like cobwebs, glimpses of people who had his height but not his heart, his long legs but not his laugh. No matter how hard I looked, he wasn't here.

My footsteps reverberated down the curving hallway. As I reached for the doorknob of the music classroom, someone shoved me from behind. I went sprawling on the tile, banging my knee and slamming my elbow. My whole arm sang from the impact, my fingers going numb.

"Watch it!" I scrambled up, cradling my arm, and whirled to see who'd pushed me.

Bree Carlson. Of course. Silky hair and wide eyes and a honeyed voice hiding a poison tongue. Confident she was Broadway-bound and talented enough to make it happen. Simon's ex.

One of many exes, to be honest, but the only one who'd tried to win him back. She took a step forward, deliberately crowding me.

"What is your problem?" I snapped.

"You are," she said, her voice higher-pitched than usual. "Where's Simon?"

"He moved."

"He didn't move," she snarled. "It's been more than a week, and nobody's heard a word from him. He won't answer any texts. He left his dog. He left his car. He left in the middle of the season without a word to his coach or his team. He would never do that. I *know* him."

"Simon knows a lot of girls." I shook my head with mock pity. "All of them just as well as he knows you."

But they didn't know him. Not the way I had.

"The two of you disappear, and now you're waltzing around

10

like nothing's changed. Nobody would have missed you," she added, lip curling. "But his whole life is here. Why are you back instead of him? What did you do?"

I left him. She was right—everything Simon loved was here, and he'd given it up, and I'd let him. The guilt dragged at me more every day. I slung my bag over my shoulder and reached for the doorknob, the ever-present ache in my chest climbing into my throat.

She shoved me again, but this time I was braced for it. I swung my backpack at her shoulder, feeling it connect with a thump.

Bree shrieked and clawed, snagging a fistful of hair. Her nail raked my cheek and I swore. It felt good to fight, to finally give action to my anger. I rammed an elbow into her stomach. Hit her with my bag again. Shoved until her spine hit the cement-block wall, and shoved again for good measure.

Walkers rarely need to fight, but younger sisters do, and Bree had nothing on Addie. She blinked back tears and panted, but went still.

"Get this straight. I didn't do anything to Simon." I stepped away. "And if you touch me again, you'll need another nose job."

She shook back her hair, voice wavering. "Where is he?"

"I don't know." Admitting it hurt worse than the scratches she'd left.

"Del! Bree!" Ms. Powell, the music teacher, strode toward us. Her normally cheerful face was creased with concern. "What's going on here?"

"She attacked me!" Bree said. "I was just standing here and she went crazy. She's unstable." She raised a trembling hand, letting a few tears fall before wiping them away. Despite having a good five inches on me, she managed to make herself look small and vulnerable.

Bree played all sorts of roles in school productions. The helpless victim was another act, and any other teacher would have bought it.

Lucky for me, Ms. Powell wasn't like the other teachers. She was a Free Walker—a rebel working to undermine the Consort, our leaders. Yesterday she'd told me Simon was alive, and my Walk had proved it. Now I needed answers, and she had them.

Her expression gave nothing away. She inserted herself between us. "Do you have any witnesses?"

Bree shook her head. "But—"

Ms. Powell cut her off. "The minimum suspension for fighting is five days, I believe. For both parties." She paused to let that sink in. "Aren't auditions for the spring musical this week?"

Bree's nostrils flared. She leaned around Ms. Powell, saying, "Everyone knows it's your fault, you violent little freak."

"That's enough," Ms. Powell said. "Bree, I'll see you in class. Use the rest of the lunch period to cool off."

Bree turned on her heel and stomped away.

Ms. Powell unlocked her door, waving me in. "After you."

Once I was inside, face-to-face with the only person who had answers, my questions wouldn't come. I sat at the battered upright piano, resting my fingers on the cool ivory keys, not playing a note.

Ms. Powell's classroom was lined with shelves of instruments and cabinets full of sheet music. The piano was tucked into the far corner, angled so she could keep an eye on the class; a door in the opposite corner led to her office. Untidy rows of desks filled the center of the room, a lectern was at the front, and she leaned against it, watching me expectantly.

"Bree started it," I said.

"She got you pretty good." She gestured at my stinging cheek. "You wanted to talk?"

I swallowed, unable to find the right words. Finally I blurted, "Powell Station is in Seattle."

Traditionally, Walkers were named after big pivots in their hometowns. But it was always their first name, never their last. I hadn't thought twice about Ms. Powell the orchestra teacher. Like an Original, I'd seen what I expected, not what was real—and Ms. Powell the Free Walker had used my weakness against me.

"Seemed fitting," she said, giving her baton an experimental flick. "A Powell at Washington High."

"It's not your real name?"

"Real enough." She raised her eyebrows, a mild reproof. "I'm assuming you have more important questions than my name."

I gripped the edge of the piano bench to keep from shaking. "I saw him. One of Simon's Echoes."

The corner of her mouth twitched. "Doughnut Simon. Cute."

"You were right. He's not terminal."

She inclined her head. "And?"

"How is that possible? The Consort confirmed the cleaving. Did he outrun it?"

It takes time for a world to unmake itself. When a Walker cleaves a branch, cutting the threads connecting it to the rest of the multiverse, the destruction isn't immediate. A major, complex world could take days to fully disintegrate. I'd told Simon to run, hoping I could find a way to return and save him, but it had been a wild, foolish hope, like trying to stop a tornado with your bare hands.

Ms. Powell shifted. "Not exactly. The important thing is that he's safe."

Joy rushed in, heady and bright, and I leaped up. "Can I see him? Can we go right now?"

"It's not that simple. We need a little time."

I thumped down again, my happiness snuffed. "We? The Free Walkers, you mean. You're the ones who got him out? How did you do it?"

"Carefully." Before I could press for specifics, she held up her hand. "That's all I can tell you for now. You're going to have to trust me."

"Trust you? You haven't even told me your real name. You've been watching me all year and you never said a word." I paused. "Mr. Samson didn't want to retire, did he? You bribed him, or threatened him, or something."

"Hardly. He retired and we took advantage of the situation." Ms. Powell brushed at her cloud of wiry blond hair, impatient. "I wasn't sent here to watch you."

I snorted, and she peered at me through her cat-eye glasses. The lenses were Coke-bottle thick, but now I wondered if she even needed them. If anything about her was what it appeared. She'd shown up at the beginning of the school year and fit in perfectly.

Too perfectly.

Only a Walker would be able to blend in the way she did. We were experts at hiding in plain sight.

"My assignment was to monitor Simon. You were . . . a happy coincidence. A bonus."

I blinked. Simon? I was the one who could Walk. Simon couldn't even hear pivots. The Walkers didn't know he existed—his father had made sure of it.

Maybe his father was the key.

"Because his dad was a Free Walker?" Was. Dead for seventeen years, captured by the Consort and executed for treason. Until a month ago, Simon had no idea.

"Gilman Bradley was a good man in an impossible situation, much like his son is now. He was captured as part of a broader attack against the Free Walkers. It's taken us years to recover. It was imperative we not engage with Simon, for his own protection, but we've needed to watch him more closely as he's aged."

"You knew about his signal flaw?"

Everything in the Key World—people, objects, oceans—resonated at the same perfectly stable frequency. As a Half Walker, Simon's signal was unusually loud, so he created more Echoes than most people. For reasons we couldn't understand, his signal carried a flaw that was amplified and transmitted through the multiverse, affecting any world containing one of his Echoes, growing increasingly unstable over time. It's why he'd cleaved himself—to silence the damaged signal and stabilize the worlds.

And the Free Walkers had known about it. We'd thought Monty was our only option; the only person we could trust, and it had backfired horribly. The familiar anger swelled and found a fresh target.

"Why didn't you help him? Why didn't you say something?"

"We didn't realize the flaw would become such a problem; once we did, we weren't sure we could trust you. This conversation alone is a huge risk."

The feeling was mutual. If the Consort knew I was talking to a Free Walker, they'd throw us both in an oubliette. But desperation trumps caution, especially when your hand is lousy to begin with. "You let me think he was dead!"

"Yesterday was the first time you've shown up for school since the cleaving," she said. "Besides, we weren't going to endanger our network and our most valuable asset before we were certain you wouldn't reveal us to the Consort."

"He's not an asset," I said, shoving away from the piano. "He's a human being. And we both know the Consort would kill Simon the minute they laid hands on him. I'm not about to go running to Lattimer."

"Glad to hear it," she replied.

I folded my arms and studied her. She was too calm. She'd

known exactly what I would do when she dropped her bomb-shell, and she'd prepared for my reaction.

But she was right—telling me was a risk, which meant she was expecting a payoff.

"You didn't tell me because you felt sorry for me. What are you after?"

Nothing makes you more vulnerable than ignorance. Mine had allowed Monty to manipulate me, and I wasn't going to repeat the mistake. Besides, it's always easier to bluff when you know the cards you're holding.

Ms. Powell set the baton down, her eyes behind the thick glasses boring into mine.

"We want you to join the Free Walkers. Help us destroy the Consort."

"You're joking," I said, a too-nervous laugh bubbling up. "You can't destroy the Consort. It's suicide."

Without the Walkers, the Key World would be destroyed. Without the Key World, the multiverse would crumble.

"Not just suicide. Armageddon. You people really are crazy." I edged toward the door, but she moved quickly to cut me off, holding her hands out as if trying to calm a spooked animal.

"We saved Simon, didn't we?" she said. "Is that something a bunch of crazed anarchists would do?"

I paused.

"Think about all the lies the Consort has told you, Del. All the secrets they've kept. Is it such a stretch to think they lied about us, too?"

She took a step toward me and I eased away, nearly tripping over my backpack. "We're trying to save the multiverse, and Simon as well. But we need your help."

Walkers are trained to think about consequences. Every action has a consequence; every choice makes a world. I wasn't even sure what Ms. Powell wanted me to do. But the only thing that mattered was getting back to Simon. I'd save him, then deal with the fallout.

Before I could reply, the bell rang, and we both winced at the noise. "Think about it," Ms. Powell murmured as my classmates began trickling in.

"Missed you at lunch," Eliot called as he set his books on the desk. I came around the side of the piano, and his mouth dropped open. "Your face!"

In my shock, I'd forgotten about Bree's scratch. I ran a finger over my stinging cheek. "Is it bleeding?"

"A little." He grabbed a tissue from the top of the piano and handed it to me. "What happened?"

I rolled my eyes. "Bree."

"You need to go to the nurse," he said.

"It's nothing," I said as Bree sidled into the classroom. I bared my teeth at her. "It won't happen again."

She blanched as she took her seat.

Gently Eliot turned my face to inspect the marks. "It looks terrible."

"Thanks. I'm not self-conscious about it at all."

His hand fell to his side, his voice turning overly casual. "You never said where you went during lunch."

I tipped my head toward the front of the room. "Needed to ask Ms. Powell a question."

"Some question. I waited all period," he said. "Were you Walking?"

I avoided his eyes, but I couldn't hide the bitterness leaching into my words. "Where would I go?"

I'd loved Walking, once. Infinite worlds, infinite possibilities. The freedom of slipping through Echoes, witnessing the power of a single choice unfold. But the thing I loved had taken the boy I loved, and the shining possibilities had tarnished. Even if Walking brought me back to Simon, the damage was done.

"Wish I knew." His tone changed, determinedly cheerful. "What were you asking Ms. Powell about?"

Lying to your best friend, even for a noble reason, is never a pleasant feeling—and I'd had plenty of experience doing so. Eliot had risked his life and his future with the Walkers to help me. I wasn't going to ask him again. And a small part of me worried that if he knew I was looking for Simon, he'd try to stop me. So I lied to Eliot, and I lied to myself, saying it was for the best.

"My composition," I said. "I'm supposed to perform it for the class, but I need someone to play the counterpoint."

"No problem. I'll do it," he said as the final bell rang.

The thought of anyone else playing the song Simon and I had written together felt wrong. It would *sound* wrong, even if Eliot hit every note.

Still, he looked so eager to help. It was another attempt to prove our friendship was back to normal, but the effort only highlighted how far off track we'd gone.

Now that I knew the truth about his feelings, I could see the signs and hints I'd missed for years: The casual touches that unsettled him, the way he watched me when he thought I wasn't looking. The way he bristled, ever so slightly, when someone mentioned Simon's name. The way he treated me like something fragile and rare.

I wasn't fragile, but our friendship was. I was cautious now, in a way I'd never been, questioning my every move. I swung between extremes: too awkward, too familiar, too remote, too warm. Terrified I'd lead him on, terrified I'd lose my best friend.

Terrified I already had.

"Sounds great," I said, mustering a smile as Ms. Powell started class. She avoided my eyes the entire hour, her genial, frazzled teacher's facade firmly in place while we reviewed for a test. Only when class ended did she look my way.

"Del, a word?" She glanced at Eliot, hovering nearby. "I've got time after school today, if you want to work on the Debussy piece."

"I do." I touched the fine silver chain around my neck, the pendant my Free Walker grandmother had left me. Answers, finally. "Thanks."

"My pleasure," she said. "I'm looking forward to it."

Not as much as I was.

CHAPTER THREE

Worlds are made by choices both big and small. A pivot forms the instant a decision is made, but it takes on its final resonance gradually, as consequences unfold. Deciding between a hamburger or a hot dog seems minor—but if you choke to death on the hot dog, the effect is huge, and so is the pivot.

High school is full of choices. Some feel monumental but aren't; some feel insignificant but alter everything. Originals don't notice pivots. They move through life seeing only the consequences that affect them directly. Walkers, on the other hand, can't create worlds. We can only visit them. It's for the best; otherwise we'd be paralyzed by the weight of our decisions.

Ms. Powell's choice to tell me about Simon hadn't made a new world, but it had scrubbed this one clean. It had helped me shake off the haze of sadness and self-pity I'd been lost in, and it felt good.

Except for the part where I had to lie to Eliot. Again.

"You're sure you don't want me to stick around?" he asked, zipping his coat. The bulky parka obscured the breadth of his shoulders, but not his uneasiness. "We could practice the duet once you're done with Ms. Powell."

"We can practice at my place," I said. "I'll call you when I get home—unless you want to come back and give me a ride."

"Now you're just being lazy." He grinned.

"It's freezing." The weather had turned while I'd hidden away in my room. No snow yet, but the cold was bitter and relentless, stripping the last of the leaves from the trees, forcing me into even more layers than usual. "I don't know why you won't drive to school. You've got the car."

"Do you know what the administration charges for parking permits? Do you know how many movies I can buy with that money? If you hate walking that much, get your own license." He paused, as if he'd heard his own words for the first time. "Regular walking. Not ours. I didn't mean—"

"I know."

He didn't move as the hallway emptied around us. "Do you? Hate Walking?"

"Kind of pointless," I said. "Nobody hates gravity, right? Same thing."

"Gravity's a constant. Walking's a choice."

Simon was my constant. If Walking helped me find him, there was no other choice.

"Go on," I said, giving him a shove to lighten the mood. "If you don't quit hovering, I'm going to return the favor. Sneak into your room and smother you while you sleep."

"I'd rather you not smother me," he said with a strange half smile. "Sneaking into my room's okay, though. Any time. Open invitation."

22

I drew back. "Eliot . . ."

"Relax, Del," he said, shoulders dropping. "I get it. I'm not going to chase after you while you're still in mourning."

"I'm not!"

He shook his head. "Simon's gone. I know you need time. That's okay. I'm not going anywhere."

My throat ached, but instead of telling him the truth, I said, "You deserve better."

"We're the best, right?" he asked, and I nodded mutely. "What could be better than best?"

"But . . ."

He held up a hand. "I just declared my intentions, Del. Give me a few minutes to feel like the hero before you shoot me down."

I couldn't help laughing, and a smile broke across his face.

"Ms. Powell's waiting," I said, waving vaguely toward the music wing.

"Yeah." He nudged up his glasses, shifted from foot to foot as if uncertain how to end the conversation. I could practically see him sorting through the possibilities: Handshake? Hug? Wave? Pat on the shoulder? What was the message hidden in each?

Finally, he slugged me in the shoulder, with a sheepish grin. I rolled my eyes and punched him back, just as gently.

"Later," he said, and headed out.

Navigating our friendship felt like crossing a minefield without out a map, testing every step, a single offhand comment enough to set off an explosion. But I cared too much to stop searching for a way through.

Hefting my violin case, I started for the music wing, but not before I caught sight of Bree at the end of the hallway, arms folded and eyes narrowed. I flashed her a toothy smile, flipped her off, and headed to Ms. Powell's office.

Answers, finally. Ms. Powell knew where Simon was. She might even take me to him.

Her classroom door was closed, and I took a moment to settle myself, smoothing down the unruly tangles of my hair. Deep in my chest was the tiniest ember of hope, brightening with every second. Before it could flare up and burn out, I pushed open the door.

The room was empty.

I'd never noticed how different her class sounded. Most of Washington High droned softly, like a beehive, the corridors and classrooms crowded with overlapping pivots. Ms. Powell didn't generate pivots, and Simon's ability to consolidate Echoes had eliminated many of the others. The result was a quiet room, interrupted by a few sharply ringing pivots. So many clues, but I'd been too dazzled by Simon and too distracted by my troubles with the Consort to notice.

I ran my hand along Simon's desk, listening. In his absence, my classmates' pivots were creeping in again. But Simon's pivots were louder than the rest. Each led to a world he'd created, simply by making a choice. If I crossed any of them, I could see his Echoes.

I wanted the real thing.

Memory flashed through me—Simon's thumb brushing the

corner of my mouth, an instant of startling, electric attraction. I pressed my fingers to my lips.

"How did you get rid of Eliot?" Ms. Powell asked from the doorway, interrupting my reverie.

I bristled at her tone. "I told him you were helping me with my phrasing in the Debussy."

"Good." She locked the door behind her.

"I don't like lying to him."

"Measure eighteen is marked *en serrant*. You should be picking up speed there, not just volume. Try to match the two." She spread her hands wide. "Now you're not lying."

I bit back my protest. "Are we going to see Simon? You said—"

"I said it would take time. A few hours isn't enough."

A few hours was too much. "Then why am I here? You want me to help you? I'm not doing a damn thing until you can prove Simon is okay."

"You've heard his Echo," she said, pulling her phone from her pocket. "What more proof do you need?"

"That tells me he's alive. Not that he's safe."

"Simon is safe because we have very strict protocols for contacting each other. In the interest of *keeping* him safe, we're going to continue following those protocols." She gestured to a wavering rift on the far side of the piano. "Let's Walk for a bit, and I can answer some of your questions."

I drew a deep breath. Like it or not, Ms. Powell had control here. I needed her on my side. I needed to play nice. "Okay."

She gave a satisfied nod and tapped her phone screen. A single, sustained note—a G-flat, mournful and wavery—filled the air. The pivot pulsed in response. I signaled when I'd fixed the frequency in my mind. *Like riding a bike,* I told myself. Riding a bike off-road and potentially over a cliff.

Ms. Powell checked one last time to make sure nobody was watching from the hallway, and gave me a thumbs-up. "See you on the other side."

I saw when she caught the edge—a hitch in her movements and a slight curling of her fingers as she found the right Echo, widening the pivot as she eased inside.

When she'd disappeared, I took one last look at Simon's desk, envisioning him sprawled there, long limbed and laughing, and pressed my fist against my heart. Then I pulled myself through the pivot, following her lead.

On the other side the classroom was equally deserted. Ms. Powell was paging through the sheet music on the piano, waiting for me. Around us the frequency throbbed in a steady rhythm.

"Who's teaching if you're not here?" I asked. Ms. Powell interacted with Original students and staff all day, but her impressions wouldn't last in the Echoes—countless versions of Washington High were missing a music teacher.

"Nobody. I keep a letter on my desk in the Key World, explaining my sudden resignation due to urgent family matters. It's been here since the day I started, so every Echo that's sprung up since my arrival has one. When administrators in those worlds find it, they hire a sub." She shrugged. "It's not strictly necessary, but we like to be inconspicuous, even in Echoes."

"Do all the Free Walkers masquerade as Originals?"

"Very few, actually. We have people working undercover in every Consort—"

"Even ours?"

"Even yours. But the majority tend to live in Echoes. It lets us limit our interactions with non-Walkers, so the repercussions are more manageable. This is the longest I've been in the Key World in years."

"Don't you get frequency poisoning?" Even the most stable Echoes would make a Walker sick over time. Minor bouts, like the one I'd suffered fixing an inversion, would put you out of commission for a few days. Major ones could rob you of your hearing and your sanity. "You should be a raving lunatic by now."

"We have ways to counteract it," she said, toying with her earring. "I'll show you later. For now, let's focus on the cleaving. Or rather, the not-cleaving."

We wandered through the school. Class was out for the day, and while there were still people around, teachers and custodians, students with detention or clubs, none of them noticed us. I could see how living in Echoes was easier—and how lonely it must be.

Ms. Powell stopped in front of the library. "Cut site," she said, pointing to a bank of lockers. A place where an Echo had been cleaved. The only sign was a barely perceptible line a few inches in front of the metal doors, hovering like spider silk. Invisible, unless you were looking. "Have you ever felt one before?"

"With my dad, when I was little. We've checked a few in training, too."

"How did they feel?"

"Rough." The pads of my fingers tingled at the memory. "Like burlap, you know?"

"Cleavers cut the strings of an Echo and reweave the fabric of the parent world. Because it's man-made instead of naturally occurring, the patch isn't as finely woven as the surrounding fabric."

"That's why cut sites are weaker? Because the fabric's not as dense?"

"Partly. You've learned about the energy transfer in your Consort classes, correct?"

"The basics."

When an Echo forms, it creates energy, which circulates between the existing branch and the new offspring like sap through a tree. That energy bolsters the Key World, protecting it from unstable frequencies. When Cleavers cut the strings between two realities, they direct the energy back into the parent world, use the weaving to seal it inside, and allow the cleaved Echo to unravel.

"One of the problems with cleaving is that not all of the energy can be harvested. Some percentage always escapes during the reweaving, so the cut site is never quite full strength."

I hadn't heard that before. "Still better than letting an inversion take root. Or leaving the edges unwoven," I said. "The energy would be wasted otherwise."

The smile she gave me was almost triumphant. "Not necessarily. Feel it," she said, and pointed at the lockers.

My hand inched toward the cut site, and the frequency around me quieted, the faintest of diminuendos. The air split beneath my touch, and the strings vibrated in perfect unison. Listening with my fingertips as well as my ears, I found the cut site. Instead of the coarsely woven fabric I expected, a line of tiny bumps pressed against my fingers, firm but resilient.

"Knots," Ms. Powell said when I twisted to look at her. "The threads are tied, not woven."

"This is a cleaving?" That couldn't be right. But the odd seam was silent, like any other cut site.

"A cauterization. The Echo on the other side of this cut site still exists."

I snatched my hand away. "How is that possible?" And if she was right, did it mean Train World, where I'd left Simon, was intact?

"Cleaving requires that you cut all the threads at once—you need all the strings of a cut site free in order to weave the edges together. But a cauterization cuts only a few threads at a time, knotting each half. Once that's done, the Echo is untethered."

"Doesn't it unravel?"

"No. Both sides are knotted, so both sides remain intact. The energy stays within the cauterized Echo, and once the seam is finished, it's a completely independent, self-sustaining reality."

I reached into the cut site, examining the knots again, trying to sense the world on the other side.

"You cauterized Train World?"

"Yes. My team found Simon shortly after you and Addie returned. The process was a little trickier, because you and Simon had already cut the strings. As you know, he makes worlds stronger, which bought us extra time."

Exactly as I'd hoped. I pulled my hand free as my knees gave out. I slid down to the floor, my back against the lockers. "You saved him."

"We did."

I hadn't believed her before now—not truly, not in my bones—but I did now, and the knowledge knocked loose a chunk of the sorrow I'd carried, dissolving it to tears.

Ms. Powell was nice enough to look away while I pulled myself together. Once I did, I asked, "Can I cross over?"

"Once a world is cauterized, there's no getting through again. It will grow, and generate Echoes of its own, but there's no going back."

"He's trapped there?" Had she given me hope only to shatter it again?

She touched my shoulder, her words a rush of reassurance. "We pulled Simon out before the cauterization was complete. He's lucky we were monitoring him—it was a close call."

"So let's bring him back," I said, rising to my feet.

"It's not safe for him here. Not while the Consort exists."

"Then I'll go to him."

"And join the Free Walkers?"

Becoming a Free Walker meant living in Echoes, hiding

from the Consort, leaving behind my family and Eliot and the plans we'd made. If I joined the Free Walkers, I wouldn't just be a troublemaker. I'd be a criminal, and I'd spend the rest of my life running.

"You make it sound like it's all or nothing."

"There's no middle ground here, Del. Either you're ours, or theirs."

"Why don't you tell people about cauterization?" I asked. "The Consort's convinced you want to destroy the Key World because you won't cleave. If you explain—"

"You think they don't know? The Consort knows all about cauterization, and it's only made them more desperate to stop us." Her gaze bored into me. "Tell me why the Consort cleaves."

"To protect the Key World from Echoes," I said automatically, a response drilled into me from my earliest days.

"Why else?"

I thought back to all the textbooks I'd skimmed. "To harvest their energy and bolster the Key World."

"Exactly. They want to capture as much of the energy as they can, and they get it at the expense of the Echoes. Cauterization would cut off the supply."

"Then why cauterize? If we need that energy, why wouldn't we continue cleavings?"

"Because the Echoes need it more. They need it to live."

I looked at her blankly. "But they're not—"

"Echoes aren't merely copies of Originals. You know that better than anyone."

I thought of Simon, of all the versions of him I'd met, each distinct and vivid and whole. "I know. They're real."

"They're more than real. They're alive. The Consort knows it, just as they know cleaving—the great and sacred duty of the Walkers—is murder."

CHAPTER FOUR

SOME SONGS YOU LOVE FROM THE INSTANT you hear them. Six notes in, part of you rises up and says *yes*. Before the melody's complete, before you've heard the lyrics or the bridge, something within you recognizes it as part of your soul, as if it's been waiting for you all this time.

Ms. Powell's words were like the chords to a song I'd always known but never heard. Still, the logical part of my brain resisted.

"Echoes aren't alive. They don't exist until their world has formed. They can't survive unless they're tethered to an Original. When we cleave, they don't even notice they're unraveling."

"With cauterization, they *don't* unravel. Once the strings are knotted, the Echoes are as alive as you and me."

"That doesn't make sense." I didn't doubt Simon's Echoes were real. I'd watched one of them cleave, and the horror of the moment had stayed with me. But real and alive were *different*. Alive meant independent. It meant Simon's Echoes could survive without him.

It meant I hadn't just cleaved Simon's Echo in the park that day. I'd killed him.

"When we cleave, they unravel. When we cauterize, they

live. Even if their Original dies, a cauterized Echo can maintain their signal and live out a natural lifespan," Ms. Powell said.

A horrible thought struck. "Is Simon dead? I can hear his Echoes, but if he was in Train World . . ."

"Simon's alive. We pulled him out of Train World before we cauterized it, I promise you."

Relief washed over me, but only for an instant. "Wait. Are you saying the Consort's been slaughtering Echoes? For years and years? My parents? Addie? Me?"

Every Echo we'd cleaved. Billions of lives in each one, unraveling to nothingness. Billions dead, by our hands.

My own hands began trembling so badly, my fingers blurred. I was going to be sick.

I bolted for the girl's bathroom and barely made it in time. When I was done, I sank down on the tile floor, spent and shaking, my breath coming in desperate pants.

The door opened and Ms. Powell came in. "I'm sorry," she said, crouching next to me. "I shouldn't have sprung it on you. There are better ways . . ."

"To say I killed a planet's worth of people? Next time try a greeting card." My stomach heaved again, but there was nothing left to throw up.

"Come on," she said, helping me to my feet. I hobbled to the sink and rinsed my mouth out, as if I could wash away the taste of what I'd done. Simon and Iggy, fading to nothingness as they played near the pond. A playground full of children. I'd killed them.

I scrubbed my hands over my face. "It's murder. It's genocide."

"You didn't know," she said, handing me a towel, calmer and more reasonable than anyone should be. Then again, it wasn't news to her. "Even most Cleavers haven't been told."

I *had* known, deep down. From the minute I'd watched Park World Simon fade, I'd known cleavings were wrong.

And they were still happening. "Do my parents know?"

"I doubt it," she said. "Outside the Major and Minor Consorts, very few people know the truth."

I gripped the edge of the sink. The girl who stared back from the mirror didn't look like me. She didn't look like a murderer, either, but it turned out she was both. "If it's such a secret, how did the Free Walkers find out?"

"A Consort physicist with a theory and a conscience. It was generations ago, well before I was born. The discovery created a schism within the Consort; in the end, those advocating cauterization were branded heretics. They fled to save their own lives. We've been considered traitors ever since."

"Why don't you tell people? Every day you keep quiet, we cleave more Echoes. More people die. The Consort might be evil, but most Walkers are decent people. They'd stop if they knew the truth." My parents would never allow it. God knows Addie wouldn't.

"Do you think we haven't tried? We can't force people to believe."

"You won't have to force them. Just explain, like you did with me."

"You had the benefit of growing up with a Free Walker. Your entire childhood, Monty was counteracting the Consort's influence. Haven't you ever wondered why you and your sister turned out so differently?"

Addie had been four when we moved in with my grandfather. She'd started school soon after, leaving Monty and me alone.

"Monty wasn't raising me as a Free Walker, he was manipulating me into finding Rose." I clutched my pendant so hard the tines bit into my palm.

She looked away. "He was also teaching you to value lives instead of taking them. He gave you tools that most Walker children never learn."

I thought back to the Walks we'd taken when I was little, the songs he sang, the tricks and shortcuts he'd shown me. All because I was his best, brightest girl.

Or so I'd thought.

"Hum a tune both deft and kind," I murmured. "Monty wouldn't let me cleave. He taught me how to tune instead."

"Cauterization's not the only thing we do. Often, tuning a world is enough to protect it from the Cleavers, and it takes far less time."

"Why not cauterize every Echo? Set them free?"

"Because the drop in energy to the Key World would leave it too vulnerable. Protecting the Key World *and* the Echoes is a balancing act. Until we convince the Walkers to stop cleaving, the best we can do is to head off as many cleavings as possible."

Addie's project, I realized. Lattimer had asked her to help

find the Free Walkers, and now I knew why. They were interfering with his cleavings.

Gently she said, "It's an imperfect solution, but we do the best we can. We cauterize the most unstable Echoes before the Consort can cleave them, and tune the ones we can save."

I leaned my forehead against the cool tile wall. "But if the Consort knows the truth, why are they still cleaving?"

"Their only concern is protecting the Key World. If that comes at the expense of every other branch in the multiverse, so be it."

"Obedience, diligence, sacrifice," I recited. The Consort's watchwords.

"The Consort views untethered Echoes as an abomination—people without souls." Her mouth twisted. "As such, the idea of entire branches filled with them doesn't appeal. It's not only the physics they object to; it's the ethics."

"So you want to take them down."

"Sometimes a world has to be torn down in order to make way for a new one. Remember, a Consort member usually holds his or her seat for life, and they choose their own successors. We'd hoped, years ago, that your grandfather would be named to the Consort. He was well-regarded by the woman who held the seat; he had the support of his colleagues. Nobody knew he was a Free Walker. Everything was falling into place."

Which was usually the time things fell apart, in my experience. "What went wrong?"

"Lattimer," she said. "We'd been so focused on Montrose

getting the Consort seat, we forgot about the other two members—but Lattimer hadn't. He'd convinced them he was the man for the job, and promised to put an end to the Free Walkers as proof. On his orders, the Consort launched a massive, coordinated attack against us. They caught Gil, your grandmother went on the run, and Monty's chance at the Consort seat disappeared along with her. Countless Free Walkers were captured and interrogated, which led to more arrests and more cleavings. It's taken us years to recover, and we've learned our lesson. Caution takes time."

"And haste leads to unexpected consequences," I said. Another proverb.

"Exactly. Your textbook got that right, at least. Now you understand why we can't rush off and see Simon."

The mention of his name sent me reeling again. I'd killed his Echo when I cleaved Park World. Every time my father and Addie cleaved, they killed people. My mom planned their Walks to help them kill with maximum efficiency. Eliot, my classmates, and I were all training to do the same. Our lives were built on murder.

"You can't blame yourself," she said, as if she could hear my thoughts.

I could, actually. I did. "Were you born a Free Walker?"

"Yes. My parents left the Consort before I was born. I've never known anything else."

She'd never cleaved a world. Never killed anyone. Her sympathy was theoretical, and she had no idea what it felt like to carry that kind of weight.

"All those people . . . ," I said softly.

"You had no way of knowing. Now you do, and you have the power to change it. You can help us."

"It's not enough." Nothing I did would make up for how casually, how thoughtlessly I'd ended lives.

She shook her head. "The past is a hungry creature. If all you feed it is regret, it will consume you. Let it fuel you instead."

She steered me out of the bathroom and back to the pivot. As soon as we returned to the Key World, my phone started buzzing with texts from Eliot.

"I have to tell him." I needed to hear that the wrong I'd done wasn't the entirety of who I was.

"Not yet. It's not safe."

"He's as trustworthy as I am. More, actually."

"You're an Armstrong."

"That's Monty," I said. "I'm a Sullivan."

"Not to us," she replied. "Will you help, now that you know the truth?"

Truth is as fluid as water, as faceted as diamonds, as flawed as memory. That's what Monty always said. And my truth was, I would have helped them anyway, to save Simon. But now I would do it to save myself.

"Yes."

She sagged with relief. "I'll work on setting up the meeting with Simon. I know you must have more questions—"

"I have a million questions," I said. "So does Bree Carlson. She's not going to quit looking for Simon."

She tapped the desk, skeptical and impatient. "Do you really think she's a threat?"

"I don't think so. But . . . can't you guys do something to get her off my case? She's come after me twice today."

"I'll see what I can do." Ms. Powell took my hands in hers. "Are you sure you're all right? Finding out about the cleavings is a shock."

My stomach twisted. Shock didn't begin to describe it.

My phone buzzed again. "Eliot," I said, suddenly desperate to escape. "I should go."

"We'll talk soon," she said. "But in the meantime, you cannot tell anyone, Eliot included." I opened my mouth to protest, but she continued. "Please don't make us regret trusting you. It could ruin your chance to see Simon again."

I swallowed, nodded, and stumbled from the room.

I couldn't tell Eliot, but the knowledge of what I'd done burned in my veins like poison. I needed to get it out, to confess.

Who did you confess to, if you had to keep a secret from the world?

Someone from another world.

CHAPTER FIVE

DUSK WAS FALLING WHEN I REACHED THE cemetery, despite the fact it was only late afternoon. The streetlights flickered on one by one, too weak to pierce the gloom on the other side of the wrought-iron fence.

My breath hung in smoky puffs. I hunched my shoulders against the cold and peered through the bars, looking for a familiar shape. But the graveyard was deserted.

The massive, rusting gate stood open a few inches. I tugged on it, wincing at the shriek of metal. I'd forgotten how loud it was, or maybe the shadows and silence only made it seem that way.

The cemetery wasn't large—tucked beside a neighborhood church and boxy older homes, bordered by a stone half wall and a row of trees at the back. Many of the gravestones scattered throughout were crumbling, or worn smooth by time and grief. Only a few were still legible, including a small marble rectangle set into the ground. Someone had swept away the old leaves, unlike many of the other headstones, revealing the crisp engraving.

AMELIA LANE

BELOVED MOTHER

I knelt and traced the letters, listening to the pitch of this world, where Simon's mother hadn't escaped the cancer ravaging her body, and grieved all over again. This Amelia had been as real as the one I visited each day, and her son felt her absence as painfully as my Amelia did her Simon.

"I'm so sorry," I whispered. "Nobody told me the truth, and I was too stupid to see it for myself, and now . . . I don't know what to do."

I wondered how much this Amelia had known, how much of the truth she carried with her. Echoes held the memories of the lives they'd led before the choice that formed their world, so she would have remembered Simon's father and her involvement with the Free Walkers. Would she have known that she was an Echo? Would she have felt second best?

"I wish you were here. I wish you could tell me what to do next. I wish I'd known sooner, and I wish I could have saved you." My breath hitched, and I pressed the heels of my hands against my eyes. "I wish I could have saved all of them."

"If wishes were horses, beggars would ride," came a familiar voice behind me, and I jolted.

Simon—an Echo of my Simon, dark hair jaggedly cut, dressed head to toe in black, carrying a sketchbook and the weight of this world. He'd told me once that he came here every day to sketch. I'd hoped to catch him, but after everything I'd heard today, the sight of him was a shock.

"What does that even mean?" I asked after I recovered.

"It means . . . I don't know, honestly." His mouth curved as he helped me up, his dissonance rocking me back on my heels. "My mom used to say it whenever I wanted something I couldn't have. I think it's about how wishing is easy. Making it happen is harder."

I brushed at my muddy knees. "No kidding."

"What are you doing here, Del?"

I looked at him then, the line of his jaw, the scar at the corner of his mouth, and longing and guilt clamped like a vise on my heart. Real. Not just real. *Alive.*

"You remember me."

He patted the sketchbook under his arm. "I never forget a face."

I hadn't told him my name, on my last visit here. He'd known it nevertheless, seen me before we touched, and I'd missed both signs completely. It had alarmed me then, but now I took it as a good sign. I searched his face for any indication that the message I'd sent through Doughnut World Simon had worked.

But the light was dim, and my heart was heavy, and all I could see in his gaze was sympathy.

"What are *you* doing here?" I asked.

"I was drawing." He hefted the sketchbook. "I lost the light, so I left. Came back when I heard the gate. What's wrong?"

"Who said anything was wrong?"

The corner of his mouth lifted. "People don't hang out in cemeteries unless something's wrong."

"You do."

"My mom's here. Can't get much more wrong. Who are *you* grieving, Delancey Sullivan?"

My head snapped up, and I wondered if one of my wishes had been granted. "Whole worlds."

He bent and removed another leaf that had scudded across Amelia's grave, then took my hand and led me to the stone wall. "Tell me."

I boosted myself onto the rough-hewn ledge, pleased when he sat close enough that our sides pressed together, shoulder to knee. He touched the scratch on my cheek, his artist's fingers featherlight, eyebrows drawing together.

"It doesn't hurt," I assured him.

"What does?"

"I did something horrible." As small talk went, it sucked. But his mother's death had stripped this Simon clean of small talk. He didn't waste time on insignificance, or false consolation.

"Can you undo it?"

I had a fleeting, fanciful image of reweaving the threads I'd cut, but Walking wasn't time travel. The world I'd cleaved was gone, as impossible to recover as a tear in the sea. "I'm too late. I thought it was the right thing, but it wasn't. And now I have all this blood on my hands, and no clue how to live with it."

He smiled, a wry, tired hitch along one side of his mouth. "You're not going to tell me what you did?"

"You wouldn't believe me."

"Figures." He looked out over the graveyard, the deepening twilight turning the headstones blue-black, the lights at the entrance casting ineffective circles on the ground. "I guess if you can't make it right, you make it so it can't happen again."

Which is what the Free Walkers were doing. But Ms. Powell had said cauterizations held back energy that strengthened the Key World. The cut site was left weaker. Without the Key World, the entire multiverse would destabilize, strings disrupting each other until there was nothing left. Were the Free Walkers—with the best of intentions—destroying the very thing I was sworn to protect?

But who protected the Echoes? Walkers believed in obedience, diligence, and sacrifice—but how much sacrifice was too much? "Do you believe in necessary evils?"

He squinted. "Fooling people into thinking evil is necessary seems pretty evil. Not sure about the necessary part."

"What about the greater good?"

"Depends on whose version of good we're talking about. Everyone's the hero of their own story, aren't they?"

"Not me."

He slipped an arm around my shoulders. "You didn't know what you were doing."

"Oh, I knew." My fingers on threads that split and sheared and unmade a world. "But I didn't know what it meant."

"Why not?"

"Because that's what I was told!" I chose the words with care. "The people I . . . work for. They told us we were doing a service, we were helping people. And instead . . . it was exactly the opposite. They've been lying to me my whole life."

Fury broke through my shock and horror. No wonder the Consort wanted to eradicate the Free Walkers. The Consort held

45

sway over the Walkers by telling us we were heroes, telling us what we wanted to believe. If we thought otherwise, they'd lose control of us, and of the multiverse. An unwelcome truth is the most effective weapon of all.

"You can't give a kid a box of matches and not expect them to burn down the house," he said. He tucked a lock of hair behind my ear, hand lingering along my jaw. I closed my eyes and savored the sensation, though it wasn't my Simon. His fingers smelled of turpentine and pencil lead, but the touch was so familiar, even if the sound was wrong. I pressed my cheek into his palm and drew strength from it, the first bit I'd had in days.

"I have to make it right."

I hadn't known, but now I did. If I sat by and let the cleavings continue, I was as evil as the Consort.

"We'll fix it," he murmured, fingers weaving through my hair. "And then we'll be good."

We'll fix this, and we'll be good. My message to Doughnut Simon, echoing back across the multiverse to me.

My eyes flew open and I bolted upright. "Simon?"

"I'm right here," he said, like I was a child waking from a nightmare. Maybe I was.

"Can I ask you a strange question?"

"You've cornered the market on strange questions," he said. "One more won't hurt."

"Do you dream about me?"

He rubbed the back of his neck, not meeting my eyes. "Not as much lately. Sometimes I think about what I'd say if I saw you again. Thought about giving you back this—" He fished in his pocket, and I knew instinctively what he was going to draw out.

When he stretched out his hand, the pale yellow star I'd folded for him rested in his palm. The breadcrumb I'd needed. I reached for it, but his fingers curled protectively around it.

"—But I'm keeping it. It reminds me of you."

"What else did you want to tell me?" I choked out. If I could send Simon a message through his Echoes, maybe he could send one to me.

He ducked his head. "That I've missed you. That I'll wait as long as you need. That you should go ahead and kiss me."

I laughed despite myself. "I'm closer every day."

He tucked the star away again, the Key World frequency chiming as he did, counteracting the dizziness that was starting to encroach on me. "You should be closer *now*."

He slid a hand around the nape of my neck, and I leaned in, pouring as much promise into the kiss as I could, the faintest hint of rosemary on his lips. Then I broke away, and he studied me again.

"I won't see you again, will I?"

I shook my head. One kiss—a kiss he asked for, whether it was a request from my Simon or from his heart—felt right. Any more would be using him.

I slid off the wall. "Not here."

"Del," he said, grabbing my wrist, the warmth in his voice transformed to worry. "Be careful. Of everyone."

CHAPTER SIX

I'D VISITED AMELIA EVERY DAY SINCE SIMON'S disappearance. Simon had asked me to take care of her, but I would have done it even without my promise. Helping her was the one thing I could do to make up for all she'd lost. Selfishly, spending time with her helped me, too. There was nobody else I could share my grief with: not Eliot, whose feelings were too raw to hear about how much I missed Simon; not Addie, who worried about my mental state; and definitely not my parents, who were completely in the dark, consumed as usual by their work.

The cottage lights glowed warmly, like she'd left them on for me. I headed around back, and before my hand touched the doorknob, a woof and a thud announced my presence.

I let myself in, bracing against the counter as eighty-five pounds of chocolate Lab hurtled toward me.

"Hey, Iggy. How's she doing today?" I knelt and scratched his ears, kissed the top of his head, and pulled a dog treat out of my pocket. Iggy snatched it up and burrowed closer.

"I'm hanging in there," called Amelia from the family room. She was sitting on the couch, laptop propped on her knees, medical dictionaries at her side. Before she'd gotten sick, she'd managed a pediatrician's office; after the diagnosis she'd decided to do transcription from home. "I thought I'd try to do a little work, get back into a routine, but . . ."

But her heart wasn't in it. I understood. Iggy must have heard the quaver in her voice, because he bounded back across the room. She held up a hand. "No food on the carpet, Ig."

He snuffled and dropped the treat exactly where the linoleum met the rug, giving her his most winsome expression.

"Beast," she said affectionately. "Eat up."

The biscuit disappeared, and a moment later he'd planted himself at Amelia's feet.

"I swear you're the only one he listens to."

"He's a good boy. Most of the time," she added, scratching his head. Her hands looked thin and pale against his dark fur. Her hair had grown back enough that she rarely wore a scarf anymore, the short blond strands emphasizing the blue of her eyes and the delicacy of her features. "Rough day?"

"Weird day." I bit my lip. As cruel as it was to hold back the truth, asking her to live with more uncertainty seemed worse. She wouldn't be able to see Simon, if he stayed in the Echoes. Then again, knowing he was okay would give her a boost. I stood, wavering. "How was yours?"

"Slow. There may have been some napping involved." Her sheepish grin was so like Simon's that my heart twisted. She motioned to the couch, unwilling to be diverted. "Tell me about the weird day—and how you got that scratch on your cheek."

I grimaced. "Bree Carlson. She's got it out for me."

"Bree. She was . . . late summer, wasn't she? The actress?" At my nod, she mused, "I never met her. But she was very persistent, if her phone calls were anything to go by."

"Still is." I definitely wasn't going to tell Amelia about Bree looking into Simon's disappearance. "Did you take your medications? Do you want some tea?"

"I wouldn't mind a fresh cup."

I returned to the kitchen and put the kettle on, fending off Iggy's whimpering pleas for a walk. "In a minute, fella."

"Something's wrong, isn't it? More than Bree."

I busied myself with the tea. "What do you remember about the Free Walkers?"

She stood slowly, and joined me at the counter. "Why do you want to know? Have they approached you?"

To spare us both from a lie, I didn't answer.

"I see." She nudged me out of the way and started assembling a tray: spoons, cups, milk, and sugar. "Gil was working with them long before we met. The Consort had assigned him to investigate the pivots stemming from the crash. You know how rigid the Consort is about Walkers and Originals mingling. He would never have asked me out if he hadn't been a Free Walker."

She chuckled, the sound rueful. "Simon got his charm from his father, you know."

"What did you say when he told you the truth? Or did you catch him Walking?" The way Simon had caught me.

"He told me. He had to, really. I knew he was keeping something back—I was only getting a fraction of him, and I wanted the whole. So I broke it off, and he told me everything."

"Did you think he was crazy?"

"At first." She ran a finger over her wedding band. "Eventually I believed him, and when he explained about the Free Walkers, I believed in them, too. They were so dedicated, and passionate . . . it was impossible not to be swept up in it. I helped, you know. I wasn't just the girl on the sidelines."

I must have looked puzzled, because she laughed. "How do you think you ended up with pivots all over your house, Del?"

"That was you?" Walker houses didn't typically have a lot of pivots, but ours did. I'd always assumed it was due to the fact that it was old—plenty of repairmen had passed through our doors, and their choices littered the house, same as their cigarette stubs and Styrofoam coffee cups.

"Did you think Gil was only interested in my looks?" She smiled. "I believed in the Free Walkers' cause. Forming pivots in houses—so they could move in and out without the Consort noticing—was an easy way for me to help.

"And then I got pregnant with Simon. It must sound crazy, but we were so happy, despite the danger."

"But . . . your Echoes . . . they were pregnant too."

She folded her hands and met my eyes. "Yes."

"Gil couldn't be with them. They were alone." It seemed selfish, somehow, and irresponsible. Two words I'd never have used to describe Amelia. "You were okay with that? Choosing for them?"

"I chose for myself," she said. "Walkers don't have to weigh their decisions, and neither do most Originals. They don't know that the power of their choices crosses worlds. I loved Gil, and I believed we were building a life together."

"Your Echoes couldn't. They'd be single moms."

"They had my memories; they knew Gil, and what I'd done. They would remember our time together as if it was their own. Having Simon meant they would have a piece of Gil in their lives forever—that's what I gave them, and it was the right thing to do."

"How do you know?"

She met my eyes. "Because it's what I would have wanted in their place."

"But—"

"I'm not sorry I did it," she said, lifting her chin. "Not when the result was Simon."

"Me neither," I said softly. The irony was, her Echoes—the ones who had lived—still had a Simon. She was the only one who had to grieve.

She dusted off her hands to show the topic was closed. "And then, Gil was gone."

"What happened?" I asked, welcoming the change of subject. I'd heard Ms. Powell's explanation, but it seemed vital that I hear Amelia's version too. The personal cost instead of the political one.

"I'm not sure. In the months before Simon was born, we were making progress—converting some high-ranking official, cauterizing a major branch before it could be cleaved—but the Consort always managed to get ahead of us. The official would disappear. We'd save one Echo, and three more would be cleaved. Monty was going to be named to the Consort, and then Lattimer got the job. They'd found . . ." She trailed off. ". . . something. A fail-safe, Rose called it. But a few days after Simon was born, Gil vanished."

The kettle screamed, and I turned it off, willing her to continue.

"He'd always been careful to keep me hidden from the Consort—he wasn't living here, and he wasn't always able to get away. Rose kept checking on me, but I knew this was different. Nothing would have kept him from his son. When Monty came looking for Rose, I cut off the whole group. I told him if a Free Walker contacted me or came near Simon—ever—I'd tell the Consort everything I knew."

I didn't doubt it. She might have been frail, but there was steel in her spine.

"Why did you stay?" I asked. "Why not pick up and move to the other side of the country?"

"I thought Gil might come back," she said quietly, and twisted her ring. "Besides, running would have drawn more attention, especially from your kind. Walkers worry about change, not consistency."

In my mind I overlaid her story with what Ms. Powell had told me, the picture slowly coming into focus, the overlapping parts adding depth and clarity. Only one thing didn't fit.

"What was the fail-safe?"

"Gil never said, exactly." She rubbed the back of her hand across her forehead, her voice turning vague. "There was a lot he didn't tell me, you know. He wanted to keep us safe, and the best way to do that was to keep us hidden."

Whatever it was, the fail-safe hadn't worked. Amelia looked pale—I'd pushed too hard, called up too many memories.

"Sit down," I urged, guiding her toward the table. When she was seated, Iggy's head on her knee, I poured out tea and placed the cup in front of her. "I have to stop the Consort."

She nodded, absently rubbing Iggy's ears. "They're dangerous."

"I know. But I can't let them keep cleaving. Not when—"

"I didn't mean the Consort. They need to be stopped. I don't deny it. But . . . I've given the Free Walkers everything, and they've failed, time and time and time again. It's one thing to sacrifice for a cause, but sacrificing for a lost cause is a different thing entirely."

"I understand." But I couldn't allow myself to believe it was lost, because that would mean Simon was lost. That the wrong I had done could never be made right.

"You're my last tie to him, you and this ridiculous dog. I couldn't bear it if you were another pointless casualty."

"What if . . ." What if I could bring him back? To keep myself from asking, I hugged her carefully. "I won't be."

CHAPTER SEVEN

A MAZDA CONVERTIBLE SAT IN THE DRIVE-way, gleaming red where the porch lights glinted off it. I sighed and let myself in the house.

"Hey," Addie called from the couch. She smoothed her hair down, cheeks turning pink. "Laurel's here."

"I noticed. Hey, Laurel."

"Hi, Del. How's it going?" Laurel didn't bother fixing her hair, dark curls corkscrewing in every direction, or her smudged lipstick.

"It's going." I threw my coat on a hook and headed to the pantry for a sugar fix. My talk with Ms. Powell and the Walk to see Cemetery Simon had left me dizzy in more ways than one. I needed to counteract the frequency poisoning. "Don't let me interrupt."

It wasn't that I disliked Addie having a girlfriend. In the short time she and Laurel had been together, she'd been happier—and easier to be around, since Happy Addie and Nitpicky Addie couldn't coexist.

And I couldn't have picked a better girlfriend for her than Laurel, an apprentice Archivist. In some ways she reminded me of Eliot—supersmart, a little spacey—but she was much more easygoing than he was, comfortable in her skin and in speaking her mind. Most importantly, she was crazy about Addie.

But watching the two of them together made the ache of losing Simon sharpen until it felt like a knife between my ribs.

I grabbed a box of graham crackers and a tub of Nutella, careful not to listen too closely to their murmured conversation. People in new relationships want everyone to be as happy as they are, and I was too exhausted to play along.

When I emerged from the pantry, Addie was sitting at the kitchen island and Laurel was standing next to her, their fingers intertwined.

"Are you sure you're okay?" Addie asked, brow furrowed in concern.

"Fine," I said shortly, finally noticing her clothes. Black pants and a loose-fitting black sweater, red-gold hair pulled back in a neat bun. Ballet flats instead of her usual heels. Polished and lovely, as always, but it was an outfit you could move in. Could run in, should things go wrong. "You were cleaving today."

My voice wobbled alarmingly. How many people had died, how many worlds unraveled in the hours since Ms. Powell had told me the truth? I bit my lip until I tasted copper, the secret threatening to burst free. Addie would never cleave again, once she knew the effects.

And then what would we do? Addie was too well-regarded around the Consort to simply quit. Lattimer had singled her out for a special project, the one that had brought her and Laurel together, but she'd barely spoken about it. If she were to stop cleaving, or disappear altogether, the Consort would investigate. Walkers worry about change, not consistency, Amelia had warned. I couldn't afford more scrutiny now.

"I know the idea of cleaving is hard for you, Del, but it's my job. It's more than a job, actually. It's a—"

"I know. A calling. Mom read the same scriptures to both of us." I pushed away from the table, took in the empty room. "Where are they, anyway?"

"Mom and Dad? Working late."

"As usual." For once, I was relieved their Consort duties took precedence.

"Not usual," Laurel said. She wandered over to the stove and poked at whatever was steaming on the back burner. "A Tacet."

"A what?"

"A Tacet," Addie said. "I just got back to regular duty, so I don't know all the details, but the Consort's planning a major cleaving."

"Tacet means 'silence,'" Laurel added. "They're silencing the Echoes."

"Which branch?" I choked out.

"A whole bunch. We're getting double or triple the usual requests." As an apprentice Archivist, Laurel maintained all the records of Consort activity in the Echoes: cleavings, exploratory walks, branch maps. "Coordinating that many cleavings takes a lot of prep work."

"Why would they do it?" I asked.

They exchanged glances, and Addie said, "The official story is that they're trying to contain damage from the anomaly. A Tacet transfers a lot of energy to the Key World. Reinforces the weak spots."

"And unofficially?"

"The Free Walkers live in the Echoes," Laurel said flatly. "Nobody knows where, but if you cleave enough branches . . . you'll hit something."

Addie frowned at her.

"Unofficially," Laurel amended. "And theoretically."

"When?" I asked, wondering if I had enough time to warn Ms. Powell.

"Three weeks, at least. It's a complicated operation," Addie said. "On another note, Shaw stopped by my desk today. He wants you back in training."

I mashed a thumb into my graham cracker, scattering crumbs. "Soon."

"The Consort's taking apprenticeship applications," she said. "You need to get moving on yours."

"Have you decided where you're applying?" Laurel asked.

"Not yet."

Addie swung into big-sister mode. "Del, you can't put this off. If you don't start showing up to class, the Consort is going to slot you in wherever they need warm bodies. And right now, they need Cleavers."

"I'm not cleaving."

"If your ranking's high enough, you can transfer to another

Consort. That's what I did," Laurel said, dimpling. "It's worked out pretty well."

I scowled. "Maybe I'll apply for an Enforcement position."

Laurel's smile fell away. "I'm not sure you're cut out for Enforcement. They're pretty . . . hard-core."

"Relax," I said. "The Consort wouldn't let me within three Echoes of an Enforcement position. Can you imagine me trying to make other people follow the rules? I'll figure out something."

Laurel wound a curl around her finger. "My advice is, don't rush it. Take your time."

"She needs to choose." Addie turned to her. "It's a big deal."

"Exactly," Laurel said. "It's her whole life. Why should she settle for something other than what she really wants? I didn't."

Addie's expression softened, and she leaned her forehead against Laurel's shoulder.

"It's your future, Del," she said. "Don't let someone else choose it for you. Not after everything Simon did to make sure you'd have one."

CHAPTER EIGHT

My SUSPENSION FROM THE CONSORT WAS meant to make me a better Walker. Instead, I'd become an imposter. Judging from the looks Eliot gave me on our way into training the next day, I wasn't a very good one.

Even before our train pulled into Union Station, I could hear the cacophony of pivots, each with their own distinct pitch. Some squeaked; some boomed; some were so low-pitched I felt their vibrations in the soles of my feet. Almost a century of choices, layered on top of one another until the air felt cobwebbed with them.

Once we were outside, the sensation eased slightly. We made our way to the Consort's headquarters, a discreetly expensive-looking building in the Loop. The glassed-in lobby, the guards behind the desk, and the Impressionist paintings on the walls indicated to passersby that Consort Change Management was a staid, reputable firm catering exclusively to its clients, so move along please.

Its clients were Walkers. The CCM building housed our school, our archives, our laboratories, our government . . . it was essentially a Walker embassy, a foreign land hidden in the middle of Chicago, fluent in secrecy.

"You're nervous," he said as we approached the building.

"Tired. Laurel and Addie were on my case last night."

"About what?"

I shrugged. "What else? My future. Or lack of one."

We slid our ID cards through the scanner at the front desk, and the guard waved us through. Somewhere in this building my grandfather was locked away. I'd expected to sense some hint of his presence, as if the atmosphere would turn charged simply because we were under the same roof. My skin prickled, ice and nerves, but it wasn't Monty. It was the effort of stepping back into my old life. Too much loss, too many truths.

Across the lobby, a tall girl with a line of piercings in both ears and her black hair in a pixie cut lounged on one of the leather couches. She spotted us and sprang up, crossing the room in long, lithe strides.

"Hey, sexy!" Callie enveloped me in a hug. A beat too late, I hugged her back, and she frowned. "Where the hell have you been? Shaw said your suspension ended more than a week ago."

"Frequency poisoning," Eliot said swiftly. "Her parents wouldn't let her come back till she was one hundred percent."

She raised one dark eyebrow. "If you say so. How'd you convince them to let you back in?"

"My stellar personality?" I offered.

"Right," she said. "All sorts of crazy stories floating around about you."

"Leave her alone." Eliot folded his arms across his chest and stared Callie down.

She tipped her head to the side and studied him, not missing the way he'd stepped in front of me, or the warning in his tone. "Whatever you did, I'm glad. Things here could use some shaking up."

I'd shaken things plenty, but I appreciated the sentiment.

"It's good to see you," I said, and meant it. Callie Moreno was one of my favorite classmates—snarky and smart and practical, with a wild streak that kept life interesting. Eliot was always my first pick on Walks, but Callie ran a close second.

"What have I missed?" I asked on the elevator ride up to our classroom.

"The usual. Hookups and breakups and a whole lot of obsessing over class rank and apprenticeships. People are freaking out."

"But not you?" I asked.

Callie smiled brilliantly. "Why would I? They know I'm good. They'd be stupid to put me—or you—anywhere but the Cleavers. The Consort's dull, but they're not stupid."

"No," I murmured as the doors slid open and we filed into the hallway. "That's the problem."

Eliot gave me a sideways glance. Ahead of us, Callie breezed through the open doorway of our classroom, while I froze in place.

Immediately Eliot halted. "Del?"

My voice scraped. "I didn't think I'd come back here. Ever."

It was a second chance—something Walkers rarely got. But

it's better to make fresh mistakes, no matter how painful, than to repeat old ones.

"You belong in there. The longer you wait, the more they'll stare."

He pushed me toward the classroom, his hand on the small of my back. I lifted my chin and stepped forward, free from his touch. I wanted to return under my own steam and on my own terms.

The room was smaller than I remembered, as if I was viewing it from a distance. A thick oval conference table dominated the space, the seats half-filled with my classmates.

All chatter stopped as I hung up my coat and hat, the movements jerky and self-conscious. I took a second to wrestle my static-ridden hair into submission and arrange my expression into something closer to happiness than dread before turning around.

Callie hip-bumped me. "Looks like those stories weren't so crazy after all. What have you been up to?"

My reply was more defensive than I would have liked. "Nothing!"

"Exactly." She gestured to the front of the room. Next to the projection screen hung a battered whiteboard. A numbered column ran down the side, and next to it, the names of every person in our class.

Except me.

"Maybe Shaw has been too busy to put my name back." My throat felt dry, my skin hot.

"Your name's been up there since the day you were reinstated," Eliot said, hovering next to me. He spun his mechanical pencil with sharp, jerky movements, like he always did when stumped. "Shaw's been waiting for you."

"Why would he take you off the list?" Callie asked. "There's no reason."

Unless they knew about Ms. Powell. Unless I was about to vanish from the Walkers like my name had vanished off the board, like Gil Bradley had vanished from Simon's and Amelia's lives.

"Your guess is as good as mine," I said finally, the words swallowed up in the silence around me.

"I bet—" Callie began, but a big, barrel-chested man wearing a lime green Hawaiian shirt and cargo pants entered the room, shutting the door firmly behind him.

"Let's see that homework, people. We've got a lot to cover." Shaw, my instructor, clapped a meaty hand on my shoulder. "Good to have you back. How are you?"

The question seemed genuine enough. His eyes didn't leave my face, and I had a feeling he knew more about what had happened in Train World than he'd told my classmates.

"Getting there," I said in a low voice. "Did I do something wrong? My name's not on the leaderboard."

He glanced at the front of the room, annoyance tightening his features. But when he turned back around, his expression was smoothed out again. "Administrative glitch," he said. "I'll sort it out. Have a seat."

Across the table Eliot shrugged.

"Big day, people. Your latest inversion analysis should be in that pile." He pointed to the stack of papers in front of him. "We're in the home stretch. Your final project before we start preparing for the licensing exam is to select a world for cleaving, make your case, win approval from the Consort, and perform the cleaving."

Callie sat up, glowing with excitement like the sun's corona. "Ourselves? Seriously?"

"We'll break down the process so I can help you with each step, but yes. By the time you're done, you'll have cleaved a world on your own."

I pressed my hand to my mouth, trying to quell the sudden rush of nausea.

"You okay?" Eliot mouthed.

To my right Logan Koskodan asked, "Cleavers work in teams—will we?"

"Not this time," Shaw said. "You'll have support nearby, but this will be a solo cleaving."

Madison Russo, sitting across the table from me, frowned. "But I'm applying for a medical apprenticeship. Do I really need to know this? Medics only Walk in an emergency."

"We don't always end up where we expect." Shaw's eyes flickered to me. "It's best to be prepared for anything."

You're heading into infinity, Monty had told me once. *There's no way to prepare for it.*

I fumbled for the bottle of water in my backpack, hoping it

would wash away the sour taste filling my mouth.

"Ready? Good," Shaw said, not waiting for a response. He hit a button on his computer, and a diagram appeared on the screen behind him. "Somebody tell me why we just spent a month on stabilizing inversions. Eliot?"

"Cleavings unravel fastest at inversions," he said. "If you don't stabilize them before the first cut, you run the risk of unraveling the wrong world or allowing the inversion to spread."

"Exactly. Correct, then cleave."

Before Shaw could continue, I asked, "If inversions can be fixed, why don't we repair Echoes instead of cleaving them?"

Eliot dropped his pencil. Shaw's tone was carefully neutral as he said, "Good question. Theories, anyone?"

The entire class looked at him blankly.

"Come on, now," he said, more amiably. "We haven't covered it yet, but you should have some ideas. It's a safe bet you'll be seeing questions like this on the ethics portion of your exam."

"Fruit of a poisonous tree," said Callie. "A flaw in an Echo's frequency is passed on to any Echoes that spring from it. Tuning would fix one Echo but leave the rest unstable. Cleaving cuts off the problem at its source."

"But what if there's another way to fix the flaws?" I'd heard Callie's rationale a million times, but I had witnessed entire worlds disintegrating into ash. "We could save all those people."

"What people?" Logan said. "Echoes don't even notice when they're cleaved."

"Dying in your sleep doesn't make you less dead," I snapped.

He lifted a shoulder. "You can't kill what's not alive. Besides, if it's us or them, I choose us."

I bit back a snarl. I'd been as blind as Logan, once. But recognizing the truth didn't do much good if I couldn't act on it.

"You've both raised good points." Shaw broke in. "Fact is, it comes down to numbers. The Originals' population is increasing exponentially; so are pivots and branches. But the Walkers aren't. Every day, we fall a little further behind the multiverse, and the only way to keep up is to cleave."

My outrage sparked and crackled like a lit fuse. Shaw believed what he was saying, the same way people believed in the sunrise: It had always been there, so it always would be. We had faith in the Consort, in our traditions and our "innate superiority." But our faith was nothing but a trick used to manipulate us. The fuse inched closer to an explosion.

Intent on controlling my temper, I didn't notice the door swinging open, or the chill in the room, or way Shaw stiffened until I heard a familiar voice say, "Sorry to interrupt. We need Delancey Sullivan, please."

Randolph Lattimer. Head of the Cleavers, enemy of the Free Walkers, all-around horrible human being. And he wanted me, which could only mean disaster.

He stepped inside and beckoned to me with a sharp wave. Behind him, a small, white-haired woman waited, hands folded over an ivory-topped walking stick, her mouth pinched with annoyance. Councilwoman Crane, the Walkers' so-called ethicist. As if the Consort had any ethics.

Shaw inclined his head, the fluorescent lights glinting off his scalp. "Go ahead, Del."

I tried to stand, but my legs were too watery to hold me. To cover, I asked, "Should I bring my stuff?"

"That will be easiest," Crane said, glancing over the top of her glasses. It was hard to imagine she knowingly sentenced Echoes to death on a daily basis. She looked like a sweet little old lady, with her snowy hair and the silver brooch at the neck of her silk blouse. If you weren't a Walker, you'd think she belonged at a garden club meeting, or worked for the historical society.

Callie nudged my foot with hers. I forced a smile, as if acting normal could make this normal, when normal had been shot to hell.

I grabbed my coat and bag and made my way around the room. Eliot reached his hand out, a quick brush of fingertips along my sleeve.

I met his eyes. Unlike Callie, he wouldn't be fooled with a smile. Once you've glimpsed something's true nature, it's hard to see the veneer as anything but false, no matter how bright the shine.

CHAPTER NINE

A M I IN TROUBLE?" I ASKED COUNCILWOMAN Crane as they escorted me to the elevator. She seemed like the type who might rap my knuckles with her walking stick if I sounded impertinent, but Lattimer was the type to slit my throat while he made small talk. I'd take my chances with the cane.

"Only if you've done something wrong," Lattimer replied before Crane could answer.

"My name's missing from the leaderboard."

"That's not a punishment, Delancey. It's an expression of gratitude." He withdrew a key card from his suit jacket and slid it through the reader. A tiny red light switched to green, and he pressed the button for the sixteenth floor, where the Consort met. I'd been there twice before: once for my suspension and once for my reinstatement.

"I don't understand." My coat felt too heavy in the close quarters of the elevator, my scarf like a noose.

Crane spoke in the raspy alto of a former smoker. "You agreed to help us with the aftermath of the anomaly. The opportunity has arisen for you to do so."

I'd agreed to help, thinking I could find out the truth about the Free Walkers. But now I had the truth—and zero desire to help the Consort do anything except self-destruct. "Isn't that what the Cleavers are doing? Why do you need me?"

The doors slid open, depositing us in a familiar black-and-white-tiled hallway. Lattimer ushered me past the Chamber of the Minor Consort, the formal meeting room where they handed down their decisions, and directed me to a nondescript door at the far end of the corridor. "The Cleavers are dealing with the effects; we would like your assistance in rooting out the cause."

"In return, you'll have our thanks," Crane said. "Which out-weighs any ranking you might hold in class."

A bribe, same as they'd done with Addie. Offer us a treat to do their dirty work.

Lattimer swiped the key card again, punched in a code, and the lock turned over with a thunk.

"I don't think—Mom?"

The room was smaller than the Chamber, but equally stark. Plain white walls, black-and-white-tiled floor, no doors except the one we'd passed through. And sitting on the far side of the table, clasped hands visible under the glass tabletop, were my parents.

"Hi, kiddo. Sit, sit." My dad patted the chair next to him, but I stayed standing, trying not to look like I was about to run.

Behind me, Lattimer locked the door again. Running was out.

At the head of the table sat the third member of the Consort: Councilwoman Bolton, the scientist, her smile a sliver of white against her dark skin. "Apologies for interrupting your training, Delancey. Especially on your first day back."

I nodded, not sure how I was supposed to respond.

Lattimer remained standing, and everyone's attention shifted to him—a wordless acknowledgment of who held the power. His silver hair was swept back, his pale eyes shrewd. He was old, but there was nothing frail about him. Unlike Monty, his age gave him an air of command, of cold iron will and calculation. "You were reinstated more than a week ago."

"Del's been through a lot," my father said. "She needed time to recover."

"A prudent course," Crane agreed, settling in at the end of the table. "The Consort is grateful for your help in apprehending your grandfather. I know it was a difficult time, but you handled it as a true Walker should."

"Thank you," I said, the words stiff and ungainly.

"Tell us again about the moment you realized he was dangerous," Lattimer said, smooth as a well-honed knife.

A command, not a question. Typical Consort-speak.

Addie, Eliot, and I had all given reports about what had happened, making sure our stories were straight, concealing the truth about Simon and my solo Walking. We'd rehearsed it like a sonata, and now I performed it again.

"We went to the school for more training." *We went to the school to fix the anomalies Simon kept triggering.* "Mom had told us to stay out of the Echoes, but we thought we'd be safe." *We knew time was running out.* "The inversions were spreading so quickly, we decided to fix them on our own." *Telling you would land us in prison and get Simon killed. So we did it ourselves.* "The Train

World inversion was too big for us to handle, but Monty refused to let us tell you, or cleave it." *He'd told me to run there with Simon, and then everything fell apart.*

"You became suspicious," Lattimer prompted, but his eyes narrowed.

"Eliot distracted him while Addie and I went through to stabilize it, but . . ." I lifted my hands helplessly. "The inversion was out of control. Addie figured out the anomaly was somewhere within that branch just as the threads split. We escaped, and Addie performed an emergency cleaving on the Key World side. Monty was furious, so I knew something was off. I brought him to another Echo and he confessed. That's when you found us."

"Yes," Lattimer said. "The cut site is weaker than we'd like, but considering the circumstances, you did the best you could."

"Thank you," I said again, fighting off the sensation that the walls were inching closer.

"Montrose mentioned the Free Walkers to you when he confessed." Bolton peered at a report, then glanced up sharply, braids swaying. "We believe the anomaly was their attempt to destabilize the Key World, and by extension, the Walkers."

I didn't reply.

"Coming to terms with your grandfather's betrayal must be quite difficult," she said, the slightest note of compassion in her words. "I'm sure you're very angry with him."

"I don't think about him," I said. Which was a lie, and Lattimer knew it, and judging from the look my parents exchanged, they knew it too. But an obvious lie is like a magician's patter—misdirection, to conceal the greater, more important trick.

It worked. Lattimer smiled, indulging me. "I see. Nevertheless, Delancey, it's the Consort's duty to think about him. We've questioned your grandfather about his affiliation with the Free Walkers, but he refuses to answer."

My stomach lurched. If Monty talked—and the Consort listened—Addie, Eliot, and I would end up in prison alongside him. We'd counted on our manufactured reports and Monty's history of dementia to keep us safe, counted on his remorse to keep him quiet. Now that I was locked in a windowless room with a bunch of murderers, it seemed like a miscalculation.

I slipped my hand into my pocket and curled my fingers around the origami star within. "Monty's stubborn. That's not a surprise."

"True enough," he said. "But your grandfather's silence endangers us all. We believe the Free Walkers have developed a weapon, and he knows about it."

"Monty never mentioned anything about a weapon," I said truthfully.

"He might have called it something else," my dad said. "You know how he was, always talking in puzzles. It might not be a thing at all, but a plan, or a technique. Whatever it is, kiddo, we need to figure it out."

"Uncovering the Free Walkers' weapon could shift the course of the multiverse," Bolton said. "As you said, your grandfather's quite stubborn. He's refusing to speak with anyone except you."

"Me?" My shock was genuine.

Crane replied, "He'll give us the information we seek, so long as you're the one interviewing him. Otherwise . . . silence."

"Why me?" I looked at each of them in turn, and finally my mother leaned forward, sliding her hands across the table as if reaching for me.

"Because he loves you, Del," she said, soft and cajoling. "He knows what he did was wrong. He knows you must feel so, so betrayed, and he wants to make amends."

In a million worlds, I could never forgive Monty. "I'm supposed to care what he wants?"

Lattimer spread his arms wide, palms up. "You agreed to help us."

"Monty doesn't know anything. He's bluffing."

"We don't believe that's the case." He paused. "Would you turn your back on us, and the Key World, for the sake of a grudge you bear a harmless old man?"

"With all due respect, Councilman," my father said, "harmless old men don't serve life sentences."

"There's no place more secure than an oubliette. Even Montrose realizes there would be no point in trying to escape, and Delancey will be well looked after."

"Why can't Addie do it?" I asked. I'd edged away until my hip bumped the wall, but it was useless. I was as trapped as Monty.

"Your grandfather is insistent on this matter: He'll speak only to you. He believes you're the one he's most wronged."

I snorted. Monty was after something, and it wasn't redemption. He'd taught me too well, and I knew, as surely as I knew the sound of the Key World or the feel of Simon's hand in mine, this was one of his schemes.

"Tell him to find some other way to ease his conscience."

Lattimer flicked a piece of imaginary lint from his suit, as if brushing away my answer. "A Walker's duty is to protect the Key World, Delancey. It is our calling, and now you are being called. Unless you've decided you no longer want to be a Walker."

My mom stiffened at the implication, my father frowning alongside her.

"Of course I do!" I twisted the hem of my sweater. Dealing with Lattimer was like playing an especially challenging violin piece, and I was out of practice—stumbling over passages I should have sailed through, missing the delicate shadings that gave a phrase its meaning, so focused on the playing that I forgot to perform.

I needed to hit the right note. Refusing to help would invite dangerous attention; caving too easily would make him equally suspicious.

Propping my hands on my hips, I asked, "What if I go in there and listen to his spiel, and he doesn't tell us anything?" Us. As if the Consort and I were on the same team.

"He's aware of the consequences if he reneges."

"What if he lies? He does that, you know. A lot. It's kind of his specialty."

"Let us worry about the accuracy of his information. Your only concern will be to keep him talking."

As long as he wasn't talking about me and Simon. If I wanted to control the information Monty was passing along to the Consort, I'd have to get involved.

I bit my lip, glanced over at my parents. My father stood. "Could we have a few moments alone with Del?"

"Of course," Crane said, before Lattimer could object. "We'll wait outside."

"Thank you. We won't be long."

"See that you aren't," Lattimer said, keying in the code to open the door. "Time is of the essence, Foster, as you're aware."

My mom scrambled to her feet as Crane and Bolton rose. We waited in silence as they filed out. I listened for the sound of the lock engaging, but it never came. Our privacy was a gift bestowed; it could be taken away at a whim.

"I'm not convinced this is a good idea," my father said. "Are you sure, Winnie?"

"Del needs to think about her future," my mom answered, like I wasn't standing three feet away. "The licensing exam is a few months away, and then she's off to her apprenticeship. This will boost her chance at a good assignment."

"Is interrogating Monty the best way to do that? She should be focused on her training."

"She needs closure," my mom said, and turned to include me in the conversation. "We'll be able to put this whole episode behind us and start fresh. It'll be good for all of us. What's more, it proves your loyalty to the Consort."

"Does it need proving?" I asked.

"People talk, Del. The rest of us have our reputations to fall back on, but you . . ."

My reputation wasn't great to begin with. Trust my mom to always keep an eye on the bigger picture.

"I thought this was about letting Monty make amends," I said, and she had the grace to look ashamed.

"Forget about Monty," Dad said. He wrapped an arm around my shoulder. "Do it for yourself. For your future. You can make a difference, kiddo."

Amelia had thought so too, and it had cost her everything. Would I pay a similar price if I allied myself with the Free Walkers?

My father opened the door, and Crane and Bolton returned. Lattimer was nowhere in sight.

"I assume you've come to a decision," Bolton said. She tipped her head to the side and waited for my response.

For the first time I felt a shift in power. The Consort needed me in a way they hadn't before, and the knowledge gave me confidence. I straightened my shoulders and met her gaze.

"When do I start?"

Crane sniffed. "Now, naturally."

CHAPTER TEN

Now?" MY MOM'S VOICE JUMPED AN OCTAVE. "She needs time to prepare."

"Delancey's made her decision. Nothing will be gained by waiting," Crane said.

"What are we supposed to say to him?" Mom asked.

Crane's wrinkles deepened in confusion. "You and Foster won't be accompanying us. Montrose's demands are quite clear—he'll speak with Delancey, and only Delancey."

"You can't seriously expect us to let her deal with him alone," my dad said.

Crane drew herself up. One of the benefits of absolute power is that nobody questions your decisions. The downside is that nobody points out when you're being an idiot, and it was clear the councilwoman didn't like the sensation.

"You have my personal guarantee no harm will come to her. I trust that's enough to satisfy your concerns," Bolton said smoothly, leaving no room for disagreement.

"Of course," my mother said, but she clutched her pendant and edged closer to my father.

I bit back the urge to remind all of them I was standing right there, perfectly capable of speech and forming my own, very definite opinions about my safety. In my experience, however, adults only ask your opinion if they think it matches their own.

"Delancey." Crane's inflection was perfectly neutral. No hint of a question, only a prompt.

What would Ms. Powell want me to do? Assuming the Free Walkers had a weapon, they didn't need details about their own weapons—they needed to know what the Consort was planning. But what people *don't* know reveals as much as what they do. The Consort's questions were as important as Monty's answers. I could pass along both.

"I'm ready," I said.

My mom hugged me. "Remember, he can't hurt you."

No, Monty couldn't hurt me. Not any more than he had already.

"Later," I said, and waved halfheartedly.

A pair of guards stood at attention next to the elevator. One of them—a woman with long, blunt-cut black hair and a thick fringe of bangs—looked familiar. At first I couldn't place her, and then the memory clicked. She'd escorted me to my disciplinary hearing. She probably thought I was being taken into custody. They followed us inside and positioned themselves on either side of me.

Crane withdrew her ID and slid it through the reader, then pressed an unlabeled black button.

The light changed from red to green, and the elevator sank smoothly. "Where are we going?"

"Sublevels," Crane said crisply.

"I thought those floors were parking." The Consort Building had assigned parking spaces in an underground garage—using public parking, where people had to choose their spaces every day, raised too many opportunities for change—but not many Walkers used them. Our kind traditionally lived near train lines, so most people didn't bother driving into the city.

"The first level is," Crane said. "The rest are restricted."

"Guess I'm special," I said. The display above the doors had stopped at B, for basement, but we were still sinking. My chest tightened, and the elevator car felt increasingly small.

When we stopped, the doors opened on a sterile, echoing corridor. Two more guards were positioned at the short end of the hallway, a few feet to my left. To my right, the corridor stretched at least a hundred feet, windowless doors spaced evenly along both sides. Unlike the regular security force, the guards here wore unrelieved black. Everything else here was blindingly white—white tiles, white walls, white doors. The only sound was the buzz of fluorescent lights overhead. The icy, overprocessed air stung my nose.

Lattimer appeared through the door opposite the elevator. Upstairs, his suit had appeared black—here it seemed to absorb light, an aura in reverse.

"Randolph," Crane said. "I believe everything is in order."

He closed the door behind him. "It is."

"I'll leave her to you," Crane said. She and her escorts stepped back onto the elevator, departing swiftly and silently.

"Hello again, Delancey. I'm so glad you came," Lattimer

said, with a smile that was meant to be warm but only made cold sweat bead along my spine. "Let me take your things."

I handed over my coat and bag to one of the guards, who took them into the control room while I inspected the hallway. The corridor stretched away from us in an unbroken line—no intersections or corners, every door visible. I counted eight on each side, a total of sixteen. Small, for a prison. "These are the oubliettes?"

"In a manner of speaking. The oubliettes are located in an Echo; we've manipulated the fabric of the target world, unraveling all threads not directly related to the cell itself. Then we create a single pivot in and out, leading to the room you're about to enter. It allows us to transfer food and other necessities between the oubliette and the Key World, and we can remove the prisoner if we need to converse with him. Each Echo is monitored to ensure that no further pivots are created. It's the perfect prison."

I'd known oubliettes were Echoes, but I hadn't realized they'd physically altered the world itself. I couldn't fathom that kind of precision, but Eliot might. I'd have to ask him.

"Don't the prisoners get frequency poisoning?"

"We choose Echoes with a pitch similar to the Key World, for minimal exposure. But to be perfectly honest, most inmates aren't here long enough for frequency poisoning to become an issue."

Apparently a lifetime sentence meant a short lifetime, not a lengthy sentence.

"Which one is Monty?"

Lattimer pointed at a door halfway down the corridor. Suddenly I was grateful I hadn't had dinner yet.

"Each cell is outfitted with recording equipment. I'll be monitoring it from the control room," he said, as if this was a comfort. "I'll be able to see and hear everything that happens while you're inside."

Since I'd come here to make sure Monty didn't tell anyone about Simon, I was less than comforted. "What do I do once I'm inside?"

"Be encouraging. Empathetic. Let him unburden himself to you, no matter how outlandish his claims."

"Outlandish?"

"He's a cunning old man, Delancey. His confession will be short on remorse, and long on excuses."

"It's all going to be lies? You said this was urgent."

"It is. But if he knows that, he gains the advantage. For now, let him talk. Let him believe you forgive him. He'll be more receptive to your questions."

"What questions?"

"Ask him about the Free Walkers. What they're planning, where they're hiding. How they communicate. Ask about Rose, and the weapon they were working on before she vanished. Even the smallest detail helps." He handed me a tiny beige earpiece. "This will allow me to feed you more questions during the interrogation."

So much for pleasant conversation. I slipped the earpiece in and let my hair fall forward. "He's not going to tell you anything."

"Not me. You."

"What are you going to do with those details?" I asked. "Chase Free Walkers?"

"If that's where he leads us, certainly."

I wound my fingers together, trying to keep from shaking.

"He's already inside and restrained," Lattimer added, escorting me to the cell door. "There's nothing to fear."

People kept telling me not to be scared, but the more they insisted, the more I doubted. But I wasn't going to let Monty see it. I lifted my chin and opened the door.

The room was as white as bleached bone and smelled like fear. Monty sat on the far side of a long, narrow steel table. His face split in a broad smile, though his lips were chapped and raw-looking. Gray cotton scrubs hung limply from his frame, and his arms looked spindly. But his eyes were keen as ever as he watched me cross the room.

"Del," he rasped. "I'd get up, but . . ." He lifted his hands, and I saw the metal cuffs circling his wrists, the chain that looped through one of the rings soldered to the table edge.

My feet squeaked on the tile floor. It slanted ever-so-slightly to one side, angling toward a drain set in the floor. I shuddered.

"Are you okay?" I asked without thinking.

"I'm better now."

This wasn't what I'd expected. I'd imagined him in a jail cell, wearing prison orange, tired and remorseful and lonely—but not shattered. I'd imagined feeling smug. Vindicated. Instead, horror crawled from the base of my spine to the nape of my neck on countless tiny feet.

Had Gil Bradley endured this too? Thinking of Simon's father reminded me of Simon, and the pity welling up around my heart receded.

"Why am I here?"

"I've missed you," Monty said. "I want to make amends."

"It's too late." The words felt sharp as blades in my mouth. Even so, I wondered: If it was too late for Monty, was it too late for me? Cemetery Simon hadn't thought so.

"Keep him talking," Lattimer's voice in my ear was so close, I flinched. Monty's eyebrows lifted at the movement.

"Nothing's done," Monty said solemnly. He glanced up at the camera embedded in the corner of the ceiling. "I've had time to think about what happened. I didn't understand before, but now I do. It's not too late."

He'd said that before, as the Consort had dragged him away. *It's not too late. He's more important than you know.* A warning prickled along my scalp. I had to steer him away from mentioning Simon in front of the cameras. "You can't undo this," I said. "You betrayed everyone. You used me."

"I wanted your grandmother back," he said petulantly. If this was Monty's idea of making amends, the Consort's plan would never work, because I'd strangle him before he gave up any real information. "You never knew her, or you'd understand. Rose and I are two halves of a whole. Montrose and Rosemont. We were meant to be, she always said. The universe itself wanted us to be together."

He'd said the same about me and Simon, but only to manipulate me. "The universe doesn't want anything," I said. "This is all your fault. Don't try to make it sound grand and important."

"But it *is* important," he said. "If you'd lost your other half, wouldn't you do anything to get him back?"

I didn't want to answer. Didn't want to think of Monty

and me having anything in common. I had limits, didn't I?

"Not if it meant destroying the multiverse," I finally said, my voice rusty as an old hinge.

He placed his hands flat on the table, fingers spread wide. "I didn't know the anomaly was going to be such a problem. There were factors I didn't account for at the time."

I stared at him, translating his ambiguity. He hadn't known about Simon's flaw, he meant, that his frequency would unbalance entire worlds.

"I understand now," he said softly, urgently. "I know what I did was wrong, and I want to help set it right again."

"Who needs your help?" I said. "I'm managing fine on my own."

"Are you, now?" His shoulders slumped, but his eyes flickered to mine, sharp and curious. "I suppose so. Moving on, then?"

"I'm not living in the past," I said. "Or chasing ghosts, the way you did."

"Rose isn't a ghost," he snapped.

"No. She was a Free Walker, like you. And she left. Did you ever think about that, Monty? She took off and left you to take the fall. You always say that you two were halves of a whole, but . . . she didn't seem to think so. That's just a story you tell yourself."

"The past is prologue," he replied, rapping the table sharply. "Shakespeare said that, and he was right. It's important that we learn from the stories of our past, Del. Our roots—who we were—determine who we are now. Our roots tell us where to go."

Lattimer's voice crackled in my ear. "Ask him about the Free Walkers. I want names."

I nodded understanding. "The Free Walkers are your roots. Who did you work with, back when you actually did your own work instead of manipulating teenagers?"

"You already know all the names you need to." He settled back in the chair as comfortably as if we were sitting at the kitchen table. "The only one that matters is Rose. Isn't that right, Randolph?" he called.

"Fine. What was Rose doing for the Free Walkers?"

"What needed to be done."

"That's not an answer."

He grunted and ducked his head. I knew this stage. This was the ornery phase, soon to be followed by the muddled phase. I was losing him.

"The weapon," Lattimer ordered. "I want to know what it does."

"Was she working on something specific?" I watched Monty's face for any twitch or droop that might give away the answer. "A weapon, maybe?"

He chuckled. "Anything can be a weapon, depending on who controls it. Look in the mirror."

I gripped the edge of the table to keep from throttling him.

"Where is it?" Lattimer pressed, and I repeated the question.

"No one person would be entrusted with information like that," Monty scolded. "Besides, a weapon's no use if it's hidden away. You only hide what you need to protect."

His fingers began twitching—not reaching into the strings of the world, but something far more innocuous. A melody played on an imaginary keyboard. "Let me tell you a story. I think you'll like it."

"I've heard enough of your stories," I said. "They haven't done me any good."

"That's because you don't listen. A story has more to offer than words on a page, if you pay attention. That's why things slip by you, Delancey. You're slapdash," he said dismissively. "You'll never get what you want if you're sloppy, you know. And you'll have no one to blame but yourself."

My cheeks burned at the accusation. I hadn't paid enough attention to the signs—Simon's flaw, Ms. Powell's name, Monty's deception—and it had cost me.

"This is pointless," I said, and pushed back from the table. Monty jerked upright, the chain rattling.

"Where are you going?"

"You promised to give me information."

He grinned. "And indeed I have."

"You've made excuses and insulted me. Not the same thing. I'm done." I knocked on the door.

"You'll come back, won't you?" His tone was plaintive, like a child's. "There's more I want to tell you."

"I don't want to listen."

As the guard ushered me out, Monty began whistling our old song.

Nothing's done that can't be un-,
Nothing's lost that can't be found,
Make a choice and make a world,
Find another way around.

Lattimer strode toward me, not bothering to mask his irritation. "You were supposed to draw him out, not get into a shouting match."

"He's not going to give us anything. This was a waste of time."

"I disagree. He said you knew all the names you needed to—what did he mean?"

"Exactly what he said," I replied. "Rose is the only name he mentioned. Nobody else matters."

"Not to us," Lattimer said. "You'll have to go back in."

He reached for the door again, and I crossed my arms.

"He's done for today," I said. "Early evening is his worst time. Once he starts with the singing, he's useless."

Useless was an exaggeration. Monty was slipping, but he would have rambled on for as long as I'd stayed. The more incoherent his story, though, the greater the chance he'd let slip something valuable—and dangerous.

"Finding that weapon and locating the Free Walkers are crucial to our plans," Lattimer said, and his eyes met mine, steely and cold. "If you can't get the information from him, I will."

CHAPTER ELEVEN

My PARENTS SPRANG TO THEIR FEET AS SOON
as I returned.

"How was he?" Mom asked.

"More importantly, how are you?" said my dad, wrapping
his arms around me.

"I'm fine," I said, unsure if I should tell them how diminished he seemed. "Monty . . . is Monty. A cell won't change him."

It was true. Even in an oubliette, he was still scheming, still
searching for Rose. I was the one who'd changed. I didn't need
him anymore.

"Delancey's too easily led by her emotions," Lattimer said.
"He'll make use of that, to everyone's detriment."

"Considering the situation—" my father began.

"I'm sure next time will go more smoothly," my mom said
swiftly, cutting him off.

"Next time? I'm not going back in there." I didn't want to
witness his decline, or risk him giving away the truth.

"The visits continue," Lattimer replied. "I will make sure
your grandfather understands better how to conduct himself.
You will practice holding your temper."

He left without further good-byes, and my mom frowned. "Don't let your grandfather get under your skin."

"You want to deal with him? Be my guest. I'd rather be at school."

"That's saying something," my dad said, forcing a laugh.

"He doesn't want to deal with me," Mom said, her words edged with hurt. "He won't even let us visit."

I hadn't thought about how it would make my mom feel, to have her own father shut her out and betray her people. Her guilt probably rivaled Addie's.

"He's impossible," I said.

"Find a way to make it work," she said. "Having a Consort member's support will open up all sorts of doors, but only if you succeed. They care about results, not intentions."

Once again my dad stepped in, trying to defray the tension. "Why don't you head back to class? You could catch the last hour, at least."

"No way. I got yanked out by the Consort on my first day back. I go in there, and they'll treat me like a circus freak."

"I'm sure that's not true," Mom said.

"Really? Don't people look at you strangely now? Don't they watch you out of the corner of their eyes, or go quiet when you walk past?"

She folded her arms. "My work speaks louder than anything they could say."

"Or maybe you're not hearing it."

She looked at my dad, who lifted his hands and eyebrows in

unison. "Fine. Today only. You'll be back in class on Saturday, no excuses."

"Whatever. Can we get out of here now?"

"You can head home," my dad said as they exchanged glances again. "We have work to finish."

The Tacet. "Addie said the Consort's planning a big cleaving. Tons of branches?"

My dad nodded. "A project this complex requires a lot of planning. Every branch has to be analyzed, every cut orchestrated. It's hard to pull off correctly, but the results will be worth it."

The results would be catastrophic.

"You've already done the crazy hours thing," I said. "Can't someone else handle it?"

If I couldn't tell them the truth, at least I could steer them away from committing more cleavings.

"It's only a few more weeks," Mom promised, her expression softening. "Besides, when the Consort asks . . ." She trailed off, and I knew she was thinking of Monty. She straightened her shoulders. ". . . we're happy to help."

To prove her loyalty, she meant. We were all paying for Monty's sins, and in the process, committing our own.

CHAPTER TWELVE

OUR RAMSHACKLE QUEEN ANNE WAS DARK when I arrived home. No lights, even on the porch. No sound once I'd let myself in, except for Amelia's pivots quivering and rustling like the wind through grass.

What would happen if the Free Walkers brought down the Consort? Would there be a place for my family? Would they take it? Walking shaped every aspect of my parents' lives. The Free Walkers would unravel their world as swiftly as a cleaving, and I didn't have a clue if they'd be able to knit it up again.

I was starving, so I munched a piece of peanut-butter toast while I turned on every light in the house. The shadows fled, but my dark thoughts lingered, and my footsteps sounded too loud. I needed music.

The honeyed wood of my violin felt warm and reassuring as I positioned it under my chin. Without thinking, I began to play Simon's song.

We hadn't meant for it to sound sad—some phrases were sly, some were merry, some were tender—but the ache of missing him found its way through my fingers, turning the notes unbearably wistful.

I heard Eliot let himself in, but I kept playing, improvising well beyond the tune Simon and I had written together. I was on my own.

"Sounds good," Eliot said when I'd finished.

It sounded incomplete.

"You're out early." I tucked the instrument into its case.

"Shaw let me go." Eliot unwound his scarf and threw his coat in the chair. "Which you would know, if you'd checked your phone. Tell me what happened."

"Cocoa?" I replied.

He groaned but followed me into the kitchen, squirming on the kitchen stool while I warmed cocoa and sugar and milk on the stove. "You're killing me. Why'd they yank you out of class?"

I passed Eliot a mug dotted with extra marshmallow fluff, just the way he liked it. "Lattimer wanted me to visit Monty. Technically, the Consort asked, but it was totally his show."

He choked on the first sip. "You said no, right?" he asked between coughs. "Because if there are two people in the world you should be avoiding, it's Lattimer and Monty."

"I wish. There was no way out of it."

"This is not going to end well," he said. "No prison visit ever does."

"This one certainly didn't."

It took a moment for my words to register. "You've already gone in?"

"Monty won't talk, and Lattimer basically said I could do it or leave the Walkers."

Eliot scowled. "He wants something."

"Yeah. The Free Walkers. They have some sort of weapon, and he wants to find it before the Consort's big cleaving."

"Not Lattimer. Monty. What's he after?"

"Forgiveness," I said, making air quotes.

His brow furrowed. "Monty's crazy, but he's not stupid. You're never going to forgive him, and he knows it. What's he really after?"

"Same thing as ever. Rose."

"Rose is dead," he replied. "There's no way she could have lasted in the Echoes for this long. Even if she had, Train World..."

Was gone, along with everyone in it.

He broke off and ducked his head. "I'm sorry."

"Don't be," I said, and turned the mug of cocoa around and around. Not telling Eliot the truth left me feeling wormy and small. "How was class?"

"Who cares? How was Monty?"

"His usual awful self," I said. "I lost my temper and bailed. Lattimer was thrilled."

"What did he say? Monty, I mean."

I snorted. "He kept going on about stories, which is Monty-speak for lies."

Eliot nudged his glasses up. "Maybe not. What exactly did he say?"

"He called me slapdash." The accusation stung, hours later.

"He insulted you? Doesn't sound like him. And it's a crap way to earn forgiveness."

"He doesn't care if I forgive him. He wants to mess with my head. It's his only form of entertainment."

"There's got to be a reason," he said. "We just don't see it yet. What else did he say?"

Anger blurred my memory. "He talked about stories, I guess. He said they were more than words on a page. And he called me sloppy." *You'll have no one to blame but yourself.* . . .

"Words on a page," Eliot repeated. He spun the stool in a circle as he thought.

"You're going to make yourself dizzy." I put out a hand to stop him, and he grabbed my wrist.

"He wasn't insulting you, Del." He lifted my hand with his, pointing to the bookshelves in the living room, filled with neat lines of matching leather-bound books. "He was telling you where to look for clues."

"The journals? You think he left me a message in their journals?"

Eliot nodded, his eyes lighting up at the prospect of a fresh puzzle. "Better make popcorn."

An hour later the popcorn was gone. I rummaged through the pantry looking for more snacks. Eliot sat at the kitchen island surrounded by haphazard piles of leather-bound journals and a mess of papers, his face bathed in the blue glow of his screen.

"Rose took nearly two hundred Walks in the six months before she disappeared." He groaned and took off his glasses, rubbing at his eyes. "At least the data sample's sufficiently large."

"Do you really think there's a pattern?"

"There's always a pattern," he said, resuming his usual hunt-and-peck. I tossed a bag of Oreos on the table—another sign that life hadn't returned to normal. Three months ago my mother would have taken a flamethrower to any processed snacks that crossed the threshold of our kitchen. But baking had fallen by the wayside, and now our pantry looked like any other family's. I kind of liked it.

Careful not to scatter crumbs, I ran my finger over the pages of my grandmother's journal. Traditionally, Walkers kept journals as a record of their personal Walks, but Rose's felt more like a scrapbook. Scattered among handwritten reports were recipes, notes about patients, brief snippets of songs, even photographs. Mom had told me Monty was the more free-spirited of my grandparents, but if this book was any indication, Rose was the definition of eclectic.

Now that I knew where she'd gone, Rose herself had become the true mystery. The woman in these pages didn't seem like a rebel. She was a healer. A mother and a musician, happiest in her work and in her home. Happiest with my grandfather, certainly.

And yet she'd run.

People—Originals and Walkers alike—are contradictions. They hold within themselves a jumble of impulses and beliefs; circumstances polish some facets and chip away others. But amid the jumble lies their heart, diamond hard and incontrovertible. Like a kaleidoscope, the aspects of a person can shift and reform, but the center holds true.

It was easier to see in Originals, because we could compare versions. I'd met countless Simons, and no matter how different he appeared, each at their core was strong and sharp and challenging. Walkers were fixed, their alternate, contradictory selves existing only in imagination.

Or in stories.

The woman in this journal was more than a contradiction. She was a careful construction of a life, a tale meant for an audience.

She was a lie.

"Rose knew the Consort would read these," I said, fixing myself a cup of coffee. "They'd analyze the Walks she took, same as we're doing."

Eliot looked up. "So they're either fake, which means we're wasting our time, or they're genuine, which means they're useless. Which means we're wasting our time."

"Rose was a medic," I pointed out. "She shouldn't have taken this many Walks." Walker medics served multiple teams, so they usually stayed in the Key World unless called out for a specific emergency.

"Fakes, then." Eliot pushed the laptop away. "But why bother making up an entire book of bad data? Why did Monty send us here?"

I stared at the scatter of pages in front of us. Two hundred Walks. For a medic, that alone was suspicious. "Maybe it's not completely fake."

Eliot started to pace around the island, pencil spinning. I

frowned into my mug and waited, but the pacing didn't stop. His lips moved silently.

I finished my coffee and poured another cup. He kept going.

"Hey—" I said, but he held up a hand to silence me. "You're going to wear a groove in the floor."

Impatient, I pulled out a fresh sheet of paper and listed Rose's Walks again—just the numeric frequencies. There was no pattern, no cluster of worlds or range of pitches she seemed to favor, and I huffed in irritation. When I was done, I had a list of random numbers and Eliot standing over my shoulder, smelling of pine sap and buttered popcorn. "Solved it yet, Genius Boy? Because I'm stumped."

Wordlessly he pulled the pen out of my hand and drew a thick black slash through two of the Walks.

"Hey! I actually worked on that, you know."

"Del, look." He ran down the paper, crossing out the duplicate frequencies. "Signal to noise. The real information is here, but you have to dig through a lot of meaningless stuff to get at it."

"I don't understand."

"The Consort would have read these journals, same as us. So it means anything obvious is probably useless—like Echoes she went to more than once. The Consort would assume they're important, but their true purpose is to throw Lattimer off the trail and obscure the real data."

I studied the remaining frequencies. "Those are the Walks she actually took?"

"Some, yes. But I'm betting we need more exclusion criteria."

"I don't speak genius," I muttered. "Translation?"

"We need another filter. Other ways to separate out which frequencies are important and which are camouflage."

"She took this one with Monty," I said, pointing to one of the numbers at the bottom. "According to his notes, it was their last Walk together before she left. Is it important?"

"He said her story was the one that mattered, right?"

I nodded and stuffed another Oreo in my mouth.

"If we cross out any Walks they took together . . . ," Eliot said.

I leaped up and grabbed Monty's journals from the living room.

"Read me the frequencies from each trip," Eliot ordered, and I obeyed. He crossed out batches, pen flying over the paper. "I'm dropping any world they both visited, even if it was at different times."

"Do you think she really went to these places?" I asked when he was done.

"Hard to say. It's possible she wrote down frequencies that fit the code, rather than places she visited."

We stared at the list in silence.

Eight frequencies in all. I wrote them on a fresh piece of paper, but they still didn't reveal their secrets.

"I'm not seeing it," he said around a mouthful of Oreo. "Are these a map? Was this her escape route? A list of worlds with Free Walker outposts?"

I stared at them, trying to discern a pattern. "We could check them out. See what we find."

He sprayed crumbs across the table. "That's a terrible plan. We don't know what we're looking for. You want to show up with a sign that says 'Honk if you're a Free Walker'?" He shook his head. "Not to mention, neither of us is licensed. I'm not going to let you—"

"Let?" The warm, easy feeling between us vanished. "You don't 'let' me do anything. You're not my mom. You're not even Addie."

His shoulders tensed. "No. I'm just the guy—"

The back door slammed open with a noise like a gunshot. "Damn it, Del! Have you completely lost your mind?"

CHAPTER THIRTEEN

ADDIE STOOD IN THE DOORWAY, VIBRATING with outrage.

"I take it you talked to Mom and Dad," I said.

She stomped inside, Laurel behind her looking amused and resigned in equal measure.

"Cocoa?" Eliot asked her. "This part takes a while, sometimes."

Laurel stifled a laugh.

Addie ignored them. "You should not be working for Lattimer."

"You are," I pointed out. "You asked me to help, remember? How is this any different?"

The project is done. I'm back to regular apprenticeship work."

I hadn't known that. "Did you have any luck? Find any Free Walkers?"

Her complexion cooled from feverish to impassive ivory. "No. We ran out of leads to follow."

The best lies look identical to the truth, only better. It's not about telling people what you want them to think—it's about telling people the story they want to believe. Addie was too straightforward to be any good at it; she assumed a lie was truth's opposite instead of its mirror. I'd had years of experience. I knew better.

Eliot did too, thanks to my terrible influence, and didn't bother to hide his skepticism. "You didn't find anything?"

Her eyes were a murky green instead of their usual jade. "Nothing we could pursue. The point is, you shouldn't be working for Lattimer."

"Why not?"

"Because you're a kid. You don't even have a license."

I stifled the urge to remind her she was no longer in charge of me. "I will soon. Aren't you the one who wanted me to think about my future? If I do this, I can write my own ticket."

"Technically speaking," Eliot put in, "we all work for the Consort. This is a specialized assignment."

"This is Monty," Addie snarled. "And a *terrible* idea."

"What does he think Monty knows?" Laurel asked. "Even if he had been working with the Free Walkers, they would have scattered as soon as he was arrested."

Her tone made it clear she knew the truth about the anomaly—and Simon. I glared at Addie, who nibbled a thumbnail and avoided my eyes.

"A weapon," I said into the sudden quiet. "The Consort thinks Simon's dad built a weapon before he was captured, something the Free Walkers would use against them. Lattimer thinks Monty has information about it."

"I don't care if he does or not. Find a way to get out of this," Addie said. "Digging around in Free Walker stuff is dangerous."

"We're not."

Addie arched her eyebrows. "And you're looking at Rose's journals because . . ."

"Homework," Eliot said quickly. "For Shaw."

"Leave the lying to Del," Addie said dryly. "In fact, leave this alone completely, both of you. Before somebody gets hurt."

"Too late," I shot back. "Somebody already has, in case you've forgotten. His name was Simon. Ring a bell?"

Eliot put a hand on my arm, but I shook him off.

Addie's shoulders sagged. "Del . . ."

"Oh!" said Laurel, overbright and obvious. "This is cute! Did you two come up with it?"

"With what?" I asked, tearing my gaze away from Addie.

"This song." She tapped the list of frequencies and hummed lightly. "Sorry. It's a thing I do when I'm bored at work."

"We didn't write a song," Eliot said. "What kind of thing?"

"I get stuck doing a lot of data entry—coding navigation reports and cleavings paperwork and stuff. Which is okay, I guess, but they all start to look the same after a few hours, so I made up a game. Each frequency corresponds to a note, more or less. Like this one is a G-flat." She sang it, her voice a clear, sweet soprano. "And this one's a D. Put enough of them together and they make a song."

"Like sight reading?" Eliot asked.

"Yeah. It's not hard; the trick is to remember which range

of frequencies correspond to each note on the scale. A generator would do the job, but it sounds nicer if you sing it."

"Can you sing this one?" I pushed the paper toward her. My pulse was thrumming so loudly I wasn't sure I'd be able to hear her.

She looked over at Addie, shrugged, and began to sing—just the notes, not the words—but I knew the tune immediately. Judging by the look on Addie's face, so did she.

Nothing's done that can't be un-,
Nothing's lost that—

Laurel broke off. "Where's the rest?"

"We know the rest," I said softly.

"Where did you get those frequencies?" Addie demanded, reaching for the last remaining journal. I snatched it away just in time.

"It's mine," I snapped. "Monty sang it to me, not you."

"That is brilliant," Eliot said. "Freakishly brilliant, but still."

"Well, Monty's a freak," Addie said. "It fits."

Laurel glanced around—me clutching a twenty-year-old book to my chest, Addie grim as death, Eliot staring at the mess of papers like he couldn't tell if they were a bomb or a birthday present.

"Somebody should explain to the new girl," she said.

"Rose left us a code," I said. "She converted the frequencies to notes and made a song out of it. But she only put the first few measures in the journal."

"And Monty taught the rest to Del when she was a kid," Addie said.

"What's the message?" Laurel asked. "Rose's location?"

"No way. Monty knew this was here," Eliot said. "If it could have helped him find Rose, he would have used it a long time ago."

"It's not a map," Laurel said. "But it could be."

We all looked at her blankly.

"Every note on the scale resonates at a different frequency. But they're rough approximations—a plain middle C won't match an Echo. The frequency needs to be much more specific."

She took a blank piece of paper and drew a staff, then sketched in the melody she'd sung. "See? Individually, they're too general. But if you combine them into a single chord . . . an octad, I guess you'd call it . . . they'll generate a more distinct frequency." She drew a chord, eight notes stacked together like a blobby, upright caterpillar. "It might be enough to pinpoint a specific Echo."

"Not from a piece of sheet music," Eliot argued. "The range of possible frequencies would be too broad. It's dependent on who's singing, or what instrument you play it on. Middle C resonates differently if you play it on a guitar or a flute or a cello."

I touched his hand. "Or a violin."

"Exactly," Eliot replied, and looked at me again. "Oh. *Oh.*"

"Rose's frequencies," I said. "Rose's violin."

Every violin has its own voice; like fingerprints, no two are exactly alike, which is why people will pay millions for a genuine

Stradivarius. Monty had given me my grandmother's violin as soon as I was big enough to play it. I didn't know if I should be touched that he'd trusted my eleven-year-old self with something so irreplaceable, or furious he'd been manipulating me for so long. I was leaning toward the latter.

I led the way to the music room and took the violin out of the case, the burnished wood familiar as an old friend. I used Rose's pendant to tune it, trying to keep frustration from stiffening my fingers.

"I can record your playing and combine the frequencies digitally," Eliot said, laptop at the ready. "It shouldn't take too long to process."

I tucked the instrument under my chin, lifted the bow, and Addie spoke.

"Even if you're right—and I refuse to believe that the Free Walkers would be so stupid as to use a *nursery rhyme* as a secret code—but if this works, what are you going to do? Chase down the frequency? Find this weapon, if that's what it is? What then? Lattimer will know you're up to something. So will the Free Walkers. Do you have any idea how much trouble you'll be in?"

She knotted her fingers together, face pinched with worry. "Del, stop and *think*. Haven't you learned anything?"

The lessons that stick are the hardest to learn. Simon had taught me how to see the truth of a person, because he'd seen me. He'd taught me how to sacrifice—to look beyond myself and focus on the good. But he'd also taught me how to fight. *You play until you hear the buzzer.*

I looked up at Addie—really looked—and saw the fear behind her anger. She'd never been scared before, not like this. I wondered what she'd seen during her special assignment to frighten her so deeply.

"Don't you want answers?" I asked.

Laurel took Addie's hand, the gesture so simple and automatic my throat ached.

"Of course I do," Addie said.

I rubbed my thumb along the ebony frog of the bow. "The Consort's not going to hand them over like a bag of jelly beans. We have to find them ourselves."

"And what happens when you get caught?"

"All I'm doing is playing the violin."

Before she could protest further, I nodded to Eliot and drew the bow over the strings, the notes rich and clear. I tried to envision my grandmother standing in their room, playing for Monty, sending out a message that might never be found. Had she meant it for me?

I played the song three times, stopping at Eliot's signal. "Got it," he said, and tapped furiously at the keys. "Give me a minute."

A minute was all it took for Addie to start in again.

"Let's say you find this weapon. You'd have to give it to Lattimer. Who you *hate*. Is that really your plan? The Free Walkers won't let it go without a fight."

The sound of Eliot's typing stopped abruptly, then started again. The comment needled me. Finding Simon wasn't my endgame. *Being* with him was, and unless the Free Walkers succeeded, that wouldn't happen. If keeping Lattimer from finding this weapon would help, I'd do it—even if it meant leaving this life behind.

I tucked the violin back into the case, lazy and cool. "I can handle the Free Walkers."

"You won't need to," Eliot said, his voice a mixture of disappointment and relief. "It didn't work."

"What?" I peered over his shoulder. "It didn't generate a frequency?"

"Not one specific enough to identify an Echo. This one is too short."

I sank onto the arm of the chair. "It worked. It made perfect sense. And it was totally wrong?"

"Not wrong." Laurel said, studying the screen. "Incomplete. You'd need at least one more frequency, maybe two."

"Monty lied. Again," I said flatly. I'd fallen for it. *Again*.

Eliot shook his head. "He's playing a game. Bet you he's got another puzzle waiting for your next visit."

"He's in for a long wait," I said. "I'm not asking Monty for a damn thing."

Not when I could ask Ms. Powell instead.

CHAPTER FOURTEEN

We NEED TO TALK," I TOLD MS. POWELL THE next day after orchestra.

"I agree. You had quite the afternoon."

I gaped at her. "You heard?"

"I have an eclectic group of friends," she said. "Did you have a nice visit?"

"It was interesting." I rubbed at my throat, where my violin had left a fresh welt. I had fallen out of practice.

"I'd love to hear more about it." She glanced around the still-crowded room. "After school?"

Eliot was putting his cello away, out of earshot. I wondered what story I could give him this time. "I guess so."

"Great," she said, and turned to one of the violas, so breezy and dismissive I wasn't sure we were on the same page.

Eliot waited until we were in the hall before asking, "Everything okay after I left last night? Did Addie lighten up?"

"Addie never lightens up," I said. "She thinks this is going to be a disaster."

"She's probably right," he said as we headed toward second period. "Can you do me one favor?"

"Of course."

"Tell me what we're after."

I stopped. "The frequency. The map. Whatever it is Rose hid."

"I mean, what is our objective? Are you trying to get in good with the Consort? Find this weapon, or whatever the journals lead to, so you can hand it over to Lattimer and get a gold star?"

"No!"

"Then what are we doing? Because the only other reason I can think of is that you're hoping to join up with the Free Walkers."

I felt for the pendant at my neck. "The Consort . . . they're not what you think."

"I don't know what to think, because you won't tell me what's going on."

"It's complicated."

He threw open his locker and pulled out his physics textbook. "It's really not. Either you're a Walker, no matter how creeped out you are by Lattimer and the cleavings, or you're a Free Walker, and you leave. Permanently."

Some music is more about the silence than the sound; some conversations are more about the words left unsaid. Eliot was telling me that, if I left, I'd be on my own.

"I need a little time, that's all. To figure things out."

"Think fast," he warned.

"Yeah. Hey, I'm going to stay after with Ms. Powell again today. I want to work on my sonata."

He paused. "The Debussy? You nailed it in class."

"The phrasing's tricky," I started to say, and he cut me off.

"You do not need help with a sonata," he said. "You definitely don't need help on the same piece twice in one week. What are you up to?"

"I'm meeting with Ms. Powell," I said. "She wants me to make up the time I missed while I was out."

His eyes narrowed. "You're Walking."

"I'm . . ."

"Do what you want," he said coldly. "Chase after Free Walkers, Walk by yourself, play your sonata. Just do me a favor?"

"Anything," I whispered.

"Don't lie to my face, Del. Because you're right. I *do* deserve better."

Lunch with Eliot was a frigid, miserable, silent affair. Music theory wasn't much better. And I didn't have to lie to him after school, because he was nowhere to be found.

"Where's Eliot?" Ms. Powell asked.

"Excellent question," I muttered. "It would be easier if you'd let me tell him."

"Too risky," she said, buttoning her coat.

"No bag?" I asked, hefting my own backpack.

"Always better to travel light," she said, and we headed out on foot.

After a few blocks, I realized our destination. "We're taking the train?"

"Eventually. We have to Walk to the right Echo first. We'll cross again once we're on the correct train."

"While it's moving?"

"Harder to track pivots in a moving object," she said. "The train schedules have to match up between Echoes, or you end up on the tracks."

Which was exactly why Walkers never used mobile pivots. Any Walk could lead you into danger. It was part of the reason we navigated by familiar routes so often—moving between known, mapped pivots was safer, if less efficient. But Ms. Powell seemed confident, so I didn't question her further.

We crossed through outside the station, waiting as the Echo train squealed and thundered to a stop. Once we boarded, I automatically reached for my ticket, despite the pitch buzzing in my ears. "No need," she reminded me.

I slid my train pass back into my bag and followed her to a vestibule at the far end of the train. The metal handrail was cold to the touch, and I pulled on my fingerless gloves, swaying from side to side. Ms. Powell checked her watch. "About five minutes," she said. "You should hold on to my arm as we cross, but in case something goes wrong, here's the pitch."

She played the frequency on her phone, its shrillness competing with the shriek of the wheels. The doors opened and the conductor strolled through, oblivious to our presence. "Tell me about seeing your grandfather."

"How did you hear?"

"I told you before: We have people inside CCM. Not many, and their access is limited, but they keep us in the loop."

I wondered if I knew them—if I'd been interacting with Free Walkers all along.

"How was he?" she prompted.

I gripped the metal railing. "I think they've tortured him. The cell that connects to the oubliette looks like an operating room. There are restraints on the table."

"That would fit with what we know about the Consort's methods," she said, her usually ruddy cheeks turning pale.

"I didn't want them to torture him. I hate him, but not like that."

"Your visits are probably protecting him from further interrogations. Tell me about the setup. We've never been able to get someone into the sublevels before—at least not in and out."

I thought of Gil Bradley, trapped in one of those cells, awaiting execution. I didn't even know what he looked like, but I couldn't help imagining a thirty-year-old version of Simon, and my heart stuttered as I described the layout, including the cameras and guards. "They monitor everything," I said. "ID cards to get in and out, video feeds in all the cells. They only have two people watching the hall, but they don't need any more than that."

"Don't sound so defeated, Del. Information is power, and this is more than we knew before. What did Monty say?"

I folded a star out of notebook paper. "He gave me a message.

A puzzle, and when I solved it, I found a frequency hidden in Rose's journal. In a song."

She nodded. "We use that technique to encrypt locations."

"Well, this one's incomplete. The chord wasn't complex enough to match an Echo."

Ms. Powell, I noticed, did not look surprised.

"Do you know where it leads?" I asked.

"In a general sense. That's what we want you to help us with."

"Help you how?"

She looked out the window at the warehouses flashing by. "I'm not really the one to ask."

"Who is?"

"The people we're going to meet."

My heart stuttered. "Simon?"

She smiled like a child with a secret. "Among others."

"You said it would take time! Not that I'm complaining."

"The Consort's planning a Tacet, as you've probably heard. Our timetable has moved up."

My stomach pitched but my voice was even. "You're sure Simon will be there?"

"That's what I've been told. We're going to meet with my contact. She'll take you to another meeting site, and the people there will transfer you to the Echo where Simon will be. He'll be doing the same on his end."

"That sounds . . . elaborate."

"It is. It also makes it difficult for the Consort to trace our movements."

Before I could ask more about Simon—or the secret Echo—the crackling loudspeaker announced the next stop. "Here we go," Ms. Powell said. "Feel the pivot?"

I did—a rent in the air, a foot away from the compartment door. Ms. Powell edged toward it, her face stern with concentration, and I put my hand out, searching for the catch and pull of the new frequency. She checked her watch again. "On three. I'll pull you through, so hold tight."

"Got it."

"One . . . two . . . three!"

She lunged forward and I was dragged in her wake, the cacophony of the multiverse swallowing me. An instant later we were through both the pivot and the doors, stumbling down the aisle of the next compartment. The seats were crammed full, but nobody batted an eye at our appearance. Ms. Powell leaned weakly against the door we'd circumvented.

"They say it gets easier," she said, "But I've been doing it my whole life, and I always think it's going to be my last Walk."

I sank down onto an empty seat, my knees wobbly. "I'm not sure I can do that again. What if we'd gotten the timing wrong?"

"Some questions are better left unanswered." The train jolted to a stop, the station visible through the windows. Two guys—nearly identical with their buzz cuts, broad shoulders, and a distinct lack of neck—were standing on the platform, scrutinizing everyone who exited the train. They had the same stance you saw rent-a-cops use—flat stare, feet spread, hands behind their back—but their heads were tilted to the side.

"Our contact's a few cars down," Ms. Powell said. "We'll go as soon as everyone's settled."

I flattened myself against the wall as a group of chattering senior citizens entered. I glanced out the window again, but the rent-a-twins were gone.

The train started with a jerk, and people shuffled into the seats. Ms. Powell began making her way along the center aisle. I trailed behind, distracted by all the pivots created by the new passengers.

Unease rippled through me. If a single person made contact, the entire train would see us.

We made our way across the compartment and into the next vestibule, the chill air like a slap. Ms. Powell hauled open another set of doors, then stopped. I peered over her shoulder, curious about the delay. Halfway down the compartment, a harried-looking mom was wrangling two rambunctious toddlers and an enormous stroller. She'd managed to block the entire aisle, take up four seats, and spill Cheerios everywhere. They crunched underfoot as the train swayed. The other passengers tsked and gaped, but nobody offered to help.

The doors at the far end of the car slid open, revealing the guys from the platform. They stepped inside, forming a surly barricade, and my uneasiness grew.

Ms. Powell pointed to the upper level. "Let's wait up there till this clears out."

I backed into the staircase, the stainless steel walls cold and claustrophobic. Peering around the corner, I saw the men scrutinizing each seat, every face. One of them closed his eyes and tilted his head.

"We need to reach our contact," Ms. Powell said. "You're scheduled to jump in a few minutes."

My nerves stretched tighter at her words. The creak-clatter of the train, the passengers' conversations, the static and blare, the pitch of the world—it was overwhelming. I tried to focus on Ms. Powell's instructions, but then, unmistakably, I caught a wisp of the Key World's frequency.

"Something's wrong with the pitch," I said. Squeezing my eyes shut, I cocked my head to the side and listened closely.

Just like the rent-a-twins.

My eyes snapped open.

"Walkers!" I hissed, ducking back in the stairwell. "The guys by the door."

Ms. Powell froze, then glanced casually at the end of the compartment. "How can you—"

"The one on the left is listening." I knew the motion, because I'd done it a zillion times. "He's trying to pick up our frequency."

And judging from the way they were moving toward us— steps slow and menacing—they'd found it.

"Did they follow us?" I asked.

"No. I was very careful. They could have followed our contact. Or someone tipped them off."

The stroller-toting mom was still blocking the aisle, but not for long.

"They might not know there's two of us," Ms. Powell said.

"Head back the way we came, and get off at the next station. I'll deal with the guards."

"How? With your baton? What about finding Simon? What about your contact?"

"Simon will be kept safe. But we can't afford to lose you, either."

The conductor called out the next stop, and the upper-level passengers began collecting their bags, shuffling toward the stairs. In a moment I'd be forced into view.

"Go," she hissed. "Go now!"

I pulled up my hood and kept my back to the guards, hoping the other passengers would block me from sight. Tugging the door open, I chanced a quick look back. Stroller Mom had cleared out of the way. One of the guards put a hand to his hip, revealing the stun gun there.

The Consort's enforcement branch didn't carry regular guns. Too risky—a stray bullet could hit a bystander. Few things created an Echo as strong as an unexpected death, and they wanted to avoid such things at all costs.

They wouldn't kill us. They'd capture us. Put us in a cell like Monty's, drain in the floor, restraints on the table, and find out what we knew.

I ducked into the next car, twisting to avoid the other passengers, and ran through as many compartments as I could.

The train squealed to a stop. The doors slid open. I jumped to the pavement, glancing around wildly. Several cars back, one of the guards climbed down, Ms. Powell slung over his shoulder.

Two more Walkers approached him, and I dove back into the vestibule before they spotted me.

Guards must have been waiting at every platform from here into the city. If I tried to leave, they'd hear my Key World signal and track me down. If they could ID me, they wouldn't even have to give chase. They could wait until I went home—or go after my family.

Anonymity was my only defense.

Where was the second guard? Looking for Ms. Powell's contact, or coming for me? The train started again, and I stumbled, grabbing on to seat backs as I made my way through the car. The conductor's voice crackled over the speaker, announcing that the rest of trip would be a nonstop express into the city. I couldn't get off even if I wanted to.

The doors behind me opened, letting in the Key World frequency. For the first time in my life, it signaled danger instead of safety.

No time to look back. I joined the crowd, careful not to touch anyone, hoping the guard wouldn't be able to pinpoint my signal amid the others.

Through the doors. Into the next car. Another vestibule. Another car, and I hauled on the doors.

They didn't move.

I was out of cars.

But not out of trains.

We'd always been taught that people made a lot of decisions at train stations—but it turned out the trains themselves carried a lot of pivots too. Maybe people were making big life choices while the car rocked its way toward the city, or maybe they were deciding to nap. I didn't care what decisions the passengers had made, only that they'd made them.

The trick was matching schedules, Ms. Powell had said. But I didn't know the schedules anywhere except the Key World, and if I tried to go back there, this guy would follow me. I'd have to pick a familiar frequency—one where the world was similar enough that the trains probably overlapped.

I reached into the nearest pivot.

The door at the other end of the car opened, and the guard stepped through.

On instinct, my trembling fingers caught Doughnut World's thread, and I stumbled through.

The compartment I landed in was empty except for a group of girlfriends, dressed for a night on the town. I gasped in relief, then sprinted to the other end of the train, scenery blurring.

Ms. Powell was gone. My one link to Simon, gone. I bent over, hands on knees, fighting for air and control.

Behind me, I heard the sound of the pivot opening. The guard had tracked my signal, followed me through. Doughnut World wasn't the refuge I'd hoped.

I took off again, searching for a clear pivot. The train shook, throwing me into one of the seats, but I scrambled up and kept moving.

I found a rift, slender but strong, in the next car.

"Stop!" shouted the guard, twenty feet behind me. "Identify yourself!"

I didn't look. I didn't think. I heard the whine of his Taser charging, and I lunged at the pivot, taking hold of the first string I found. I half-Walked, half-fell into nothingness . . .

. . . and slammed into the wall of a boxcar, landing on the wooden planks, splinters gouging my palms. Pale bars of sunlight shot through the slats onto the floor, and the air smelled of dust and machine oil. A freight train.

I was trapped. There was no door to the next car; no way to get out if the guard followed me. The best I could do was jump and hope I survived the fall.

Over the roar and clatter of the wheels, I heard a scream that ended as abruptly as it started. I pulled myself up and peered through the back slats of the car. A hundred yards away, the guard who'd been chasing me rolled limply along the ground. Then he lay silent and unmoving on the tracks.

He'd Walked into thin air. If I'd waited ten seconds longer, I would have met the same fate.

I always think it's going to be my last Walk, Ms. Powell had said.

They had taken her. I sank to the dirty floor. She'd been good to me. She'd been *honest* with me, and she'd tried to help, and now . . . either the Consort would kill her, or they'd interrogate her and *then* kill her. All because she'd tried to help me.

I pressed the heels of my hands against my eyes, trying to hold back tears, but I couldn't help the scream of frustration that burst from my chest.

My only ally, my link to the Free Walkers, my chance to reach Simon, all of them gone. I was more alone than ever.

The train headed into the city, and I sat in the cold, echoing boxcar, trying to figure out my options.

By the time the skyline slid into view, I'd eliminated all the unlikely ones and zeroed in on the most impossible option of all. The only one left.

Monty.

CHAPTER FIFTEEN

I ENDED UP IN A FREIGHT YARD, SOMEWHERE on the southwest side of Chicago, numb with cold and shock.

I'd been so sure of myself. So confident that this time I would fix things instead of breaking them. I would bring Simon home. Now he was farther away than ever.

I wondered what had become of Ms. Powell's contact, or the other Free Walkers involved in the transfer. If the Consort had traced them back to Simon. The worry was like a kick to the stomach.

As the train slowed to a crawl, I threw my weight against the door, forcing it open. Stacks of metal containers, like children's blocks, towered above me. In the dusky half-light, their colors appeared muted, their shadows ominous.

The car lurched, throwing me into the wall and sending my backpack sliding across the floor. At least we weren't moving any more.

Muscles cramped, head ringing, I jumped out. Gravel scattered underfoot. The first step was getting back to the Key World before the frequency poisoning disabled me. I hitched my bag over my shoulder and made my way out of the massive, fenced-in lot. I spotted a highway overpass nearby and headed toward it.

We had a similar one back home, so if I found a pivot, it would be a relatively safe journey back.

Fifteen minutes later I was standing underneath a massive concrete bridge in the Key World, clutching my phone, trying to explain to Eliot how I'd landed so far from home.

He found me in an IHOP, warming my hands on a mug of heavily sweetened tea, pausing only to shovel in bites of syrup-drenched pancakes.

"This is the most repulsive thing I've ever eaten," I said as he loomed over me. "It's delicious. Want some?"

He didn't sit down. He didn't greet me. He stood in the bustling restaurant and stared at me like I was a stranger. I set my fork on the plate, tossed a twenty at the cashier, and followed him out to the car.

"Can you turn the heat on?" I asked when we were buckled in, my voice small in the dark interior.

He jammed the key in the ignition and cranked the heat. But instead of checking his mirrors and executing a textbook three-point turn, he glowered.

"Explain."

I held my hands up to the vents, but the numbness wouldn't go away.

Ever since Ms. Powell had revealed herself, I'd tried separating the various parts of my life: Simon and training and the Free Walkers and Monty and Amelia and my family, each in their own cocoon. But instead of protecting what mattered, the divisions had cost me, time and again.

Now it could cost me Eliot.

Instead of lying, or asking him to trust me, I did what I should have all along—I trusted him. Exhaustion made my words thick and clumsy. "Ms. Powell's a Free Walker."

Eliot blinked. "Come again?"

"Ms. Powell's a Free Walker. She was sent here to keep an eye on Simon."

He scowled. "And you know this how, exactly?"

"She asked me to join them."

His jaw clenched, as if he was biting back words. His eyes took on the cool, distant look that meant he was sifting through possibilities, analyzing data, figuring out the best approach to the problem.

I was the problem, and watching Eliot try to solve me was unsettling.

"When?"

"You believe me?"

He jerked his shoulder, the only outward sign of the anger he was filing away to process later. "Either you lied before, or you're lying now. You had more to gain by keeping Ms. Powell a secret than you do by outing her. And this is your pattern, isn't it? Hide the truth until you're in so much trouble you can't handle it?"

There's always a pattern, he'd said.

"She told me the day I came back to school."

His hands tightened on the wheel. "When she held you after class? She wasn't giving you pointers on the Debussy. She was giving you the hard sell."

"She didn't need to give me the hard sell," I replied. "You've seen what the Consort does. What they did to Simon's family."

"What Monty *says* they did. You're taking the word of a lunatic."

"Amelia's not a lunatic. She corroborated everything he said."

"Everything Amelia knows about the Consort, she learned from Simon's dad. She's completely biased. It's natural she'd blame them, now that Simon's gone."

"Simon's not gone," I snapped. "The Free Walkers rescued him from the cleaving."

Eliot went very still, eyes closing briefly. When he opened them again, they were filled with pity. "Is that what she told you? Ms. Powell's manipulating you, as much as Monty ever did. I went back to the Depot. I checked the cut site myself. Nothing is broadcasting at that frequency. I know you don't want to believe it, but there's no way Simon survived."

"He did," I said. "Because of the Free Walkers. They're not anarchists. The Echoes are alive, Eliot, and every time the Consort cleaves a branch, billions of people die. At our hands."

His sympathy evaporated. "Prove it. Show me data. Evidence."

I bit my lip.

"Even if I believed you, the Consort's protecting the Key World. The Free Walkers are saving Echoes at the expense of *reality*. They may have a different goal than Monty, but they're equally crazy."

"They aren't crazy. They've found a better way to handle the Echoes—one that leaves them alive and still protects the Key World."

"There is no better way," he said. "I know you've got issues, but cleaving is necessary."

"Was it necessary for them to take Ms. Powell?"

His eyes widened. "The Consort captured her? How? When?"

"An hour ago, maybe two. We were Walking to meet Simon."

He hammered a fist against the dash. "You're like a little kid! A stranger comes up in a big white van, offers you Simon-shaped candy, and you jump right in. You went Walking with a bunch of people you don't even know, and you didn't tell anyone where you were going?"

"Would you have preferred I sent you a text? 'Out with rebels, back for movie night, your turn to pick'? We were on a train. She was handing me off to a contact who would take me the rest of the way. A bunch of Consort guards got on too, looking for us. Or our contact. Ms. Powell said they've been hunting Free Walkers lately."

Addie's project, I realized. They'd had more success than she imagined.

He grabbed my arm. "The Consort knows you were there?"

"I wouldn't be breathing if they did. One of the guards chased me, but when I jumped pivots to another train, he fell. I think . . ." I swallowed hard. "I think he's dead too."

Eliot groaned, dragging a hand over his face. "Better and better. You're involved in the death of a Consort guard."

"I kept my hood up and my face hidden. The only guard who saw me is the one who fell."

He took several slow, deliberate breaths. "What about Ms. Powell?"

"I saw them carry her off. I think she was unconscious. But if she's not already dead, she will be soon. I'm not a genius, Eliot, but I can add two and two."

He peered out into the parking lot, as if someone lurked behind the shadowed lines of cars. "So can the Consort. She's a teacher at our school. You don't think they're going to be suspicious when they realize you had daily contact with a Free Walker? What if she talks?"

"I don't know."

"You're screwed, Del. They'll bring you in by lunch tomorrow."

He was right. "We need help. The Free Walkers are still out there. If we can contact them, they'll know what to do."

"Who's this 'we'?" He threw the car in drive and headed for the expressway, every movement furiously controlled. "You're the one who drank the Kool-Aid, not me."

"You don't believe me?"

"I don't know," he said. "But even if it's true, it doesn't change anything."

"Are you kidding me? It changes everything! It's like someone deciding that E equals mc-squared is actually E equals mc-cubed."

"You suck at physics," he said. "Do you have a clue what that formula means?"

I picked at a hole in my sweater. "Light's fast, or something."

"Something," he grumbled. "Yes, *something*."

"My point is, if scientists one day said, 'Hey, you know what? Light's slow!' You'd have to rethink all of physics. Come up with totally different rules."

"Except that most physicists won't kill you over the theory of relativity. The Consort absolutely will."

"And that doesn't bother you?"

"Of course it does! But I'm not going to risk my life for some crackpot theory."

"They're not crackpots."

"They're as nuts as the people who think we faked the moon landing, only more dangerous." I started to protest, but he held up a hand. "You *want* to believe them, so you don't care about facts. But I need proof, and you don't have any."

"Actually," I said, trying not to sound smug, "I do."

CHAPTER SIXTEEN

When I'd left Simon in Train World, I'd given him my backpack, stuffed with Walker tools. Since then I hadn't Walked enough to build up a new bag of tricks. Monty had once told me that a good Walker did more with less, and right now my tools were definitely falling on the "less" end of the spectrum. Then again, I didn't feel like much of a Walker.

"I haven't replaced Monty's picks yet," I told Eliot as we crept toward the darkened school. We'd used Monty's lock picks last time we broke into the school. There'd been a basketball game tonight, but no one had stuck around to celebrate a victory. The team's record since Simon disappeared had been nightmarish.

"Better think of something," he replied. His words were stilted and stiff.

"Here." I gestured to a pivot hovering a few feet from the back entrance of the field house. He took my elbow, as lightly as possible, like he couldn't stand to touch me, and I led the way through.

The truth can claim as many casualties as a lie. I'd lost Eliot's trust, and he'd lost his hope. I didn't know if we could recover either.

We arrived in the same Echo Ms. Powell had taken me to on

our first Walk—a pitch I would never forget. I rummaged in my backpack.

"I got nothing," I muttered. My phone, some notebooks, a couple of candy bars. Origami paper and a length of kitchen twine, because you never knew when string would come in handy. The papers we'd used to decode Rose's journals and a half-used jar of raspberry lip balm.

He peered over my shoulder while I cursed the fact that I had twelve different hair elastics and seven pencils, but no lock-picks. Then he reached around me and plucked out the reports we'd looked at the day before.

"What—"

Without a word, he pulled off the paper clips and held them out.

"Genius," I said. "As usual."

He didn't reply.

"You have to talk to me eventually."

"I don't have to do anything," he said. "And especially not because you tell me to. I'm only here to keep the Consort from coming after us. We *both* had contact with Ms. Powell. Guilt by association."

I worked the wire into a rough approximation of a lockpick. "I'll take the blame," I said. "If this doesn't work, I'll make sure they know it was all me."

"You think they'll buy it?"

"Well, one of us is a fantastic liar. Better I try to sell them a story than you."

The makeshift picks took more time than I liked, but finally we were in. We made our way swiftly across the deserted basket-ball court, the air thick with pivots and memories and tension.

"What are we looking for?" he asked.

"You asked for proof," I said, leading him through darkened hallways. "I'm giving you what you want."

He scowled. "I gotta work on my communication skills."

"Hush," I said as we stopped outside the library. "I need light."

He held up his phone, casting a faint, grainy glow. I reached into the air, relying on sense memory to guide my hands, looking for the shift in density that would reveal the cut site.

The only sounds were Eliot's breathing and mine, and the rustle of pivots around us. My hands skimmed through empty space, until something caught on my fingertips like a snagged piece of silk. The seam in the world that would restore Eliot's faith in me.

Gently I parted the air, holding it open. "There's your proof," I said with a nod. "Go ahead. Feel."

One hand still clutching the phone, he reached into the cut site, skepticism etched across his face. His fingers splayed wide, searching through the strings.

His brow furrowed. His mouth fell open, then clamped shut. "How?"

"I don't know. Ms. Powell didn't get into the specifics. But there's your proof."

He continued to examine the cut site and the seam. I could see him sorting through theories and analyzing the data. He prodded the air, muttering to himself and to the strings them-selves, as if they might answer his questions.

Finally he turned to me. "It's amazing. The Echo's still there, on the other side?"

"According to Ms. Powell, yes. And I believe her. Simon's Echoes still have a signal. They're alive."

He shook his head, trying to take it all in. "You're saying the Consort's been killing Echoes for years. Since . . . always."

"Exactly! But the Free Walkers are trying to change things."

Eliot snorted. "You might not have noticed, but the Consort's not a fan of change."

"So you think we should go along with them? Keep killing?"

"I think we should be smart. We need to stay alive—and under the radar." He nudged up his glasses. "And that starts with figuring out how to keep the Consort from connecting Ms. Powell to us."

I considered this. "Powell wasn't her real name, and I don't think she was carrying ID. She made a crack about traveling light. Besides, she was never a Consort Walker, so they don't have records of her. They might not be able to track her here."

"What if they put out a police report? Have you seen this woman; please call CCM? The school's going to report her missing. Someone will put it together."

"Unless the school *doesn't* report her missing," I said, and set off for the music wing.

He fell into step beside me. "Why wouldn't they?"

"Because she resigned."

A few minutes later we were back in the Key World, standing in front of Ms. Powell's office.

"Ms. Powell was leaving? Were you going with her?" Disbelief tinged with hurt. Maybe he hadn't given up on me after all.

"No, and no. She left a letter in the Key World so it would propagate through the Echoes. It explained why she disappeared, so they could bring a sub in faster." I bent over the lock, working my paper-clip picks as quickly as I could.

"Why would it matter? They're only Echoes."

"That's the point. She didn't think they were 'only' anything."

Once the door swung open, I pulled down the shade and locked the door behind us.

"Not a lot of pivots in here," Eliot said, surveying the cluttered room.

"She wouldn't have made any, and I doubt she had kids in here very much." Lying in the top drawer was a pale blue envelope, the principal's name written across the front in navy ink.

It wasn't sealed—the back flap was tucked inside—and I carefully withdrew the letter. "She wrote it by hand."

"So?"

"So, that's good. More convincing." I scanned the paper. "She says she has to leave due to urgent family business—an ill relative—and she doesn't know if or when she'll be able to return. She even apologizes for any disruption it might cause."

"Touching," Eliot said. "Drop a bomb and walk away. No wonder you got along so well."

"I'm not bailing on you."

"Not today. But once you find the Free Walkers, what then?"

"I haven't gotten that far," I said. "Ms. Powell said they needed my help. So I help them."

"And leave?"

Rather than answer, I slid the letter back in the envelope. "We need to put this in the office. The sooner they think she's left, the less chance they'll think she's missing."

"Fine. Let's plant it and go."

"Not yet," I murmured, turning in a slow circle. "There's got to be more information here. Some link to the Free Walkers, something we can use to get in touch with them."

"What kind of link?" Eliot asked.

"A big red folder labeled 'Top Secret Free Walker Contact Information,' probably."

He scowled, and I threw up my hands. "How the hell should I know? They're a secret organization, Eliot. They don't want to be found."

I stared at the gray metal desk in front of me, mounds of sheet music and batons, a tangle of strings and rosin cakes and reeds. A pile of ungraded essays sat on one corner.

"This is going to take forever," Eliot said, skimming over the files in the drawer. "These papers haven't been touched since the nineties."

"Then look at the stuff from this year. She had a tuning fork," I said, striking it on the desk corner. The Key World frequency rang out.

"Most Walkers do. So do music teachers." Eliot paused. "Hold on."

"What?"

"This score. It's original. And the notes are in Powell's writing."

"You think it's a map?"

"Possibly. I'd need to analyze it to be sure."

"Take it," I said, and he stuffed the papers into my backpack.

From the shelf above the desk I took down a picture of Ms. Powell at our first orchestra concert. Someone had snapped it while she was in the midst of conducting, her hair swinging wildly, her arms uplifted, her face fierce and proud.

We'd sounded amazing that night. She might have faked her teaching credentials, but in that moment she'd been completely genuine. It was the only personal thing in the room.

"Why do they need you?" Eliot asked abruptly.

I set the picture back. "What do you mean?'

"You said Ms. Powell told you the Free Walkers needed your help. Why?"

"I don't know," I admitted. "She was about to tell me more when the guards came. I'll be sure to ask the Free Walkers once I track them down."

"We're wasting our time," he said.

Exhaustion was creeping in, turning me short-tempered. "Leave if you want," I said. "But I'm staying until I find something that will lead me to them."

"You don't need to," Eliot said. "If you've got something they need—scores, or secrets, or something else—the Free Walkers are going to come for you. It's just a matter of time."

He was right. I only hoped they found me before the Consort did.

CHAPTER SEVENTEEN

Days until Tacet: 22

Heading into CCM the next morning, I felt like I'd been hit by a train too. The late night with Eliot, the fear of discovery, the deepening realization that Ms. Powell was gone, all combined to make my hands shake. But no one looked twice as we checked in at CCM's front desk; no one was waiting to take me into custody. For now, we'd gotten away with it.

"What have you two been up to?" Callie asked when I slunk into the room behind Eliot, head bent and shoulders hunched.

"Nothing."

"You look like shit. Both of you." When Eliot didn't respond—or look at me—she leaned in and whispered, "Fight? Are you two . . ."

"No," I said firmly.

She raised an eyebrow. "Is that why you're fighting?"

"We're not fighting." Fighting would clear out the wound. Despite showing him the cut site, Eliot was still angry, and with every clipped answer, our relationship festered.

I'd thought working together would help. We were always

a good team, but helping the Free Walkers wasn't a common goal, proof or no proof. If anything, I'd made things worse. He'd tolerated my obsession when he could chalk it up to a delusion, a part of the grieving process. Knowing it was real—and that I hadn't trusted him despite all we'd been through—was a blow we might not recover from.

"Work it out fast, whatever it is," Callie said, and gestured to the board. Our team assignments for the day were written out, and as usual, Callie, Eliot, and I were together. "I'm not losing my ranking because you two can't get your act together."

"Thanks for the support," I muttered.

She nudged me. "Your name's still not on the leaderboard. Should I be worried?"

"About me?" I made a brushing-off gesture, laughed too loudly. "Cal, I'm touched."

Her smile was as forced as my own.

Shaw strolled in, followed by my father and the rest of his team, Cleavers named Clark and Franklin. "Dad?"

"Cleaving Day," Shaw called, and the air crackled with anticipation. "We have a team here—led by Del's father—who are going to walk us through a real cleaving, step by step."

I gaped at my dad, who gave me a cheerful wave. His smile faltered when I didn't return it.

"But—"

Across the table Eliot coughed loudly, a warning to stay calm.

I gripped the arms of my chair. He was right. I couldn't afford to draw any more attention to us. Somewhere in this building, Ms. Powell was locked up, or worse. Unless I wanted to join her, I needed to look like a team player. So I shut my mouth and avoided my father's gaze while Shaw reviewed the ground rules and target frequencies. Eliot leaned back and took notes, as always, but I couldn't hear over the drumming of my pulse.

"Remember," Shaw said, "your role today is strictly observation. For safety reasons, we've chosen a relatively stable world, instead of one that's badly deteriorated. Even the most routine cleaving can be dangerous, so it's important we stay together and follow directions exactly. Got it?"

All around the table, heads bobbed agreement, but I held still, feeling as fragile and wavery as antique glass. Eliot cleared his throat, and I nodded in time with the rest of the class.

"Great. Let's roll, kids."

Shaw strode to the coatrack and shrugged into a canvas duster, clamped a cowboy hat on his balding head, and beckoned for us to follow. Everyone scrambled up. Only Eliot and I hung back.

"Can you handle this?" he asked as I struggled into my coat.

"Nothing I haven't seen before." But my jaw was clenched so tightly, it hurt to speak.

My dad caught us at the door. "You don't look happy to see me, kiddo. Are you too cool to have your old man visit?" His voice was teasing but his expression was worried.

"Just surprised," I managed. "You didn't say anything this morning. Aren't you supposed to be swamped?"

"Not so busy I couldn't make time for my little girl."

I managed not to snort, but before he could respond, his Second Chair, Clark, called him over.

"Let's get moving," Shaw said.

The elevators ferried us downstairs in groups. When we reassembled in the lobby, Shaw played our target frequency one last time, and led us out into the city.

The Consort worked hard to keep CCM as pivot-free as possible, so we had to leave the building before crossing over. Today Shaw had selected a passage inside the Pedway, a series of pedestrian-only tunnels that ran beneath the city. Some parts were well-trafficked, but on a clear, sunny, windless day, the corridors were pretty much deserted—which meant nobody noticed when, in groups of two, we started down the covered stairways and vanished from sight. It was classic Walker logic, using expectation to camouflage the inexplicable.

On the other side of the pivot, we arranged ourselves in a half circle, Shaw at the center. He did a quick headcount and then led us aboveground, emerging along Michigan Avenue.

I bit my lip. This Echo sounded fine. It looked exactly like Chicago should on a winter weekend—noisy and crowded and cheerful as tourists made their way to the Art Institute or skated on the pop-up rink the city constructed each year. Earnest young lawyers and finance guys, with their canvas messenger bags and wool overcoats, dodged the crowds impatiently. There was nothing wrong with this familiar bustling world.

Except that we were about to destroy it.

"Where's the target?" I asked Eliot as we followed Shaw,

who was deep in conversation with my dad and his teammates. My feet refused to keep pace with the rest of the class. Eliot kept dropping back to check on me, but the best I could do was hover on the periphery.

Several yards ahead, Callie called back, "Were you asleep? Millennium Park."

"That's five square blocks. Be specific."

"The pavilion."

I winced. I loved the Pritzker Pavilion, the futuristic outdoor concert hall, with its undulating curves and shimmering metal finish. It looked like music felt, rippling and twisting and alive.

Eliot and I saw concerts here every summer, stretching out on the lawn, lying back under impossibly blue skies with the sound of the lake and the city throwing the music into sharp relief, our fingers sticky from eating caramel corn. He might not believe me that Echoes were real—not yet, anyway. But his fingers brushed mine in silent understanding, and I knew he didn't want to watch it fade any more than I did.

"All right," boomed Shaw, when we reached the amphitheater. Despite the tourists wandering the park, we went unnoticed as we took center stage. "I'll hand this over to Mr. Sullivan."

"Call me Foster," my dad said. "Who can tell me the first step in a cleaving, once it's been officially sanctioned?"

Someone called out, "Find and fix the inversions."

"Yes. For today, assume that we've handled them. What's next?"

"Locating the breaks," Callie said. "You want to start the

cleaving at the weakest spots, so you can maintain proper tension on the threads."

"Excellent. You can be first up to check the break we're using today."

She followed him stage left and touched the handrail of the stairs leading offstage. The instant she made contact, she shuddered dramatically, then grinned. "It's not that bad. Like swimming in cold water."

"Del? Eliot? Give it a try."

We made our way over, both of us taut with nerves. I could hear the twang of the break before I touched it, and once my fingers brushed against the icy metal, an erratic pulse traveled up my arm. A shock, like Callie had said. Instinct took over and I hummed, trying to find the right frequency for the string.

Eliot stepped on my toe, breaking my concentration. "Sorry!" he called as I yelped.

Callie was staring. My father was staring. I didn't dare look to see what the rest of the class was doing. Instead, I elbowed him. "Klutz," I said loudly. "Your turn."

"You okay, kiddo?" my dad asked, motioning for Clark to take over. He guided me away from the group, and I braced myself against an angular steel post. "You look white as a sheet."

"It hit me harder than I expected. I'm good."

"If you're sure," he said, peering at me in concern. I waved him off, and he went back to the break, helping each kid find the correct strings.

Eliot joined me at the edge of the stage. "What were you doing?"

"Tuning, I think." I'd corrected the pitch of a world plenty of times, but it had always been deliberate and difficult. Here, in a relatively stable world, the effort was minimal. "Not on purpose—it was a reflex."

"Yeah, well, quit having that reflex. Not in front of this many witnesses."

We rejoined the group just as my dad pulled a slender metal disk, the width of a matchbook, out of his pocket. "You've all seen one of these before, yes?"

"It's a divisi knife," Logan said, edging forward. "For cutting the threads."

My dad handed him a piece of linen twine. "Hold it taut," he said, and addressed the entire class, holding the silvery circle for us to see. "The edges are notched, with blades hidden inside. This allows you to manipulate the divisi without slicing off a finger, or wasting time opening and closing the blades. Once a cleaving begins, there's no stopping it. Your only recourse is to keep cutting and weaving. If you don't, *both* sides of the cut site will unravel."

I shuddered. A Consort team had finished the cleaving I'd started in Park World. If they hadn't, the damage would have been worse.

But there was a better way. Simon had strengthened Train World after we'd broken the strings, holding it together long enough for the Free Walkers to cauterize. He'd saved countless Echoes.

Simon was proof of the Consort's lies—lies my father believed. He had no idea what he was teaching us to do.

With a last, puzzled look, my dad continued. "The idea is

to separate the strings you want to cut, and fit the blade around them, like this. . . ." He demonstrated with the length of string Logan was holding out, the divisi tucked in the curve of his forefinger and thumb, slipping it into place. "In a real cleaving, you'll cut a handful at a time. Take the side that connects to the stable Echo, the one you're trying to preserve, and trap it against the heel of your hand, maintaining the tension."

My classmates crowded around to get a better look, Callie towing me along.

"What do you do with the other threads?" asked Eliot.

"Nothing. Once you've cut enough of them, the cleaved world will unravel. Your focus should be on the Key World side of the strings so you can weave them back together. Watch."

With a twist of his wrist, he sliced cleanly through the twine. The upper half dangled limply from Logan's left hand, but the lower half was held taut between his right hand and my father's.

"That's the basic technique," Shaw said. "We'll be practicing it in class, so don't worry. By the time we're done, you'll be able to cut the strings in your sleep."

"What about the weaving?" Callie asked. "When do we get to see that?"

"Right now," my dad said. "Reweaving is the trickiest part, because the unraveling has already begun—"

"Excuse me?" Maddie raised her hand. "Why don't we cleave from the stable side? Wouldn't it be safer?"

"It would," my dad said. "But in this case, it's a trade-off. We need to maximize the energy transfer of a cleaving, and working from the stable side limits the amount we can harvest. Additionally, we want the fabric to be as seamless as possible, to minimize weakness."

We must have looked pretty clueless, because he chuckled and continued. "It's like this stuffed panda Del had when she was a baby. Remember that thing, kiddo? You loved that little guy. You used to take him everywhere, and your mom was constantly having to fix pieces that were falling off, or spots where the stuffing came out."

"Dad. Seriously?" The tips of my ears burned with embarrassment.

"I remember that panda," Eliot whispered, grinning. "Stewie, right?"

"Anyway, no matter how carefully Winnie stitched that poor bear back up, those were the parts most likely to split again. How many times did Mom reattach his ear, Del? Five? Six?"

I closed my eyes and wished for a lightning strike.

"Cleavings are the same way," my dad continued. "Exposed seams are the most likely to fray again, so the goal is to complete as much of the reweaving as possible before you cross the exit pivot, leaving only a tiny amount of finishing on the stable side."

"Stewie," Logan mouthed, and I flipped him off.

Callie took mercy on me, asking, "Will we be able to see the reweaving today?"

"You'll see the effects of the cleaving, but not the actual thread work. It's done by touch, not sight."

"You won't be staying until the end, either," Shaw said.

145

"We'll cross back and finish watching from the stable side."

Logan groaned, but Shaw simply adjusted his hat and said, "Sorry, guys. Safety first. Ready, Foster?"

My dad glanced at the other Cleavers, who nodded, their divisis in hand.

"I'm going to initiate the cuts here, at the break. Once that's handled, we'll work our way back to the pivot we used to access this world, cleaving as we go."

He reached into the break with one hand and held the divisi lightly in the other like a magician would hold a coin, for the audience to admire. His hands were broad, but they moved with astonishing delicacy, twitching as he sorted through threads too fine to see. When he found the ones he wanted, fingers crooking in a familiar gesture, he transferred them to his divisi hand and spoke over his shoulder.

"As you watch, take special note of how the unraveling spreads—where it wants to go, how we shape it."

I felt hot, despite the biting air and the pale sun, sweat collecting between my shoulder blades and at the backs of my knees and along my hairline. There was no shape to a cleaving. Shape implied order. This was a return to chaos, no matter how carefully he handled it or how meticulous our notes. We were supposed to fight entropy, not welcome it in with open arms.

This was murder, and we were all complicit.

Shaw took over the narration as the men formed a loose triangle around the break. "They'll approach from three directions, in order to maintain even tension on the strings."

I opened my mouth, preparing to scream, but Eliot whispered, "You *can't*."

His words brought me back to myself. I'd give away everything if I spoke up now. I'd save one world and reveal the Free Walkers. I pressed a fist against my mouth, and he squeezed my other hand tightly. I gripped back, pouring all my anguish into the gesture.

"Once the initial cuts are made, the First Chair handles the warp, the Second Chair handles the woof, and the Third Chair guides the unraveling strings out of the way, so they're not caught in the repair."

The Cleavers reached into the break, divisis at the ready. My throat constricted, air wheezing in and out.

"Del?" Callie's voice sounded as if she were standing on the lawn of the pavilion, a hundred yards away. I turned, trying to place her, but my vision swam, and the stage tilted underfoot. "Del!"

I closed my eyes seconds before my knees buckled. I felt Eliot's arm come around my waist, and I listened.

Silence.

The silence of an indrawn breath, of anticipation, of the instant before the music begins.

And then the cleaving started.

The noise was raucous, a bow skidding wildly across the strings, splitting and squealing. I clapped my hands over my ears, buried my face in Eliot's shoulder.

"Is she okay?" Dad called. The concern in his voice was tempered by the strain of managing the strings. "Is it frequency poisoning?"

"She's sick," Eliot said. "She's felt lousy all day. I'll take her back."

"We stay together," Shaw said, over the rising noise. "She'll have to hang on until we're done here. Give her some chocolate. The rest of you, quit staring and pay attention."

"Don't look," Eliot murmured, wrapping his arms around me.

But I needed to see. This is what my people had done, and I needed to bear witness. The Consort sent teams to cleave every day, all day, around the world. I'd focused so intently on the pain of Simon's disappearance, of making reparations, I'd let myself forget it was still happening. Every moment I held back, every time I waited or didn't speak up or fumbled a chance to find the Free Walkers, I was letting this happen.

If I couldn't stop it, I could at least pay attention. Someone should mourn these deaths, and today it would be me.

White noise filled the air, the hiss and crackle of a radio, and the colors of the park, already muted by winter, began to drain away. The team worked quickly, their fingers deft and sure, the divisis glinting and hovering like dragonflies. The bridge, a gentle swoop of silvery wood and brushed steel, writhed and sagged. The people atop it were oblivious to the movement, and their own colors—a bright orange coat, a teal-blue beret, a forest-green parka—faded to gray.

I bit my tongue until I tasted blood.

Eliot squeezed my hand, but I didn't pull away. The world around us flickered and faded as I stood fast.

One by one, the people on the bridge disappeared, bursts of

colorless static around them like ghostly fireworks. The curves of the pavilion drooped above our heads.

"Head toward the exit pivot," my father said. "It gets easier as you go—the tension in the lines becomes more manageable, and you get into a routine. Cut and loop and weave and move," he chanted as we crossed the plaza surrounding the Bean, a jelly-bean-shaped sculpture and the main attraction of Millennium Park. The skyline, already distorted in its mirrored surface, twisted in on itself like a Möbius strip—but when I looked up, it was the buildings themselves sinking into the ground, spreading like lava.

We crossed Michigan Avenue, pacing ourselves so that the team's movements, their careful steps and precise gestures, never ceased. We were like an amoeba, a shifting mass that left behind a smeared, ugly trail.

We reached the stairwell, and my dad jerked his head toward the pivot, his hands still in motion. "Once we've sealed the strings of the pivot, this world will finish unraveling on its own. Based on the strength of the signal and the stability of the Echo, it should take longer than usual for it to cleave—I'd estimate a week before it's gone."

I straightened. A week. We might be able to come back and save this world in seven days, if I could find the Free Walkers.

"In a minute, I'll send you all back through, and wrap up here with my team. We'll rejoin you for the last few steps on the stable side of the pivot, to finish it off properly. We want to make sure that the cut site is reinforced against any sort of inversions or instability."

"What if one of you had gotten sick?" Callie asked, with a

sidelong glance at me. "Do you really need three people?"

"In an emergency, a cleaving can be handled safely by one person," Shaw said. "That's part of why the Consort expects you all to learn. If you Walk somewhere critically unstable, you need to be able to act, regardless of where you're apprenticed. But it's preferable to have a three-pronged team, plus a navigator and medic on the other side. Speaking of medics, Del, Callie, Eliot—I want you three through the pivot first. The rest of you follow at regular intervals. Go!"

Eliot didn't waste any time. Gripping my hand, he led me through the pivot, letting the air shift and part around us, humming the Key World frequency. The world sighed, settled, and welcomed us back.

"Sit," Callie ordered, helping me down the stairs. "You are the whitest white girl I've ever seen right now. You look like a freaking vampire."

She handed me a chocolate bar from her backpack, but I waved it away. Sugar could reverse frequency poisoning; I wanted to reverse time. I stood up, and she shoved me back down, hands on shoulders. Eliot paced and scowled, lips moving silently.

"You really aren't cut out for this, are you?" Callie asked.

I drew my hand across my mouth, battling back nausea. "Guess not."

"She got sick," Eliot called. "Frequency poisoning or food poisoning or the flu."

Callie scoffed. "Bullshit. Come up with a better story than that, because Shaw's going to want to know what's going on in about three minutes." She shook her head. "What the hell is wrong with you two? We were *good* together. Then Del gets booted, then she comes back, then she's off the leaderboard, then you two aren't speaking, and then you have some sort of . . . what? Episode? Breakdown? Whatever the problem is, figure it out, because if I'm going to cleave with you, I need to be sure you're not going to get us all killed."

She stood up and pointed a finger at me. "Playtime's over."

I leaned my head against the cold metal handrail. "No kidding."

Shaw ordered us back to CCM before my dad and his team were finished. Callie and Eliot stuck close, saying little for the entire return trip. But when we arrived in the lobby, no amount of evasion was going to save me. Lattimer approached us, his face a mask of concern.

"Shaw called in a request for an emergency medical evaluation."

"Del wasn't feeling well," Callie said. "He wanted her checked out, to make sure it wasn't serious."

"I'm better now," I protested. Showing weakness around Lattimer was like blood in the water.

"You don't look it," Lattimer said.

"It's frequency poisoning," Eliot said, and did his best impression of my mom. "I told you not to overdo it. She doesn't listen, sir."

"It sounds as if a break is in order," Lattimer said. "You'll sit out class tomorrow. I can use your assistance with other matters."

"Other matters?" Callie asked, and Eliot glared at her.

"Nine o'clock, as before," Lattimer said, ignoring both of them. "Make sure you've got a firm grip on your temper."

As soon as the medic checked me over, force-feeding me cup after cup of sweet, inky tea, Shaw sent me home with Eliot, and stern instructions to rest.

"You're going to join them, aren't you?" Eliot said as we made our way through Union Station. I didn't need to ask who he meant.

We boarded the train, the memory of Ms. Powell making me check over my shoulder every few minutes. I didn't reply until we'd found our seats.

"I can't even find them."

"Do you really want to spend the rest of your life hiding? Being hunted? You'll have to leave everything behind, or you'll have to lie, every day, for the rest of your life."

"According to you, I am an excellent liar."

"I'm an excellent juggler," he said, "but you don't see me joining the circus."

"I can't cleave."

"Then don't be a Cleaver," he said. "Be a navigator. Be a medic. Be a teacher."

"I don't like little kids."

"Be an ethicist. You want to change the Consort, that's the way to start."

"By admitting I know something the Consort has been covering up for generations? I don't think that's the path to career longevity."

"The only upside to working with Lattimer is that you've got your pick of apprenticeships. Choose one you can live with."

"That's not a solution. Being a Walker means supporting the Consort, and the Consort wants us to cleave." My voice broke on the last word.

"I get what this is doing to you. I do," he said, pulling me into him. "But you have to play along, at least in public. Shaw's going to put it together. Callie's halfway there already."

"She's my friend. She wouldn't—"

His words ruffled my hair. "Callie is as pigheaded as you are, and if she thinks you're going to hurt her chances, she will throw you under the bus. Any one of them would."

"But not you." I sat up. "You're on board?"

He sighed deeply. "The Free Walkers aren't my fight. But you, I'll help. I'll run the scores we took from Ms. Powell's office later tonight and see where they take us."

Us. I leaned my head against his shoulder and tried to ignore the prickling behind my eyelids. It's not only the demons who have the power to break you. It's the small, unexpected kindness, the flame that throws the darkness into relief.

CHAPTER EIGHTEEN

At my request, Eliot dropped me at Simon's house, where Iggy romped about in greeting. He must have sensed my mood, because he settled almost immediately, pressing against my legs as I went in search of Amelia.

"I'm down here," she called from the basement. "Laundry never ends. Even when it's just me."

I made my way down the narrow stairs. Washing machine aside, the basement was clearly Simon's domain. Carpet remnants covered the floor, and in the middle of the room sat an ancient, ugly, comfortable-looking couch. The coffee table was nicked and scratched, and back issues of *Sports Illustrated* were scattered everywhere. A weight bench sat in one corner, the bar still loaded with iron plates; a drum set collected dust in another. I could picture Simon and his teammates here, watching ESPN and playing Nerf basketball. I could imagine him bringing a girl down here, and I quashed the jealousy that welled up—not of the phantom girl, but of the time they'd had together.

I turned my back on the couch and the ghosts. Along the opposite wall, Amelia was standing in front of a dryer full of towels, folding them carefully and setting them in a basket.

"Let me help," I said, joining her. I'd smelled this fabric softener on Simon's skin so many times, and without thinking I pressed my face into a washcloth, inhaling deeply.

When I looked up, Amelia was watching me wistfully.

"I do the same thing," she said. "Sometimes I go into his room, and it smells just like him. That boy smell, you know? I close my eyes, and he's standing next to me. I can't even wash the sheets, because I'm afraid I'll forget."

"Me too," I said, twisting the cloth in my hands.

She blinked rapidly and picked up the basket. "Any progress with the Free Walkers?"

I shook my head. "I'm sorry."

"Don't apologize. I'm sorry it didn't work out like you'd hoped."

I took the laundry basket, over her protests, and followed her upstairs. "Do you want me to put on tea?"

"Please," she said, and left to put away the towels. I filled the kettle, the surface as mirrorlike as the Bean had been today. When she returned, she arranged cups and saucers on a tray, and added a plate of shortbread. "The Free Walkers must seem exciting to you, and a better alternative than the Consort, but it's not an easy life. The longer you live with a deception, the more real it becomes."

"Like Monty?" I carried the tray to the table in front of the couch.

"Your grandfather's a special case," she said. "He was never as passionate about the Free Walkers as your grandmother. She believed in the cause, and he believed in her."

"Why did the Free Walkers abandon him?"

"I cut ties with the Free Walkers after Gil was taken, so I don't know what happened. But I can tell you, they're not a sentimental group. They can't afford to be, considering who they're up against. Reaching out to Monty would have made them vulnerable."

"And my grandmother would have been okay with that?"

"That part surprises me," she admitted. "I can't imagine Rose not getting a message to him somehow, even if it was only to say she was safe."

"Unless she couldn't."

Amelia looked down at her cup again and said nothing.

But the Free Walkers had contacted me. They'd sent Ms. Powell after Simon; they thought I could be valuable.

"I think she left a message for me," I said. "Not me, specifically. But someone. Monty, maybe."

Amelia set her cup down with a clatter. "What kind of message?"

"A puzzle. When I solved it, I found a frequency."

"Oh?"

"The frequency's not complete; I'm guessing Monty has the other part."

She twisted her wedding band absently, lost in thought.

"Lattimer thinks the Free Walkers hid a weapon. Maybe the frequency tells where it's hidden."

She frowned. "Gil always said the truth was the only weapon they needed."

"Not according to Lattimer. They hid *something* in the Echoes, and I need to find it before the Consort does."

"Stop looking," she said sharply.

I must have looked shocked, but she touched her ring again and stared into her tea.

"The Free Walkers will get you killed, Del, just like they do everyone else. I am begging you—forget about this frequency and anything else having to do with them. Let their secrets stay hidden so you can stay alive."

CHAPTER NINETEEN

FEELING BETTER?" LATTIMER GREETED ME THE next morning.

"Like a new person," I lied, trying to appear nonchalant as the guards escorted us downstairs. Addie handled people better than I did, and I channeled her now, down to the way I tucked my hair behind my ears and folded my hands. Clearly they hadn't tied me to the incident on the train. Yet.

"How many people do you keep down here?" I asked as we approached Monty's cell. Ms. Powell had been stunned, not shot. She might be locked behind one of these doors. If she was alive, would she give me up?

I quashed the thought. That kind of thinking would lead me to the same place as the Consort; taking lives for my own preservation.

"The number varies. Your grandfather is our most recent arrival. We have the capacity to take more prisoners, but that hasn't been necessary for quite some time."

Assuming he was telling the truth, Ms. Powell wasn't here. Which meant she was probably dead. Fighting to keep my voice level, I said, "What am I supposed to ask him about today?"

"Our first priority is this weapon. What it's capable of, where it might be hidden. How to defend against it. Barring that, information about the Free Walkers he worked with during the anomaly would be helpful."

I'd have better luck asking him where to find the local unicorn herd. "I'll do my best."

Lattimer handed me the earpiece. For an instant I saw myself as he must—young and foolish and pathetic—and my hands curled into fists as he opened the door.

"I didn't think you'd come back," Monty said as I crossed the floor, my boots squeaking on the tile.

"Neither did I." I slipped into the chair opposite him.

"Randolph's leash is shorter than you realized, eh?" He sounded amused.

I bristled. "I thought I'd give you another chance. Tell me about the Free Walkers."

He scrutinized me, but I kept my face impassive.

"I've told you everything you need to know. You too," he added, tipping his head back to address the camera.

"Tell me again," I said. "I'll get you started. You were a Free Walker."

He hummed lightly, as if he didn't hear me.

"You've already confessed," I pointed out. "Seventeen years ago. It's not news to anyone."

"Then don't waste my time asking about it," he snapped. "What other questions does he have?"

159

The earpiece stayed silent.

"Are you in contact with any Free Walkers now?"

His eyes gleamed. "The only person I'm in contact with is you."

Guilt by association, Eliot had said.

I pressed my fingers against the tabletop to keep them from trembling. "The Consort thinks you had help during the anomaly. That you couldn't have done it on your own."

"Hard to believe, isn't it?" He grinned, letting me sweat. Payback for the last visit, for turning him in, for failing to find Rose. He lifted a shoulder. "How many times have I told you? Anything is possible."

I exhaled in a rush of relief. "You haven't had any contact with the Free Walkers?"

"One," he said. "An old friend, but according to Randolph, he's already been seen to. The rest want nothing to do with me.

"I'm tainted," he continued, and for the first time I saw real sorrow cross his face. "Don't you think if I could have gotten back to them, I would have? Avoided everything you went through?"

"You don't have any way to find them?" I tapped the table lightly, emphasizing the next question. "Not even a map?"

The tiniest of smiles, the faintest of nods. "If I knew where to find them, the last person I'd share it with is Randolph." His eyes flickered to the ceiling, then returned to me. "Why did you come back? It's not as if you need *my* help. Isn't that what you said last time?"

I didn't reply.

He shook his head. "I've told you everything you need to know."

"Not everything. Not about the weapon, or where it's hidden."

"In plain sight, I'd imagine. You'd be amazed at what people overlook, Delancey, even when it's right under their noses. Even you." His gaze turned distant, his face went slack.

I didn't buy his performance for a second, but I played along, gentling my tone.

"They wouldn't keep it in the Key World." I touched his sleeve. "Grandpa, even *part* of a frequency would help."

"And what do I get?" he asked, quarrelsome and deceptively old. "I've lost everything, Del. My Rose, my family, my home." He rattled his chains, the sound almost merry. "My freedom."

"Your grandfather will never see daylight again," Lattimer snarled. "Make that absolutely clear."

"The Consort's already cut you a break, letting me visit. They're not going to let you out."

"I'm not asking about *them*," he said. "If I'm to betray a great cause, I need an incentive. What do I get from you?"

Son of a bitch. He wanted me to help him escape. If he thought I could break him out of an oubliette, he really was crazy. There's impossible and there's *impossible,* and this fell into the second camp.

"I don't have anything to give," I said quietly.

"Then you're no good to me," he said. "Come back when you've got something I want, and we'll make a trade, Delancey. Until then, I've nothing more to say."

. . .

Lattimer met me at the door. "That was a shorter visit than I'd anticipated."

"He wasn't in great shape today. It's hard to know how much to believe him, when he's in and out like this."

"Perhaps he'll be more forthcoming on your next visit," Lattimer said.

"He doesn't want to see me again. You heard him—he wants more, whatever more is."

My freedom. Come back when you've got something I want. I might as well help him fly to Mars, or sprout gills and ferry him to Atlantis.

"The Tacet will begin in mere weeks. If you fail to glean any useful information from these sessions, we'll have no use for him. Be more persuasive next time."

CHAPTER TWENTY

WALKERS ARE USED TO KEEPING SECRETS. WE go through our days knowing the world we inhabit is one of many, the lives we see are only one possibility, and reality is more complicated and entangled than anything Originals could imagine. We know all of this, and we keep it to ourselves. Most days the power of those secrets fizzed in my blood like champagne.

But knowing the truth about Ms. Powell ate through me like battery acid. Concealing her death didn't just feel sneaky, or sad. It felt deeply, deeply wrong. The Consort had taken her life, but we'd taken the chance for people to mourn her.

The orchestra room had an air of freewheeling, good-natured chaos. At the podium, Principal Sayers, a thin man with a dusting of dandruff on his shoulders and a fondness for knit ties, spoke with a woman who didn't look old enough to drive, let alone control sixty-odd teenagers.

Eliot bent and murmured, "Looks like they bought the note."

"Great," I said, but the words lacked conviction.

The sub looked fresh out of college—but drab and lifeless,

especially compared to the memory of Ms. Powell. I searched her face for a sign she knew me, but her expression was frozen in terror. When Dr. Sayers introduced her with a brief speech about Ms. Powell's unexpected departure, the baton trembled in her grip. Probably not a Free Walker plant, then.

By lunchtime, the school was buzzing about Ms. Powell's absence. The usual rumors sprang up: rehab or an affair with a student or something equally scandalous. Eliot listened, genuinely baffled. "How do they come up with this stuff? Anyone with two brain cells to rub together would know better."

"You're giving them too much credit."

By the time we were headed back to music, with our pocket-size sub and Bree's big mouth, things had shifted from speculation to accusation—and I was at the center of it. People fell quiet as we passed, whispers swelling in our wake. My skin itched under their scrutiny.

"This is not good," Eliot said out of the corner of his mouth. "They're looking at us. Nobody ever looks at us."

"As many of you have already heard," Dr. Sayers began, launching into the same speech he'd given in orchestra, "Ms. Powell has been called away due to a family emergency. She has resigned her position effective immediately."

"What kind of emergency?" Bree demanded.

Dr. Sayers tugged at his maroon knit tie before answering, "According to her letter, the situation came up quite suddenly."

"Her letter? She didn't call? Or tell you in person?"

"I admit it's a shock," he said, looking chagrined, "Not to mention highly inconvenient, but—"

"It's not a shock. It's weird. And it's a lot like Simon Lane."

"Maybe they're together," snickered a pothead senior whose attendance was even more sporadic than mine. "Holed up in some hourly motel, and he's hot for teacher."

One of his friends leaned across the aisle to high-five him, braying with laughter.

Bree wheeled on him. "Shut your mouth, you cretin."

The principal cleared his throat. "I can assure you that Ms. Powell's absence is perfectly legitimate. I think it would be best for all involved if we look forward instead of back," he added. "Ms. Powell may not have shared information about her home life, but that was her right."

"I bet she shared with Del," Bree said. "She was Ms. Powell's favorite, after all."

A murmur of assent rippled around the room.

"Sorry," I said, shrugging. Next to me Eliot went still. "I barely saw her outside of class."

"What about Friday? I could swear I saw the two of you walking downtown. Wouldn't she have told you if something was going on?" Bree asked.

Now the principal turned to me. "Del?"

"Orchestra," I said. "There's a Debussy sonata she wanted me to polish up; she thought I had a shot at getting into a conservatory. But she didn't say anything about family stuff."

"Such a weird coincidence," Bree said sweetly. "I mean, you

were the last person to see Simon before he disappeared. You were the last person to see Ms. Powell before *she* disappeared. Better look out," she said to Eliot. "The people she likes don't seem to last long."

He nodded. "Imagine what happens to the people who piss her off."

"Enough," said the principal. "This is not a good use of our time. Ms. DeAngelo will be your teacher for the rest of the year, and I'm sure she'd like to get started."

But he watched me as he left, narrow-eyed and thoughtful.

"This cannot be good," Eliot said at the end of the day. He leaned against the locker and stared at the light fixtures, pencil spinning faster and faster. "I told you Bree was a problem."

"Bree is not a problem," I replied, throwing a book in my bag and slamming my locker. "Bree is an annoyance, same as always."

"Two people have disappeared from this school in the last month. You have connections to both of them. People are going to ask questions."

"Amelia has answered the questions about Simon. And Ms. Powell wrote that letter. No matter how they analyze it, it won't come back to me. The Consort's the problem, not some drama queen with an unrequited crush and an ax to grind."

"Strangely, I do not find that reassuring," he said.

I pulled on my coat, wound my scarf around my neck, and set off, Eliot easily matching my pace. "If we want to avoid the

Consort, we need to figure out where that map leads. The Free Walkers are the only way out."

"For you, maybe."

Not for Eliot. Even knowing the truth, he was still unwilling to cast his lot with the Free Walkers. And if Eliot couldn't be convinced, what chance would the Free Walkers have with the rest of our people?

CHAPTER TWENTY-ONE

Days until Tacet: 18

THE FUNNY THING ABOUT TROUBLE IS HOW quickly it grows, like a snowball rolling downhill, swelling and silently picking up speed, and you only notice a split second before you're flattened.

Trouble likes you to know it's coming, but only if you can't run.

I should have known something was off when I saw how cheerful Bree looked, two days later, standing outside math class with her friends, marking my progress. It's never a good sign when someone who loathes you looks happy to see you, but my mind was too full of maps and secrets to pay attention.

Trouble likes it when you don't pay attention.

I slid into my seat, pulled out my notebook, and started doodling Rose's song. Late in the period, a squawk and crackle rent the air. I jolted in my seat, my heart kicking like a jackrabbit, looking for the pivot.

"Yes?" called Mrs. Gregory. I slumped. The intercom.

"Delancey Sullivan to the office, please," came a nasal, disembodied voice.

Bree sat a little straighter, tossing her hair over her shoulders.

"Naturally," sighed Mrs. Gregory, and waved me toward the door.

One of Bree's friends leaned over and whispered something in her ear. She nodded in reply, but didn't giggle. Whatever triumph she was feeling—and it *was* triumph, I could see it in the lift of her chin and tilt of her shoulders—it was strained.

I grabbed my bag as I left, texting Eliot as I went.

Trouble. Office.

"Go ahead," the secretary told me when I arrived. "You know the way."

Even if I hadn't—which I did—Principal Sayers was waiting outside his office.

"Thanks for coming in, Del." He followed me inside and shut the door behind us. I dropped into my usual seat. A quick glance at the two plate-glass windows, blinds open, showed that the office staff was planning to watch our conversation, even if they couldn't listen. Instead of sitting behind the desk, the principal lounged against the corner, trying to look casual.

Walkers know that keeping your options open is a literal thing: Indecision manifests as eddies of air, pivots caught in a formative state. The air around Principal Sayers was thick with uncertainty.

"Did I do something wrong?" This was a different kind of trouble than the Consort. A wrong answer here wasn't going to get me killed. But I remembered the satisfied look on Bree's face, and stripped the sulkiness from my voice.

Trouble loves when you're overconfident.

"We're hoping you could help us answer some questions. About Simon Lane."

I said nothing.

"We understand that you two were seeing each other?"

"Yes."

"Have you heard from him since he left?"

I ducked my head, trying to look embarrassed. "No."

"Did you know he was going to transfer?"

"We weren't big on talking about the future."

His face turned a red so dark he nearly matched his tie, and he cleared his throat. "I see."

"Simon left more than two weeks ago. Why are you asking me about him now? Is it because of Ms. Powell?" I scoffed. "The stoner kid's not exactly reliable, you know. That much pot would make anyone paranoid."

He sniffed. "Ms. Powell's departure is inconvenient, not sinister. We're concerned because Simon hasn't checked in with anyone since he left."

"Does he need to?" I asked pointedly. "His mom signed off on the transfer, right?"

"She did. But considering her situation . . ."

"Amelia's cancer," I said, and he shifted, as if saying the word out loud might make it contagious.

"It's important Simon is adequately supported during this difficult time. We'd like to help."

I scoffed. "Bull. You're not worried about his support

network. You want Simon to come home because the basketball team has lost their last five games."

"I like to think of Washington as a family," Principal Sayers said stiffly. "And when our family loses a member, it's important that we understand why."

"Simon *has* a family. And I doubt she appreciates this kind of harassment."

"We're not harassing anyone, Del. There are some irregularities"—he tapped a file on his desk—"and we're trying to sort them out."

I glanced at the cream-colored folder, suddenly nervous. "What kind of irregularities?"

"I can't share the specifics." He slid the file beneath another stack of papers. "We're simply trying to ensure Simon hasn't come to harm. If we can't resolve this—establish some kind of contact with Simon, or verify his whereabouts—I'm afraid we may need to involve the authorities."

That's trouble for you: a swift, sneaky son of a bitch.

The bell had rung while Sayers was grilling me. In the hallway outside the office, a small crowd had formed—Bree and her friends, mostly, and a good chunk of the basketball squad. Eliot shoved through the gawkers and dragged me away, his mouth a flat, angry line

"What happened?" he asked.

"There's some sort of problem with Simon's records, and

now they're worried he's dropped off the radar, " I said through gritted teeth.

He whispered, "Do they think you killed him?"

"He's not dead," I pointed out. "Can you do something? Work some computer magic? They're going to keep hounding Amelia."

"I don't think the records are the problem," Eliot said. "Nobody's heard from him."

I ran through possible explanations, trying to find one that would hold up against Principal Sayer's scrutiny. "Maybe Amelia can say his relatives are homeschooling him."

"They're not worried about his course credits. He's old enough to drop out, and they know it. They think he's *missing*."

"Fabulous." I looked around, reflexively. I did it all the time, searching for Simon in the halls or on the street. Knowing is not the same as believing; if it were, no one would ever hope, or have their heart broken. "Ms. Powell was going to ask the Free Walkers to help us out. Guess she didn't get the chance."

"What if we took a picture of an Echo Simon—something with the date visible in the frame?" he asked.

"Like a kidnapping victim?"

"They want proof of life, don't they? Why not give it to them?"

Bree—and the rest of the school—wanted more than a photograph. They wanted answers. They wanted Simon to come back, lead the team to victory, and be everyone's favorite guy. They wanted life to be the way it was before.

I did too.

"If wishes were horses," I mumbled.

"What?"

"Nothing." We rounded the corner into the hallway where Simon's locker stood. Wishing wasn't going to bring him back, no matter how often or how desperately I sent up a plea to the cold and feckless multiverse.

That's what I thought, anyway.

And then I saw him.

Simon.

My Simon.

Standing by his locker, mobbed by people—Bree included. I could only see his hair, brown as cattails, and his smile, sharp and sly.

I froze, my heart beating so hard and fast that it must have been audible in space, terrified I was hallucinating, terrified I was dreaming, terrified I might wake up.

His eyes met mine across the hallway, crinkling slightly.

"Del—" Eliot reached for me, but I shook him off. As in a dream, my feet moved without thinking. Slowly at first, stumbling and shuffling, then faster, my boots ringing out on the linoleum in the suddenly quiet hallway. The crowd parted, and he was steps away, and I was running, heart in my throat, tears in my eyes.

He opened his arms and I practically flew into them, fusing my mouth to his. The Key World frequency rang through his touch, traveling through me like a nuclear blast. His hands went around my waist and he lifted me up, spun me around, and pressed me into the lockers, fierce and possessive and almost punishing. I twined my arms around his neck and breathed in the scent of snow and canvas, so different from the soap I was used to, and my brain stuttered. His mouth never left mine, and the kiss was like none we'd ever shared—a clashing of tongues and teeth and strange tastes. I gasped for air, drew back to look at the face I'd only seen in dreams and Echoes for far too long.

I ran my fingers over his cheeks, along the line of his jaw, through the softness of his hair, longer than I'd remembered. "You're here," I breathed.

"I'm here," he said, his mouth curving slyly. I traced his lips, swollen from our kiss, my fingers lingering where his scar should have been.

Should have been, but wasn't.

I drew back as the heat fled. With shaking hands, I pushed my hair away from my face, searching his eyes for some explanation.

"Miss me?" He moved in for another kiss.

"I don't miss," I murmured.

And punched him square in the face.

END OF FIRST MOVEMENT

BEGIN
SECOND
MOVEMENT

CHAPTER TWENTY-TWO

BLOOD POURED FROM SIMON'S NOSE. SOME-
one in the crowd shrieked, reminding me that our reunion—and
my punch—had been a very public one.

"What the fuck?" he snarled, cupping his hand against his face.

I scrambled away. "Who the hell are—" I started, then
thought better of it. "Who the hell do you think you are?"

"Simon Lane, obviously," he said, taunting even as he tried
to stanch the bleeding. "I thought you wanted me to come home.
That's what I kept hearing, anyway. Hell of a greeting."

He grabbed my wrist, dragging me toward him again. The
sound of his frequency—an exact match to the Key World—
scrambled my brain for a moment.

But only a moment. I thrashed, stomping on his foot with
my boot. He let go, and I turned so my back was to the crowd
instead of the wall. Dangerous to be so exposed, but more dangerous to be trapped.

"Del?" Eliot said from behind me, half-appalled, half-
delighted.

A circle formed around us. Simon pinched his nose and
scowled. "What's the problem, Delancey?"

"You," I spat, ignoring the crowd. All the digs my classmates had made about me in the past—every whisper, every snide remark, every hushed rumor—were repeated now, loud and clear, aimed directly at me.

I didn't care. All I cared about was that the Simon in front of me was wrong. Completely wrong, and impossible, and an impostor. "You're the problem. You walk in here and expect me to believe nothing's changed? I'm not stupid. Everything's changed, especially you."

"He hasn't," Eliot said softly, urgently, hands on my shoulders. "It's him, Del."

"No, it isn't." My eyes burned. "What do you want? Why are you even here?"

Lazily his eyes traveled over me, from the crown of my head to the tips of my boots. But those eyes—the cold, dark blue of deep water—weren't appreciative, but calculating. The kind that would root out your softest places and scrape them clean. "There's no place like home." He glanced around at the crowd, then back at me. "Let's finish this somewhere more private. The equipment room, maybe?"

"I'm afraid that won't be possible," said Principal Sayers. "Fighting is an automatic suspension, as you're both aware. It's good to see you, Simon."

"It's good to be back."

Ten minutes later I was sitting in my usual spot in the office, my hand throbbing in time with my head. This time Sayers had closed the blinds, shutting me out. Through the door I could hear the impostor pleading my case—an impossible situation veering further into unreality.

"The rules are very clear, Simon. Physical fighting, no matter who instigates it, is an automatic suspension for both participants."

"She wasn't fighting," he said. "It was my fault."

"I have at least twelve witnesses who say otherwise. There's not a mark on Delancey, and you should be in the nurse's office right now, getting your nose checked out. At least let them bring you an ice pack."

"She punched me, sure. But I deserved it. I might have gotten a little . . . carried away . . . when she kissed me. If you know what I mean."

There was a pause. "You're saying you made an unwanted advance toward Delancey Sullivan, and she was defending herself?"

"It won't happen again, sir."

"I should hope not"—a frosty note entering his voice—"because that, too, is a suspension."

"The thing is," the imposter said, "I'm not technically a student. Not until I re-enroll. You can't suspend me."

A few minutes later the door swung open. "Delancey, based on Simon's account of the incident, you will not be suspended. I do need to ask if you'd like to press charges against him, however. Should I call the authorities?"

"God, no," I said. "He won't try it again."

"Then you're both free to go." Sayers massaged his temple

as if a migraine was brewing. "Simon, I will assume that once re-enrolled, *you* will be a model student. There will be no warnings or second chances. For either of you."

I murmured my understanding alongside Simon. He reached out as if to take my arm, but I jerked away.

"Locker," I said. "I need to get my stuff."

He tipped his head in acknowledgement.

"Is it broken?" I asked, gesturing to his nose.

He touched it gingerly. "I don't think so."

"I'll try harder next time."

Eliot sprang up from the bench as we emerged from the office. "Are you suspended?"

"No," we chorused, and I glared at the imposter.

"Good," Eliot said. "I don't know how we'd explain this to your parents. I don't know how to explain it to me."

"He's not Simon," I said, grabbing my coat from my locker and heading outside. "Does that clear it up?"

"Less than you'd think," Eliot replied.

"I'm Simon," the guy said. "Just not the one you're used to. Never bothered you before."

I ignored him.

"Del," Eliot said. "His frequency matches perfectly."

Simon looked at me. "What gave it away?"

I tapped the corner of my mouth. "Every Simon I've met has that scar. Who are you?"

"Simon Lane."

"That's not possible," Eliot said as we strode toward my

house. "The definition of an Original is that there's only one of them." A thought struck him. "Are you a twin?"

He scoffed. "Twins with the same name. No. But you're getting warmer."

I shoved him. "This isn't a game, asshole. Tell me who you are."

"I'm the Original. The one you get all hot and bothered for? He's the Echo."

CHAPTER TWENTY-THREE

GRIEF IS LIKE A BLACK HOLE. EVERY PANG of sadness, every minute of loss, I'd stuffed down in my core, until the pain coalesced into something dark and dense and powerful, drawing me in more deeply, until I was too numb to escape.

Now the black hole threatened to turn itself inside out, emotion bursting from me like a supernova, wiping out everything in its path.

"You're the Original?" My throat was so tight I could barely breathe, but laughter erupted anyway, wheezy and high-pitched. I tried to swallow it, but it just kept coming, taking over my chest in jagged gasps, a cross between a sob and a scream. I shoved him into a thorny-looking shrub and stalked away, Eliot chasing after me.

"We need Addie," he said.

"I need a baseball bat," I said. The taste of . . . whoever the guy was . . . lingered. I spat, trying to get rid of it. "And a toothbrush."

"His frequency checks out. I think he might be right."

"Simon is not an Echo," I shouted. "Simon is real. He's alive. And he's waiting for me to find him."

"We already found him," came a voice behind me. "Why do you think I'm here?"

"You're a Free Walker." I didn't bother hiding my scorn.

"If you're going to get picky, a Free Half Walker. But close enough, yeah. When we lost . . . Ms. Powell, you called her?"

I nodded. "Is she . . ."

"Dead," he confirmed, and the mocking note dropped away.

I pressed my fingers against my eyelids as he continued. "When we realized the meeting had gone sideways, they sent me. Your contact managed to escape. You're damn lucky they didn't get you."

"I ran," I said numbly. "Took a chance and landed in a box-car. The guard chasing me missed the train and died."

"So I heard."

"Free Walkers work in cells," Eliot said. "They should be cutting off contact, not sending help."

"They should. But Del's special," he said, giving the word an unpleasant twist. He turned to me. "And so is your boyfriend."

"Special how?" I demanded.

"We need your help."

"Fine. Take me to him, and I'll do whatever you want."

"Not that simple. There are things we need to take care of here. Seeing your Echo can wait."

We'd reached my house, the driveway empty. I considered slamming the door in his face, just to make my point. But if he was my only link to the Free Walkers, I couldn't shut him out. Not yet.

Once we were inside, I tossed my bag and coat on the floor, then whirled to face him. "I don't care what you say. Simon's real."

"Real, yes. Original, no." He turned to Eliot. "You analyzed his frequency during the anomaly, right?"

"I did," Eliot said, hanging up his coat on the rack, his words careful and deliberate. "He resonates at the Key World frequency."

"So do I," Not-Simon pointed out. "But when you ran a deep analysis on him, you found a flaw, didn't you?"

"That's not proof," Eliot said. "Echoes resonate at an entirely different pitch. His tries to shift, but self-corrects each cycle."

"Guess you're not the genius everyone says. He's been here so long that he's taken on the Key World frequency, but his true frequency keeps trying to get through—the flaw is the alternate pitch, trying to reassert itself and failing."

"I don't care what his frequency sounds like," I said. "He's an Original. That scar—the one you don't have—every one of his Echoes has it. If you're the Original, shouldn't they be scar free?"

"It would depend on when the branches were formed," Eliot mused. "And when he got the scar."

"He was a baby," I said desperately. "He made a grab for Amelia's cat and it took a swipe at him."

"Makes sense," Eliot said. "An event that early would affect most of his Echoes."

"Because," I said with a pointed look at Not-Simon, "he's an Original."

"He's the Echo that will destroy the Consort. Why do you think the Free Walkers have been watching him so closely? It's not because they think he's dreamy." Not-Simon lounged against the kitchen island and gave me Simon's charming, mischievous smile.

"It's his dad," I stuttered. "Gil Bradley was important, and that means Simon's important."

"Why?"

"Because . . ." I trailed off. "Because he can Walk?"

"All hybrids can Walk. We can't hear pivots—not even me—without a device. But we can cross them if a Walker guides us. We can even manipulate the threads."

"There are more hybrids?"

"In the Key World? Some. We're kind of a rare species."

"Pregnancy's hard for female Walkers to sustain," Eliot said. "The change in frequencies is dangerous for the fetus. But for the men . . ."

"Male Walkers can father children with Originals, and the pregnancy proceeds normally. And every one of their Echo children carries the Walker gene. So technically, there's a lot of us. Just not a lot of Originals."

"That's not proof!" I shouted.

The angrier I got, the wider he smiled. It ripped something inside me, to see the face I loved turn cold and mocking. "How about this? Your Simon never noticed you, did he? For *years*. You guys went to the same elementary school, and he didn't even know your name. Either of you."

"We don't hang in the same circles," I said. Next to me, Eliot looked dismayed. "I didn't like it, but it's not actually a surprise."

"Isn't he supposed to be charming? Everybody's favorite guy? Friends with the entire school? The only two people he ignored . . . were the Walkers."

"He knows my name now," I said.

"And when did he learn it? When did he look at you—actually

look at you, not through you or around you or past you?"

"Park World."

"That was the anomaly," he said. "The anomaly and the fact that he's a sucker for sad little kids, since he was one. Poor fatherless Simon Lane, always wondering why people leave." He shook his head in disgust. "Here, in the Key World. When did he look at you?"

I closed my eyes. Impossible to think with that face in front of me, cruel and enthralling. "Music class. Ms. Powell paired us up, and he turned around and—"

"His legs banged into yours."

"You were there?"

"In a manner of speaking."

"Synaptic Resonance Transfer," Eliot murmured.

He nodded. "SRT lets him see his Echoes, and I'm looped in too. It's stronger between us because our frequencies are nearly identical. He touched you, and then he saw you. Sound familiar?"

I couldn't speak.

"He kept getting my name wrong," Eliot said. "I thought he was being a dick."

"He was," Not-Simon said with a grin. "Let's see . . . what else? I have perfect pitch. Simon's tone deaf because his frequency's off. He couldn't find middle C if his life depended on it."

Something was shifting inside me, some rearrangement of everything I'd known, like tectonic plates shaping the earth. It took all my concentration not to let the pieces scatter completely.

Eliot stepped in, taking over while I tried to find my footing on the newly treacherous ground.

"That's anecdotal," Eliot said coolly. "Unlike Del, I need something verifiable."

"The flaw. You've verified that already. It's the frequency of the Echo he came from."

"How'd he get here?"

His expression hardened. "Ask him."

"I thought you had all the answers," Eliot pointed out, arms folded.

"Doesn't mean I'm going to give them to you."

"Fine," said Eliot. "Can you at least tell us what you're doing here?"

"I told you—we need Del to help us find something."

"The map frequency? The one in my grandmother's journal?" I asked. "I've already got it. Take me to Simon and it's yours."

He looked startled. "You figured it out?"

I nodded, finally feeling smug.

"Well, bully for you. But we've already got that one. We need the other two."

"Two?" Eliot said, and smacked his forehead. "Of course. Three notes in a chord; three signals to triangulate the frequency."

"Congratulations, Einstein." Not-Simon turned to me. "We need Monty's part of the frequency. Since you're the only one who has access . . ."

"Not an option," I said.

Eliot held up a hand, like a traffic cop. "Where does the map lead?"

"Get me those frequencies, and I'll tell you."

"You want her to retrieve a frequency to complete a map, but you won't tell us where it leads? Del, you can't be okay with this."

I paused, toying with my pendant. "Who has the third signal?"

Simon's mouth twisted, a smile gone wrong. "Gil Bradley."

"Your dad's dead." I paused, realizing how insensitive it sounded. I couldn't be that callous toward someone with Simon's face. "Sorry."

"I know. We'll take care of it after we get Monty's part."

"I want to see Simon," I said. "Not after we unlock the map. Before."

"I'm not here because I'm a nice guy, Del. The Free Walkers don't work that way. Get the frequency from Monty, and then we'll talk reunions."

"Monty won't give us the frequency," I said. "Trust me on this."

"Why not?"

I looked at Eliot, who waved his hands in a "might as well" gesture. "He wants me to help him escape the oubliette. He won't give me the frequency until he's free."

Simon dragged a hand over his face, the gesture so familiar my heart squeezed. "Guess we're gonna have ourselves a prison break."

CHAPTER TWENTY-FOUR

W E'RE NOT BREAKING MONTY OUT OF prison," I said. "We'll find the frequency some other way."

"There is no other way." Not-Simon helped himself to a pop from the fridge and a cookie from the jar on the counter, as familiar in my home as Eliot.

"How did you know—" I pointed to the cookie.

"How do you think? We've gone into Echoes of your house more times than I can count, looking for Monty's frequency. It's not here."

"Maybe you haven't figured out how to crack his code."

"Nice try, Nancy Drew. It's not here. He memorized it, which means we have to spring him."

"This isn't the Three Stooges," I said. "We can't pry the window out and have him climb over. It's an oubliette, four stories below ground, surrounded by guards."

"Good thing you know your way around," he said.

"Why don't we focus on the other frequency?" Eliot said. "The one less likely to end in certain death."

"Gil's?" Not-Simon frowned. "We've looked over his place too."

"His house? Did he even have—oh God. You went through

Amelia's place?" I said, outraged. "You could have led the Consort right to her."

"We haven't, though. She's fine." But he looked away, his swagger gone.

I sank into my chair. "What am I going to tell her?"

"Better think fast," Simon said. "The prodigal son returns? Phone's going to be ringing off the hook."

"I should be the one to tell her," I said, and pushed up from the table. "We can go now."

"Heartwarming reunions later," Simon said. "We need to—"

The sound of someone rattling the back door interrupted him.

"Hide!" I whispered, but Simon merely took another swig of pop and smiled.

"I'm done hiding," he said. "Why do you think I came back?"

The door swung open, and Addie breezed in. "Del, you could have opened—" she called, and then caught sight of the ghost sitting at the kitchen table.

Addie took Simon's resurrection about as well as I could have hoped.

Which is to say, she didn't punch anyone.

So, better than me.

Instead, she stood in her coat and hat at the kitchen counter while I brought her up to speed. Her icy calm was belied by the fact she was white-knuckling her purse strap the entire time I spoke.

When I finally ran out of explanations, she took a deep breath, set down her purse, and hung up her coat, eyes on Simon the entire time.

Then, very deliberately, she turned to me. "You people have gone completely off the rails. Del, you are not breaking Monty out of prison. It cannot be done, and even if it could be done, it shouldn't be done, because he will go right back to looking for Grandma, which means he'll wreck the Key World. *Again*. And while I would like to think that we are capable of outsmarting a dementia-riddled septuagenarian, our track record is spotty at best. Not to mention the fact, if the Consort catches us, they will kill us, and even if they don't catch us, they will hunt us across Echoes for the rest of our days. Maybe you got the gene for living life on the run, but I did not, and I have no desire to spend the next sixty years figuring out how to avoid frequency poisoning and a painful, drawn-out death."

She ended an octave higher than usual, breathless and scarlet with panic.

Simon studied her, then turned to me. "Smaller crew is better anyway."

"You don't have a crew!" Addie shrieked. "You have my sister, who you are taking advantage of. How do we know you'll even take her to Simon? The *real* Simon."

"I am the real Simon," he snapped. "And a hell of a better choice than letting her bumble around on her own. I don't have time to argue with you. We need those frequencies before the Tacet starts."

"Eighteen days? You're going to do this in eighteen days?"

191

"Eighteen days, eighteen years. It doesn't matter," Eliot said. "Breaking out of an oubliette is impossible. "

"I want to know how this happened," Addie said. "Who swapped you two? What possible purpose could it serve to move kids around the multiverse like they were interchangeable? Who messes with reality like that?"

"Your grandmother," Simon said coldly. "And my dad."

"Rose?" I said. "Rose swapped you?"

He ran his hand through his hair, baffled. "Do you guys really not know any of this?"

"Who would have told us?" Addie asked. "Monty?"

Simon rolled his shoulders, working out kinks. "About seventeen years ago, the Free Walkers were reaching critical mass. They were starting to look like they could be a real threat to the Consort, converting high-level Walkers to their way of thinking. My dad had met my—Amelia—during the Washington Station train crash a couple years prior, and they'd fallen in love. She got pregnant, and they thought—" He shook his head at their foolishness. "They thought they were going to get a happy ending.

"Right after I was born, the Consort figured out he was a Free Walker. A sympathizer tipped him off, gave him a head start, so he ran. Dropped off the radar. But the Consort wasn't giving up. They went scorched-earth on every Echo he might be in—they cleaved anywhere he'd visited, any Echo he'd run a navigation report on.

"He'd befriended a lot of Amelia's Echoes, and he went out to check on one of them, see how she and the baby were doing."

"Her Echoes were pregnant?" Eliot shook his head. "He's like the world's biggest deadbeat dad."

"Amelia knew what she was getting into," Simon shot back. "The Consort almost caught up with him in that Echo. He'd visited before, and it was just . . . luck, or the opposite of luck, that they arrived while he was there. They cleaved it, but there was no time for him to cauterize it. He had to leave her behind."

"She couldn't Walk," I said, sick at heart. "But the baby was a hybrid."

"She begged him to take the baby, and he did. How could he say no?" He scrubbed a hand over his face, fatigue turning his skin dull. "The Consort was going to find him again. He knew the clock was ticking, and he knew they'd find Amelia and me eventually, no matter how well he'd hidden us. But if they did, all the Free Walkers' research into hybrids would be for nothing."

"What kind of research?" Eliot said sharply.

Simon ignored the interruption. "Rose knew the Consort would come after her soon enough, so the two of them came up with a plan. She took me into the Echoes, and rather than let Amelia suffer, they left your Simon in my place. Then Gil let himself be caught."

Silence took over as his words sank in.

"Seems like a sucky plan," I said.

"Once they had Gil, they stopped looking," Addie said softly. "He redirected their attention."

"What if it hadn't worked?" I asked. "They would have killed my Simon as easily as you."

He jerked a shoulder. "Which would have been sad, but not

fatal to the cause. If my Echoes die, *I* carry on. If I die, every one of my Echoes unravels. Hiding me was the only way to save us."

The logic behind it was irrefutable, but also unsettling. For all their talk of Echoes being real, the Free Walkers seemed willing to count their lives as less valuable.

"No offense," I said, "But what's so special about hybrids?"

"Everything," he said. "We boost the signal of a world. We can Walk and tune and cauterize, as long as we're paired up with a full-blooded Walker. And unlike your kind . . . there's plenty of us. We have Echoes. Lots and lots of Echoes."

"You solved the population crisis," Eliot said. "If hybrids were allowed to cauterize, you could take a three-man cleaving team and split them."

"One Walker, two hybrids," Addie mused. "Triple the effectiveness. Assuming you could convince them to join up."

"I'm very convincing," Simon said with a leer.

Addie rolled her eyes.

Simon shrugged. "Echoes won't cleave. They'd be killing versions of themselves."

"So the Consort can't admit Echoes are real, because it would mean an end to cleaving, and they can't ask Echoes to cleave. And they won't give up cleaving, because the Key World needs the energy transfer," Eliot said, in the methodical, "piece it all together" way he used when helping me with my homework.

"Powell got that far with you, huh? Good."

"But that doesn't explain why they sent you back now. Or why they took so long."

"After the first Tacet, we were in a shambles. We couldn't have organized a bake sale, much less a rebellion. The Consort thought we were finished, and we let them think so while we rebuilt. The harder they came down on people, the more sympathetic we looked. You spend years crushing the little guy, and people start to think you're a bully. You might have noticed that despite the fact the Consort calls us terrorists, we haven't done anything yet."

"Yet," Addie said.

His smile chilled my blood. "Yet."

"Well, do it without my sister." She turned to me. "Del, I don't know if I believe him, but even if I did, they're as ruthless as the Consort. They stole a child. They left Monty behind to be tortured. This guy probably has Stockholm syndrome."

"Addie's right," Eliot said. "I don't trust them."

I looked at Not-Simon. Original Simon, but not *my* Simon.

His gaze was flat and uncompromising. "Never said they were nice. But they stand on the side of the good. Where do you stand?"

With Simon. All I said was, "How do we get Monty out?"

Not-Simon's shoulders eased, and I realized he'd been more worried about convincing us than he'd let on. "I've got some ideas. First, let's go meet my mom."

CHAPTER TWENTY-FIVE

Do you think she'll know?" Simon asked as we stood in front of Amelia's house.

"I did." I wrapped my arms around myself, partly from cold and partly from nerves. "She's known you a lot longer."

"Not me," he said, simultaneously withering and wistful.

"She'll know," I said. "Maybe we should skip this. It won't make her feel any better, not once she knows you're . . . you."

"What if it makes me feel better?" he asked.

"You have feelings? I hadn't noticed."

"Nobody asked me if I wanted to be taken, you know. Nobody asked if I wanted to grow up on the run, or spend years trying to fix worlds I don't belong in."

I blinked. "They saved your life."

"Yeah, and for what?" he asked, and stalked toward the house.

His response caught me off guard, and I raced after him, calling, "Go around the back!"

Before he could knock on the door, I caught his hand, the sensation alien and familiar at the same time. I let go and slid between him and the screen, careful not to touch him again.

"You can't barge in there," I said as Iggy began to bark. "Let me talk to her first."

For a moment I was sure he would push me aside. But he stepped back into the shadows, shoulders hunched, and made a shooing motion.

I cracked the door open just enough to let myself in, but Iggy threw himself against me, protesting loudly. "Give me a minute, boy." I pulled a treat out of my coat pocket.

"Del," said Amelia, poking her head in the kitchen. "What's wrong?"

"Something came up," I said.

"Something bad?"

"Something . . . unexpected." I motioned to the living room couch. "We should sit."

Her eyebrows arched. "The only time people want me to sit is when they're about to give me bad news."

Did this qualify as good or bad? "It's about Simon."

She crossed the room and sat, hands folded tightly in her lap.

"I told you the Free Walkers approached me," I said. "But not why. I didn't want to get your hopes up. They gave me proof that Simon survived the cleaving."

She raised a hand to her mouth, took several trembling breaths.

"He's alive, Amelia."

"Is he—"

"Safe?" She nodded. "I think so. They think Simon's . . . important."

"Useful," she said flatly.

"Probably. They wouldn't help him if he wasn't."

"Can he come home?"

I covered her hands with mine. "Not yet. They've got some plan to stop the Consort, and they won't bring him back until they've seen it through."

Her expression, hope and longing and grief woven together like a braid, didn't change. "Have you seen him?"

I looked down. "Not exactly."

"Something's changed," Amelia said. "That's why you're telling me now."

Iggy agreed. He sprang up and hurtled through the house, crashing into the back door, baying wildly.

I twisted to look at him, and saw Simon's profile silhouetted in the window, pacing back and forth.

I took in Amelia's too-quick breaths and her pale, set face. She didn't need to know every last detail. Later, when she'd recovered, I could tell her about the frequencies. Not-Simon was enough of a shock for one night.

I finally said, "The school was asking questions about Simon. They were looking more closely at his transfer, wondering if there's something off."

"They've been calling," she admitted. "I was hoping it would blow over."

"Amelia, he disappeared and nobody's heard from him. His teammates, his coaches, his friends . . . people are suspicious. They want proof he's okay, and the Free Walkers sent it."

"I don't understand."

The words felt unreal in my mouth, but I said them anyway, furious at the Free Walkers for putting me in this position. "They sent another Simon. He's not ours, but he's here, and he wants to see you."

Iggy's body thudded against the door, again and again.

"Another Simon?" She covered her face with her hands.

"You can say no," I told her. "If it's too much, if you're not up to it, I can take him somewhere else. I'll understand."

"He won't," she said, dropping her hands to her lap. "My son."

My head snapped up. Had she known about the swap? No. Her grief was too deep, too all-encompassing to be faked.

She wiped away the tears and squared her shoulders. "He's outside? Sending Iggy into fits?"

"He has that effect on people," I said. "He's not like our Simon. He's angry. At everyone." He's broken, I wanted to say, but didn't. "His life has been . . . not easy."

"Sometimes the only way to survive something terrible is to pretend that you already have," Amelia said. "Let him in, Del."

"Are you sure?"

She stood up with an effort, tried to smile. "I'm ready."

I caught Iggy by the collar. "Settle down, you nut. He's not who you think."

Opening the door, I poked my head outside. "Where'd you go?"

"Here," he said, stepping into the porch light. Iggy went rigid at my side. "Did you tell her?"

"Some of it. She knows you're not him. Don't tell her about the switch, please. It's too much for her."

"I'm an asshole, not an idiot." His voice was harsh as the night air.

I stepped back, hauling on Iggy's collar, and Simon entered.

"Hey, dog," he said. Iggy nosed his hand, sighed, and sat back on his haunches. "He's not biting my hand off, at least."

"Iggy's nicer than I am. Come on."

I led him across the family room. Once I'd felt like a stranger here, unsettled by the easy affection between Simon and Amelia, so different from the tension that ran like an electrical current through my own house. Now Amelia had brought me into that warmth, and the need to protect it—and her—was overwhelming.

Amelia was standing where I'd left her, arms wrapped around herself, eyes bright with unshed tears, her skin so pale I could see the tracery of veins along her temples. Her jade-green sweater dwarfed her tiny frame, making Simon seem even bigger. It was like watching a panther and a dove face off, and I wasn't entirely sure this Simon wouldn't pounce.

"Simon," she murmured.

He jerked back, his shoulders broad and tense beneath the heavy canvas jacket he wore. He looked over at me, eyes wild as the sea.

"I don't know what to call you," he blurted. "Mom? Mother? Amelia? Mrs. Lane? Mrs. Bradley?"

"We can rule out Mrs. Bradley," she said. "Your father and I never married, not officially."

"But you have a wedding band."

"Yes. He gave me this. And you." She twisted the slim gold ring. "Mom, if you want. Amelia's fine, if you're more comfortable."

He nodded, but didn't say which one he preferred.

She stood stock-still, drinking in the sight of him, and he stared back, unabashed and disbelieving.

"Come and sit," she said, gesturing to the couch. Joy broke across her face like a sunrise, tears caught on her lashes. With halting steps, he joined her.

"Tell me about you," she said. "I want to know who you are."

"Simon Lane," he replied.

She reached out and brushed a stray lock of hair away from his face. "There are a million Simon Lanes. I want to know who *you* are."

"I'm the one . . ." He trailed off and exchanged glances with me. "I'm just me."

"How long have you been with the Free Walkers?"

"Ever since I can remember." He chose his words with the same care Walkers did, weighing the possibilities of each one, measuring out meaning.

"That must have been a difficult way to grow up. Uncertain."

He lifted a shoulder. "I never knew any different."

Lie. He knew exactly what he'd missed out on; he'd compared his life to Simon's and found he'd drawn the short straw. But he spared Amelia, and my anger deflated slightly.

"You should have," she said, her voice thick with emotion.

"It wasn't so bad," he said. "I got to see the multiverse. How many people like me can say that?"

"There's nobody like you," she said. "Isn't that the point of all this? Every life matters."

He studied her for a long moment. "I suppose so."

She took his hand in hers. "Have you seen him?"

There was no need to clarify "him." Other Simon shook his head. "Not yet. But they won't let anything happen to him."

The look that passed between them was so fraught—tender and awkward and longing—that I backed into the hallway, wanting to give them privacy.

Iggy padded after me, whining softly. I examined the lineup of Simon's school pictures, watching him grow from a round-faced kindergartener to the lean, driven boy I knew. So easy to picture his arms coming around me, his fingers tangling in my hair, sinking back against the broad planes of his chest. Safe, with Simon. Happy, with Simon. Without him, nothing of the sort.

"I should get home," I said, returning to the living room. "My parents will be home soon, and I need to keep up appearances."

Simon stood to leave, but Amelia kept hold of his hand. "Where will you go?"

He looked at me, and I said carefully, "Simon needs to re-enroll in school. I'm sure the administration will want to follow up, and it would look better if you were living here when they came calling."

Amelia closed her eyes for the briefest of seconds, long enough that she missed the hurt that flashed in his eyes.

"I can figure out something else," he said in a low voice. "It won't be more than a week or two."

She frowned and looked at me. I shrugged.

"Stay here, " she insisted. "I want as much time with you as I can grab."

Other Simon insisted on walking me to the end of the driveway.

"What's wrong?" I asked.

"Can't I be gentlemanly?"

"You don't know how to be gentlemanly. And you don't like me enough to bother. Are you going to ask her about the map frequency?"

"Soon."

"You said we didn't have a lot of time."

"Don't rush me," he snapped. "I deserve a few days. This was my home."

I brushed my hand over the rough canvas of his sleeve. "Thanks for not telling her."

He stared at the frozen grass. "She thinks I'm an Echo."

"She thinks you're the child of her Echoes," I said. "Which makes you her child, in a way."

"I *am* her child. They were tight, weren't they?" He glanced back at the house, naked longing on his face.

"I don't think they had anyone else. Not really." Secrets have a way of hiding their keepers. Amelia knew the truth about the Walkers, and it put her in a different world from Originals, even as they occupied the same space.

"Do you think I should tell her?"

"Why? To make yourself feel better?"

"You don't think she deserves to know?"

"Amelia *deserves* to grow old with her son, but she's not going to get that. The least we can do, in the time she has left, is not tell her that her real son was kidnapped and the kid she spent her life raising belonged to someone else."

"No," he said, steel in his voice. "The least we can do is take down the Consort."

Something he said earlier came back to me. "You're not in this to save the Echoes, are you?"

"Sure I am. I'm not going to get sappy about it, but they're killing off entire worlds. How do you not try to save them?"

"You believe the Free Walkers the way I believed my parents. It's how you were raised." He didn't know anything but fighting and surviving. "But you don't just hate the Consort because of cleavings, or how they treat Echoes. It's personal. It's payback—revenge for everything they took from you."

He faltered for a split second before going on the attack. "You talk a good game, but the truth is, you're doing this to save your boyfriend. Do you ever think about what this fight could cost you?"

A chill that had nothing to do with the weather worked its way over my skin. "Every day."

"It's not only your family. Your sister, or Eliot, or whatever life you've got planned out for yourself. It could cost you Amelia. If we lose, you'll spend your life running. Amelia will die alone because you wanted to hook up with your Simon."

I stared up at the sky, imagined a life as desolate and lonely and transient as a comet, all ice and dust and flare, consuming itself. I imagined a life without Simon, and it seemed equally cold. So I gave the only response I could.

"I love him."

He snorted. "That's the *stupidest* reason. You won't last five minutes with us if you're going to go around quoting pop songs and greeting cards."

"Don't interrupt me," I snapped. "I love him. I don't care if he's an Echo. He's a whole person, and the multiverse is filled with people who love Echoes, and if I think Simon's worth saving, they all are. There's nothing stupid about loving someone."

"It makes you weak," he said.

"Bullshit. Look at Monty—what he endured, how carefully he planned, the sacrifices he made. Granted, he's insane, but he sure as hell isn't weak. And what about Amelia? She's lost everything. Most people would have shut down by now, but she's welcomed us both in without a hint of bitterness. Imagine how hard tonight was for her, but she did it. It's not hatred or revenge powering them—it's love, and it gives them the strength to do impossible, terrifying things."

I dragged in a lungful of cold air, let it shock my system, and said what I'd been too afraid of saying until now. "Now it's my turn."

CHAPTER TWENTY-SIX

Days until Tacet: 15

ORIGINAL SIMON'S RETURN WORKED THE magic we needed—the school left Amelia alone. Simon's old teammates treated him warily, hurt that he had abandoned them, bewildered by his sudden preference for me over the team. We were conspicuous. People watched us now and whispered in a way the old Simon wasn't used to. The new Simon didn't care. He was too focused on planning the prison break and spending time with Amelia.

Meanwhile, I was recruiting help. Or trying to.

"Where are Mom and Dad?" I asked Addie when we returned from training later that weekend. She and Laurel were baking cookies, and unlike Addie's solo efforts, the entire kitchen was covered in flour and sugar. I dipped a finger into the batter and tasted. "Needs more vanilla."

She swatted at me with a towel. "I hope you washed your hands. Work, obviously. The Tacet's two weeks away."

"Why aren't you there?" Eliot asked.

Laurel handed Addie the beater, saying, "A lot of the

information is classified, and we don't have clearance. So we tend to finish early."

"What sort of information?" Simon asked.

"Nothing I'm sharing with you," Addie said sharply

"Don't be like this," I said. "We could use your help."

"With what?" She threw up her hands. "Do you even know what you're doing?"

Eliot nodded agreement, and I shot him a dirty look. "We're getting the frequency from Monty."

"Right. Tell me again where it leads?"

I looked at Simon, who leaned forward and stole a glob of cookie dough, but didn't reply.

"You don't have a clue where it leads, do you?" she asked him.

"I know exactly where it leads. And I know the plan," he said, his smile more like a snarl. "Not that I'm sharing with you."

Turning his back on Addie, he slanted a look at Eliot. "I need someone to run the tech," he added. "I've got equipment, but my hands will be full."

"Use a Free Walker," Eliot said.

"I could," he agreed. "But I want the best, and that's you. Besides, you've got a personal stake here." His tilted his head toward me, and I fought the urge to brain him with a cookie sheet.

Eliot's jaw tightened. "You can't tell me what you're after, I'm not getting involved. I can't believe you would, Del."

"Eliot . . . ," I started, but he folded his arms and stared at his shoes.

Simon turned to Laurel, who had been quietly scooping out cookie dough.

"No way," she said, and laced her fingers with Addie's. "We've had enough close calls lately."

Addie shook her head in warning. I started to press for details, but Simon cut me off.

"So that's it. None of you will help?"

"Sorry," Laurel said.

"I'm not," Eliot replied.

Simon made a noise of disgust, and I nudged him. "You've had seventeen years to acclimate. We need a little time."

"You don't have it. We have fifteen days before the Tacet."

"Then make us understand," I said. "Give them some answers."

He dragged a hand over his face. "The Free Walkers are planning to move against the Consort. It has to be soon, because they want to stop the Tacet. And no," he added, "I'm not telling you the plan. Don't ask. But we need those frequencies before we can do anything."

"Because the weapon is there?" I asked.

"The weapon . . . ," he snorted. "No. The combined frequencies lead to our fail-safe. We've gone down this path before, during the last Tacet, and Free Walkers have long memories. Before people would commit to this plan, they wanted a way out. An escape plan, in case the Consort won again."

"I thought you guys were all in," Eliot said. "Devoted to the cause."

"Do you know how long the Free Walkers have been around?" Simon retorted. "Generations. Some of them, like Powell, have families. So yeah, they believe in the cause. But they want to protect their kids, too."

"And this frequency helps . . . how?" Addie asked.

He narrowed his eyes and ground out the words. "It's the First Echo."

The oven timer dinged, but nobody moved.

"Nice try," Addie said after minute. "The First Echo is a myth."

My heart sank. She was right. Simon and the Free Walkers were delusional, and I'd risked my life for nothing.

"No," Laurel said firmly. She rescued the burnt cookies, gathered her thoughts, and spoke. "The First Echo exists in a technical sense. The Key World's been branching since the beginning of time, so logically, one choice—one Echo—preceded the others. But it's impossible to trace back, because the number of realities generated since then are nearly infinite."

"Impossible," I said dryly. "There's that word again."

"It's like the Holy Grail. Lots of Archivists try to find it—they write algorithms and crunch the data on one of the Consort's supercomputers, but nobody's ever been able to find it."

"Cleavers think it's a sign that the multiverse is unknowable," Addie said. "A gift to be revered, not analyzed."

"Well, you're both wrong. It exists," Simon said. "Gil and Monty stumbled across it, eons ago. Fate, or destiny, or dumb luck. Who knows? But once they found it, they knew the Consort would cleave it."

"A branch that old and complex would be a gold mine," Eliot said. "The energy transfer would be huge."

"The loss of life would be huge," Simon returned. "So they split the frequency into three parts, and each took one: Gil, Monty, and Rose. Unless all three of them agreed, they'd never be able to find it again."

"Like activating the missile on a nuclear submarine." I said. "You need two people to turn the keys."

Simon nodded. "Once we have the location of the First Echo, we can send the nonessentials there while we launch our attack against the Consort. If we win, they come home. If we fail, they can cauterize it and start over. Do it right this time. First Echo, second Eden."

"You'd never be able to come home," Addie said, turning pale.

"Exile's better than death," he said.

"What if you do?" Eliot asked. "What if you fail, and you all run away to the First Echo? The Consort keeps cleaving. Nothing changes. Who stops all the future Tacets?"

"You understand we're not planning to fail, right?" Simon asked.

"No," Addie said, her voice cracking. "You cannot do this. I don't agree with the Consort, but there must be a better way to deal with this than outright treason. There's got to be a way to fix it from within."

"Spoken like an insider," he said. "You don't know how ruthless they've been to our people."

"I know exactly how ruthless they've been," she said. "I've

seen the people they send after Free Walkers; they're fanatics. They believe what they're doing is ordained."

"Which is why we have to force their hand."

"And start a new revolution in the process? Even if you win, you'll have a target on your back."

"She's right," Eliot muttered. "You'd do better to win people over."

Simon said, "Free Walkers have been trying to win people over for decades, and it's gotten them nowhere. Which is why we need to get Monty out."

"It's an oubliette," Laurel said. "There's no breaking out. There's no breaking in. It's like the crown jewels, or Fort Knox or . . . something."

"Fort Knox is empty," Simon said. "And the crown jewels were swapped out for fakes years ago."

Eliot blinked. "By Free Walkers?"

"By the Consort. Where did you think CCM got their money from?" He shook his head, dismayed. "No wonder you all fall in line. You're as gullible as preschoolers. We need to do this, and we need to move. So who's in?"

The silence was flat and stony. I stared at each of them in turn. Eliot wouldn't meet my gaze. Addie fumed silently, her eyes narrowed to slits. Laurel worried her lower lip between her teeth.

"Eliot?" I asked. "Please. It's the last thing I'll ask you for, I swear."

"Don't say that," he replied. "Can you guarantee they won't come after my family?"

"Absolutely," Simon said. "We protect our people."

"I'm not your people," he said with a slow, reluctant nod. "I'm Del's."

I went up on tiptoe to hug him. "Thank you," I whispered, and his arms came around me.

"I'm going to be pissed if you die," he murmured.

"Me too."

Simon cleared his throat. "I need an ID. Something that will get me past the front desk at CCM."

"I know someone," Laurel said, and Addie hissed at her. "What? Just because you don't like going to bars doesn't mean I can't."

I grinned at Addie. "She is definitely a keeper."

She didn't smile back. "It'll never work."

"Never's a big word," I said.

"I don't understand why we can't try to fix the Consort," she said. "Why do you have to tear down everything the Walkers have built?"

"Bad beginnings lead to breaks," I said. "Isn't that what we're taught? The Walkers are built on a bad beginning. Let's push the reset button."

I reached for her hand, but she yanked away from me, her voice shrill enough to shatter glass. "You are a sixteen-year-old girl, not the leader of the rebel forces! This isn't one of Eliot's movies. This is real life, and you know what happens to the rebel forces in real life? They get outgunned, they get massacred, and then they get forgotten."

Laurel opened her mouth to speak, then shut it again. Eliot ducked his head, distress furrowing his brow.

"Wow, Addie. Thanks for the support." I turned to Simon, who was lounging against the counter looking mildly curious, at best. "Let's go. We can finish this at Amelia's."

He straightened and offered me his arm. Before I could move, Addie blocked my way. "How do I support you if you're dead, Del?" Her eyes glittered with tears and terror. "It isn't a question of believing in you. It's me, being selfish. I've seen what they do to Free Walkers. And I can't stand the idea of them doing it to you."

I exhaled slowly, and my anger went with it. "My odds aren't terrible, Addie. I had an amazing teacher."

"Who got caught. He wasn't that good."

"I'm talking about you, moron. You did the best you could, even when I was a pain in the ass."

"You're still a pain in the ass," she said, but her voice cracked, and she smiled when she said it.

"I was never going to have a place in the Consort," I said. "You know that. I've never had it in me, the way you do."

"If you'd just go along," she said desperately. "If you'd just try, Del. It doesn't have to be all or nothing. We can make people listen. We can change their minds, but we have to be patient."

"Every day we wait, more Echoes are dying."

"Better them than you," she said.

Next to me, Eliot made a noise of agreement.

"What are you going to tell Mom and Dad?"

My stomach bottomed out. "I hadn't thought about it."

"You have to tell them," she said. "I know you're not close, but put yourself in their position. Do you really want the news coming from Lattimer? Or a Consort guard?"

"What do I say?"

"Tell them the truth," she urged. "You've never tried to explain Simon, or the Free Walkers. You assume they won't understand, but you haven't given them a chance."

"I have! But they don't listen. It's never that I do things differently—I do things *wrong*. That's never going to change, no matter how I explain it."

"Try. Once. If they don't listen, you can leave with a clean conscience. Otherwise, they'll keep cleaving. And when the truth finally comes out, they'll feel terrible. If you can convince them now, they might become allies, instead of enemies."

"If." Such a small word, easily dismissed. But "if" made entire worlds. "If" changed the course of the universe. One breath, two letters, three strokes of a pen. And contained within was more power than a star. I bent my head. "I'll try."

CHAPTER TWENTY-SEVEN

Days until Tacet: 11

THE NEXT FEW DAYS PASSED IN A BLUR OF training and school and furtive, meticulous preparation. Simon returned to school, but not the basketball team—his "transfer" made him ineligible to play for the rest of the season, no matter how hard the school petitioned the conference.

"Thank God," he said when I met him outside the coach's office.

"You don't like basketball?"

"I don't give a hot damn about basketball. I have bigger things to worry about than a carnival game on steroids."

"I think it's supposed to be fun," I said as we headed back toward my locker. "Don't you have fun?"

He draped an arm over my shoulder and eyed Bree as we passed her in the hallway, gave her a lazy, inviting nod. "Sure. But it's a little more horizontal."

"Gross," I said, shoving him away. "Can you please try not to make things worse around here?"

"Saved your ass, didn't I?" He popped a can of Coke and

drained half of it while I sputtered in outrage. "How are things with Addie?"

"Better, I guess. She's not actively trying to stop us."

"Was that a possibility?" The rumble in his voice sounded like a threat.

"If she thought she could get me to stay, maybe. But she knows better."

"Good."

"You don't get frequency poisoning," I said, tugging my locker open and changing the subject. "Why the sugar addiction?"

"Grew up that way."

So had Ms. Powell. The memory prompted another question. "How do the Free Walkers deal with frequency poisoning? They can't go around mainlining corn syrup."

"They've got a few tricks. Tuning strategies, earplugs, devices, surgery. The longer they spend in Echoes, the more drastic the treatment. None of them are perfect solutions, but they keep people sane." He considered. "Mostly."

"Other hybrids are immune too? Or is this a result of the swap?"

"All hybrids. Yet another reason we're good at cauterization. Now lay off. You're starting to sound like Eliot." He glanced around, scowling. "Where's Einstein, anyway?"

"Going over the tech."

"Right. He's done that a hundred times already."

"You think he's lying?"

"Hardly. He can't even lie to himself."

"That's not a bad thing." I swung my backpack over my shoulder, and we headed toward the commons.

"We all lie to ourselves. It's a survival technique. Anyway, I'm glad he's gone. I need to talk to you."

I wondered what lies Simon was telling himself—and what lies I believed. "Oh, well. As long as it works for you."

"If we're going to sell this," he said, ignoring my sniping, "you and I need to sell it. Nobody's going to believe that we took off together if you keep glaring at me like that. They'll think you killed me and buried the body in a shallow grave."

"Tempting." I tilted my head back and batted my eyelashes. "Better?"

He dropped onto one of the benches. "Sit on my lap."

I glowered at him. "I'm not a Pekingese."

"The last time you touched me, you nearly broke my nose. Time to make up some ground." He nodded toward Bree, who was watching us from across the commons, eyes narrowed.

"I'm not kissing you," I said through a smile as brittle as winter leaves.

"Pretend you're kissing him."

"But I'm not."

"You've done it before. Twice, if memory serves. Imagine you're sending a message: one to him and one to the world."

So my words *had* gotten through. "Does he always see me through your eyes?"

"Only once we touch. Then it fades in and out, like a radio

signal. Contact boosts it again, like when you recharge the stars you leave in Echoes. So if you want to have a conversation, you're going to have to use me."

A thought struck. "Did you see me? When Simon was here and we . . ."

"Oh, yeah." He grinned. "Good times."

"Can you block it?"

He shrugged. "If I try hard enough."

"Try harder," I ordered, and my heart went abruptly, painfully still. "Were you influencing him?"

His smile dropped away. "Echoes are alive, and part of being alive is making choices, mistakes and all. Denying someone their choices is like saying they're more houseplant than human."

My blood started moving again. "Thank you."

"You're welcome." He grinned again. "Feel free to show your gratitude by kissing me. Bree's watching, you know. Showtime."

A quick glance over my shoulder proved him right.

Instead of flipping Bree off, I tugged my sleeves down until only my fingertips were poking out. Simon looked up at me, cocksure and expectant.

I traced his cheekbone, his jaw, the line of his throat, letting his signal travel through me. Slowly I bent until my lips hovered next to his ear. His hand curved around my hip, blatantly possessive.

Threading my fingers through his hair, I murmured, "The next time I kiss you, it's going to be in person. And it's going to be amazing. And I don't want this guy watching, so figure something out."

When I pulled back, irritation and admiration warred in his eyes. I gave him a languorous smile, one full of promises meant for someone else. "Showtime, remember? Sell it."

His grip tightened for a minute, and then he stood up, drawing me closer, dipping his head so that his words resonated against my neck. "I'm not a messenger boy."

"Then stop telling me to send a message." I faked a giggle. "Let's go save the world."

"Take a last look," he said. "You going to miss this place?"

I pictured Eliot and me testing his maps, making fun of our classmates, planning Walks and swapping stories and arguing about movies. I pictured years of watching Simon without being seen, and the few brief weeks where his eyes followed me. When he'd taken my hand and led me away, and I'd believed, only for a moment, in happy endings.

"Some of it, I suppose. Mostly not."

"Keep the good memories," he advised. "The other stuff is deadweight. Regret only slows you down."

Later that night I stopped by Eliot's and found him tinkering with the Free Walkers' technology, exactly as he'd said he would. The familiar sight of him, hunched over the keyboard, cajoling the software to behave, swamped me with nostalgia.

"How many times is this?" I teased from the doorway. "A thousand?"

"Thousand and one," he muttered.

"You can hack a baby monitor to play HBO," I said. "You've got this."

He shrugged and went back to hunting and pecking. I looked over his shoulder at the stream of computer gibberish and then flopped back on the bed.

"I can't decide if I like him more or less than the old one," he said abruptly.

"Definitely less," I said, staring at the ceiling.

"But that makes me like him more," he replied.

"You're not making sense."

He turned to face me. "*You* like him less, because he's not the one you want. But since I wasn't a big fan of the Original—or the Echo, or whatever we're calling the Simon who started this whole mess—this guy seems like an improvement."

"Really?" I propped myself on my elbows.

"Well, I could do without the whole prison break," he said. "Addie's right, you know. It's not going to work. And it's not worth your life."

"Does that mean you won't help?"

"This is a no-win situation for me. If I help you, I lose you. If I don't, you end up dead." He threw his arms wide. "The only way to save you is to stop you."

I sat up fully now, temper rising. "I don't need to be saved. Try it and see how far I run."

He drew back as if I'd slapped him. "You're asking a lot, you know."

"Then forget I asked." I reached for my backpack and he tugged it away.

"Right," he scoffed. "I'll forget how my best friend went on a suicide mission because I wouldn't help her. I told you I'm in, and I'm in. But quit asking me to be happy about it."

"I wish you'd come with me. After."

"Never going to happen," he said gently. "My life's here."

"But we're a team." It wasn't enough of a reason, and I knew it, but I couldn't help asking. "Always have been . . ."

"Always will be. Exploring's your thing. I'm the navigator, and that means I stay behind."

"But you could . . ."

He touched my cheek, equal amounts of regret and resolve in the gesture. "I'm nice, Del. But I'm not that nice."

CHAPTER TWENTY-EIGHT

MY PARENTS WERE WAITING FOR ME WHEN I arrived home, wearing the expectant look that typically signaled I'd screwed up.

"What did I do?"

"Nothing," my dad said, too quickly. "We haven't gotten much time with you lately."

I wondered if Addie had prompted this sudden desire for quality time. But I'd promised I would try to talk to my parents, and considering how much time they were spending at work, this might be my only chance.

"Are you hungry?" my mom asked. "I can fix you some leftovers."

"What's going on?"

"I wasn't sure you'd eaten." She bristled. "Forgive me for wanting to make sure you had at least one healthy meal."

My dad laid a hand on her arm. "Winnie."

She took a deep breath. "Councilman Lattimer paid me a visit today."

"Oh?" Somehow I managed to go hot and cold at the same time.

She busied herself assembling a plate of spaghetti and meatballs. "He wants you to visit your grandfather tomorrow."

I pushed away from the island. "Tomorrow? That's too soon!"

"I know you're not looking forward to it, but the Consort needs to act quickly. We're less than two weeks away from the Tacet."

"We shouldn't even be having a Tacet," I said, seizing the opening. "Most of those Echoes aren't hurting anything."

"Statistically, any branch of the size we're cleaving is likely to contain several unstable Echoes," my dad said. "They'll only destabilize over time."

"So the answer is to kill them because they *might* pose a threat?"

"Nobody's killing anything." My mom set the plate down with a clatter. "Monty put this into your head, didn't he?"

"I can think for myself. And I think Echoes are as real as we are."

"They aren't, kiddo," my dad said. "You don't kill a shadow when you turn off the light. The object is still there."

"They're people, not objects!"

"They're not born, and they don't truly die. So they can't be alive." He was so patient, so certain.

"How do you know? Who gets to make that call?"

My mom stalked across the room as if she was leaving the discussion entirely. My father motioned for me to stay where I was. She went up on tiptoe and pulled down a massive leather-bound book.

"Here," she said, carrying it in both hands. "This is the scripture that tells how the world began."

She set the book on the table and opened it, turning the tissue-like paper as carefully as my father handled the threads. She read in her crisp alto.

"'In the beginning was the dark, and the Lord spoke and chose the light, and the world cleaved, and the song of the new world was pleasing to His ears. Worlds begat worlds like the branches of a tree, and each favored branch was touched with His song. He anointed the ears and hands of His most favored children, and granted them freedom to Walk among the branches so they might preserve and magnify His song.'"

She passed me the open book. "See for yourself."

"I haven't read this in years," I said, turning over the pages. It looked like an illuminated manuscript, drawings crowded around the sides of the verses.

"Probably your first day of training," my dad said. "Reading the opening verses is part of the invocation. You'll read it again at your convocation, when you begin your apprenticeship."

"It's ancient," I said, closing the Bible. "And it's not an excuse."

My father covered my hand with his, trapping it against the gilt-embossed leather. "We were chosen, not by the Consort, but by something greater, to do this. Every religion in the world has Walkers. Every one of their sacred texts confirms that this is our calling."

"It doesn't say we're supposed to kill people!" I yanked my

hand free. "What if preserve means to *protect* the Echoes? To help the multiverse expand? What if there was a way to separate the Echoes from the Key World, and let them carry forward on their own?"

My mom looked faintly repulsed. "Sever the threads between them? Del, an untethered Echo would be a person with no soul. It would be cruel to force that on any creature."

"But if they could survive . . . doesn't that mean cleavings would be murder? Because we're taking away their chance to live?"

"It's not that simple," my dad said. "Consort scientists have been studying this phenomenon for longer than any of us have been alive. The ethicists, too. Do you really think they'd sanction cleavings if that were true?"

They were so earnest. They were as certain in their belief as I was, and arguing further was pointless.

People see what they want to believe, hear the truths that confirm their own ideas. Walkers relied on that trait to deal with Originals, but the Consort used it to control us, too.

"Del, sweetheart . . . these are natural questions to have, especially as your apprenticeship draws closer. Nobody wants a Cleaver who can't think for herself." My mom forced a smile. "If cleaving isn't the path you want to pursue, we can find you something else. Navigation, maybe."

"Mom, please. I suck at navigation."

"I'm sure you'd be very good. It's a question of applying yourself."

I rolled my eyes. So much for giving them a chance.

"We want you to be happy," my father added. "To find your calling, the way we have. If Monty's muddying the waters, it's for the best tomorrow is your last visit."

"Maybe it is," I murmured, and went to warn Simon that our deadline had changed.

CHAPTER TWENTY-NINE

Days until Tacet: 10

AMELIA AND SIMON WERE FINISHING BREAK-
fast when I let myself in the next morning.

"Are you hungry?" she asked. "I made plenty."

"No, thanks." I couldn't have forced food past the lump in
my throat. Instead, I looked around the kitchen, cluttered and
warm and familiar. If we won, we could come back here. If not,
this was the last time I'd see the apple-green walls, the chipped
sink, and the pictures of Simon stuck to the fridge. The last time
I would see Amelia.

She frowned. "If you're sure— Iggy! Down! Bad dog!"

Iggy dropped to the floor, mouth full of sausage links, too
blissed-out to look ashamed. I cocked my head at Simon in a
silent question—had he asked her about Gil's part of the map
chord?

He shook his head and reached down to pat Iggy, ignoring
my scowl. We were running out of time.

And then I understood. The longer he put off asking Amelia
for the frequency, the longer he could pretend this was his life.

"What is it?" Amelia said, glancing between us. Neither of us replied. I stared at the toes of my boots, unable to meet her eyes, hearing the quaver in her voice. "You're leaving, aren't you? But you just got here."

The chair creaked as Simon shifted his weight. The tension smothering the room made it clear she wasn't talking to me. Simon stared at his half-eaten stack of pancakes.

"Amelia . . . ," I said, trying to catch Simon's eye. He refused to look at me. "I told you that I found a message from Rose. Part of a frequency."

"I remember." She twisted her ring nervously.

"I thought Monty had the other half. But I was wrong. He had one *third*."

Her hands fell to her lap.

"And so do you," I said. "Gil gave you his key, didn't he? To pass along to Simon."

She tried to smile. "He knew you'd come for it eventually."

Something clicked inside me, like a tile in a mosaic. If Gil had known, so had she: A Simon other than the one she'd raised would return.

"But we looked," Simon protested. "We've checked everywhere."

"All you had to do was ask," she said. "I always loved to watch him Walk. He would reach into the air and find another world. It was like magic. You have his hands, you know."

Simon looked at his fingers as if he'd never seen them before.

Gently she slipped off her wedding ring and ran her thumb

around the edge. Then she held it out to him, a gold circle shining at the center of her palm.

"Your wedding ring?"

"I never take it off," she said. "I'd imagine my Echoes feel the same way. Go ahead."

He took it and inspected the inner surface. "The frequency's engraved."

She laughed. "The clerk at the jewelry store thought we were a very strange couple."

"You played dumb when I asked you about the frequency," I said, unaccountably hurt. "Why would you lie?"

"I'm tired of sacrificing the people I love. I thought if I kept quiet, you'd be kept safe."

"What changed your mind?" Simon asked.

"You won't change yours." She brushed the tears from her cheeks. "I'll sacrifice whatever I have to, if it gives you a fighting chance."

CHAPTER THIRTY

THE BEST LIES REQUIRE BELIEF—BOTH THE deceived's *and* the deceiver's. You have to become the person you're pretending to be, so that your actions are second nature, as smooth and fluid as a magician's scarf. The barest hesitation will break the spell.

That's how Monty had lasted so long. He wasn't playing the addled grandfather—he *was* the addled grandfather. He'd found that facet of himself and polished it to a high gleam, blinding us to his other aspect, the Monty who was driven and desperate and shrewd.

Even now he was teaching me. When I entered CCM, I let myself be the Del I needed Lattimer to see: young, scared, and in over her head.

Because it was the truth. Just not the whole truth.

"I trust your parents have given the school a plausible excuse," Lattimer said when he met me in the sublevel's arctic hallway.

"Probably. School isn't exactly my priority these days, sir."

"Not a priority, but important nevertheless. We have neither the time nor the resources to devote to the more mundane aspects of your education."

I could never figure out if Lattimer bought his own lies. Was he so convinced that the Walkers were doing the right thing, he genuinely believed the Free Walkers were a threat to the Key World? Or was he more concerned with keeping his hold on power, on letting his view of the world stay intact? It's hard work, rebuilding your beliefs when they've been smashed into dust. I could almost—not entirely, but almost—understand how he had justified the Consort's actions to himself.

I didn't doubt he would destroy anyone who threatened his certainty. He'd guard that even more fiercely than the Key World itself.

"Shaw says you're doing well in class. You haven't reported more bouts of frequency poisoning."

"No, sir. I've been careful."

He paused outside Monty's cell, handing over my earpiece. "Today is your grandfather's last chance. Feel free to make that fact clear to him. If he doesn't provide us with actionable intelligence, I'll finish his interrogation personally."

I swallowed hard and kept my voice steady.

"What can I offer him?"

"Excuse me?" he replied, startled into a direct question.

"I grew up with Monty. I know how to make him behave, and it's not threats. Forcing him to do something doesn't work nearly as well as offering him a treat. A bribe."

"Very well." He waved his hand. "Offer him whatever you think will be most effective."

"He wants out," I said.

"Then offer him his freedom. We won't grant it, but he doesn't need to know that."

I suspected he already did.

"Now. I want all the information on this weapon that you can pry out of him. I want details—and anything he can tell you about a man named Gilman Bradley."

I tucked my hands into my pockets to hide their trembling. "You think he knows where this guy is?"

"Gil went to his grave years ago. But he was your grandfather's navigator, and by all accounts, the creator of the weapon we're seeking. Information about him might help us locate it more quickly."

"I'll do my best," I said.

Lattimer opened the door, and I edged past him, hands still in my pockets, toying with an origami star to settle my nerves.

Monty sat, chained to the table, chin on his chest. He looked even smaller than usual, and when he lifted his head, a yellowing bruise circled one eye.

"You came back."

"I did."

"I told you not to."

"And yet here I am."

He leaned back in the chair, careful and stiff. I hadn't expected him to be so slow, hadn't calculated for it. Not good. "What have you brought me?"

"An offer," I said. "Tell me what I want, and I'll get you what you want."

"You know what I want."

I looked straight at him, until he returned my gaze. "Lattimer wants information. He wants to know about Gil Bradley's weapon. He says he can get you out of here if you cooperate."

His eyes narrowed. "Does he, now? And I should trust him?"

Monty's hands lay clasped on the table, cuffs around both wrists. I covered his hands with mine. "Trust *me*."

As I spoke, I fished a set of paper-clip picks from my sleeve, my movements concealed by our joined hands and the bulk of my sweater. His eyes flew to mine.

"My freedom," he said.

"In exchange for the information we need. We're running out of time." I nodded encouragingly and slipped him the picks. "So I need you to focus. Try to remember anything you can about the weapon, or the frequency it's in."

"It was so long ago," he said piteously. He twisted his wrist to make the keyhole more accessible. "My memory . . . my ears. They're not what they used to be."

"Push him," Lattimer ordered.

"You have to give them something," I said, raising my voice as the lock clicked, loud as snapping bone. "What about the weapon Gil Bradley developed? Can you tell me about it?"

"It wasn't ready," Monty said. "Even before Gil was taken, they knew they needed time to . . . refine it. To figure out how it could best be used. So they waited and kept it hidden. So well hidden, the Consort doesn't know what they're looking for."

"Wait's over. We need specifics, not vague hints." *Something that will draw the Consort's attention away from Simon.* "I'm not going anywhere until you tell me."

Monty's mouth worked soundlessly, his eyes growing distant and watery. His hands, I noticed, were perfectly steady.

"It's a kind of circuit breaker," he said finally. "Diverts all the energy in a branch away from the parent world and back into an Echo. The Key World relies on that energy, so it's a bit like cutting off the food supply."

My stomach dropped. Was this true? Amelia was convinced there was no weapon, and I'd never expected Monty to give the Consort real information—but even his lies had the ring of truth.

"They're going to starve the Key World? Why?"

He shrugged. "Because the Consort's greedy. They can't leave the Echoes well enough alone, so we wanted to turn the tables. Once the Walkers have seen the light, they'll reverse the process."

He looked down at his wrists, his carefully arranged hands hiding the fact the cuffs were open.

"Is that enough?" he asked, voice quavering as if answering had worn him out. "Will that satisfy him?"

I checked my watch. Enough time had passed for Eliot to work his magic.

"I'll ask."

I knocked and the guard opened the cell door. Lattimer stepped out of the control room and headed for us.

"Councilman," I called, hand on the doorframe, wedging a paper star into the lock so it wouldn't catch. "How'd I do?"

"Quite well," he said. "I'll admit, I didn't expect him to capitulate so quickly. You're very persuasive."

I edged closer to the guard, wrapping a lock of hair around my finger. "What about the circuit breaker? Could it work?"

"We won't know until we examine it," Lattimer said. "Press him for more details. How big it is, how we can trace it."

"I don't think he knows. Or if he does, he's forgotten."

"Then jog his memory."

"Do I have to go back?" I asked, swaying. "I'm not feeling great."

Lattimer scrutinized me. "You look feverish."

I touched the back of my hand to my forehead. "Could I have a glass of water?"

He jerked his head at the guard closest to the elevator, who nodded and went upstairs. I lifted my hair off my neck and fanned myself. "It's really hot down here."

He stepped away, grimacing. "I assume this is some sort of illness you contracted at school?"

"There's a virus going ar—" I staggered into the remaining guard, knocking him into the wall. He righted us, but not before I unclipped the Taser from his belt. With a quick pop and crackle, he went down.

"Delancey!" Lattimer snarled. "You're—"

"You told me to think about my future," I said. "I've decided to branch out. So to speak."

CHAPTER THIRTY-ONE

LATTIMER REACHED FOR THE PHONE AT HIS waist, but I fired the Taser again, and he hit the ground with a cry and a full-body shudder.

Snatching his ID, I ran to Monty's cell and threw open the door. He was sitting at the table, exactly as I'd left him.

"Get up! We have to go!"

He sprang to his feet, but I saw the wince and heard the hitch in his breath. "Wanted to make sure it was you coming through the door. You don't give a man many hints."

"We were on camera," I said, hustling him out of the room. "What was I supposed to do?"

"It's a good start," he said, standing over Lattimer's still-twitching form. "But like I said, Del. Slapdash. It's important to be thorough in your work."

Before I could stop him, he yanked the Taser from my grasp and hit Lattimer again. I winced at his shout of outrage.

"Quit it," I said. "We looped the CCTV from this hallway to buy some time, but it's not much. We need to move."

I swiped Lattimer's ID, and the elevator slid open to reveal an empty car. "Ready?"

"What about the other guard?" he asked as I shoved him inside.

"He'll be back in a minute." Klaxons sounded, and the elevator started upward of its own accord. "Less than a minute."

"Lattimer's card has an override," Monty said. "Special privilege for Consort members."

"Why do you think I took it?" I snapped, slamming the card through the reader and mashing the emergency stop button. The elevator alarm joined the general one, layers of cacophony drilling into my skull. Painful, but it would help to conceal our trail.

"We're trapped!" he shouted over the melee. "What's your plan, Delancey? Shoot your way out with a toy gun?"

"We'll Walk out," I said as a ceiling panel opened overhead.

"But first, we're going to climb," Simon called down.

Monty gaped. "You found him."

"Nope." Simon lowered a rope ladder. "I found her."

I shoved Monty. "Grandpa, come on. The override will only last until they bring in another Consort member."

"How did he get in?" Monty asked, heading clumsily up the rungs.

"Friend of a friend of Addie's got me the ID." With a grunt, Simon hauled Monty through the ceiling hatch. "Guards were so focused on Del coming in, they didn't pay much attention to little old me. Waited until her elevator came back, got in, and didn't hold the door for anyone else. Been waiting up here ever since."

I started after Monty as the elevator began moving again, the emergency alarm falling silent.

"Clock's ticking," he said as he helped me onto the roof, pulled up the ladder, and fastened the ceiling panel in place.

"Where's the pivot?" Monty asked.

"Wherever I choose," he said. "Del?"

"Ready." I took Simon's hand, tuning out the blare of the alarm and the whir of the elevator machinery. Tension radiated down his arm, and then I heard it. A hiss and a pop, the sound of a choice being made, a few inches in front of me.

Swiftly I reached inside the new pivot and hummed. This was the trickiest part. Simon couldn't exist in same space as his Echo—their differing frequencies would put too much strain on the fabric of the worlds, especially in such close quarters. We also had to find a world where this elevator wasn't working, or it would be a repeat of my time on the freight train. I'd already picked a frequency we knew would be safe. Now I stepped through the formless space, bringing Simon with me, Monty trailing behind.

We'd practiced, of course, but this was different. My balance was unsteady, making it hard to maintain my course. And there was always resistance. Even though this version of Simon moved more easily through the worlds than my swapped one, it was a slow, grudging passage.

We burst through like a cork from a bottle, and dropped several feet to the empty car. Quickly Simon pulled up the ceiling panel and lowered us through, then jumped down.

"How much time left?" I asked. He pressed the button for the ground floor. Moments later we stood in what used to be the

238

Consort's lobby but was now a department store, my homemade OUT OF ORDER sign prominently displayed on the doors.

"Before they find this place? Give them three minutes, tops, to figure out the ceiling trick. Another three to get up there and track the frequency."

"I like it here," Monty said, fingering a display of silk ties. "Sounds busy."

"It's going to get a hell of a lot busier if we don't move," I said.

Simon pulled a heavy, fleece-lined sweatshirt and a pair of gym shoes from his backpack and shoved both at Monty. "Put these on."

Outside, the wind whipped through the corridors of the Loop, biting into our skin, snatching our breath.

"Union Station," Monty said at the next intersection. "Easiest thing in the world to lose them there."

"They'll be expecting us at Union," Simon replied. "It's the first place they'll go. Too much surveillance."

"How do you propose we get out of the city, then?"

"We don't," I said, and towed him down Wacker Drive. "Time for you to keep your end of the bargain, Monty. I want the frequency."

He scowled, a familiar, mulish look on his face. "How do I know you won't leave me to be captured again? You can be a spiteful girl."

I stopped in the middle of the sidewalk. People swerved around me without realizing it, a boulder in a stream. "True. But I keep my promises, unlike some people."

"We'll get you to the Free Walkers," Simon said. "But we had a deal."

Monty eyed Simon, then me, his fingers fumbling. "Can't we get somewhere warm?"

This was another trick, another way to show me he was in charge. But I'd had enough of Monty's tricks.

"Have a nice what's left of your life, Monty," I said, and started moving again.

"Del!" He chased after me. "Pen and paper?"

"Tell me as we go," I said, pulling out my phone. He rattled off a series of numbers, and I keyed them in.

A few blocks away we approached a gray limestone building, dwarfed by the steel-and-glass skyscrapers but beautifully ornamented.

"The Board of Trade?" Monty asked.

"Fourteen million trades a day," I said. "Fourteen million pivots in the pit alone."

"We can't get on the trading floor," Monty said irritably. "That's restricted to traders. And too crowded."

"That's why we're playing tourist," Simon replied, and ushered us through the doors.

The overheated lobby felt good after the frigid outdoors, but we couldn't afford a moment to thaw out. Traders in polyester blazers and oversize IDs rushed past, clutching coffee and antacid. The number of pivots was incredible, an irregular, jarring stream of pops, like a toddler with Bubble Wrap.

"Observation deck," said Simon, unfazed. He led the way

upstairs. I kept throwing glances over my shoulder, looking for any sign of Consort guards, listening for another note from the Key World.

Snatches of conversation filtered through, and as we reached the enormous plate-glass window overlooking the trading pit, I began to match up conversations with the pivots that trailed them.

"Let's get pizza for lunch! Isn't Chicago deep dish, like, legendary?" The air whooshed and crackled like dry wood catching fire.

"Can we just go back to the hotel, please?" A soft sigh of a pivot.

"Everyone make sure they have a buddy, and let's go back to the bus." Staccato strikes as a group of elementary-school-aged kids paired up and filed out.

"Easy pickings," I said to Monty. The sheer number of pivots would muddy our trail.

"Hurry it up," Simon said.

The field trip had cleared out, leaving a gap in the crowd. I checked my phone and found a safe pivot—Simon might be immune to frequency poisoning, but Monty and I weren't. The more stable, the better.

"Don't rush me," I muttered, but very faintly, I heard a shift in the world's pitch, a new note breaking into the regular tone.

The Key World frequency.

The Consort guards were here.

Swiftly I slid my hand into the pivot, found a signal at random, and pulled us through.

The room itself was similar, but the crowd was different—

adults in suits, eating hors d'oeuvres and quaffing champagne. The air here was as lifeless as the conversation.

Monty grabbed a stuffed mushroom as we ran out.

Simon started for the street, but I tugged him back. "The pit."

"Too many people. We need to run."

"Monty can't sprint across the Loop," I retorted. "Look at him."

He was slumped against the wall, huddled into the heavy sweatshirt, struggling for breath. The plea in his eyes was genuine.

Without waiting for a reply, I headed down to the packed trading floor. Easily three stories tall, with giant monitors and tickers everywhere, paper slips ankle deep. The shouts of the traders were overwhelming, and it was hard to say which was stronger: the scent of panicky financial types, or the sound of the pivots, dense with static.

We didn't bother with subtlety. I ducked behind a wall of wildly gesturing traders and grabbed the first pivot that caught my ear.

The mood here was as bright as the pitch itself, the trading excited instead of desperate, but I didn't stop to figure out why— once I'd made sure Simon and Monty were behind me, I took another pivot, and another, shifting through Echoes so rapidly they seemed to blur. It was the kind of challenge I'd enjoyed as a kid. The floor shifted and slid as we moved, like walking atop wet sand.

Sometimes it's the act of choosing that saves you, not the choice itself. Sometimes your only option is to move, and move fast, because if you don't stay ahead—or at least get out of the way—the world will collapse beneath your feet.

Hard to say how far we'd Walked, but by the time we were done, we'd passed an art gallery, countless law firms, a vacant lot, and a gym. We stopped in a restaurant.

"Rest," Monty wheezed, and leaned heavily on the bar.

Simon poured him a glass of water from a nearby pitcher. Monty drained half, wiped his mouth on his sleeve, and started digging through a bowl of mixed nuts.

"I suppose you've got some grand plan, Delancey. You're not just dragging an old man across the city in the dead of winter?"

"Would you rather I send you back?" I checked my watch. "Yes, we have a plan."

He grunted. "You've found your boy."

"He's *not* my boy," I said firmly, and Monty paused, eyeing him with fresh curiosity.

"You're the Original, then?"

Simon checked the window for any sign of the Consort. "That's me."

"Impressive," Monty said. "Gil always was the sentimental sort."

"You really didn't know about the swap?"

He popped a pistachio in his mouth before answering. "Rose never said a word. I put it together on my own, right about the time my granddaughter tried to murder me."

I shook my head. "Slapdash, Monty. You should have figured it out years ago."

"Fight later," Simon snapped as the guards appeared outside. "Run now."

We dashed through the kitchen and out the back door, the guards in pursuit, Monty leaning heavily on Simon. Despite the big leap in worlds, the Loop felt the same: skyscrapers and bitter wind and traffic and people and the damp, funky smell of the river a few blocks away.

"Cab," I said as we ran, deliberately bumping into a banker, wincing as his briefcase banged my knees. Monty and Simon followed suit.

Once we were all visible, I stepped into the street and hailed a cab while Simon gauged the progress of the Consort guards. "Hop in."

Simon and Monty climbed in after me and slammed the door. I leaned forward to direct the driver. "Navy Pier."

"Cutting it a little close," Simon said.

I dug two bags of M&M's out of my backpack and tossed one to Monty. "I didn't think they'd find us so fast."

"We're moving too slow," Simon said.

"Sorry to be such an inconvenience," Monty grumbled around a mouthful of candy. He twisted to look out the back window. "They're following us."

"I'm sure. We've got to get back to the Key World," I told Simon, blinking away the spots clouding my vision. "I'm already feeling it."

"Almost there," he said.

The other cab was only a few cars behind us. I slipped the driver a twenty. "We're in a hurry."

He nodded and punched the gas, speeding through a yellow light. The other cab, snarled in traffic, stopped for the red, and my breath came easier.

"Navy Pier," Monty fussed when we arrived at the massive brick entrance of the park, Lake Michigan cold and choppy a short distance away. I threw a handful of bills to the driver, and we hustled Monty down the main walkway without responding. "Are we going on the Ferris wheel?"

"Better," Simon said. "We're going on a cruise."

Even though Lake Michigan turns dangerously frigid in winter, it rarely freezes solid—which means the boat tours along Navy Pier run year-round. It wasn't my idea of fun, but it served our purpose.

Minutes before the ship set sail, we boarded with tickets Simon had bought the day before. I watched through a porthole as the Consort guards arrived just as we glided away, safely out of reach.

I dropped onto a blue-velvet bench, fighting the urge to curl up and sleep.

"You've bought us a few hours at most," Monty said, "They'll board when we dock again and pick up the trail."

"You're welcome, you ungrateful old man," I snapped. "Keep it up and I'll push you overboard."

Monty toyed with the zipper of his sweatshirt and scowled.

"We're untouchable for the next ninety minutes," Simon said, taking over. "By the time we dock, we'll have laid fifty false trails. They won't know which one is the right one, and we'll have pivoted away."

Monty thought it over. "Not bad," he said. "But there aren't fifty pivots on this ship. These people aren't making choices, they're admiring architecture."

"They don't need to make choices," said Simon, and pulled a deck of playing cards from his backpack. "I do."

"Even his little choices make worlds." I took the deck from him. "As long as I Walk through, we'll leave a signal."

"But his Echoes . . ."

"I stay here. Del Walks through, tweaks the strings so it won't transpose, and comes back. You do the same. The trails don't have to lead anywhere. They just need to give us time to get away."

I said, fanning out the deck like a street corner shyster, "Pick a card, any card."

"Every card," Simon corrected me.

I lost track of how many trails we left. Definitely more than fifty, each crossing taking a toll on Monty and me. Ten minutes before we docked, I slurred, "Talk about cutting it close. Close shave. Close knit. Clothes horse."

"You're losing it," Simon said as I leaned into him. "Open up."

"Aaaaaahhhh." I opened my mouth wide, sticking out my tongue. "You're like the hottest dentist ever."

"And you're like the town drunk. Here."

I took the small plastic bottle he handed me. "Enabler."

"It's a glucose solution. Like sugar, only super concentrated. Bottoms up."

I gagged at the taste of chemical fruit, but managed to get it down. Simon passed Monty, sitting on a bench nearby, a bottle of his own. He seemed to be feeling okay, which struck me as unfair.

"Better?"

I leaned my head back against the seat, letting the sugar hit my system and steady my thoughts. "You're not actually a hot dentist."

"I am hot," he pointed out. "But no. Not a dentist."

"We need to go home," I said. "Not that I have one."

"Few more minutes and we'll Walk. Hang in there."

I closed my eyes but jerked upright when I felt his fingers brush against my neck. "Hey! Perv."

"Sorry," he said, holding his hands up. "Thought I'd try your pendant."

"You don't have one?" I fished the necklace out from beneath my sweater, and he lifted it over my head.

"Don't need it."

He tapped the miniature tuning fork on the back of the seat. The soft, sweet peal was a welcome relief, and my muscles eased slightly.

Monty straightened. "I gave you Rose's pendant. I'm not all bad."

"Bad enough," I said, as Simon settled the necklace around my neck again. "Don't think I broke you out because you're forgiven, by the way. You're a means to an end, as far as I'm concerned. Same as I am to you."

"As long as we understand each other," he said, but there was an underlying melancholy to his words.

Simon glanced out the giant porthole, and I followed suit. The dock was in sight, a contingent of Consort guards waiting for us. "Almost done."

We couldn't cross back directly to the Key World—the Consort would almost certainly have guards waiting there. Instead, we ducked through a pivot near a stairwell, ending in a flat, stable world. The massive Ferris wheel still rotated slowly, and the line of tourists wrapped around the redbrick building, even in the cold, but there were no guards to be seen.

We pushed our way through the crowd, down the gangway, Monty and me leaning on Simon as we made our way to the fleet of taxis waiting in the parking lot. Minutes later we were speeding out of the city.

"Here," Simon told the cab driver as we crossed over the border to Evanston. He paid the driver and handed me out the cab, then tugged Monty out. "Last one," he promised, and I blinked at him. "Key World, Del."

My arm felt heavy, as if it had fallen asleep. I reached into the pivot with a trembling hand, whispering, "Please."

The string leaped under my fingers, bringing an instant of clarity along with the familiar frequency. Heart soaring, limbs buoyant, I met the Key World with arms outstretched and breath locked in my lungs.

There were no Consort guards here, just apartment buildings and a mishmash of boutiques and offices and restaurants.

Overwhelmed—exhausted and sick and heartsick—I sat down on the nearest stoop. Monty leaned into the building and muttered to himself.

"Our contact will be here any minute." Simon said. "Let's get you something to eat."

He tried to haul me up, but my legs wouldn't hold me, and I crumpled back to the curb. "Del, come on. Stay with me."

He grabbed another bottle of glucose and tried to pour it down my throat, but I turned away, the smell making me gag.

Over his shoulder, the air glimmered and twisted like a candle flame. My vision narrowed, the world slipping away, Simon slipping away, my muscles cold and rigid and the blackness taking over like a starless night. I'd scattered my stars across the multiverse, as if they were endless. But nothing is endless, not the sky or the stars or worlds, not even love, because I was going to die here and never tell my Simon that I loved him, singularly and endlessly. Wasteful, really, not to say what is etched on your heart. Words only carry weight once they're heard. I'd been freer with my stars than my words, and now both were fading.

I closed my eyes.

Someone cursed, and I felt a stinging at the nape of my neck. I heard the sound of my pendant striking metal. The clear, sweet sound of the Key World rang out, like the sparks of a campfire floating into the night sky.

And then everything—sparks, sound, sensation—faded.

CHAPTER THIRTY-TWO

Days until Tacet: 8

WESTLEY AND BUTTERCUP GOT IT WRONG:
Life is not pain. Life is rare and glorious and precious. But coming back to life is a *hell* of a lot of pain—the price extracted for cheating death, for regaining the precious thing you wasted.

Frequency poisoning made everything hurt, even the parts that couldn't feel, like eyelashes and toenails. It was like thawing out from frostbite, every single cell readjusting and finding its proper pitch, its own little world coming into tune. Finally the pain subsided enough that I could move my fingers. My fingers, no more, a faint scrabble against cheaply woven cotton.

Sound filtered back in: muffled footsteps, a drip like a leaky faucet, two voices murmuring nearby, their conversation drifting over me in tatters and bursts.

"... worse before she gets better ..."

"... you promised ..."

"I don't ... the safety of the entire ... risk ..."

"... might die, and you're okay ..."

"... very little in this situation ..."

All five fingers worked now, and I gathered the blanket in my fist. The conversation broke off. A door opened and shut again with a decisive click. A familiar hand took mine, gently tugging the fabric away.

"How are you feeling?" Simon's voice.

"Cold," I said, wondering if the word would come out as gibberish. There was the snap and rustle of a second blanket being shaken out, and a soft, welcome weight from my neck to my toes. I sighed in relief.

"Better?"

My mouth felt dry as paper, my lips cracked. "Took their time finding us."

"Security procedures," he said, his voice heavy but his touch light as he brushed my hair back.

This time I forced my eyes open, struggling to keep the room in focus. Lamplight coated everything like honey, soft edged and rich. Even Simon, who sat next to me in his canvas coat, shoulders hunched, face haggard. "Where are we?"

"Free Walker base camp. This the infirmary."

The infirmary looked a lot like a hotel room. To my left was a small nightstand, the kind that usually held a Bible and phonebook in its single drawer, and a second bed with a cheap printed coverlet; a desk and a dresser topped with an outdated TV stood along the opposite wall. The curtains were drawn, a sliver of daylight visible along the edges. "Did Monty—"

"They picked him up too. He's down the hall." He started to say something else, but stopped.

"How long have I been out?"

"Day and a half."

My arm felt stiff and painful. With an effort, I turned my head to look, and blinked. A needle was sunk into the crook of my elbow, held in place with an X of white medical tape.

"IV?"

"Glucose solution. Gotta get you better."

"Right," I said, even though the thought of lying in this bed for the next . . . rest of my life . . . sounded nice. Peaceful. But lying in bed was not the way to find my Simon. "No rest for the wicked."

"Del—" he said, and broke off.

Alarm stirred within me, shaking off the haze. "What's wrong?"

"Nothing," he said, and rubbed his forehead.

"Doesn't look like nothing," I said. The low light had turned his blue eyes nearly black, and shadowed the bones of his face so they were more prominent than usual, as if he'd lost weight.

But I'd only been out for a day and a half.

The part of me that had turned hard and parched and brittle in the last month softened, as if it had finally felt rain. In the faint light of that tiny room, hope took root and sent out a tentative, tremulous leaf toward the sun.

"You're him," I said softly, and his eyes snapped to mine. "You're *you*."

Time stretched out, looping and curling and twisting back on itself, my breath caught in my chest, and the space between my heartbeats felt as vast as the multiverse, like he was forming a world just by answering—but there was no choice. There was only the truth, waiting to be spoken, waiting for the world to start again, waiting for the impossible to take shape in the inches between us. The impossible: believed and then seen, dazzling as the sun at midnight, or a constellation cupped in your hand.

"I'm me," he said, the words an exhalation.

"You're mine. My Simon." My voice cracked.

"Always." His hand curved along my cheek, as strong and warm as I remembered, and his thumb swept underneath my lashes, rubbing away tears.

"You're not dead."

"No."

"I'm not dead."

"I don't think you get an IV in heaven," he said. "So, not dead."

I didn't need to look for the scar. I didn't need proof, because miracles don't need proof. But the sight of the faint, raised line at the corner of his mouth was the last thing I saw before he drew closer, bending over the bed, smelling like soap and sunshine, and then my eyes shut again because the thing I knew best about Simon was how it felt to be touched by him, and this . . . was my Simon.

His mouth was gentle and sweet and tentative, and then less tentative. He tasted like spiced honey, soothing and stirring all at once, his hands weaving through my hair and sliding along my neck, my skin glowing wherever he touched. I opened my eyes for the briefest second, but my vision blurred, want and tears and joy making it impossible to see. My blood sparkled, so buoyant I thought I might fly away. I pulled him onto the bed with me, anchoring myself with his weight, kissing him so deeply I lost track of where I ended and Simon began.

"Easy," he murmured, nipping my collarbone, but I didn't want easy. We treasure what is rare or fleeting, and then we step away from it, for protection. We lock it away, treat it with kid gloves, guard it carefully. But love cannot be locked away; a heart withers in isolation. We'd fought for this moment. We had risked and we had sacrificed, and after all we'd gone through, anything less than everything was wrong.

I wrapped my arms around him, urging him closer, and he shifted until we were both lying stretched out on the bed, facing each other, his breathing short and quick, his mouth never leaving mine. I slid my hands under the edge of his shirt, felt the play of muscles under his skin as he shifted against me. A sharp pain lanced through my arm. "Ow!"

He froze. "Too much?"

"Arm," I said, and he stood, examining the blood welling up.

"You pulled out the IV. I'll get the medic."

"No. I don't want to see anyone but you."

He sighed. "Fine. Keep pressure on it, or you'll have a hell of a bruise."

I reached for a tissue and pressed it against the wound. "Did you get a medical degree while you were gone?"

He gave me a small, reluctant smile. "My mom's had plenty of IVs."

"Oh, I'm sorry," I said, but he waved the words away, then covered my hand with his.

He looked the same—his hair was a little longer, his bones a little more pronounced, as if his time among the Free Walkers had stripped away the softness and left behind something finely honed, but his eyes were the same as ever, thickly lashed and a deep, startling blue, full of challenge and amusement and warmth. I couldn't believe I'd confused, even for a second, the other Simon with him.

"Why didn't you tell me?" I asked, as he stretched out next to me, propping himself on an elbow. "Why didn't you say something the minute I woke up?"

He shrugged, his expression clouding. "Thought you could use a little time to adjust."

"That's crap," I said. "I've been looking for you since the minute Ms. Powell said you were alive. I don't need to adjust. I need you."

He touched his lips to mine. "Even if I'm an Echo?"

"You're Simon Lane," I said. "I've wanted you for three years. I don't care if you're an Echo or an Original or a hybrid or a talking bear."

"It would be easier, though," he said, the words so low I could barely make them out, "if I were an Original. If I were him."

"I know you're tone deaf, but listen to me. I don't want him. I want you." I cupped his face in my hands. "Didn't you tell me once that it's always better when it's a challenge?"

He grinned, wicked and hot, and dragged me closer. When

we came up for air, breathless, my mouth swollen and his hair a mess, I said, "We're good now, right?"

"Yeah." He looked at me. "You're still pale. Let me get someone to fix the IV."

"I need to rest, that's all. Stay with me."

So he lay back on the bed and tucked my head under his chin. My cheek pressed against his chest, his heartbeat steady and his arms strong, and for the first time in weeks, I was happy.

His breath ruffled my hair. "How's my mom?"

I paused and laced my hand with his. "She's . . . okay. She misses you, but she gets it. She knows this is safer."

He didn't say anything for a long time, working through the implications, gathering his thoughts and marshaling his feelings until he was centered enough to ask, his voice as tight as the arm he'd wrapped around me, "Does she know? About the switch?"

Sometimes it seemed as if people were made as much of secrets as they were blood and bone, as if, under the skin, we were just as unknowable as the multiverse. "We didn't tell her. But sometimes, the things she says . . . I think she knows."

"She's not my mom, is she?"

"Of course she is."

"No. He's her son. And she knew it all along. I was someone she was . . . looking out for."

"That's not true. I've seen her nearly every day since we lost you. She's grieving. Not for some other version of you, not the idea of her son. You. You, specifically. She misses everything about you—how much you eat, and the way you leave your socks in the living room, and your terrible cooking. She might have known you were swapped, but it didn't matter. You are her son."

"I miss her," he said. "And Iggy, too."

"They miss you." Trying to lighten the mood, I added, "I've seen a million baby pictures."

"Not the one—"

"In the tub? Oh, yeah. You were very cute."

"I've grown a lot."

"I'm aware." I smiled. "We'll find a way to bring you back. You'll see them again."

"I don't think so," he said.

"We're in the Key World right now," I pointed out. "Nobody's panicking about the anomaly."

"We're not in the Key World." He gestured to a small box on top of the television. "That thing is broadcasting the Key World frequency, to help you heal."

They've got a few tricks, Original Simon had said. The sort of tricks Eliot would love, I thought wistfully. "What about you? The Consort thinks the anomaly isn't a problem anymore."

"This thing." He held up his wrist and pointed to the black rubber strip circling it, a small red light blinking erratically. It looked like the pedometers we had to wear in gym class. "It tunes me, somehow. Changes the strings around me to compensate for the flaw, but it has to be reset every time we Walk."

I stared at it. Addie had tried, once, to fix the break in an Echo Simon. The strings connecting anyone to their world extended a few feet around them, making it possible to stabilize an Echo's

257

break even if it was in a person. But altering an *Original's* string was unheard of—one of our greatest taboos. The idea made me faintly queasy.

"We never adjust an Original's strings," I said. "It's—"

"Good thing I'm not an Original," he said with a wry grin. "They won't let me go home. Not yet, at least. Not until they've beaten the Consort."

"Why?"

"They won't tell me. They need me, though. They've put me through a bunch of tests. They've analyzed my frequency the way I used to watch game tapes—picking apart every little detail. They've made me Walk; they're teaching me how to work the strings."

My thoughts felt tangled, and I tried to sort them out, but my brain was too fuzzy and exhausted to make sense of what he was telling me.

"Back up and tell me what happened after I left you." I slugged him in the arm. "I'm still mad about that, by the way."

"I thought I was keeping you safe."

"I thought you were *dead*." I hit him again. "I thought I'd killed you."

The shock gave way, my resolve crumbling like a sand castle before waves, and I started to cry.

"Not dead," he said into my hair. "And it wasn't your fault. I broke the strings, not you."

I felt his heartbeat as if it were my own, wiped my face, and tried to focus. "How did you get out?"

He shifted. "I watched you go, and then I took off. All that basketball conditioning came in handy."

"Glad to hear it."

"I wanted to see if my mom was at our house, but she wasn't. Some family lived there. They had little kids. Twins." He trailed off. "The Free Walkers said it's because I'm a hybrid—I boosted the signal, so the world didn't unravel on my side as fast as it did on yours, but it didn't feel slow.

"I was sitting on the steps, watching the world go . . . wobbly. And all of a sudden, Ms. Powell was there. She looked like some crazy thrift-store version of a SWAT team, dressed in black. I thought I was hallucinating."

He took my hand again. "I heard about the train."

I bit my lip and nodded.

He continued. "I thought she was an Echo, but she headed right toward me, told me we needed to move fast. She had a group with her, and they spread out. It looked like they were fixing inversions, but it turns out they were cauterizing."

"But your frequency was disrupting everything. How did they stop it?"

"She tuned me," he said. "Put her hand a few inches away from my chest, wiggled her fingers, and the inversions stopped. Then she brought me to a camp."

"Not here?"

"Not at first. They moved me every night; reset the tuner each time. We landed here a few days ago."

"That fits," I said, mind reeling. "Ms. Powell didn't know

where you were. She could only tell me you were safe."

"I am. So are you."

"If they could fix you, why did they wait for so long?"

"No idea. I think they didn't expect the damage to be so bad. And it's not a permanent solution."

"It's better than nothing. They should have reached out sooner. You're valuable to them—they should act like it." I let my hands wander over his chest, as if by touching him, I could remind myself he wasn't a dream.

"Del . . . ," he said, interrupting my fascination with the way his collarbone met his shoulder. "They keep saying they need me to defeat the Consort, but . . . I can't. I don't know anything about being a Walker."

"You'll learn," I said. "If the other Simon can do it, so can you. I'll be your personal tutor."

"Oh?" He grinned. "What if I'm a slow learner? You know what they say about jocks."

"One-on-one private sessions," I said. "Lots of them. It's the only answer."

"I like the sound of that." He kissed me, then rolled off the bed. "Come on. Time to go for a walk. A regular one, to see the sights."

"Now? Why?"

"This could be my last chance to know more about the Walkers than you. I'm not wasting it."

Gingerly I swung my legs over the edge of the bed. "Shouldn't I be meeting with someone? Debriefing, or giving a statement?" A thought struck me. "Where's the other Simon?"

His mouth twisted. "You mean the real one?"

"You're real," I said firmly.

"Am I?" Doubt diminished his voice.

"Yes. It isn't about strings. Being *you* makes you real. And mine."

"Definitely yours." He pointed to the door connecting my room to the next. "There's a medic in there. We should keep it down."

I nodded as he opened the door to the hall and checked both directions, beckoning when it was clear. My legs felt a little wobbly, but that was common, considering the frequency poisoning.

My room was at the far end of the hallway. We crept past the medic's closed door and toward the lobby. Away from my room, the true frequency of this world asserted itself, a low droning that vibrated against my skull.

"Pool's empty; the fitness center has, like, one elliptical and a few weights. Laundry's there; kitchenette's on the other side— but it's really just a microwave and a sink." He pointed to each one in turn. "Conference room is there, but it's usually locked."

"Do you always stay in hotels?"

"Not as far as I can tell. One place was a school; another was an apartment building. Nursing homes, storage units . . . I keep hoping for an IKEA, but they've never found one that's not packed all the time. I think the base camp moves around a lot— they've only been here for a month or two—and they keep the location a secret, even from most of the local Free Walkers."

"Where is everyone?" The lobby was empty. A fake Christmas tree, dusty and forgotten, stood next to a cold fireplace.

No one was at the front desk, but behind the office door I could hear voices.

"People are always holed up in meetings or going out on jobs," he said. "Usually I'm training, but not since you came in."

"How many people are staying here?"

"Thirty, maybe? Forty?"

"That seems like a lot. I thought Free Walkers operated in small groups."

"We usually do," said a voice behind us. "But now is a time for amassing forces."

I twisted around. An old woman stood in the doorway of the conference room. She was dressed like she'd raided an army surplus store—olive drab pants, stout boots, a flannel shirt. A long, silver braid fell over one shoulder, reaching past the hem of her cargo vest. Her skin had the appearance of crepe paper, thin and soft, spotted with age. But her eyes were clear and curious, the sort of green-brown that some people would call hazel and some would call mud.

Eyes like mine.

She must have been watching for a sign that I knew, because she smiled, her face crinkling all over. I'd seen that smile—minus the wrinkles—every day on my way to breakfast, in her wedding portrait.

"Grandma?" The word trembled in the air, hanging like the opening note of a performance.

"Rose," she corrected me, in a rusty voice. "It's a little late for me to start playing granny."

CHAPTER THIRTY-THREE

As a child, I'd dreamed of finding my grandmother. Of restoring my family to the way it was supposed to be. My daydreams always included a grandmother with a soft lap who wrapped me in her arms and smelled like fresh-baked oatmeal cookies, whose voice was a lullaby to keep shadows at bay.

Rose was none of those things. No lap to speak of—she was thin to the point of bony, even in her baggy pants and layers of shirts, and her manner was equally sharp. She held herself with an unnatural stillness, watching everything and revealing nothing, studying me as closely as I studied her. Despite the lingering smile, the tension between us turned the air thin, as if we were on two, equally high mountaintops—with a hell of a lot of valley between us.

I lifted my chin. She and her Free Walkers had saved me, but I hadn't done so badly: brought her Simon, brought her Monty, brought her the coordinates she needed. I could play our reunion as cool as she did. "Thanks for the rescue."

"You're welcome. You're supposed to be in the infirmary."

I lifted a shoulder. "I got bored."

"That happens frequently, by all accounts."

"Not mine," Simon said, his voice hard as granite.

She smiled—not the wide, welcoming smile of her portrait, but something indulgent. "Not yours. Del's antics are well-known, even to us."

"They're not antics," Simon put in. "She nearly died bringing you the information you wanted."

"Free Walkers 'nearly' die every day," she said. "Some of them sail right past nearly, in fact, like Powell."

Questions whirled in my head, almost painful in their jumbled rush. I fastened on the most obvious. "I thought you were dead," I blurted.

She smiled again. "Monty told you I wasn't."

"Monty is not a reliable source. And nobody told me otherwise. Not Ms. Powell, or Other Simon—he always talked about you in the past tense."

"Did you ask him?"

"No. Because *I assumed you were dead.*"

"Stop making assumptions," she said, "and ask better questions."

I turned to Simon. "You knew?"

He held up his hands. "I was going to tell you. There was a lot to catch you up on."

I'd fallen into the same trap as Originals—assuming what I'd seen and heard was real, without ever questioning it. What else had I missed?

"Why did you wait so long to help him?" I asked.

"We hadn't realized the signal flaw would manifest so dramatically. Once we figured it out, you two were already close, and we thought it best to monitor you instead. Powell was preparing to extract Simon when you and your merry band tried to repair the anomaly—it's why she was on hand to save him."

"Why wait to tell me he was okay? You let me think he was dead."

She said coolly, "Everything we do is about balance. Between the Key World and the Echoes, between secrecy and truth, between risk and reward. We judged the risk of bringing you in was finally worth it."

Not me. The information I had.

"You needed Monty's and Amelia's frequencies."

"Partly. We also needed Simon's cooperation."

I turned to him, eyebrows raised.

"I told them we were a package deal." He scowled at Rose. "Some grandmother you are."

"I haven't been a grandmother for a very long time," she said stiffly, and then her expression softened. "But I am grateful to you for bringing Monty here."

"Where is he?" I asked. If Simon was with me, shouldn't Rose be taking care of Monty? "He wasn't in the infirmary."

"He's resting. As you should be." Her mouth lifted wryly. "I trained as a medic, Delancey. I'm capable of caring for my husband without help. As it happens, his hearing loss protects him from frequency poisoning—his symptoms were nowhere near as severe as yours."

"Why didn't you come back for him? He's lost his mind looking for you. He nearly ended the world!"

"Monty's always been a romantic. I haven't had that luxury. Our mission was of greater consequence than my feelings." She glanced at Simon. "It might sound cruel, but you would have done the same. You already have."

The pride in her voice made it sound as if I'd passed some sort of test—one I'd had no idea I was taking. Unease rippled through me, a pebble dropped in deep waters.

"I'm glad you're here," she said, as if she sensed my wariness. "You've had a difficult time, but we're nearly through the worst of it. Thanks to you, we're ready to defeat the Consort."

Before I could ask her more about it, a wave of exhaustion swamped me. Simon's arm came around me and I leaned into him, the solid warmth I'd been longing for, the only refuge I had anymore.

"How did you survive the frequency poisoning?" I asked. "Nobody can last in the Echoes for as long as you did."

She came closer, close enough for me to catch the faintest whiff of lilacs. "They don't hurt if you can't hear."

I stared as she pushed back the hair above her ear. A small plastic device was embedded in her skull, tiny wires leading beneath the skin.

"A hearing aid?"

"Not exactly. It's similar to a cochlear implant. It filters out bad pitches and substitutes the Key World frequency. Much more advanced than when I first started out."

"What did you use then?" I asked.

"A needle," she said, running a finger along one of the wires.

"Piercing the eardrum is crude, but effective. Unfortunately, it's also temporary—you have to repeat the procedure every few weeks, and there's always a risk of permanent deafness. I was happy to upgrade."

My stomach did a slow, unpleasant tumble.

"Do all of you . . ."

"The ones who live in Echoes, yes."

I thought back to Ms. Powell's wiry mass of hair. It must have concealed the implant. She wasn't kidding when she said the Free Walkers had ways to counteract frequency poisoning. I wondered if I'd get one too.

A girl, dark blond hair piled in a messy bun, clipboard in hand, stepped out of the front office. "Rose? We need to do a final— Oh. You're awake."

Whoever she was, she didn't sound thrilled about it. She looked at me over the top of her bright red glasses, unsmiling.

"I'll be there in a moment. Delancey, this is Prescott, my assistant. We'd be lost without her."

"Nice to meet you," I said, not meaning it.

"You too," she replied, equally insincere. I expected her to go back into the office, but she stayed at the counter, clipboard clutched to her chest. "You knew my mom."

I looked at her blankly. "I don't think . . ."

Simon squeezed my hand, and I saw it. The curly hair. The thick glasses. The offbeat shoes.

"Ms. Powell," I said softly. "I'm sorry."

"Yeah," she said, expression hardening. "Me too."

She turned to Rose. "I've got those schematics, when you're ready."

"I'll be there shortly," Rose replied. Then, to me: "We should get you back to the infirmary."

"I'm a fast healer," I said, watching Prescott disappear into the office, shoulders stiff.

"You get that from your grandfather," she said.

"And my dad," I said with a pang of guilt. By now the Consort would have told them what I'd done. They'd probably been questioned, along with Addie and Laurel, and Eliot, and all of my classmates.

"Foster's a good man," she said. "Too trusting, I think, just as your mother is too dedicated to principles she won't examine."

"Are they in danger?"

Her mouth thinned. "They'll be questioned, but it's no secret your relationship has been strained. I'm sure most of what the Consort tells them will come as a complete surprise, and once Lattimer realizes that, they'll be released. It's likely they won't rise much higher in the ranks, but it's for the best. When revolutions turn bloody, it's the figureheads who have the furthest to fall."

If she was trying to make me feel better, it wasn't working.

"What about Addie and Eliot?"

"Addison's work for Lattimer helps her case. The technology Eliot used was ours, and it's already been retrieved. There's nothing to tie him to the escape, especially since he was at school when it happened."

I swallowed. Safe, then. As safe as I could hope for.

"That's the last we'll speak of them," she said. "From now on, they need to be as dead to you as you are to them."

"But—"

"They'll be watched," she said. "The Consort will use them for information and then as leverage. The only way to protect them is to forget they exist."

"Is that what you did? Pretended we were dead?"

"Pretending isn't enough. You have to believe it."

Simon's hand tightened on mine. "What about my mom? What if they trace me—the other me—and figure out she's connected?"

"We've scrubbed all the security tapes from your escape, so they won't ID him."

"What about the school? Won't they ask questions after I take off again?"

"Hold on," I cut in. "Isn't Other Simon here already? That was the plan."

"He changed the plan," Rose said, her displeasure clear. "He returned to the Key World, where he's watching over Amelia and making a show about pining for Del. When the time comes for him to join us, nobody will question it." She smiled. "It helps that you broke his nose, of course. Adds such credence to the notion of a volatile, impetuous romance."

Simon looked at me askance. "You broke my nose?"

"Bruised," I said. Original Simon must have blocked their connection that time. "Believe me, you deserved it."

His expression turned thunderous, and Rose cut in. "The

important thing is that we're now in a position to move against the Consort."

"The Tacet's scheduled to start in a week," I said. "How are you going to stop them?"

"We're going to do more then stop the Tacet. We're going to crush the Consort and rebuild the Walkers." Her words took on a smooth, rhythmic cadence—urgent and stirring, like an old-time preacher. "In the beginning, Walkers were called to protect the multiverse—all of creation, not only the Key World. The gift we were granted was a healing one. To cleave isn't only to cut, but to bind and bring together, to join and to make whole. We were meant to explore the multiverse, to learn and protect and make better every world we pass through. We were born to fight entropy, to weave it back into order and beauty. That is our calling, not destruction and death. And so we shall."

Silence followed her words, the kind of hush usually found in a church.

"That's not what we're taught." I said, thinking of the leather-bound Bible in our living room. "I'm not saying the Consort is right—but they've been teaching the exact opposite for generations. They have books and writings and scripture to back up what they say. How are you going to convince anyone to listen?"

"Because we have proof. Think about it, Delancey—the Free Walkers have never attacked the Consort, or the Walkers in general. We've never done anything to damage the Key World. And yet we're branded as threats and traitors. Why is that?"

"They're afraid of you," Simon answered.

Rose smiled, brilliant but weary. "They're afraid of *you*. Hybrids are the future of the Walkers. The Consort has chosen to deal with the population crisis using brute force. They see Half Walkers as a weakening of the line, but the truth is, you're more powerful. You make cauterization possible, and your Echoes mean the population crisis is a moot point." She shook her head. "You and your kind could save us all, if we'd let you."

"Telling them Simon could preserve Echoes won't change their minds."

"Showing them will," she said grimly. "We just need to get their attention."

"You've *got* their attention. They're planning the Tacet because they're afraid of you. How are you planning to stop it?"

Rose's eyebrows snapped together, the same as my mom's whenever I talked back. "Let us worry about the details. It's time for you to rest."

She took my arm and angled me toward the infirmary. I jerked away.

"I'm not tired!" I sounded like a little kid up past bedtime, but that's how she was treating me. "We have a right to know what you're planning."

"No, you don't. You're not a Free Walker yet."

"I brought you the frequency. I brought you *Monty*. I turned my back on the Walkers. My friends. My family. What else do I have to do to prove myself?"

"You're inexperienced. We can't send you out without the proper training." More gently she added, "This is a marathon, not a sprint. Once we've dealt with the Consort and you've caught up, you'll have plenty of opportunities to help."

"You mean once you trust me."

Simon squeezed my fingers, but I was done being careful. Careful worked for Addie, maybe, and Eliot. But careful made you hesitate, and if I'd learned anything in the past few weeks, it was that hesitation could be as deadly as haste.

"I trust you, Del," Rose said, but there was a precision to her words that underscored everything she wasn't saying. She didn't believe I could be helpful; the Free Walkers didn't trust me *or* believe in me.

"Then tell me what the plan is."

"I've told you all you need to know. You are both guests here—valued guests—but we expect that you'll abide by the rules we've set." She stopped herself from adding "or else," but it hung in the air between us.

Simon shifted closer to me. If you didn't know better, his movements would have seemed lazy, but it was the opposite— fluid and easy, an archer drawing a bow and taking aim without spooking the rabbit.

She was small and white-haired, but Rose was no rabbit. Instead of spooking, she gestured toward the infirmary. "We can talk more once you've rested."

I was planning to do a hell of a lot more than talk.

CHAPTER THIRTY-FOUR

ROSE RETURNED ME TO THE MAIN INFIRMARY—
a generic hotel room, identical to mine, but every surface was covered with regimented rows of medical supplies. A middle-aged woman wearing a lab coat and mom jeans startled when she caught sight of me.

"Rose! I had no idea she'd left!" She opened the door connecting our rooms, like she was making sure I wasn't there. "I'm so sorry!"

"Del has a mind of her own," Rose said, waving away the apology. To me she said, "Rest now. Pushing too hard will turn you into a liability."

There was no room in the Free Walkers for a liability.

"Come on," Simon said, in a voice I'd heard him use to charm everyone from the lunch lady to my mother. I couldn't tell if he was using it on Rose or me—or both. He looped his arm with mine. "I can't see you that sick again."

Rose spoke to the medic, their voices too low to hear, and then embraced me. She felt wiry and strong, so different from Monty's hollow fragility. "I'll check on you later," she said. "We'll catch up."

She marched away, and my breath eased.

"Let's get you settled in," the medic said. Simon frowned at her, and she took a step back. "You heard your grandmother."

"I'll take care of Del," he replied, and steered me back to my room.

She scurried after us, a fluid-filled plastic bag in hand. "You need your IV. We'll use the other arm this time."

"No thanks." The crook of my elbow still felt tender from where the needle had gone in, my skin reddened from the tape.

She took an alcohol wipe from the nightstand. "Your system needs more glucose."

"I feel fine," I protested. "Getting out of bed helped. And the pitch here is good." Which was true—with the Key World frequency filling the room, I was stronger and steadier than I'd been in the lobby.

"I'll stay with her," said Simon. "We'll let you know if she feels lousy."

"Rose's orders," she said, brightly rigid.

Everything about the base camp felt temporary, like the Free Walkers didn't want anyone getting too comfortable, like they were ready to run at a moment's notice. Unsettling as the sensation was, tethering myself to the bed felt worse.

She folded her arms. "Do I need to ask your grandmother to come back?"

I didn't want to see Rose—not until I'd had a chance to process what she'd told me, not until Simon and I could make a plan. I was as much an outsider here as I'd been back home. Giving in,

I stretched out my arm and winced when the IV found its vein. The sugar hit my system in a cool, smooth rush, and I sighed deeply.

"You okay?" Simon asked, brow furrowing.

"Maybe I overdid it," I admitted, and leaned against the headboard. The medic tsked as she left, closing the door behind her.

Simon bent to kiss my forehead. "I thought you were feeling better."

"Thought so too." I reached for him, and he lay down next to me.

"What's next?" He traced my features, the gesture soothing my frayed nerves.

"Don't know. It's like Addie says—I didn't *think*. I assumed they'd want me here. They'd let me help."

"Rose wants you here. She was worried about you."

I shook my head, heavy and slow. "She wanted Monty, so she used us. Monty used us because he wanted her. They're the perfect match."

"Not as perfect as us." Simon ran his fingers through my hair, coaxing out the knots.

"You really told her you wouldn't help without me?"

"She's pretty cold, Del. She didn't want Monty—she needed him. She let him sit around for twenty years before she brought him in. I wasn't going to take any chances with you."

"Still the guy all the girls want," I murmured. "Even grandmas."

He chuckled as I burrowed closer, trying to soak up his warmth, The IV chilled me from the inside, a thread of cold running through my core, impossible to dispel.

My eyelids grew heavy, images of Simon in Train World springing to life with each drowsy blink. Even knowing he had survived wasn't enough to erase my guilt. "Should've stayed."

"At home?" I felt him draw back and tip my chin up, but I couldn't summon the energy to meet his gaze. "Why—"

"Not home. Nothing there. Train World."

His voice was warm and worried, and very far away. "Del, you had to go. I told you to go. You would have died."

"So would you."

"But I didn't," he pointed out.

"I knew he wasn't you." The words came with an effort, thick and sludgy. "That's why I broke his nose, mostly."

"Mostly broke?" He sounded amused.

"Mostly him. Little you."

"You were breaking my nose a little bit too?"

It was too much trouble to answer. Ice slipped and spread through my veins, carrying me further into sleep.

"Del?" Simon's hands on my shoulders, shaking me. Simon's fingers on my pulse. A crack of brightness beneath my lids, and a pinching sensation as I drifted away.

Someone was shaking me. Calling my name and shaking me, and I dragged the blankets over my head, a fuzzy cocoon. Warm again, I realized, finally. The cold in my blood was dissipating.

If I ignored Addie for long enough, she usually gave up. Playing possum bought me at least ten extra minutes of sleep. Long enough for her to go downstairs and complain to my parents, who would finish their coffee and their discussion before coming upstairs.

On days she was especially annoyed, she'd smack my shoulder or punch me in the arm. Rip off the covers and tickle my bare feet. But she'd never actually slapped me. Now she did, a stinging against my cheek that faded almost as soon as it registered.

I did not like it.

Instinctively I pushed away the hand before the next blow landed, and my fist shot out.

At least I thought it did. The punch sailed through the air with all the speed and force of a wet dishcloth.

Simon chuckled, but there was more relief than humor in it. "You're okay?"

I forced my eyelids open. Not Addie. Simon. "I would be if you'd stop hitting me."

"You passed out." Once again, he was pressing a tissue against my arm.

"I was sleepy," I said, sitting up in the bed.

He leaned forward until his forehead touched mine, our lips brushing for the briefest of seconds. "You were drugged."

"What? No. Frequency poisoning," I said, but he held up the IV he'd taken out, the needle swaying like a pendulum.

"You had that thing in for five minutes, tops, and I could barely wake you up. Your grandmother had them put something more than glucose in the line."

"Why would she do that?"

"To keep you out of the way," he said grimly, handing me a Band-Aid. "You don't always listen to authority so well."

"To the Consort! But they're different."

"Are they? From where I stand, the Free Walkers and the Consort aren't that different. They're both playing God. They use people, and they walk away, and if there's any mess left behind, they chalk it up to collateral damage."

"They're not the same," I said. "They're *not*."

"Why? Because their leader is a little old lady you're related to? Because you want to think Monty wasn't all bad?"

Because I'd sacrificed too much—family and friends and future—to believe I'd traded one evil for another. "They're out-gunned. They're doing what they have to in order to survive, and protect the Echoes."

"Consider the sources. You're taking the word of a woman who drugged you, a dementia patient, and the guy whose life I stole."

"You think the Consort's a better choice? They killed your birth mom when they cleaved your home world. They killed your dad. They'd kill you, too, if they knew who you were." His words—*the guy whose life I stole*—lodged under my skin like a splinter.

"I'm not saying I want to throw my hat in with the Consort. But if the Free Walkers are going to burn the world down, I'd like to make sure we don't go up in flames too."

"Walkers believe there is a choice in any situation. Sometimes it's a choice between acting or doing nothing. Sometimes it's a choice where you can't lose—a trip to Disney World or a new car—and sometimes the alternatives both suck. But right now, for us, it's deciding who we believe: the Consort or the Free Walkers. Not their tactics, but what they stand for."

"And you can separate the two? What they want and how they get it?"

I met his eyes. "I cleaved a world, Simon. All those lives were lost because of me. Because I was careless and stupid, and they'll never come back."

"You didn't know."

"Ignorance of the law is no excuse for breaking it. One of your Echoes told me that."

"He sounds like an asshole."

"He had some anger issues," I said. "But he had a point. I treated Walking like a game, and people died. Now I need to fix it."

"Even if fixing it means being as ruthless as the Consort?"

"The Consort says we have to sacrifice anything to protect the Key World."

"Would you? To stop them and protect the Echoes, would you sacrifice anything?"

I laced my fingers with his. "Anything but you."

"Considering that your grandmother drugged you, I think you can consider yourself benched. You might spend the war in a hospital bed."

"That's why she did it." I swung my feet over the side of the bed. "They're making a move—soon—and she doesn't want me interfering. We need to find out what it is."

"She's not going to tell you anything," Simon said as I grabbed his arm and hauled myself up.

"No. But Monty might."

The medic hadn't come in to check on me, no doubt assuming the drugs were enough to keep me under control. Even so, Simon turned the lock on the door connecting our rooms, slow and silent, then fixed the chain on the hallway door.

"You're locking us in," I pointed out. "I don't think that helps."

He grinned and opened the curtains. Sunlight poured into the room—through a sliding glass door.

"Sneaky looks good on you," I said.

"Learned from the best," he replied, and pressed his mouth to mine before giving me my coat.

We slipped outside. "Is he close?"

Simon nodded. "He's in Rose's room. This way."

My hand tucked in his, he led me toward the corner room on the ground floor. The curtains were tightly drawn, giving no indication whether Monty was alone—or even inside. "Do you think Rose is still with Ms. Powell's daughter?"

"Prescott? Probably. They looked like they had a lot to talk about."

"And they're not telling me any of it." I rapped on the window. "I can't believe we're asking Monty for help."

No response from inside. I knocked again.

"Maybe he's asleep," Simon suggested. "Maybe she knocked him out too."

I knew better. "He wants to make me wait. Screw him."

I turned as if to leave, and the curtain twitched. A moment later Monty was standing on the threshold, grinning from ear to ear.

"Wondered when you'd visit," he said as he tugged the door open.

"We're not here to catch up," I said, pushing past him into the room.

Rose had gone for the upgrade—a king-size bed instead of two twins, a loveseat instead of the lone upholstered chair. But every surface was swept clean, except for a small pile of buttons on the dresser.

Monty shuffled toward the loveseat, lowering himself to the cushion with a grunt. He'd swapped the gray scrubs of the oubliette for a pair of khaki pants and a wool cardigan, same as ever. "Feeling better? You had me worried."

"I doubt that," I replied.

Simon pulled out the desk chair and nudged me into it.

"Good to see you, Simon." Monty squinted. "You *are* the Echo, aren't you?"

"How did you know?"

"If your Original had pulled that stunt with the chair, my granddaughter would have broken it over his head," he chuckled. "How'd they fix you, boy? Last I knew, the Key World was falling like the walls of Jericho, thanks to you."

Simon flashed the rubber bracelet. "Tuner."

Monty's eyes narrowed. "A little gadget fixed your frequency?"

"That's what they tell me," he replied. "Not my area of expertise."

"Clever," Monty muttered. "Altering an Original's strings isn't done, you know."

Simon's jaw flexed. "I'm not an Original."

"Exactly," Monty said, slow and thoughtful. "You're a loophole. May I see?"

Simon stuck out his wrist, and Monty peered at the device, twisting Simon's hand to study it from every angle.

"Dangerous," he said. "You could kill someone, interfering with their strings."

"Or save them," I said pointedly.

"Indeed," said Monty, and for the first time since his escape, his eyes took on their old familiar gleam.

I tugged at his sleeve. "What are the Free Walkers planning? Why does Rose want me out of the way?"

"Rose always has her reasons," he replied.

"She drugged Del to make sure she didn't interfere," Simon said.

Monty sputtered in protest, but Simon stared him down, like he was a member of the opposing team, and he thought better of it.

"You're a loose canon," he said to me, tilting his head to look past Simon. "They've got a plan and they want to execute it, and keeping you well away is best for everyone. Including you."

"What's the plan?" I asked. "Chicago is only one Consort—there are twenty-three more."

"It only takes one domino to fall. CCM is leading the Tacet, so they're the ones we'll take over."

"Take over *how*?" Simon asked.

"We have people inside. And unlike the Consort guards, our guns fire real bullets."

"You're going to kill the Consort?" I yelped.

He patted my hand. "Only if they don't cooperate."

"Oh. Well. What a comfort."

Monty ignored my sarcasm, turning to Simon. "Once the building's secure, and the Tacet's no longer a threat, they'll bring you and your Original in, make their case."

"Two Simons won't prove anything."

Monty forced a grin. "I'd imagine whatever demonstration they put on will be impressive. And once the Chicago Walkers are convinced, word will spread. The Major Consort will have to resign, and we'll be there to fill the vacuum."

I bolted upright. "That's a terrible plan. Do you really think taking CCM by force and then telling people they're murderers will make them believe you?"

"They will if the evidence is convincing enough."

"They'll shoot the messenger," Simon said. "It'll be absolute chaos."

Monty's smile broadened, a gleeful flash of teeth that set my own on edge. "So be it."

I looked at Simon. "The Major Consort will step in. They'll decimate us. It'll be a massacre, like Addie predicted." *You know what happens to the rebel forces in real life? They get outgunned, they get massacred, and then they get forgotten.*

"When?" Simon demanded, and Monty shrank away.

"Soon," Monty said. "They were waiting on Del and me to bring them the frequencies. Now they've got them, and they'll want to strike before the Tacet."

"Eight days," I said.

"The First Echo frequency has already gone out," Simon said. "I heard them talking about distributing it to cells in other countries. They're moving all nonessential Walkers over in the next few days."

Monty's gaze darted to me for a split second.

And just as quickly, I understood. "That's why she drugged me."

Simon frowned, puzzlement turning darker as he realized what he'd said.

"She wanted me unconscious so I couldn't fight back. Rose was sending me to the First Echo."

We left Monty shuffling in circles, humming a tuneless song, tugging at the buttons of his sweater. Plotting something, no doubt. Scheming was as natural to Monty as breathing, and I knew the signs. Rose didn't, not any more, but that was her own fault—and I wasn't in the mood to clue her in.

Simon chased after me.

"Del, think. If you go after Rose now, she'll do worse than drug you."

"I'm not going to the First Echo," I snapped, keeping my voice low. "If that woman thinks I am going to hide out while you go on a suicide mission, she's crazier than Monty."

"You could come back when it's over."

"Not if it fails. And let me tell you, this plan? It will fail. The Major Consort will bomb that building to dust before they agree to stop cleaving. Maybe we should bail. Put as much distance between us and the Free Walkers and the Consort as possible."

"I can't do that," Simon said.

"Why? Because you said you'd help them? They forced you to agree. You don't have to go along with it."

He ran a hand through his hair, dark strands sticking up in every direction. "Rose promised to help my mom. She said if the Free Walkers succeeded, she'd make it a priority to find a cure in the Echoes."

"She can't guarantee—" But I didn't finish, because even without a guarantee, it was Amelia's last shot at beating cancer, and I couldn't deny Simon the chance.

"Okay," I said, and gave in to the urge to smooth down his hair, just for the excuse to touch him. "We stay. But I'm not going to the First Echo. What do they want you to do?"

He shrugged. "Rose keeps saying that my existence is enough, but that doesn't make sense. When I got here—to the first camp—they started explaining the Free Walkers to me. All about cauterization, and Echoes, and why the Consort was bad, like I needed convincing, and telling me about my dad. They didn't tell me about the swap until I met Rose. And then they started training me."

"To Walk."

"Partly. But also to cauterize. As long as someone starts me off, I can manipulate the strings." His hands moved as he spoke, as deft as any Walker's, a too-vivid reminder of Train World.

"I remember," I choked out, and he took my hand.

"I was trying to save you."

"You *left* me," I replied. "Don't do it again."

"I promise." He brushed a kiss along my knuckles and continued. "They told me you were okay, but I wanted proof. I wanted to see you—if I was stable, and you were safe, there was no reason not to see you, right? But no matter how many times or how many ways I asked, all I got was Rose's speech about forgetting."

"She's gotten a lot of mileage out of one speech," I said grimly.

He tugged at a lock of my hair. "Yeah. I decided it was time to start calling some plays myself. I knew they wanted you to get Monty's frequency, which meant they were still keeping tabs on you. So I said I wouldn't help until I saw you again."

"That's why Ms. Powell arranged the meet on the train."

"And why they sent my Original back."

I laughed. "Rose must have been pissed when she realized we'd have to break Monty out." But Rose didn't seem like the kind of person who let anyone else call the plays. They needed Simon's help more desperately that she'd let on.

"It doesn't fit," I said. "Why you?"

"I'm a hybrid?" he guessed. "And an Echo?"

Which was true, but there were countless hybrid Echoes of him scattered across the multiverse. The Walkers could have brought any of them in, but instead they'd taken *my* Simon. "You were raised in the Key World. That's got to mean something."

"Let's figure it out in your room," he said. "Rose said she was going to check in on you, remember? You should be there when she does."

He was right. "Great. I'll ask her then."

"She's not going to tell you anything."

No, she wouldn't. "I know someone who will."

CHAPTER THIRTY-FIVE

WE TOOK THE LONG WAY INTO THE INFIRMARY— outside, through the patio. Simon checked the two interior doors.

"Still locked," he said. "They think you're knocked out."

"Better unlock them again," I said, and crawled back into bed as he fixed the doors. "What am I going to do about this?"

I dangled the IV line in midair.

"Lie down," he ordered.

"I'm not letting you put that thing in again," I said, clapping a hand over the crook of my arm.

"Obviously." He rumpled the covers and set it along one side of me, then climbed onto the opposite side of the bed. "You're a restless sleeper. Pulled it out while you were napping, but you didn't notice. I took care of you, thoughtful boyfriend that I am."

"Very thoughtful," I agreed.

I curled up on my side and sighed as his arms came around me. "Like this?"

He felt warm and solid, his voice rumbling through his chest and into my core. "Yep."

"What if they think it's because we were making out?"

His hand slid beneath the hem of my shirt. Sparkles hummed

along my skin wherever he touched, and he chuckled. "I'd hate to get a reputation as a creeper. You're supposed to be sedated, remember?"

"Good point," I said. But his hand stayed where it was.

Rose's muffled voice came from the main infirmary. I slammed my eyelids shut and did my best fake sleep, the one I'd perfected over years of avoiding family togetherness. A moment later, I heard the doorknob turn.

Footsteps scuffed along the carpeted floor, and the medic gave a disapproving sniff. I felt the IV line lift off the bed, and focused on keeping my breath slow and even.

She circled the bed and shook Simon by the shoulder.

"What's all this?" she demanded.

His voice was blurry with mock sleep. "She was having a nightmare."

"She pulled out her IV," the medic said. "That could have been dangerous. I have to reinsert the line."

"She's pretty wiped out," he whispered. "Can't you let her sleep? I promise to get you if she needs anything."

He must have looked pretty appealing, because her voice softened. "I suppose if she's resting comfortably . . ."

"She is," he assured her. "I'll watch her the whole time."

After she bustled out, we waited until she'd made her report to Rose. The door cracked open and closed again, but I stayed immobile, sleeping the sleep of the heavily drugged. We heard Rose leave and waited another ten minutes before climbing out of bed, my limbs growing twitchier with every second.

"I'm not letting you go back by yourself," he said as I rummaged through the nightstand.

The drawer did, in fact, hold a Bible and a phone book. But there were also several packages of glucose tablets. "Excuse me?"

"It's dangerous. The Consort is looking for you."

"They won't be watching your house," I said. "Other Simon is the only one who'll help us."

"Help you," he corrected. "I doubt I'm his favorite person."

"Another reason for you to stay here. Besides, remember what happened the last time you met one of your Echoes? The multiverse couldn't handle both signals at once, and it ripped." I shook my head and pulled on my coat. My backpack was propped in the corner, and I swung it over my shoulder. It felt good, a reminder that no matter what the Consort or the Free Walkers thought of me, I was a Walker.

Simon caught me by the hand. "According to the techs, that was because we had different frequencies. Now we match."

"Except for your signal flaw," I reminded him.

"Rose said it's safe, as long as I'm stable and we don't touch." He held up his wrist. "See? Stable. Assuming I don't punch him, we're fine. It worked okay before."

"When was this?"

"We were both here," he said. "Not ten feet away from each other, when the Free Walkers rescued you guys."

"You were here?"

He nodded. "I was training in the parking lot when the retrieval team came back. It was total chaos—medics and security and Rose and Monty, and him in the middle, carrying you. I didn't realize who it was at first, because I only saw his back. I've never seen the back of my own head except in game tapes. But I knew it was you. It's hard to miss this hair." He wrapped a lock around his finger, tugged gently. "He carried you to the infirmary, and they shut the door in my face. I went around back and watched through the window. He stayed the whole time they worked on you. Rose left—to check on Monty, I suppose. But he stayed until you were stable."

"Did you talk to him?"

"No. But he spotted me."

"What did he do?"

Simon looked away. "It doesn't matter. The important thing is, he and I were only a few feet away and the world didn't end."

"Early days," I muttered.

The Free Walker base was just off the expressway, surrounded by dingy strip malls. A few blocks away, we found a sports bar, lively but not jam-packed. Perfect for what I needed.

"Shouldn't we cross over?" Simon asked. "You're going to get sick again."

I felt steady, but popped a glucose tablet while I surveyed the crowd. "Either we steal a car or take a bus," I said. "It's easier to steal a car in an Echo."

It was early, but one guy was already hitting boozily on an exasperated waitress.

He frowned. "You're really comfortable with grand theft auto."

"Monty was a bad influence in all sorts of ways. We need to get as close as possible to your house before we cross back over, in case the Consort's watching the area."

I lifted the drunk guy's keys while his back was turned.

"What?" I said when Simon shook his head. "He shouldn't be driving anyway."

His frown deepened, but all he said was, "Lead the way."

The key remote led us to an aqua-blue Chevy. In minutes we were speeding away, Simon at the wheel.

When we pulled up outside Simon's Echo house, it was still light out. Simon stared at the drawn curtains, trying to make out the shapes inside. He dragged in a breath. "How are you feeling?"

"Okay," I said, tapping my pendant. "I've got a few hours before I'm in trouble."

"If we're not back in a few hours, frequency poisoning won't be the biggest problem we have," he warned, and opened the car door.

I followed him across the street and into the garage. I chose another pivot, and we Walked back to the Key World, where I promptly stumbled over a lawnmower, cursing.

He helped me up, then pressed a button on his tuner. Red lights chased each other across the display, then slowed to a steady beat. "I'm good," he said. "Stay still."

A minute later a single lightbulb glowed weakly, the pull-chain swinging back and forth.

The familiar, bell-like frequency swept the last wisps of fog from my brain, and my shoulders eased.

"You actually park a car in here," I said, looking around. Amelia's car, I assumed. A dark green compact, older but well-maintained. "I always assumed she didn't drive."

"Why wouldn't she drive? We keep her car in here. That's what a garage is for, Del."

"Not ours," I said. "My dad uses it for an office. Keeps a whole bunch of divisi and other tools there, and the maps for the day's Walks. We're not allowed in without permission."

Simon scoffed. "That's a man cave, not an office."

"No, it's . . ." I blinked. "It *is* a man cave."

"Oh yeah. Can't blame him for wanting a little peace, especially when you and Addie lay into each other."

Thinking about Addie cut deeper than I'd expected. How much trouble were she and Eliot in? What about my parents? Had they been taken into custody? We'd planned for the aftermath of the escape, taken steps to protect Addie and Eliot, but what if it hadn't been enough? What would happen when the Free Walkers made their move?

To distract myself, I inspected the garage. The walls were lined with gardening equipment and tools. A bike stood in the corner, covered with cobwebs, and an entire corner was crowded with sports equipment. Basketball wasn't the only sport Simon excelled at. He was a natural athlete—one of those people comfortable on any kind of court or field, his lean, easy grace an asset no matter what game he played.

He came up behind me as I was poking my fingers through the strings of a tennis racket. "You ready?"

"Yeah. I'll go in and get him. We'll Walk out through one of the house pivots, and your mom will come get you."

"I don't like the two of you Walking without me."

"We'll be fine as long as you stay away from him. I don't care what the Free Walkers have done; putting the two of you in the same room is bad news."

Rose wouldn't have let the Simons near each other if she'd thought there was a danger, of course. It wasn't their frequencies I was worried about. It was their egos.

I leaned my head back against his chest, listening to the rhythm of his heartbeat. "Are you sure you can handle seeing her? You're okay?"

"Positive. Better than okay."

I wasn't sure I believed him. *The guy whose life I stole.* The comment had stayed with me, the sort of offhand remark that should have faded but instead picked up strength, a droning in the back of my mind that built to a roar. Is that how he viewed himself? An imposter? An interloper? A thief?

Did he think he was only an Echo?

He was none of those things. He was Simon Lane, the boy I loved in any world, and what made him real was his heart, not some tangle of sound and strings. I pressed my lips to his, drawing his warmth and his breath inside me, and it underscored what I already knew. He was alive, and mine, and I'd do anything to keep him that way.

"See you in a little while," I said, and slipped out the side door, my hood up and my head down.

Nobody seemed to be watching the house—no strange vans idling at the curb, no sign of the Consort or the police. I slipped up the back steps and knocked lightly.

Iggy heard me first, scrabbling at the door with frantic barks. A moment later Original Simon answered with a scowl.

"Are you insane?" He grabbed my arm and hauled me inside. "Did anyone see you?"

"Who would be watching you? It's perfectly safe."

"Del!" cried Amelia, jumping up from the table. "Are you okay? Did something happen? Is Simon—"

"He's good," I said. "He's waiting in the garage."

She paled and took a step toward the door. "Why won't he come in?"

"It's better if we keep them apart as much as we can," I said, careful not to elaborate. Omission is always easier than an outright lie.

Original Simon started to contradict me, but I narrowed my eyes, and he reconsidered. "Why'd you bring him?"

"I needed to talk to you, and he wasn't going to let me come alone."

"Idiots," he muttered.

Iggy pressed so heavily against me that I had to brace myself against the counter. I leaned over and wrapped my arms around his neck. "I missed you too, fella. We both did." Straightening up, I added, "Can we Walk somewhere? Let Simon and his mom catch up?"

His jaw clenched, but he shrugged and pointed to the

hallway. Before I could follow him, Amelia touched my arm.

"You look tired," she said. "Are you—"

"I'm okay. I just need some answers. Once we've crossed, you can go see him."

She nodded. "I didn't get to say thank you."

"For what?"

"For saving my boys. Both of them."

"I haven't," I protested. "Not yet."

She tucked my hair behind my ear. "I saw the way you looked at Simon the first time he brought you home. Like he was playing music only you could hear. And I saw the way you looked when he was gone, like every pivot in the multiverse had slammed itself shut. You'll save them," she said, and there was a quiet certainty in her voice that made me believe her.

Maybe Simon got some of his strength from his father—Gil must have been tough to endure the oubliette without betraying the Free Walkers or his family. But a good chunk came from Amelia, simultaneously fragile and tough, who could look at me with infinite kindness after what I'd done, and what my people had done, and after she'd lost so much. She looked past what I'd taken and instead saw what I was trying to return.

"Amelia . . . ," I started to say, and her expression altered from benediction to trepidation. "Do you trust the Free Walkers?"

"To do what? Believe in their cause? Fight for it? Absolutely. But do I trust them to succeed?" She touched the bare place on her fourth finger. "I've seen them do otherwise too many times,

Del. But I believe they'll fight, no matter the cost."

"That's what worries me," I said. "Since when do the good guys act like the bad guys?"

"You thought they'd be the opposite of the Consort."

"I guess."

"Make no mistake. They're every bit as driven, every bit as ruthless and exacting as the Consort. It's natural to want people to be binary, Del. Good or evil, right or wrong. But people are like pivots—at any given moment, there are a million possibilities in play. Their choices illuminate who they are."

"So the ends justify the means? They can manipulate kids and sacrifice dads and abandon families, and we're all supposed to say, 'Well, it's for a good reason'?"

She looked out the window to the garage. "I ask myself that every day. I don't think they do it lightly. The Consort adheres to a single rule: the Key World above all else. Everything else is insignificant. They don't even have to think about it—fighting entropy is their sole consideration. The Free Walkers don't have the luxury of indifference. They believe each life matters, Del. Walkers, Originals, Echoes. Balancing the needs of the three means every single choice puts someone in danger. There are no perfect solutions."

"Only less horrible ones."

She inclined her head.

"Enough philosophy," said Original Simon. "You wanted to talk, so talk."

I hugged Amelia carefully. She looked better than the last

time I'd seen her, but she moved gingerly, as if the world was filled entirely with sharp corners and hard edges.

"I'm glad you're safe," she whispered, and released me.

"Ladies first," Original Simon said mockingly. I reached for the closest pivot and held out my hand. The brush of his fingers against my palm was gentle, but when I turned back, his face was stony as ever.

The Walk was smooth, depositing us in an empty kitchen with a lightly trilling pitch. "We shouldn't stick around here," he said. "In case I come back."

I nodded, and he led the way outside. "What did you want?"

"Did you know the Free Walkers drugged me?"

His eyebrows lifted. "Glucose solution. To rebalance your brain chemistry after the frequency poisoning."

"Sugar water doesn't knock people out."

He considered this. "I wouldn't put it past them. But they didn't do it when I was there."

Memory stirred. "When you brought me to base camp, what did you do?"

He slid his hands in his pockets, as if he was sulking. "Brought you in. Decided I'd stick around to make sure the medical team stabilized you. Then I left."

Not according to my Simon. "That's it?"

"That's it," he said. "So, you and Rose are butting heads, huh? Wish I could have seen it. What's the problem?"

"She wants to send me to the First Echo." He didn't break stride. "Which you knew."

"We'd discussed it," he said.

"And you agreed I should sit at the little kids' table?"

He raised an eyebrow. "Can you cauterize a world?"

"I can tune. How different can it be?"

"Can you fight Consort guards in hand-to-hand combat?"

I flushed, but responded, "I did okay during Monty's escape."

"Can you fire a gun? Have you ever *touched* a gun?"

"Do Tasers count?"

He threw up his hands. "What did you expect? You're a newbie, Del. You're a newbie with an impulse-control problem, and they're not going to let you in until you earn it."

So I was an outsider. Again. An outsider among outsiders, and I was beginning to wonder whether Simon and I should *stay* outsiders. We could leave both the Consort and the Free Walkers and try life on our own. I couldn't tell if the skip in my pulse was fear or excitement.

We'd arrived at my Echo house, either by accident or design, and the familiar sight brought a wave of homesickness down on me. Before I could get too nostalgic, I forced myself to remember why I'd come back. I sat on the front steps, leaned my head against the pillar.

"I'm guessing you're in on the plan to take over CCM."

He sprawled out next to me. "Yeah. Finding the First Echo was the last piece of the puzzle."

"It's going to be a bloodbath," I said.

"Not if we get our message out."

"Can't you talk to Rose? Convince her there's another way?"

"Why would I?" He stared at me, aghast. "You seem to be confused about the goal here, Del. The Consort are the bad guys. They're the mass murderers. They kill their own people rather than allow a whisper of dissent. They killed my dad. If you think I'm going to beg the Free Walkers to go easy on them, you need more sugar, because you have scrambled your goddamn brain."

"What if it doesn't work?"

"Then we'll go after the other Consorts." he said. "Seventy-five people control the Walkers and the multiverse. *Seventy-five.* How many Echoes do I have? How many do the other hybrids? They can't fight all of us. Seventy-five against infinity? I like our odds."

Seventy-five targets. My mind reeled. "You're going to kill all of them?"

"If we have to."

"The weapon Lattimer was after," I said, my voice emerging thin and panicked. "The one your dad developed? This was his plan all along—to use it to assassinate the Consorts?"

Simon blinked. "The weapon?"

"Lattimer used me to get information about the weapon from Monty. He didn't know what it was, only that your dad had been working on it before he was captured. Amelia insisted there was no such thing, and I believed her, but—" I broke off as his face contorted, a lighting-fast shift between disbelief and anger and black humor, before his mouth settled into a bitter twist.

"You don't know? Neither of you?" His laugh was so caustic it could have stripped varnish. "You've had your hands on it all along. Gil's weapon is Simon."

CHAPTER THIRTY-SIX

S IMON WAS THE WEAPON.

My Simon.

And he had no idea.

"He's not an assassin," I said through frozen lips. "He doesn't have it in him to kill someone."

Simon's brows snapped together. "They aren't expecting him to assassinate the Consort."

"Then how is he a weapon?"

"We both are," he said. The words were calm, but an emotion I couldn't name shimmered above the surface. "You've heard Rose, haven't you? Hybrids are the future of the Walkers. He and I are the proof. Once we've got the Walkers' attention, Rose will bring us out for show-and-tell."

I stared at him.

"We're proof," he repeated. "Tangible, verifiable evidence that the Consort lied. The Walkers will have no choice but to believe us, and that will be the end of the old regime."

"Lattimer said it was a weapon. Like a gun, or an amplifier, or . . ."

Gil always said the truth was the only weapon they needed.

Simon was the truth incarnate. Which made him dangerous, and put him in danger.

Anything can be a weapon, depending on who controls it.

Monty had figured it out. Alone in the oubliette, he'd put the pieces together. He'd tried to warn me, but I'd refused to listen. They'd used a reunion with me to control Simon.

"Why him? Why *my* Simon, instead of some other Echo?"

He turned away. "He sounds like an Original, so Walkers are more likely to accept him in their world."

"Great. Maybe they can start a book club," I said. Simon was keeping something back. I'd known too many versions of him not to recognize the signs. "How will you prove it? Is he going to Walk in front of them? Cauterize a world? Give a presentation?"

"Something like that." He kicked a stair tread. "If my Echoes can Walk, they're part Walker. And since Walkers are alive, no matter what world they're in, so are the Echoes."

It seemed like a weak argument to hang a revolution on, and I tried again, hoping to needle him into revealing more. "So the Free Walkers take CCM, I get shoved into the First Echo, and you . . . hang out here?"

"I've earned a break," he snapped. "I've spent seventeen years fighting the Consort. Cauterizing worlds, building net-works, with no family except the Free Walkers. I deserve a little bit of time to enjoy the life I was supposed to have. The one your boyfriend had instead."

"You're jealous of Simon."

Even in the fading light I could see the clench of muscles in his jaw. "Not jealous. But I've been running for my life while he's been hitting free throws and nailing cheerleaders. Hard to work up a whole lot of sympathy for the guy."

"He grew up thinking his dad bailed. His mom is *dying*. I wouldn't call his life easy."

"But it's *his*. A home and a family and a dog and you. It was supposed to be mine. Excuse me if I want to enjoy it while I can."

"He lost out too. You've always known who you were. He thinks he's been living a lie."

"He has." His face was flushed with anger. I couldn't blame him—he'd lost more than my Simon, no question—but one person's pain does not invalidate another's. If you break your arm, breaking your leg doesn't make it hurt less or heal faster.

And Original Simon's existence didn't undo my Simon's. "Amelia loves him. Not in place of you, not as a substitute. He's absolutely her son. That's not a lie. How I feel about him isn't a lie. It's not tied to whether he's an Echo or an Original. It's who he is."

"He didn't even see you," Simon said. "For years, he literally couldn't see you."

"But he does now. More clearly than anyone."

He reached out, his fingers hovering over my cheek. "If I'd been here, I would have seen you. From the very beginning."

"Even if you had," I said, as gently as I could, "you wouldn't have been him."

His hand dropped, his expression turning shuttered and unreadable.

"I'm sorry," I said, searching for a way to undo the damage. But it was seventeen years in the making. A few words from me couldn't begin to make reparations. "We should go."

He stood and headed down the driveway, back toward his house.

"Simon . . ." I started to follow, but he held up a hand.

"Five minutes, okay? Can you give me five minutes before we break up the happy family reunion?"

I backed away. "Sure. Take as long as you need."

He stalked off, and I stared at the darkening street, listening to the pitch of the world and the whisper of the pivots around me. If I picked one right now and Walked through, I could see my parents.

They might listen. Despite her unshakeable faith in the Walkers, my mom wouldn't refuse to hear me out, would she? I was her daughter. Rose was her mother. For once, she'd have to pay attention.

My parents were well-regarded. Highly placed. They could tell their friends, tell their teammates. Change didn't have to come from one sweeping moment. It could come from countless small ones. A single drop of water had little power—but enough of them, over time, wore away mountains.

Simon was nowhere in sight, which meant he couldn't stop me from Walking through the pivot by the mail slot and heading into my kitchen.

CHAPTER THIRTY-SEVEN

Days until Tacet: 8

Begin Tacet

HOMECOMING SOUNDS SO EASY. SO CELE-
bratory. But it's not nearly so simple, even when you know the
way. It's a kind of time travel, the person you are colliding with
the person you were, a gap between what was and what is, and
there's no smoothing over the difference.

I heard the radio first—not NPR or some other news station,
but the special half frequency the Consort used for emergency
broadcasts—the announcer's droning lost amid the hammering
of my heart.

My parents sat at the table in their usual places, ramrod
straight, food untouched.

Mom jumped up as I came down the hallway. "Addie! Did
you—"

"Sorry," I said with a weak smile. "Just me."

"What are you doing here?" she exclaimed. Her face was
blotchy, eyes swollen. "Del, of all the dangerous, irresponsible,
stupid things you could have done! The Consort is—"

My dad cut in. "Are you hurt?"

"No."

"Did someone force you? Did Monty and the Free Walkers threaten you?"

"Nobody forced me to do anything," I said, which wasn't strictly true. I would have rather left Monty in the oubliette, but getting Simon back had been worth it.

"Then why would you betray us? Those people are dangerous. They're lunatics!"

"They're not," I said. "If you would listen to me for two minutes—"

"We're past listening," she said. "You've left the Consort no choice."

On the radio, the announcer read a string of numbers, repeating them twice.

"What is that?" I asked.

"The Tacet," my dad said. "They're calling out cleaving assignments."

My knees gave way, and I grabbed the edge of the table. "The Tacet wasn't supposed to happen for another week!"

"The Consort decided it was better to hold a smaller Tacet now, rather than wait for the rest of the plans to be completed," he said.

There was no such thing as a small Armageddon.

A clammy sickness spread through me. "Aren't you supposed to be running it?"

"We've been removed from anything directly related to the

Tacet," my mother said stiffly. "The Consort feels we're a security risk."

"What about Addie?"

"Don't," she snapped. "Don't pretend you're concerned about us after everything you've done."

"I'm not trying to get you in trouble," I said. "I came because I didn't want anyone else to get hurt. The Free Walkers—"

"I've heard enough about the Free Walkers," she said.

"You haven't heard anything! They want to stop the cleavings and protect the Echoes. They found a way to do it that won't harm the Key World, and the Consort's known about it all along. They have proof it will work! If you would just listen," I said, seeing the worry in their eyes, "we could stop this before it gets worse. Please."

"Come here," my dad said, and it felt so good to let him envelop me in the familiar bear hug, to know my parents had finally heard me.

Tears of relief sprang up, and I sniffled into his shirtfront. "I don't want anyone else to get hurt."

"I know, kiddo," he said. "Monty was a bad influence, and you got caught up. We understand. So does the Consort."

I drew back. "The Consort?"

"They're willing to reduce your sentence," he said. "Maybe even grant you immunity."

"You cut a deal for me?" I asked. "You think I'm here to turn myself in?"

They looked at each other uncertainly.

"It's a generous offer," my dad said finally. "They'll let you come home in no time."

"Come home?" Out of the corner of my eye, I saw my mom pull out her phone. They hadn't listened to me at all. "Who are you calling?"

"Someone who can get you help," my mom said.

"You're turning me in? I'm not coming *home*," I snarled, twisting out of my father's arms. "I was trying to keep anyone else from dying!"

"Nobody's going to die." My dad stepped toward me, hands extended. "The Consort isn't killing anyone."

"They'll kill me." I edged around the corner of the kitchen island. Amelia had made pivots all over this house. I needed to find one. "If you turn me in, Lattimer will torture me, same as he did Grandpa, and then he'll kill me."

"Del," my mom said, desperate and raw. "We're trying to help you. To keep you safe."

"Then don't call the Consort," I begged, feeling blindly behind me. "If you love me, don't make the call."

"But—"

I didn't hear the rest of the sentence, because I was already gone.

Simon was waiting on the other side of the pivot, eyes nearly black with fury. "You are a goddamn idiot," he snarled as we tore through backyards and Echo houses. I heard my dad come through the pivot, but we were younger, and used to running, and had desperation on our side.

"The Tacet," I panted. "They've started."

He cursed. "Rose won't let that stand."

He dragged me inside a garden shed. "We need to head to the Key World. They can't follow your signal once we cross back, and I don't want the trail leading to my mom's."

He was right, and a few steps later we were standing in the Key World, on the outskirts of Simon's neighborhood. He grabbed my arm, slowing me down. Running would only draw attention.

"Of all the half-assed things to do—" Simon started to say.

"I thought they'd help!" I said, horrified by the crack in my voice.

"Why? Because they're *family*? The only person family has ever mattered to is Amelia. Walkers don't give a damn. Family's just another idea sacrificed on the altar of the Key World, no matter which side they're on."

I didn't reply, afraid I might agree.

Simon and Amelia were sitting on the living room couch when we arrived at Simon's house, his hands clasped with hers. The coffee table was littered with wadded-up tissues, and Amelia's eyes were glassy and red, but there was no time left for sentiment.

"What's wrong?" Simon sprang up.

"The Tacet's started," I said. Amelia pressed her hands to her face.

"How do you know?" he asked.

"My parents," I spat. "I went to ask for their help. I thought I could make them see reason."

"I'm sure they were worried about you," Amelia said, but Simon was already throwing on his coat.

"Sure. Worried enough to turn me in. They wouldn't listen to a thing I said."

"Can they track you here?" My Simon asked.

"Doubtful." Original Simon stuck to the far end of the kitchen, keeping as much distance as possible between himself and my Simon. Carefully I reached into the strings, searching for any sign of stress on the Key World's fabric. But the threads resonated against my fingertips, smooth and true. Rose was right: Since their signals matched, the Simons could coexist.

"If the Consort guards come here, all they'll find is the guy who dumped you and sent you into a tailspin," he continued. "There's nothing wrong with my frequency, so they won't suspect anything. In the meantime, you'll get back to the Free Walkers, where you should have stayed." He scowled. "No wonder Rose drugged you."

"She what?" Amelia said, startled.

"I'm fine," I assured her. "But he's right. We need to leave."

My Simon bent and kissed Amelia's cheek. She hugged him tightly, and then pushed away, resolute. "Go. If they come, we'll stall them."

"Don't stall," I ordered. "Don't do anything that might make them pay attention to you."

Iggy whined, and Simon tousled his ears. "Be good," he ordered, and looked up at Amelia again. "I don't want to leave you."

"Then make sure you come back."

He swallowed, met my eyes over her head, and nodded. "Love you, Mom."

"I love you too. Get out."

I looked at Original Simon, his expression a strange, sad blend of wonder and longing, like someone from the desert seeing the ocean for the first time. The life he was supposed to have was spilled out in front of him, all the emotions and grief and love he'd been denied. It wasn't only the Consort who had cheated him.

We spend so much time thinking about how the future will unfold, all the newness in the world and the frontiers to be discovered, that we forget about what came before. But we carry the past with us, the bright pieces and the damaged bits giving the world meaning in the same way hope gives it direction. Simon had a past of fleeting moments and shifting worlds; hard ground that made it tough to put down roots even now, and I watched the realization of all he'd lost hit him full force.

"Go," he said roughly, and shoved me toward the door.

We slipped back through the garage pivot and found the car, saying nothing until we arrived a few blocks from the Free Walker base.

"You okay?" I asked him.

"It's only a matter of time before they find us, isn't it? Either we beat them, or we're just running out the clock."

I leaned my head against his arm, felt him brush a kiss over my hair. "Probably. But after tonight . . . I'm not sure how much time we have left."

When we walked into the lobby of the hotel, it was clear the clock had run out.

CHAPTER THIRTY-EIGHT

THE LOBBY DOORS DIDN'T SLIDE OPEN AT OUR approach. Through the panes of glass I spotted a Free Walker I didn't recognize behind the front desk, and I rapped hard to get his attention. When he saw us, he spoke into a walkie-talkie, then pressed a button to let us in.

"Where's Rose?" I said.

"You two were supposed to stay in the infirmary," he said, trying to sound imposing. I'd been in trouble enough times to know when you were dealing with a real threat, and this guy, with his scrawny arms and nervous air, was nowhere close.

"I didn't feel like a nap. Where's Rose?"

"Right here," said my grandmother, coming around the front desk. "I suppose this is better, actually. Makes you easier to move."

"You mean because I'm conscious?" I sniped. "I'm not going to the First Echo."

Her mouth thinned. "In case you're unaware, we're in a bit of a crisis. I'm not going to waste time arguing. Why don't we leave the decision to Simon?"

She made a show of turning to him, shutting me out. "Montrose filled you in on our plans. Would you prefer Del to wait out the attack in the safety of the First Echo? Or would you like her to accompany you to CCM, knowing how desperate the Consort is to stop us, and knowing that they will kill her if we don't succeed."

He swallowed and looked uneasily at me.

"*No.*" He started to speak, but I cut him off. "I swear to you, Simon, send me away again and it will not be the Consort you have to be afraid of."

"You could come back," he protested. "Once it was safe."

"And if the Free Walkers fail?"

"Then at least you'd be okay," he said softly, and laced his fingers with mine. "I thought I was going to die, Del. Saving you was my consolation. I never expected Powell to come. Ever since, I've been living on borrowed time."

Fear, ominous and choking, rose inside me, but I said, "That's not true. We can do this, but not if you ship me off the minute things get rough. This is my life, and my choice, and I choose to stay with you."

He bent his head to mine, the kiss battling back both our fears. Then he straightened and turned to Rose.

"I told you before: We're a package deal. You try to play us against each other, and you'll need to find another Echo to put on your show."

"It's on your heads, then," she said coldly. "We have more important problems to deal with."

She beckoned, and we followed her into the conference room. Inside, the massive table was covered with whirring laptops, extension cords and power strips winding along the floor like jungle vines. The air was warm, heavy with the scent of burning dust and something electric, and two guys—one heavyset, wearing a sweat-stained blue T-shirt, the other rail thin, with the kind of seedy-looking scruff guys get when they're too lazy to shave—were dashing back and forth between the computers.

"We have a team handling sector Alpha Seven Thirty," the bearded guy said. "And another in Epsilon Twelve Sixty-Two. But we can't send another team out without spreading ourselves too thin."

"What are sectors?" I asked, and despite the heat from so many computers running, the sweat that trickled down the center of my back was icy. "What is this place?"

"Branch-based naming conventions," said T-shirt guy. "Easier to identify on a map. And this is our central monitoring system. Like your friend Eliot's phone, but more powerful. We can even tap into broadcasts from the Key World."

"You know Eliot?" I said.

"We know his tech," he said, pointing at Simon. "Impressive. We could use a guy like him."

Suddenly I missed Eliot so fiercely I could barely breathe. What was he doing now? Was he safe?

"Are we monitoring Consort communications?" Rose asked.

"Yes, ma'am." The bearded guy leaned over the table and tapped a key. An announcer's voice—the same one I'd heard at my parents'—filled the room. "They're calling out frequencies pretty much nonstop."

This time I paid attention to what I was hearing. The voice read a string of numbers—an Echo frequency, by the sound of it—paused, and then two more numbers in quick succession. A second voice repeated the numbers, confirming them, and the original voice read them again. We stood silently as the call and response continued, naming another Echo.

Simon frowned. "What are we hearing?"

"It's the Tacet," Rose said, her face ashen and resolute. "Those are cleaving assignments: a frequency, plus the latitude and longitude of the pivot they should cleave at."

I said, "Normally, Cleavers get an assignment from the Consort and the navigator prepares the Walk. They make sure that protocols are followed, paperwork is filled out, that the Cleavers go in with a specific plan for how they'll handle the strings. But this is . . ."

"Slice and dice," said T-shirt guy. "They're gutting the Echoes as fast as they can."

My parents must have been excused from cleaving so they could stay home and lay a trap for me.

"Coordinate with the Indianapolis cells," Rose said. "They should be able to cover at least two more."

"Cover what?" Simon asked.

"Cauterizations," Rose said. "We know which branches the Consort is cleaving. Our teams are cauterizing them instead—much like we did with Train World. We can't save every branch, but it's better than nothing."

"Usually we have advance notice," said T-shirt guy. "We can

get there before the Cleavers show up. Now we're scrambling."

"If you're cauterizing worlds while the Cleavers are there, what happens to them?"

Rose shrugged. "We can survive in Echoes. Why shouldn't they?"

My stomach dropped. "But the frequency poisoning! They don't know how to deal with it. And they'll be trapped."

"Every war has casualties," she said. "It's time the Consort learned what that's like."

For a moment I panicked, thinking about Addie and my parents before I remembered they'd been sidelined. But Eliot's father was a Cleaver. My dad's team—the ones who'd saved him from frequency poisoning. Nearly half the Walkers in the Consort, left in Echoes.

"Amelia was right," I said. "You're as ruthless as the Consort."

Rose's voice was cold and terrible. "How else can we win?"

Simon's hand found mine.

"While you two were off endangering yourselves and our mission," she added, "we decided to move up the strike on CCM. By tomorrow morning, all non-essentials will have been evacuated to the First Echo. A skeleton crew—Simon and his security detail and, I suppose, you—will move to a new location. The rest of us will—"

She broke off as the announcer fell silent, and a new voice took over.

"This is Randolph Lattimer. By order of the Major Consort of Walkers, immediately hold all cleavings in abeyance."

We turned in unison to the speaker.

"He's stopping the Tacet?"

Rose shushed me.

"We are aware that those who do not support the calling of the Walkers are listening at this moment, monitoring our work. I am speaking to these so-called 'Free Walkers' now.

"I am speaking to you, Rosemont."

Rose straightened, throwing her shoulders back.

A pause. A hiss of static filled the air, blotting out other noises, blotting out thought. He knew Rose was alive. He *knew*.

"Two days ago, the Free Walkers infiltrated our headquarters and freed a dangerous criminal, a man who threatened the very fabric of the multiverse. They have weakened the Key World, assaulted a member of the Consort, and even as I speak, they are killing Walkers who are performing their sacred cleaving duties.

"This is beyond treason. This is a declaration of war, and make no mistake: We shall defend ourselves and the Key World, as we have been called to do. The Tacet will continue. We will unravel world after world until we have dissolved your squalid little hiding places, all the weak spots that molder and threaten the Key World. We will silence every Echo in the multiverse before we allow you to continue this blasphemy. Every world you've ever passed through will be returned to dust."

Rose's breath came fast and shallow in the silence that followed his words.

"We will stop the Tacet when you have surrendered, and turned over your leaders, starting with Rosemont Armstrong and Delancey Sullivan."

"Like hell," Simon snarled. "This is a trap."

"I'm not a leader," I said. "Why does he want me?"

"Doesn't matter," he replied. "We're not doing it."

"Until you agree to our terms, we will continue to shear away every Echo attached to the Key World, and be the stronger for it. The Consort awaits your decision."

Rose stood, unmoving, and the techs watched her openmouthed. Simon drew me into him.

There was a rustling sound, as if Lattimer was stepping away from the mic. And then distantly: "Let them fall. Every last one."

CHAPTER THIRTY-NINE

THE NUMBERS RESUMED. FREQUENCY, LATI-
tude, longitude. Frequency, latitude, longitude. Each one a death
sentence, the matter-of-fact delivery magnifying the horror. So
mundane, so routine and bloodless.

So much death.

"You can't go," Simon said. "You can't turn yourself in."

"Send the signal," Rose said to one of the techs—the guy
with the beard, whose face was ashen. To the other tech, she said,
"Pack up. We move in fifteen."

"Move where?" I asked, but nobody paid any attention.

Rose beckoned to us as she strode toward the front desk.

"You can't turn yourself in," Simon repeated. "You're sure as
hell not handing over Del."

"Everything's in place," said Prescott, coming out of the front
office. "We're still on track."

Then she caught sight of me and scowled. "This is your fault.
Lattimer moved up the Tacet because of you."

The words landed like a kick to the ribs. I struggled to
respond, and Simon stepped in, saying, "Lattimer moved up
the Tacet because you poked the hornet's nest. You wanted

Monty out of prison—how did you think they'd respond?"

"We weren't going to spring him," Prescott retorted. "But it was the only way to get the frequency."

"You supplied Del with everything she needed to bust him out and you used me as leverage. You want someone to blame? Look in the mirror."

"Enough," Rose said. "Prescott, this is a minor change."

The girl loosened her death grip on the clipboard, but the back of my neck prickled with alarm. I knew better than anyone how big an impact came from a 'minor change.'

Rose said, "Continue the cauterizations as planned. With any luck, the Consort will believe that's where the threat lies. You'll head up the attack team, and I'll get Simon to the meet-up at the safe house."

"I should come with you," Prescott said, eyes widening in alarm.

"We need to separate," Rose said firmly. "If something should happen to me—"

"You mean if you turn yourself in," she cut in.

"I mean that getting Simon to his security team is critical. I'll take him now. The First Echo evacuation should be complete by tomorrow morning, but give them a good thirty-six hours to settle in and cover their tracks before beginning the attack. I want this building cleared out before it happens. Once CCM is secure, you proceed as planned. Am I clear?"

A message passed between the two of them, some wordless communication that had Prescott blinking back tears.

Rose gave a short, sharp nod and strode away.

We chased after her, leaving Prescott alone and stricken.

"You're abandoning ship?" I asked.

"It's not uncommon for the Consort to cleave our safe worlds. We likely would have moved in a week or so. We're accustomed to it."

"How often?"

"When I first fled, we moved nearly every day. Then, as the Consort grew complacent, we could stay in one place for months at a time. Recently it's picked up again, for obvious reasons."

I tried to estimate how many times they'd moved, but it seemed impossible. No wonder they weren't sentimental. They never stayed still long enough to let an attachment build.

She stopped in front of her room, unlocked the door, and ushered us in.

Monty was sitting on the edge of the bed, fingers sifting through the strings, brow creased in concentration. She touched his shoulder, and he tucked his hands behind him like a child caught misbehaving.

"Time to go, my love," she said in the gentlest voice I'd ever heard her use. "Have you packed?"

He looked at her blankly. "What would I bring? All I need is you."

She shook her head, her face mingling exasperation and affection, and pulled on a heavy gray parka.

I hadn't noticed before how generic and impersonal her

room looked. Not just tidy, but barren. Only Monty's handful of buttons was visible.

"Where's your stuff?" I asked.

She took a duffel bag from the closet, swinging it over her shoulder with a grunt. "Here."

"I mean your regular stuff."

She adjusted the strap. "Here."

She didn't carry anything except a go bag. She'd spent twenty years assuming that she wouldn't stay in one place long enough to unpack. The future was a gamble to Rose, I realized, and she was smart enough to know the house always won.

"Simon," she said, "gather your things. Meet us in the lobby in ten minutes. Del, stay with him."

I hadn't unpacked either, come to think of it.

"You're not turning yourself in," Simon said, not moving.

"Turn herself in?" Monty asked. "Don't be stupid, boy. Of course she wouldn't."

"I need to monitor the conference room," she said. "Ten minutes."

"Why would we turn ourselves in?" Monty said, bewildered. "After all the effort I went to getting out?"

He flapped his hands, agitated, and Rose caught them in hers. "No one is making you go back."

"Randolph is after you," he warned her, his gnarled fingers gripping her. "He won't rest until he thinks he's won."

"He won't win," she promised, the words as tender as they were fierce. "We'll start over, if we have to. But we won't be defeated."

Monty let go of her hand and looked away, nodding. One hand toyed with a button, dancing it through his fingers like a magician with a coin. But I knew better than to fall for the misdirection. My eyes were glued to his other hand, sifting and sorting the threads of the world, tiny gestures that nobody—not even Rose—noticed. It was as if he was running scales, practicing until he could play without thinking.

"It should be me," Monty said. "I'll do it. One last chance with Lattimer, face to face." The corner of his mouth turned up. "So I can get my hands on him."

"Nonsense," she said briskly, as if that put an end to the discussion. "We leave in eight minutes. Gather your things."

Simon didn't budge. "I'm not going anywhere until you promise you won't turn Del in."

"I won't turn Del in," she said with the same precision she'd used earlier. I met her eyes, the same hazel as mine, and she nodded once.

Words work strangely. The fewer words someone uses, the more their silence tells you. Lattimer's grandiose speech meant as little as his promises. But Rose's silence in the face of Simon's panic meant exactly what she'd said: She wouldn't turn me in. She'd turn herself in, and she'd expect me to do the same. Simon didn't hear it, because he only listened to the words, and not the silence around them.

"Seven minutes," I said, and we headed for Simon's room,

just down the hall. The door was unlocked—not everyone got the privacy Rose did, it seemed. Simon pulled my old backpack from the closet. "Half this stuff is yours."

"Was it useful?"

"Eliot's phone, definitely. The tech guys acted like it was Christmas morning when I handed it over. I ate some of the candy bars. I didn't try the picks or the duct tape, though. It's quite the collection." He began stuffing clothes into the backpack at random.

"I like to be prepared."

"Runs in the family, huh?" He closed the bag and pulled me to him. "Tell me this plan will work."

I buried my face in his sweatshirt, inhaling the scent of him, soap and sunshine and boy. It didn't mute the memory of the cleaving numbers, but it muffled them. How many worlds would Lattimer destroy before this was over? How many lives would unravel to nothing?

I drew back and kissed him, so hard that the memories stopped and my mind filled with Simon, with the taste of him on my tongue and the feel of his hands on my skin, blocking out the rest of the world.

When he broke the kiss, we stood for a moment, breathless and sweaty and dazed, and I remembered what had turned everything so frantic, all the awfulness we were trying to hold back, a dam trying to contain an angry river before it swept away the shore.

"It'll work," I promised, careful not to say more, and drew him down to me again.

. . .

When we reached the lobby, Rose was pacing next to a high-backed leather chair, arguing with Monty. Her head snapped up as she caught sight of us. "You're late."

"He had to pack," I said, rebraiding my hair.

From the chair, Monty snorted. I ignored him and peered around the deserted lobby. "Where is everyone?"

"Doing their part. Now we do ours."

Rose had given me a device similar to Simon's, to mitigate the worst of my frequency poisoning, but I felt shaky as we crossed the parking lot with Simon's hand at my waist. Rose strode ahead, and Monty scurried to keep up with her.

The night sky was blanketed with clouds, a hazy gray over-laying deep blue, light pollution from the city turning the horizon orange. I let the cold air fill my lungs, snapping me into alertness. "Where's the pivot?"

"A few blocks west," Rose replied. "There's a bus terminal that will make it harder to trace us."

Simon tucked my hand in his as we crossed streets and dodged pedestrians. "This isn't what I expected."

I laughed. "What did you expect? A few weeks ago, you had no idea Walking even existed."

"And now I don't exist. I shouldn't, anyway."

"Don't talk like that," I said sharply. "Your existence is the thing that's going to save us all."

"I'm not sure I care about saving everyone, Del. Just you and my mom. Besides, he's the one who's special."

My pace slowed. "He's not the only hybrid, you know. There are more of them—enough that the Consort has studied their effects on the multiverse. But you're unique. You're the only Echo with a Key World signal. You're the only one who's Walked. Cleaving and cauterization . . . those are physics. They're facts. You're a truth."

I went up on tiptoe to graze his jaw with my lips, blinking back tears before he could see them.

We kept moving until Rose halted.

"Here," she called, motioning to a rift that hovered a few feet off the ground near a ticket kiosk. We crossed over to another pivot, where Rose boosted a minivan in the time it took Simon to reset his tuner.

We ended up on the South Side, crossing over outside a convenience store. Rose and Monty bought snacks while Simon reset his tuner again, and we set out on foot through the neighborhood of neatly tended lawns and brick bungalows, their windows glowing in the darkness.

"Here," Rose said finally, gesturing at an orange bungalow with a FOR SALE sign in the yard. "It's vacant."

"How can you tell?"

"Newspapers." She pointed to a small pile of waterlogged *Tribune*s on the front stoop.

Inside, a cluster of pivots hung near the front door, another set in the kitchen, another at the stairs. Everything was perfectly staged—no family pictures on the mantle, just an assortment of candles that had never been lit. A bowl of wax fruit sat on the kitchen table, and the couch pillows practically stood at attention.

"I'm hungry," said Monty, pushing past me to tear into our supplies. He rummaged around the drawers, discovered a lone plastic spoon, and dug into a tube of cookie dough.

Simon watched him, baffled, and then turned to Rose. "What's the plan?"

"Tomorrow you'll meet up with your security detail. Once CCM is secure, you'll be brought in, along with the Other Simon, to show the Walkers the truth."

"Dangerous stuff," warned Monty through a mouthful of cookie dough.

Rose's lips pursed in annoyance, then smoothed out again. She seemed happy enough to have Monty back—there were plenty of affectionate looks and brief, fleeting moments of contact, as if she was reassuring herself he was truly here. But underneath the affection was impatience. She ran the Free Walkers with stark efficiency, and maneuvering around Monty's shambling, lackadaisical nature was slowing her down.

As for Monty . . . I wanted to know why he was keeping up the dotty, distracted routine. Was it a way to punish Rose for leaving him behind? Was he so unsettled by the woman she'd become that he couldn't trust her? The way his face lit up every time she entered the room suggested he wasn't holding a grudge.

It didn't make sense. Monty had gotten exactly what he wanted, so there was no need for the act—unless there was something else he wanted. Some new scheme.

"What exactly is it I'm supposed to do?" Simon asked.

"I can't tell you that," Rose said.

He leaned back against the counter, arms crossed, deceptively at ease. But I knew the look in his eyes. The tiniest flash of pity ran through me, for Lattimer and the Walkers and any other person—Rose included—who tried to take a single thing more from him.

"I've gone along with you," he said, pleasant as June, stubborn as February. "I've done what you wanted, to protect Del, to find a cure for my mom, and because I like the Consort a hell of a lot less than I like you. But I'm not going in there without a game plan."

"We don't have time for this," she said sternly.

I moved next to Simon, let him slide an arm around my waist and draw me closer.

"I don't think this place has cable, Rose," I said. "We've got plenty of time."

"You," she said, pointing at me, "should have gone to the First Echo. Since you didn't, you're a security risk, and I will not jeopardize our mission to satisfy your curiosity. Simon, you'll be given the information you need once you reach your team."

His jaw worked, and I knew the discussion wasn't finished, only postponed. "What are you going to do about Lattimer's offer?"

Monty paused for moment, sighed, and returned to his snack.

"I'll go, of course," Rose said.

CHAPTER FORTY

That's insane! Lattimer's not going to stop cleaving once you hand yourself over," Simon said.

"I'm aware of that." Her hands gripped the edge of the counter, despite her even tone. "But it will buy us time. Allow the rest of the Free Walkers to continue their work, and serve as a show of good faith. Randolph promised publicly to end the Tacet. By honoring our word as he breaks his, we show the Walkers we're committed to our beliefs."

"You'll show them an execution," Simon shot back.

"I'm too valuable to execute. I'm rich in secrets, and he won't want to squander them."

"What a comfort," I said.

"In the meantime, the Free Walkers will attack, just as the Consort is feeling smug and victorious. That's always been their problem; they assume people are irreplaceable. But the only one who's irreplaceable is you, Simon."

"And his Original," I reminded her.

She smiled too easily. "Of course."

Simon's shoulders tensed. "You want to play the martyr, fine. But you're not taking Del."

"I've yet to meet a single person who could make Del do something she didn't want to."

"You've met Simon," I pointed out. "He sent me back to the Key World."

"Del's decision is her own," Rose said. "But knowing her as I do—"

"You don't know her." Simon folded his arms and stared her down. "You left before she was born and didn't bother showing up again until she had something you needed."

"What about me?" asked Monty, rapping the plastic spoon against the table. "I raised her. Taught her everything she knows. Everything worth knowing, anyway. I'd say that makes me something of an expert."

"It makes you a manipulative bastard," Simon replied. "You don't know her half as well as you think."

"And you do?" Rose asked. "After less than three months, you think it's your place to decide her fate? You argued exactly the opposite a few hours ago."

"It's my place," I said, my voice overloud in the high-ceilinged kitchen. "Nobody else's."

"Delancey," Rose said, and she reached for my hand. "Free Walkers are devoted to saving Echoes. Every branch Lattimer cleaves will end countless lives. We can stop him."

"You didn't turn yourself in when you heard the announcement," I said. "How many branches has he cleaved since then? How many could you have saved, if you'd gone straight to CCM?"

Her lips pressed together, exactly the way my mom's did. "I needed to consider the larger picture."

"You needed Simon," I said calmly. He jerked, and I gave him a sad smile. "She knew you wouldn't agree to help unless you thought I was safe. Now they've gotten you out. Monty can take you to the new meet-up, and the plan can move forward."

"I don't go anywhere without you."

I took his hand, but kept my eyes on Rose. "The bigger picture. That's the same argument Lattimer uses, you know. It's how he justifies everything he does. Does it ever worry you, the way you two sound so alike? Because it sure as hell worries me."

She flushed. "If I sound like Randolph Lattimer, it's because my convictions are equally strong. More, even, because it's not tradition or fear or greed dictating my beliefs. It's the truth. One I'm willing to sacrifice myself for."

She rested her hands on Monty's shoulders. "If I can stop the Tacet and help Prescott's team complete our work, then my sacrifice means something. But I can't do it alone."

"Del," Simon said, his voice shattering.

"Enough," Monty said, face red with anger—but at whom, I couldn't tell. "Del knows what's at stake. Let her decide."

He pushed away from the table and stumped down the hallway to the bedroom. Rose followed him, turning to look at me for a long moment. "We'll discuss it in the morning."

When we were alone, Simon ran his hand roughly over his face. "Please say you're not considering this."

"What else can I do?"

"Refuse," he said. "The Free Walkers thought they could pull this off while you were in the First Echo. Let them prove it."

"While the Consort keeps cleaving?"

"He won't stop just because you turn yourself in. It's a trap."

"What if it's not? What if I can save those Echoes?"

"By dying?"

"Lattimer won't kill me," I said, hearing the quaver in my voice. "The announcement was too public; there'll be too many questions. He wants information, that's all."

"Well, as long as he's only going to torture you, I suppose it's no big deal. You want a ride over there tomorrow, or are you going to take the train?"

"Don't," I said. "You are the last person in the world who gets to give me grief."

"The hell I am!" he said. "I love you! Am I supposed to be okay with you handing yourself over to the Consort? What if I never see you again?"

"Was I supposed to be okay with you cleaving yourself?" I snapped. "Because I don't remember us taking a vote before you broke those strings. Why is it okay for you to risk your life, but not me? I can save so many lives. *Your* lives. Why would you take that from me?"

"Because I can't handle losing you again." He framed my face with his hands. "When I cleaved that world, it was to protect the entire multiverse. You'll be saving a few Echoes, if that, and only if Lattimer keeps his word. But if we wait him out and let the Free Walkers do their thing, you'll be alive to see it."

His fingertips were warm against my skin, each one an anchor against the panic threatening to wash me away.

"It's never a few Echoes," I said. "Even a single world contains an infinity."

"What about *our* infinity? We could have an amazing life together, Del. All you have to do is choose it. Choose *us*."

"I can't build a future on that many deaths," I said softly. "Your Echoes, Amelia's. Would you really want me to?"

Suddenly I was weary. I'd lost track of how many days I'd been running, how many worlds I'd crossed. They caught up to me in a rush that made me sway on my feet and grab the counter for support. It was too much to stand here in the artificial light of the kitchen and discuss my almost-certain demise with the boy I'd lost and found again.

I needed to rest. I needed the dark, where I could tell him all the things I'd been carrying, the fears and the hard truths and the soft ones as well. I needed the dark to tell him all the things he needed to hear without telling him too much.

"Let's go upstairs," I said. His eyebrows lifted, but we climbed the stairs together, wordlessly. Stupid to fight when so little time was left.

"Two bedrooms," he said when we reached the landing. "You have a preference?"

"Whichever one has a bed."

"I approve," he said, but his laughter was strained.

"Not like that," I said, smacking his arm. "I mean, not *not* like that either. I didn't mean . . . we don't have to . . . I'm not . . ."

The words tangled together, and I felt the flush creeping up my neck, along my cheeks. He touched his lips to mine.

"You're not . . . what? Ready? A virgin? That kind of girl? In the mood? Opposed?"

I blinked, overwhelmed, and he took me by the shoulder. "First step. Choose a bedroom."

I pointed to the one opposite the stairs, and he led me to the open door, then nudged me through.

Inside, the light from the streetlamp fell in thin bars across the floor. A four-poster bed, made up with a velvet patchwork coverlet and a ridiculous number of pillows, dominated the room.

"We should leave the lights off," I said. "It'll attract less attention."

"Good idea." He spoke from the doorway, both hands resting on the top of the frame, swaying back and forth.

"What are you doing?"

"Waiting for you to invite me in."

I rolled my eyes. "You're not a vampire. You can come in without an invitation."

"I could. But I won't."

"Fine. Come in."

"What's the magic word?" he teased.

I gritted my teeth. "Please come in."

"Glad to." He drew closer, his footsteps softened by the rug I'd nearly tripped over. "Long day, you."

"Better now." And it was, to my surprise. A few minutes alone with Simon were enough to restore me to the person I'd been before the world went sideways. An illusion, maybe, but a necessary one.

I'd forgotten how soft his hair was. Longer than it was when he'd left, flopping into his eyes, and I went up on tiptoe to brush it away, stepping in close enough that the heat radiating from his body warmed me.

The shadows hid the blue of his eyes, but not the gleam. They locked on mine, and my breath caught in my throat. My fingertips slid to the nape of his neck, pulling him closer, until his lips hovered a fraction of an inch from mine. He whispered against my skin. "Can I kiss you?"

I drew back. "You've kissed me a million times." Not technically, of course. My head swam at the idea of a future where Simon could kiss me a million times.

"This is different."

"Why?"

"Because this isn't the millionth time. It's the first time." His eyes met mine. "If you want it to be."

"Oh." I was grateful for the darkness now, hiding the flush of my cheeks.

"I'm not asking you to decide now," he said, taking my hands and bringing them to his lips. "But if you do—if you think you might—then I need you to choose it, every single step. I don't want you to have regrets, or questions or doubts."

"*You* want to," I said, a strange thrumming building in my blood. "You want to have sex. With me."

"I do," he said with a grin. Then, more seriously, he said, "I know I've got . . . a reputation."

"So I've heard."

He shifted, faintly defensive. "It's not as many as you think," he said. "People assume, but they're wrong. I don't brag. And even when I say I didn't, they want to believe otherwise. Guys talk."

"Girls too," I said, and his eyebrows shot up. I shrugged. "What? We have locker rooms. I hear things."

"Complimentary things?"

I smirked and didn't answer.

"How about you?" he asked.

I paused. "Walkers hook up a fair amount—at least the ones in training do. Same with apprenticeship, too, from what I hear. Most people don't get serious until they're a lot older, when they're settled into their careers."

I couldn't imagine settling down at this point. Or having a career. Or, if I was honest with myself, surviving long enough to get older.

"That's not an answer," he said. "We don't have to talk about it, if you'd rather."

"I haven't slept with anyone," I said, cramming the words together like it would speed the conversation along. "I could have, probably, if I'd wanted to. But . . . even if I can't make pivots, choices change things. It seemed like too much of a change for someone I wasn't sure of."

"Are you sure of me?"

I traced his features—the sharp line of his cheekbone, the square angle of his jaw, the curve of his lower lip, the soft skin of his neck, where his pulse beat a steady tattoo.

"I'm sure I would like you to kiss me now," I replied, and pulled him closer.

His mouth came down on mine, slow and tentative and searching, one hand cupping my face and the other wrapping around my waist, hauling me against the broad planes of his chest. My head dropped back and the world dropped away, and it was only the two of us in a strange and shadowed room, with the sound of the wind and our breathing woven together.

We stumbled toward the bed as I shoved his coat off his shoulders. It landed with a whoosh, and he pulled away, a question forming in his eyes.

I sighed. "Yes, I want you to keep going."

"You're wearing a lot of layers," he pointed out.

"Hand to God, Simon, if you ask me yes or no on every single piece of clothing I'm wearing—"

I shoved him backward, counting on the element of surprise to help me.

It worked. He fell onto the bed, arms windmilling, and then propped himself up on his elbows.

"Yes," I said, and took a step back to survey him—long limbs and messy hair and easy strength, his mouth tilting up as he watched me, his gaze so intense it felt like a spotlight, turning me visible in the darkness, heating my skin.

"Yes," I said again, and let my own coat fall to the floor next to his.

"Del . . ."

"Yes." I took a step toward him, toeing off my shoes.

His smile faltered as the air between us grew charged. I pulled off my sweater and dropped it where I stood.

Another step, and my flannel shirt joined it. "Yes."

He sat up fully, but I put out a hand to stop him from standing. "You asked," I said. "I'm answering."

His breath hitched. The cold air was a shock on my overheated skin, and I looked down at the line of clothing on the floor, a path running directly to Simon. "Breadcrumbs," I murmured.

"I knew you'd find me," he said softly.

"Of course I did. You're my home."

I took a final step, and he wrapped his arms around me, drawing me between his knees. We stayed like that, my fingers running through his hair, his head resting against my heart, a perfect, silent moment.

His arms loosened, and his fingers slid up my sides, under my tank top. I was certain the touch left a trail behind, gilt-edged and fine, and he tipped his head back to look at me.

I nodded, too breathless to speak.

He reached back and did the guy thing—the one-handed tugging off of his shirt, a twist and a shrug, the movement fluid and mesmerizing. Wordlessly I placed my hand flat over his chest, his skin so hot it nearly blistered mine. His eyes glinted, like a spark in the darkness, and when he pulled me down next to him, my blood turned to flames.

His mouth followed the paths his hands had traced, slow and deliberate one minute, light and playful the next, and it felt like the world was spinning away from me, a tumble of cravings and impulse. I pressed against him, suddenly aware how much I had to lose and desperate to be as close to him as possible.

He must have sensed it, the moment when the want turned from dizzying to overwhelming, because he drew back, the cool air rushing between us.

"Hey," he said, skimming his fingers along my shoulder, brushing my hair from my face. "Come back."

"I'm fine," I said, shaking my head.

"Fine isn't enough," he said. "We don't need to do this tonight."

But we did. And I wanted to. Needed to, actually, needed to have this night with him. There wouldn't be any Echoes of this moment. I could never travel back or capture it again, and I wasn't going to let it slip from my grasp.

Every person is the result of an entire universe's worth of choices—moments that coalesce into a life, and a life that unspools in a meandering, unpredictable line. It's the easiest thing in the world for two people to miss each other, by minutes or miles, which makes the moments when they don't miss—when strings and paths connect—even more precious.

It shouldn't happen, two people finding each other, recognizing the strange, unique harmony between them—but every once in a while, it does, because love is a singularity. Like Simon himself.

I traced the muscles in his arms, tried to memorize him like I would a new piece of music—the patterns, the rise and fall, the way each part flowed into the next. I burned this memory into my brain: Simon, eyes closed, breathing ragged, mouth blurry from our kisses.

I leaned in, molding my body against his, and his eyes snapped open. "Del," he said, voice careful and hoarse. "I told you . . ."

"And I told you yes," I reminded him.

He paused, then reached for the bag he'd brought with him, fumbling through the pockets until he emerged with a small foil square.

My mouth fell open, but I finally found the words. "Seriously? You've been on the run for weeks. When did you have the time—"

He grinned. "The infirmary doesn't just stock glucose solution and Band-Aids, you know. Figured I should be prepared."

"You're like a Boy Scout. An R-rated Boy Scout." I matched his smile. "I approve."

"I'm glad," he said, and pulled me closer than I thought was possible, until he had memorized me, lips and hands and teeth and tongue, gentle and clever and thorough, until my skin felt like starlight, my limbs heavy and soft with want.

"You're sure?" he asked, hovering over me. I nodded, but he didn't move, sweet and serious and utterly mine. "Say yes."

"Yes."

His mouth curved upward. "Now say please."

"You first." I ran my nails lightly down his back and watched the heat in his eyes blaze anew.

And then neither of us said anything intelligible for a long, long time.

The light was changing, bringing the world back with it. Simon lay across from me, head propped on an arm, his free hand sliding along my hair with slow, languorous strokes.

"You okay?"

"Very," I said, leaning in to kiss him, warm and drowsy.

"You don't regret it?"

"God, no." I laughed a little. "It's not like I expected."

"In a good way? Please say in a good way."

"I thought . . . it would make me feel complete."

"It didn't?" He sounded insulted, or worried, or both.

"I don't think part of me was missing," I said slowly. "I'm still me, all of me, but I'm part of us, too, and we're . . . different. Something new, and more. Like our song. There's a melody, and the harmony, and they both sound okay on their own. But combine them, and it's more than a series of notes. It's music."

He drew me back against him, wrapped an arm snugly around my waist. "You told me once that I saw you."

"You do." I loved the weight of him, the way his body curved around mine, our legs tangled together. Sleep was taking over now—I heard it in his breathing, in the timbre of his voice, low and gentle as a sunset, even as light peeked through the curtains. I pulled the quilt over our shoulders and sank into him. "You see me like nobody else does."

"You know what I see? Every time I look at you, every time I touch you, do you know what I see?"

I shook my head, afraid to ask.

"I see our future." He kissed the nape of my neck. "I love you for a lot of reasons, Delancey Sullivan. But that's the biggest reason of all."

I laced my fingers with his and said nothing. The tears in my throat made it impossible to speak.

Simon slept—and snored, as it turned out. It didn't matter—nothing short of a tranquilizer would have let me sleep. The sun climbed higher, but before it had left the horizon, I slipped out of bed.

Simon stirred, but I tugged the covers up around him, breathing in the scent of sleepy boy, nutty and warm, and he fell still again.

I dressed as quietly as I could, picking up the discarded trail of clothing, my breadcrumbs taking me farther away from him with every step. My chest hurt, like someone had struck me dead center, and the ache intensified as I tied my shoes and pulled on my coat. I left my bag in the corner and my pendant on the dresser. I wouldn't be needing either anymore.

Rose sat at the kitchen table.

"There's coffee," she said. "It's instant, but I made enough for two."

"He's never going to forgive me."

"You wouldn't forgive yourself if you didn't."

"Does Monty know?"

Her smile was sad and gentle, and more genuine than any she'd worn before. "He knows me," she said. "After all this time, he knows who I am. He just won't admit it to himself. People have a nearly unlimited capacity for self-deception. We all have lies we tell ourselves."

Original Simon had told me the same thing, and it struck me that just as I was more Monty's than my parents', he was more Rose's than I could ever be.

"What's yours?"

"That this is how it has to be." She traced the wood grain of the table with a thumbnail.

I leaned forward, nearly knocking over the coffee. "There's another way?"

She lifted the mug with a shaking hand. "We're Walkers, Del. There's always another way."

"What is it?" Because if there was another way to save those Echoes, I would do it. Simon or the multiverse: I knew the right choice. I was making the right choice. I'd wanted to be a Walker, and a true Walker—not one tied to the Consort, but one who understood both the gift and the burden of our abilities—would save the world. But I was also the girl who loved Simon Lane, and was loved by him, and I was still trying, desperately, to reconcile the two halves of myself.

But maybe I could love Simon best by saving the Echoes; by showing him that he was alive, and so were his people, and their existence was worth sacrificing myself for.

Rose drank, swallowed, set the mug down, and folded her hands. "I don't know. And I cannot allow myself to look for it, or I will search forever, and never act, and the world will crumble in the face of my inaction. Absolutes are easier. Hesitation is like cracks in a teacup, and all the righteousness leaks out." She met my eyes. "What's your lie, Del?"

"I'm brave enough to do this." *What about* our *infinity?*

"And why do you tell yourself that?"

"Because I need to believe I'm that person."

"It's not a lie," she said, standing. "Let's be off."

CHAPTER FORTY-ONE

I TURNED MYSELF OVER TO THE CONSORT WITH the scent of Simon clinging to my skin and his words tucked close to my heart.

"When we enter," said Rose, "it's important you don't fight. They'll take us into custody immediately. If you resist, they're likely to use force."

"They'll use force anyway," I said, remembering Monty's cell in the oubliette, the wincing stiffness of his movements. Smart, I thought, to have passed on the coffee this morning. My stomach twisted.

Rose didn't disagree.

The city was gray—gray pavement, gray buildings, gray sky. The cars sprayed gray water along the sidewalks as they sped past. The pivots that gave Chicago its familiar pulsing rhythm sounded muffled and low.

"Does it sound like there are less of them?" I asked.

"It's been a long time since I was here," Rose said. "But it would make sense that they would start the Tacet close to home."

"When will Prescott and the others come?"

"Hard to say. We'd planned to move quickly, but I would

anticipate the Consort has enacted new security protocols. It will take time to find a way around them. In any event, I can't give up information I don't possess."

"I thought you had people inside."

"We do, but we can't risk exposing them too early."

"Yeah. We wouldn't want them to go out on a limb," I said.

The smooth, familiar edifice of CCM came into view, and Rose's demeanor changed. Her spine straightened; her chin lifted—the exhausted woman I'd seen at the table was suddenly the cool, defiant leader once again. "They'll separate us, of course. Hold us individually, question us and try to match up our stories."

"What should I tell them?"

"Anything you like."

I must have looked startled, because she shrugged. "They'll get it out of you, Del. You haven't been trained to withstand an interrogation. You don't have the clearance to know anything truly damaging."

"I know about Simon."

"Not his location. Not the extent of our plans."

"That's why you said I was a security risk."

"It's the one thing we couldn't let you give away. Every Walker in the Consort will know about Simon soon, but we need the element of surprise." She tucked my hair behind my ear and straightened my collar, the way my mom always did. "Nothing you can tell them will hurt the Free Walkers, Delancey."

Frightened people tend to hyperfocus. They think staring down danger will hold it at bay. But that focus locks them in place, like a deer in the headlights, blind to the wolf sneaking up from behind.

Rose was frightened, no matter how calmly she was marching through the Loop. Intent on protecting the Free Walkers, she didn't consider there were others who needed protection—or she didn't care.

"Addie and Eliot will be in danger," I said. "And the minute they figure out who Simon is, they'll go after Amelia."

Rose shrugged. "Simon is smart enough to move Amelia to safety. As for your sister and the rest . . . you offered them a choice, and they stayed behind. It's regrettable, but the decision was theirs to make."

They were pawns. I'd fled in part to protect the people I loved, to take them out of the battle. My return endangered them all over again. I'd thought this would be a simple solution—painful, but effective. Instead I'd made things exponentially more complicated.

She sighed. "Your best bet is to be as forthcoming and consistent as you can. If Lattimer believes you're telling them everything of your own volition, he may not feel the need to dig deeper. Your biggest asset is that people consistently underestimate you, Delancey. They think you're a reckless, impulsive girl."

"And what do you think?"

"I agree." Her smile was humorless but not unkind. "It makes you dangerous, your willingness to act out of passion and belief. And it makes you powerful. I wish . . ."

"What?"

"I wish we'd had more time," she said softly. "For all that we can play with the fabric of the world, time eludes us. It's like bottling starlight. I would have liked to get to know you, Del. Monty was looking for me, but he was also trying to save you from a life as a Cleaver. He wanted better for you."

Somehow I doubted this was the future he'd hoped for. "What's he going to do now?"

"I've left him the location of the safe house. He'll take Simon there, then wait out the attack in the First Echo."

Rose was kidding herself if she thought he'd sit idly by. But wondering about Monty made me think about Simon asleep in the bed, our future playing out in dreams, waking to find I was only a memory. He must have figured it out by now. He must be frantic and furious and sick. I could envision it, because it was exactly how I had felt when he'd cleaved Train World.

"Del," my grandmother said, bringing me back to the moment, with its muffled pivots and damp concrete and gray skies. CCM stood a few feet away.

I nodded.

"Be brave," she said, and pushed open the door.

I'd expected CCM to be on some sort of lockdown—extra guards, a deserted lobby, tension ratcheted unbearably high. But we walked in, same as I had every week for the last five years. The only sign of a change was the quiet intensity of my class-mates' conversation as they huddled in the corner, waiting for their weekend training to begin.

"Remember," Rose said. "Don't fight."

The problem with abandoning your family for almost twenty years is that when you come back, you don't know them at all. You don't know, for example, that the surest way to get me to do something is to tell me not to do it.

"Rosemont Armstrong for Randolph Lattimer," Rose said, stepping up to the guard desk and laying her hands flat on the counter. "I'm afraid I don't have an appointment."

END OF SECOND MOVEMENT

BEGIN
THIRD
MOVEMENT

CHAPTER FORTY-TWO

THE GUARD GOGGLED AT ROSE FOR A SPLIT SECOND and drew his weapon, the same kind of Taser I'd used on Lattimer.

"Stay right there," he said in a low voice, keeping the gun on us while he reached for the phone. "Do not move. Do *not* move. Hands where I can see them," he said, jerking his chin at me.

I stayed perfectly still.

"Del," hissed Rose. "Hands."

"He told me not to move," I said, my voice ringing out across the tile floors.

In the corner, the buzz of conversation ceased. I swiveled toward my classmates and my fear ebbed slightly.

"Del? Del!" Eliot sprinted across the room, Callie and the others at his heels.

"Stand back!" the guard shouted. A swarm of black-and-white uniforms burst out of the door behind him.

"Why are you—" Eliot cried, as a guard shoved him away. "What are you doing?"

"The right thing." Another guard wrenched my arm behind my back. Pain shot through my shoulder in a white-hot line. I struggled, and he twisted harder.

"Delancey!" Rose snapped. She was kneeling on the floor, hands already zip-tied together behind her back. "Settle down."

The hell I would. I thrashed and kicked and scratched, breaking free for an instant. Running was futile, but I wasn't going quietly. It was time to make myself known.

I met Eliot's eyes, dark brown and anguished, and tried to smile. A crowd was forming, but another set of guards herded them toward the opposite corner, barking orders.

Someone pinned my hands behind my back, forcing me to the ground. My cheek slammed into the floor. I heard the crack of bone on marble, Eliot's shouts, Callie's cry of outrage. The guard shouting at me to be still and Rose begging them not to hurt me. I bit someone's forearm, and then pain shot through me like a sunburst, and I stopped fighting.

A pair of gleaming dress shoes and pinstriped dress pants approached. The wearer crouched, but my muscles wouldn't obey me, so I couldn't turn my head to see who it was.

Someone grabbed me by the hair, lifting me up to inspect my face.

"Delancey," Lattimer said, as warmly as you'd greet an old friend. "Welcome home."

I woke in the same room where I'd met with Monty. At least I assumed it was the same room. Interrogation cells might all look alike, and I'd never seen it from this perspective, stretched out atop the steel table.

If I'd wondered what the metal loops in the side of the table were for, now I knew. Thick leather straps held my hands and feet in place. My coat and shoes were gone, though my clothes remained. I took comfort in that, especially since I'd stolen one of Simon's T-shirts.

I lifted my aching head and looked around, then immediately wished I hadn't. To one side of the table a metal cart with wheels and drawers stood next to the wall, like you'd see at the dentist's office. I couldn't tell what was on the tray, but I was betting it wasn't a bubble-gum flavored fluoride treatment.

Sinking back onto the table, I shut my eyes against the relentless glare. The silence was tangible and expectant. The buzz of the fluorescent light overhead and my fast, shallow breaths only underscored the quiet. I was alone.

Not for long. Someone would come in to interrogate me. To untie me. I'd have to pee eventually, and then it struck me that they might not even let me have a toilet. Humiliation was probably part of the plan.

I tried not to cry. The camera overhead was recording everything, the red light like a winking eye. Lattimer was no doubt watching me, waiting until I was weakest to come in and dig out the answers he wanted.

Rose was wrong. No amount of helpful volunteering on my part was going to protect me, or convince Lattimer to go easy on a reckless, impulsive girl who had stolen his enemy from under his nose, humiliated him in front of his people, and Tasered him for good measure.

But the camera was still observing me, silent and mocking,

so I forced the tears to retreat. I was sure I'd need them later.

They'd taken my watch. I had no idea what time it was. I wondered where Rose was—if they'd tied her down like me, or if she was allowed to sit in a chair, given her age and her quiet defeat. I wondered if she was still alive, and if so, what she was telling them. *I'm rich in secrets.* They'd mine her for information until she was hollowed out.

I pressed my back against the table, trying to feel each individual vertebra. Simon was probably out of his mind with worry. Would he try to find his Original? Slip away from his security detail and approach Addie? He wouldn't be that stupid. The Consort was bound to be watching my family. He might try Amelia, but I was betting his Original had already moved her. Too much risk to let her stay at home. The other Simon might be cold, but Amelia had put cracks in his icy veneer.

Maybe the Free Walkers would rescue us. They'd have to move soon, before Rose spilled their secrets and set them back another twenty years. I wondered if they'd tried to rescue Simon's dad, who hadn't spilled anything.

I'd never even seen a picture of Gil Bradley. He'd set all of this in motion—the swapped children, the First Echo—and I didn't know what he looked like. I could guess: tall, like Simon, with the same rangy build and dark hair, the same sharp features. Simon's eyes and smile were from Amelia, his generous nature and resilience all her. Maybe he'd gotten the stubbornness—the ferocity and drive he displayed in basketball and in our arguments—from Gil.

How much of us was our past? Gil's contribution wasn't

solely genetics even if he'd never met his son. His absence shaped Simon's life as surely as Amelia's presence did. How much of me was Rose, and Monty, and their terrible tragic story? Monty's lunacy, Rose's single-mindedness, my mom's tightly bound grief, Addie's drive for perfection . . . they were all parts of me, indelible and inarguable.

I see our future, Simon had said. My heart wrenched, and hardened. Rose thought this was the only way, but she was wrong. There was always a choice, and if I had to grab the strings of the multiverse and weave them myself, I was going to find a way out of this and back to Simon, and we would make a future as wide open as the sky.

We didn't have to stay with the Free Walkers. Not after the pain they'd put us through. We could go anywhere: find a cure for Amelia, explore the Echoes. Finish school and live a normal life. I might even be nice to Bree. All we had to do was survive.

My hands curled into fists, and I stared straight at the camera overhead. "Don't be boring, Lattimer. You wanted me; I'm here. Let's go."

Then I closed my eyes and waited.

The sound of the lock releasing came more quickly than I expected. I could sense Lattimer drawing closer, stopping at my shoulder. He seemed to absorb sound. I couldn't hear his breathing, or his shoes, or even the rustle of his clothes. He smelled like dry-cleaning fluid, sharply chemical and bitter as old tea.

He was silent for a long time, and I forced myself to take slow, even breaths—not faking sleep or serenity, just making sure I didn't show any cracks he could take advantage of. I kept my face neutral, my eyes closed, and my hands flat on the table. His move, I reminded myself. He knew more than I did, and the trick was to get him to reveal it.

Finally, he spoke. "I believe you have information we would find useful."

I opened my eyes and angled my head toward him. The way he loomed overhead gave me a direct view up his nostrils, and the ridiculousness of the sight—I was about to be tortured by a man in need of a nose-hair trimmer—pierced my fear with a sliver of outrage.

Shrugging is harder than it looks if your wrists are immobilized, but I managed. "Depends on what you mean by useful."

"You know the location of the Free Walkers. You know who they are, what they're planning, and where their weapon is."

"Nothing you couldn't get from Rose, which you're going to do anyway."

"Your grandmother is an old woman. The strain might be more than she can handle. You, on the other hand, have proven quite resilient." Before I could stop myself, I jerked against the restraints. He smiled. "Let's begin. The location of the Free Walkers."

Nothing you can tell them will hurt the Free Walkers. For once, I decided to trust my grandmother.

I hummed the frequency. "That's as close as I can remember. I wasn't there very long."

He pursed his lips. "That's enough to start. Where specifically is the camp located?"

"One of those little towns outside Aurora," I said. "Clover Ridge, maybe, or something like that? An old motel, right off the expressway."

"And you'll simply turn them over? With no hesitation? I'm not sure I believe you."

"I'm not sure I care."

He reached out and ground a thumb into my collarbone. Pain exploded behind my eyes and I screamed.

"You should," he said. "You should care very much."

My breath came in ragged pants. When I could speak, I said, "They packed up and left. The minute you finished the broadcast, Rose gave the order to move out."

"And where did they go?"

"Scattered," I said. "They have some sort of protocol, but they didn't tell me what it was. They split up and meet again according to some sort of prearranged formula, but I wasn't there long enough to find out. I followed Rose and Monty."

"Ah, Montrose. The only person ever to escape an oubliette. We'll get to that in a minute. Where did the three of you go?"

The three of us. Good. He was asking questions, I noticed. Answers trumped tradition, and I hoped it meant he was worried.

"Rose found an empty house for sale on the far South Side. She didn't plan it. The more they improvise, the harder it is for you to get ahead of them."

"What was the street address?"

"I didn't pay attention. Monty's gone, anyway. No way he stayed after he realized we'd come in."

"The street address, Delancey."

"I don't know!" He reached for my collarbone again and I flinched. "It was a bungalow. White shutters, orange brick. I swear, that's all I remember." I'd been paying attention to Simon, not the street signs. Simon, whose shirt I was wearing. Simon, who needed me to be strong.

Lattimer's hand rested on my shoulder, his thumb nestled in the hollow of my throat. "Let's move on. Names, please."

"They didn't wear name tags," I said. "And there wasn't a lot of time for introductions."

Instead of hitting the pressure point in my collarbone again, he wrapped his hand around my windpipe and squeezed.

I flailed, uselessly. With my hands restrained, I couldn't push him away, and no matter how I writhed, he wouldn't release me. The world started to go black around the edges, my lungs screaming but my voice useless.

Tears leaked out the sides of my eyes, and the blackness spread, obscuring everything but his looming face.

Just as the dark overtook my vision, the pressure on my throat eased. Light returned and I gasped, the chilled air filling my lungs and making me cough, my head bouncing on the table as the spasms racked me.

When I stopped shaking, Lattimer repeated, "Names, please."

Give up the names and betray the Free Walkers. Refuse to speak and die. But he had Rose, and he had to know that she was the one with the real information. She'd told me to answer his questions, to give him what he wanted. But he wasn't after names. This was an opening act, to see how I responded. He was after something else. Some deeper, more important information.

The only thing of value that I held was Simon. I'd die if I had to, in order to keep him safe; in order to give the Free Walkers enough time to finish what they'd started.

But I really preferred not to die.

"I only heard one name. Rose's assistant, Prescott—she's about my age, I think."

"Very good, Delancey. I knew you'd be reasonable."

"Rose knows way more than I do." The words bruised my throat, but I had to ask. "Why did you want me?"

"I want to know why the Free Walkers are so interested in you, Delancey. What makes you so special?"

"Nothing," I whispered. I was a means to an end, same as I was to Lattimer. "Addie's better than I am."

"She is," he agreed pleasantly. "But you're the one they wanted. You're the one Montrose groomed. You're the one they rescued from the wilderness like a prodigal."

"They don't care about me. It was Monty they wanted, and I turned him over to you."

"Yes, you did. You hated him. Of anything you've ever told me, Delancey, that's the one thing I believe wholeheartedly."

What heart? I wanted to ask.

"Yet, you risk your life and ruin your future to break him out of an oubliette. Why take that kind of chance for someone you wanted to kill only a few weeks before? And then . . . you turn yourself in."

"To stop the Tacet."

He drew back, eyebrows lifting, and then a smile spread across his face. A genuinely delighted smile, which was somehow more terrifying than any of the smirks he'd aimed at me before.

"Why on earth would you think we would stop the Tacet?"

"You said—" I began, but stopped. I was an idiot. Simon was right. "What will the Walkers think?"

"The Walkers will think I did what was necessary to protect the Key World. Exactly as I'm sworn to."

"Or they'll think you're a liar. And they'd be right."

A muscle in his jaw jumped. "The Free Walkers have a weapon, Delancey. One they've been building for almost twenty years, and it threatens the Key World. I want to know what it is."

I thought of Amelia, wished I'd told her a proper good-bye. "The truth. That's all the weapon they need."

He smoothed my hair back, his fingers moving gently along my forehead. There was nowhere for me to go, no way to draw back from the cold, alien sensation. "I'm afraid you may have broken your cheekbone when the guards took you into custody. There's already quite a lot of bruising."

"Guess it's good I don't have a mirror, then."

"I suppose so," he said. "It's particularly bad . . . here."

He jammed the heel of his hand against my cheek. I screamed as the world went red.

And fell silent as it went away.

. . .

When I woke, I was no longer tied down to the table. I was flat on my back in a cinder-block cell, on a metal shelf meant to be a bed. A toilet in the far corner, a sink next to it. No windows. A single light in a cage, the ceiling too high for me to reach. The air was cool and stale, like it had been recirculated a bunch of times. On the floor beside me were a paper cup of water and a sandwich—peanut butter and jelly, it looked like. I sipped at the water, tiny bits, my stomach cramping with each swallow. Somehow I managed to keep it down, but I shoved the sandwich away.

A pivot hummed directly in front of the wall near my feet, and I made my way over to it. They wouldn't have been so stupid as to leave me an exit, I knew, but it didn't stop me from reaching inside. All I felt was smooth, featureless steel. No strings to part; no escape.

I lay down on the metal bed again, careful not to jostle my cheek or my aching shoulder. When he'd been here, Monty had worn gray scrubs, but I was still wearing Simon's T-shirt and my own tattered jeans. I hated how grateful I was to Lattimer for leaving me that little shred of dignity. I tugged at the neckline, trying to catch the scent of Simon, trying to remember what it felt like to be curled up in his arms, trying to tell myself I could make it back home.

Then, because there was nothing else to do, I slept, pretending the metal shelf beneath me was the bed we'd shared last night.

CHAPTER FORTY-THREE

THE NEXT SESSION WAS WORSE.

I hadn't imagined that was possible, and I'd imagined a *lot*. But I'd been raised to believe in the impossible. I'd lived it; I'd fallen in love with it. I should have known infinity had two sides, like a Möbius strip, and with a single twist life could slide from dream to nightmare.

I'd lost track of time. There was nothing to do in my cell except sleep. My useless Walker pivots transposed before I could do anything; the air quavered, like another reality might be taking shape, and fell still immediately. The threads of this world had been peeled away except for the pivot in the wall, leading back to the interrogation room. I felt for the strings, trying to understand how they'd done it, but the weave was too dense for me to find a way out.

So I slept. Sometimes nightmares came, but sometimes I dreamed of Simon, of our time together, and I woke aching and needy. Sometimes I dreamed of Addie, reading a passage from a textbook, urging me to pay attention. Sometimes I dreamed of my mom, baking cookies and brushing my hair, tsking over how messy I'd let it get, or playing scales for my dad. Sometimes I dreamed of

Eliot. *We're a team,* he would say. *Always have been . . .*

I would try to answer, but every time I woke, gasping for air.

Sometimes it was the sound of the Key World drifting through the pivot that woke me. The pitch in this world was out of tune enough to leave me nauseous and woozy. Sometimes I would curl up on the floor, one hand reaching through the rift to touch the metal door, to reorient myself. The guards would kick me out of the way as they dropped my food—always a cup of water and a not-quite-enough sandwich—peanut butter and jelly, or plain cheese, or unidentifiable lunch meat. Never enough to sate my hunger, but I didn't have much of an appetite.

The guards never spoke. The first few times they came in, I asked questions—when did I get my trial, when did I get out, had my parents been contacted—but they never answered. Lattimer never came through the pivot.

I lost all sense of time, but I'd stacked up the empty cups. Nine of them. Judging from the hollow feeling in my stomach, I didn't think I was getting three meals a day, so it followed that I was on day four or five. Long enough, I hoped, that Simon had made it back to the Free Walkers.

Cup stacking had to be the most useless PE unit ever, but it came in handy now. I sat cross-legged on the floor, building and demolishing towers, my movements as crisp and fast as possible. I played imaginary scales and sonatas on my metal bed, working through Bach and Scarlatti, the way Monty used to. Without strings to manipulate or pivots to walk through, it was the only way to keep myself sane.

The guard came in just as I was starting to build a new tower. He snorted at the sight of me, but I didn't bother to look over. This time he didn't drop off the food. He stood near the pivot, on the edge of my peripheral vision, feet planted and disdain palpable. When I finished, he barked, "Up."

I nested the cups into a single cone and set them below the bed, then clambered to my feet. "What's going on?"

"Councilman wants to see you. Put your hands behind you. Face the wall."

I did as he asked, felt the snap of metal around my wrists and the clink of the chain. Then he took me by the elbow and dragged me through the pivot, where the metal door stood open and a second guard waited on the other side.

There was a chair this time, which seemed like an improvement. They shoved me into the seat and attached my handcuffs to the table, just like Monty. He'd lasted for weeks in here. Of course, he'd already been insane. But he'd lasted, and so could I. I slouched as the guards stepped out.

"How are you feeling?" Lattimer asked when he entered, lavender silk pocket square peeking out from his immaculate suit, coordinating with his tie.

"I want a lawyer."

"We don't have lawyers."

"My mom and dad, then." They might have called the Consort, but I was still their kid.

"Your parents have dedicated their lives to protecting the Key World. You've betrayed them, and our purpose. Your family has washed their hands of you."

I tried not to let my hurt show. Emotion was another tool for him to use against me. He might be lying, I reminded myself. I had no idea what was happening outside this cell, and Lattimer was as impassive as ever. There was nothing I could glean from his appearance.

"Still cleaving?" I taunted. "How many Walkers have you lost since you started the Tacet?"

Annoyance flickered over his features, and a spark of triumph caught in me.

"Feeling spirited today? We'll have to do something about that."

"They're not going to give up, you know. They've been waiting almost twenty years for this. They won't stop because you have Rose."

He crossed over to the cart, perusing the instruments atop it, and then turned to me.

"I'd imagine not. But I hope you're not expecting another dramatic rescue. Now that we're housing such dangerous prisoners, this building is on lockdown. Essential personnel only, increased Enforcement Walkers. No one comes into this building unless they've been approved by a Consort member."

I didn't reply. Rose had been right about the protocols. She'd known it would happen this way.

"It truly is just the two of us," he said, and sat down. "Let's not waste time with the notion that the Free Walkers wield a sword of truth, Delancey. It will only end badly for you. Your grandparents hid something seventeen years ago. Something they believed could defeat the Walkers."

"Not the Walkers," I said. "The Consort."

"They're one and the same."

"If that were true, you wouldn't be worried."

He chuckled, but there was a tightness around his eyes. "I'm not the one who should be worried."

"Because you're going to kill me? Wasn't that always part of the plan? Kill me to spite Monty? Maybe as a way to make Rose talk? You're counting on them to be sentimental, and believe me, they aren't."

He sighed. "I suppose not. But you are. You're a romantic. You fought for a cause you're barely a part of; you turned yourself in to protect worlds you've never even visited. For someone who has been characterized as selfish, I think your recklessness has taken on a martyrlike cast."

"Some causes are worth fighting for," I said, picturing Simon in the half-light.

"And dying for?"

"If I have to."

He tented his fingers, tapped them to his lips. "Would your family feel the same? Do they believe in your cause?"

In the cold room, on an icy metal chair, I began to sweat. Even my insides felt slippery and feverish, and beads of moisture trickled down my spine.

"You said they'd disowned me."

"You care for them. It's a weakness, that kind of devotion. A soft spot, so easy to open up and scoop out." He caught my hand and turned it over, tracing a finger over the veins.

I jerked away. "They don't know anything."

"They don't need to. They matter to you. Your sister," he said. "Poor besotted Eliot Mitchell. Even Shaw seems to think you're worth saving. And the irony is, trying to save you is what will get them killed. I know you'll sacrifice yourself. What about the ones you love?"

"You're asking questions." My voice wavered more than I liked. "Members of the Consort never ask questions."

"We're past formalities," he replied, a gleam in his eyes. "Tell me about the Free Walkers' weapon, Delancey, or tell me who I should send the guards to pick up first. Addison? She's currently at Laurel Pruitt's apartment. They seem very happy together, you know. Tragic, really, to separate them."

"Leave them alone."

"Who, then? Eliot? He's struggled in your absence. I would be putting him out of his misery. Your parents might know more than they've admitted. Or perhaps it should be Shaw. Considering his failure to manage you over the last few years, it would be fitting to select him."

"Stop," I said, my voice low and hoarse.

"Picture your hands on the strings of their lives," he said. "Cut them or save them. The choice is yours."

I couldn't speak. The metal cuffs bit into my wrists, Lattimer smirked, and I opened my mouth, but no words came out.

"Addison it is," he said. "We might as well keep it in the family."

He stood, and the words burst out, desperate and raw. "It's the First Echo!"

I counted ten heartbeats—ten times my heart squeezed and my chill blood rushed and my lungs clamped shut. He lowered himself into the seat.

"The First Echo."

"It's proof. Rose and Monty found the First Echo, years ago." I forced myself not to mention Gil, to bury anything that might lead to Simon.

"The First Echo is lost. It's too old, too far back in the thickets of time to be found again."

"They found it," I let the words flow from me as freely as my tears. "They were going to tell the Walkers about cauterization, and if it didn't work, they'd move to the First Echo and cauterize it."

"Which would prove nothing."

"It would prove the Consorts have been lying. It would prove the Echoes aren't the enemy. It would prove we don't need to cleave to be okay. And we'd be able to start over."

"We are Walkers!" he thundered, ugly color mottling his jowls and neck. "'Okay' is a poor foundation on which to build reality. Okay is a celebration of mediocrity, and we are not mediocre. We are *chosen*."

"We're anomalies," I said. "We're a chromosome that went sideways, and we're no better than Originals. We're just different."

So quickly I barely registered the movement, he yanked on

the chain linking me to the table. I slammed into the metal face-first, pain tearing through me like a lightning strike.

Lattimer lifted me by the hair and spoke, so close I could see the flecks of spittle gathering at the corner of his mouth. "I will not argue philosophy with a child," he snapped. "The frequency of the First Echo, now, or I will use every single one of the tools in that cart. Slowly. On your sister."

"They split it," I gasped. "Rose and Monty. That's why she needed him out of prison. It wasn't love, or sentiment. She needed his frequency before you killed him."

"And now you have it too. Because there's nothing Montrose wouldn't give his best, brightest girl, would he?"

I swallowed down bile and nodded.

I had all three frequencies, thanks to Amelia. But I wasn't ready to give up the third one. Not yet. If Lattimer was desperate, the Free Walkers must be making progress. I closed my eyes, begged Addie to forgive me, and took the second-biggest gamble of my life.

The biggest one came later.

CHAPTER FORTY-FOUR

'D BOUGHT TIME. TIME FOR ADDIE AND ELIOT, time for the Free Walkers, time for Simon and Amelia.

I'd bought it with my future, and payment was coming due. The guard delivered food and a set of faded gray scrubs. Wearing them seemed like giving up, so I put the top on for as long as it took to rinse Simon's shirt in the sink. When I put the T-shirt back on, the material was still damp, no longer smelling of him—but it felt like a connection.

Another sandwich. If I ever got out—unlikely, but I let myself pretend—I would never eat another cheese sandwich again, or drink out of a paper cup. I'd have so many mattresses and blankets and pillows, my room would look like the inside of a genie's bottle.

When the guard came, and there was no paper plate in his hand, I never wanted a cheese sandwich so badly in my life.

Lattimer was already in the interrogation room, seething and toxic. The guard threw me into the chair and locked me down. I thought I saw the barest flash of pity in his eyes, but then he left without looking back. It was me and Lattimer, and the air was thick with hatred.

When he spoke, it was with great and obvious restraint, as if even one word let fly without consideration would be a killing blow.

"We put the frequencies together. Every possible combination of the two, and none of the Echoes they led to were complex enough to be the First Echo."

"Maybe your people aren't that good."

"You lied."

"I gave you the frequencies," I said. "Rose will confirm it."

It struck me Rose might already be dead, but Lattimer said, "She did. She's been unwilling to say more."

"I'm not as dumb as everyone thinks," I said. "Rose encoded it in a song, same as Monty. I found the frequencies in her journals. You must have read them when she disappeared. They were in front of you all along."

"There's a third frequency, isn't there?" Lattimer asked. I willed my expression to stay neutral. "Based on our analysis, a third component would generate a frequency as complex as the First Echo."

"If you say so."

"I do." He ran his tongue over his teeth. "I've directed my people to pick up your sister. I think we'll bring her back here. Let you have one last visit before she realizes what you've done to her."

I straightened. "Leave Addie out of this."

"I'm not the one who involved her. What is the third frequency?"

If the Consort found the First Echo, they'd cleave it, killing everyone inside, Free Walkers included. I couldn't hand it over, couldn't let him think I knew. A half truth then. "It's not in Rose's or Monty's journals," I said. "They don't have it."

"Who does?"

"You're supposed to be smart," I said. "You really don't know?"

He grabbed my wrist and squeezed viciously hard. "Tell me."

My bones ground against each other, my fingertips going numb, and I said the name on a gasp. "Gil Bradley."

The pressure eased. "Gil Bradley's been dead for seventeen years."

"Exactly. They split the frequency before you caught him. Didn't Rose tell you this?"

He let go. "Your grandmother is less than forthcoming. As was Gil. I interrogated him for months and he never said anything about the First Echo. It was always talk of a weapon."

I massaged my wrist. "They believe truth is all the weapon they need."

Maybe it was. But I didn't need a weapon. I needed a shield, and a lie would work better than the truth. Just a little longer, I told myself. Hold off Lattimer; let the Free Walkers make their move. That was the best I could hope for.

He glowered. "Why wait until now?"

Because they'd needed to rebuild. Because Simon's anomaly had made it now or never. "Because you threatened to start another Tacet."

"I've done more than threaten," he said, so confident that he leaned back in his chair to study me. "We cleaved thousands of Echoes. Not minor ones. Major branches, with countless offshoots."

I'd known it, but his casual confirmation made my stomach constrict, bile flooding my mouth. "Why?"

"Because it's the easiest way to keep the Key World stable."

"But it's wrong! Those Echoes are people. You're killing them every time you cleave a world. The Free Walkers know how to give them a life of their own."

"Hardly. Those Echoes are abominations. Soulless creatures, divorced from everything that makes them human. Allowing them to live is condoning blasphemy, and we will not stand for it."

"It's murder."

"It's a cleansing," he snarled.

"It's a lie! You've been training generations of people to commit genocide, telling them it's the only way, that it's a calling. You tell them it's *noble*."

"And it is. We cleave in accordance with our most sacred beliefs."

"I've read the scripture. That's only one interpretation." My mouth tasted sour. "We have the chance to create worlds, not destroy them. Why would you take that from us? What gives you the right?"

He leaned back, secure in his arrogance. "My predecessor. And her predecessor before her. And so on, since the beginning of our people. This is our tradition."

"Traditions can change."

"This one won't."

"The Free Walkers are going to tell everyone," I said.

"Who will listen?" He laughed at my expression. "It's not as if I'm going to repeat this conversation. And you're certainly in no position to do so. The truth will die with you, Delancey."

His suit pocket buzzed. He held up a finger, as if asking me to excuse him, and withdrew his phone. His face altered as he scanned the screen—a slight narrowing of the eyes, a thinning of the mouth. The vein in his temple pulsed.

I didn't know what was on that phone, but I liked it.

"Problem?" I asked sweetly.

"Your sister seems to have disappeared. Hardly a problem."

"Kind of sounds like it," I said. "She's not very good leverage if you can't actually bring her in to . . . lever."

"Where would she have gone?"

"No idea," I said. "She has zero interest in the Free Walkers, and they wouldn't go near her, especially now. If Addie ran, it's because she knows you're coming for her. And if she's smart enough to know you're coming, she's smart enough to know where you'll look."

She'd go where they wouldn't know where to look. Where she might find the one Free Walker in existence who might stick around.

She'd go to Amelia's.

Something must have shifted in my expression, because Lattimer's hand shot out and trapped mine. "Where did she go?"

"I don't know."

"Are you certain? I would feel quite comfortable wagering the opposite."

Slowly, methodically, he bent my index finger back, holding my hand in place. I cried out, but he ignored me and pressed harder.

"Where did she go?"

My shriek rose in step with the pressure, but I didn't answer. Not even when the bone snapped and my throat burned and my tears flowed. I couldn't trust myself to speak, so I screamed until Lattimer released me.

He stood, straightened his tie, and smoothed the lapels of his suit.

"We will find her." He paused, hand on the doorknob of the cell. "I'll have the guard bring you a comb. You should look presentable for the family reunion."

CHAPTER FORTY-FIVE

THE GUARD THREW ME BACK INTO MY CELL—I stumbled toward the bed, banging my shin on the metal edge, cradling my hand.

Already my finger was swollen, throbbing in time with my frantic heartbeat. Like a movie on an infinite loop, the moment of the bone's snapping played over and over in my head—the pressure, the tension, the flash of release, and the pain that followed, so overwhelming I could barely stay conscious.

I curled up on my side, willed the tears away. Better to be mad, I reminded myself. More useful. And holy hell, I hated Lattimer—his callousness, his cruelty, the way he used every single person who crossed his path. Maybe my grandmother was right, and the only way to save the Walkers was to first tear them down.

I summoned up every curse word I'd ever heard and some I invented on the spot. My finger was fat as a sausage, bent at an unnatural angle. We didn't get much first-aid training—that's why we had medics—but I remembered enough to know that if the bone wasn't set soon, it would heal crookedly, and I'd lose the full range of motion. Nimble fingers, open mind . . . I needed both. I'd have to set the bone.

And that's when I knew I hadn't given up. Lattimer's threats hadn't left me desolate as ashes; they had fueled my anger and my hope. Addie had run. Addie had known something was wrong, and she'd run. Lattimer had locked down the building because he was afraid. He'd thrown me in prison, but I'd broken out once. I would find a way to do it again.

After I fixed my hand.

There was nothing in my room except a stack of cups and paper plates—the cheap kind, uncoated paper kids use in craft projects. They bent under the weight of a sandwich. I'd even tried to fold some origami with them, but the paper was too thick and stiff after just a few creases.

Stiff.

Like a splint. My left hand was useless, but I braced the plate with my knee and folded it into a long, narrow rectangle, double the length of my finger. Folded over, it would act like a protective sleeve. Now for a way to hold it shut.

There was no string in the room. Not even my shoelaces, or a drawstring on the uniform I'd been issued. It was some unholy polyester, scratchy and unpleasant to touch. I tried ripping the fabric apart, but it was indestructible. If the multiverse ever fell, these clothes would be the last item to unravel.

Simon's T-shirt, on the other hand, was a soft cotton knit, so old it had worn through in spots. I hated to take it off, to lose that one last connection to him, but I pictured him looking at me, mystified. "It's a shirt, Del. Get over it."

I used my teeth to tear the fabric into strips, and began the process of setting the bone, bracing it with the paper splint, and immobilizing it with the T-shirt ties.

When I was done, I was covered in sweat. Dots of pain danced in my vision like confetti from a smashed-open piñata, but my finger was straight, tightly bound, and, I hoped, healing.

I began to plan. The next time Lattimer pulled me out might be the last. It might be Addie's last. And I wasn't going to let that happen.

The guard did bring me a comb, as promised. His eyes flicked to my homemade splint, but he left without another word. With nothing else to do, I began working on my hair, tugging out the knots as gently as I could. After everything else, it seemed silly that something as simple as a snarl would make me hiss, but it was how pain worked. You don't reach a threshold and stop feeling it. You reach a threshold and you feel everything, seventeen times more intense than before. Same as love.

Time passed. The guard delivered another sandwich. My finger continued to throb, dull unless I moved it. I dozed and kept the image of Simon's face fixed firmly in my mind.

I needed to slow Lattimer down. Give the Free Walkers time to take down CCM; give Addie more time to run. But I'd played every card in my hand; there was nothing left to bluff with.

Rose would tell me to protect the Free Walkers. Think about the greater good. Think of Addie as collateral damage, regrettable but necessary. I didn't doubt the Free Walkers, Prescott especially, would look at me the same way.

But I also knew what Addie would say, if the positions were reversed. For all her love of rules, her belief in protecting the Key World . . . she wouldn't abandon me. Family won out for Addie, in the end. Love won out. If our places were reversed, Addie would stand for me, and let the Free Walkers fend for themselves.

The rift in the wall pulsed. The guard was coming back, which could only mean they'd found Addie. The time for planning was over.

Two choices. If I were an Original, the pivot would sound as crisp and bold as a coronet. I could protect my sister, or I could protect Simon, but not both.

Find another way around.

Unless I was the target.

By the time the guard had crossed the pivot, I'd made my choice.

I shrank back on the bed as the guard reached for me. "You know the drill. Up."

I scuttled away, wedging my back against the corner, careful not to put weight on my injured hand, drawing my knees to my chest. He hitched up his belt, considering me, and then leaned in. I kicked out with both feet, catching him in the belly and sending him stumbling backward.

I scrambled up, but he recovered, grabbing for my ankle and yanking me off the bed. My head slammed against the edge and my tailbone hit the floor, so hard my teeth rattled. I blinked to clear my vision, and he hauled me up again, pinning one arm behind my back. I shrieked and kicked at the side of his knee—it hurt to do it without shoes, but he went down with a shout, so it must have hurt him more. I kicked him in the stomach, and then in the nuts, satisfaction pumping me full of adrenaline. He caught my foot and pulled, sending me reeling.

I fell on top of him, driving my elbow into his gut. His next punch grazed my arm. I drew back my fist, but his punch caught me square in the chest.

The air left my body in a rush, and I collapsed, facedown on the cement floor.

Grunting, he yanked my arms behind my back and slapped on cuffs, then hauled me upright. I dug in my heels, but it was pointless. He dragged me to the pivot, and I squeezed my eyes shut.

The air shivered. The floor under my bare feet changed from rough cement to cold, smooth tile. The guard's meaty hand squeezed the back of my neck, forcing me farther into the interrogation room.

I heard a pop and a hum, and his grip relaxed. An instant later, I heard the sound of a body hitting the floor.

"Once," said someone, more irritated than angry, "just *once* it would be nice if you did what you were told."

I opened my eyes. The guard standing before me, Taser in hand, had coal-black hair, a familiar, exasperated scowl, and green eyes filled with tears.

"Addie?"

"Obviously," she said, moving swiftly to unlock my handcuffs. "Can you walk?"

"I think so. I . . . don't . . ." I stared at her, at the bad dye job and the stolen uniform and the flat, determined line of her mouth. "How?"

The door swung open, and a second familiar head poked in.

"Hurry up," said Simon.

Despite the pain, despite the woozy feeling in my head and the spinning, swooping room, I was across the cell before I'd drawn my next breath. "Which one?" I demanded.

He kissed me in answer, brief and hard, anger mixed with relief.

"Make out later," Addie ordered, pushing me into the corridor "Which cell is Rose's?"

"I don't know." But as I oriented myself, my gaze fell on the cell that led to Monty's room. Lattimer would take pleasure in the symmetry. "That one. She's on the other side of a pivot, though."

"Then go get her. We'll stand guard."

"But . . ."

"Del, you're not in any condition to fight, and we don't have time to argue. Go get Rose."

I threw open the door to the cell—empty, as expected—and dashed toward the pivot. I couldn't feel my injuries anymore. Everything had moved into a dazed, distant, unreal place.

Rose stood as I came in, mouth open. A bruise bloomed along her jawline, and the thin skin of her arms was mottled with welts and black marks. One hand was wrapped in a dirty, sagging bandage. Her eyes were red rimmed, her back stooped, and she took a single, shuffling step closer to me.

"Addie," I said. "And Simon."

She nodded once and slipped an arm around my waist. I did the same, and we headed out.

"Come on, come on, come on," Simon shouted, waving us into the hallway. We dashed toward the elevator, where Addie was doing something to the elevator controls. The second guard—the one Simon had handled, I assumed—was unconscious and cuffed to a nearby door handle.

"Addison," Rose said, and Addie's head came up.

For a moment, Addie froze. "Grandma?"

"You have your mother's eyes."

She nodded once, sharply, filing away whatever emotion was making her hands shake. "I can't *believe* Monty was right" was her only response before she bent over the control panel again.

I leaned against Simon. "How did you guys—"

"Later," he said shortly. "Can you run?"

I nodded, and he touched my uninjured cheek. "Del—"

"I thought I was going to die," I said. "Lattimer told me the truth. He said it didn't matter, because I was going to die."

"He was wrong." Simon took my hand.

"We're not out yet," Addie warned.

"But he thought I was going to." I laughed—the kind that sounded hysterical, even to my ears. "It was my interrogation, but he confessed."

"We'll make him pay," Simon promised. "But we have to go now."

"He admitted to everything—the cleavings, the Echoes, lying to the Walkers. It's on tape."

Rose's head snapped up. "Where?"

"Here." I shoved open the control-room door.

"Del, we don't have time," Simon said, but he and Rose followed me inside.

The room was filled with computers, each screen displaying an empty interrogation cell.

"That . . . is a lot of laptops," Simon muttered. "Which feed is yours?"

"That one," I said, pointing to a screen near the end of the row. The feed showed an overturned chair and blood smeared across the floor like crushed petals. "That's where—" My throat closed.

"How do we get the file?" he asked.

I slapped the cover closed and yanked, the power cord falling away with a pop. "Like that."

"Guys!" Addie shouted from the hallway. "Move!"

The elevator doors stood directly across from the control room. Addie was hauling on one of the doors, trying to keep it open, frantically pressing buttons at the same time.

"They're trying to override the system," she said. "If the doors close, they can bring it up to the ground floor express; we'll never get out."

Simon braced himself between the doors, blocking them. "Does that help?"

"I think so." She ran an ID card through the reader.

"You did have a plan, didn't you?" Rose asked.

"I always have a plan," Addie said coldly, and popped open

the control panel. "But it didn't involve Del attacking a guard. I had to move up the timetable before they called in reinforcements."

"Sorry," I muttered. "It's not like I knew you were coming."

Addie shrugged and went back to messing with the elevator controls. I asked, "Can we pivot out, like with Monty?"

"They're expecting it. They've cleaving any Echo generated from this building right now."

"We need to get to the parking garage," Simon said, his voice strained from the effort of keeping the doors open.

"Let the elevator go," Rose said.

"We'll be trapped down here," Addie said.

Rose waved a hand impatiently. "Elevator shafts have ladders. Once they've taken control of the elevator, they'll raise it up to the main level. We'll follow behind and climb up to the parking garage. They'll watch to make sure you don't sneak out the roof again—but they won't be able to see underneath the car, which is where we'll be."

"Which means we have to get out to the parking garage before they bring the elevator back down, or we're pancakes," Simon warned.

"Can you climb?" Addie asked me.

"Yeah. Rose?"

"Of course. We'll need a distraction. Something to keep the Consort occupied while we slip out."

"Already on it," Addie said, and checked her watch. "Eliot hacked into the fire alarm system. In about three minutes, the alarm will sound for every floor in this building, and the fire department will pay a visit."

"Nice," I said.

"So we're doing this," Addie said, voice shaking. "Sending the elevator without us. If it doesn't work . . ."

"It will work," Simon said firmly, and took my uninjured hand. "Ready?"

"Ready."

Simon stepped out of the elevator and Addie pulled her key card away. Instantly the doors slid shut, and we heard the car begin its ascent. Addie and Simon pried the doors open.

There was a small drop to the bottom of the elevator shaft. Simon took my hand and swung me down, careful of my injuries.

"Rose?" He helped her down, then jumped next to us, Addie right behind.

"We need to go first," Addie said, looking at me apologetically. "We'll have to pry the door open at the parking garage."

"Stop talking and climb," Rose said.

"Are you sure you're okay?" Simon asked, but we were already starting up the ladder, so I gritted my teeth and nodded.

"How many sublevels?" asked Rose.

"Three," Addie called, already past the first door. Simon was close on her heels, but Rose and I lagged behind. The climb was harder than I expected, especially carrying the laptop.

Above us, the elevator stopped moving, and the car rocked as people stormed into it. Their shouts echoed faintly down the cement shaft.

"Climb faster," Addie shouted.

I didn't say anything—just hung on to the laptop with my bad hand and the ladder with my good one.

I heard the doors slide shut.

"They're coming back!" Simon called.

There was no niche for us to plaster ourselves into. We'd be crushed or we'd be captured, but there was no way out.

And then Rose jumped.

She landed on the floor of the shaft with a sound that made my knees turn to jelly. "Simon, throw me that stun gun."

Startled by the command, he unhooked the Taser from his belt and let it fall. Rose snatched it midtumble. "Keep climbing, Delancey."

"But—"

"If I overload the system, it'll freeze the elevator in place."

She brandished the Taser with her good hand and clambered out of sight, into the hallway.

"Move it," Simon ordered. "She'll catch up, Del."

But I couldn't. I was frozen, my arms unwilling to haul myself any farther, especially as the elevator began to slide toward us.

There was a buzz and a loud crackle, and the stench of an electrical fire drifted up. Above us, the car jerked to a halt.

"That should do it," Rose called, poking her head back in. "Let's—"

There was a horrible crack, the sound of metal connecting with flesh. Rose cried out, then fell backward into the elevator shaft.

"Grandma!" I scrambled back down the ladder, and the guard I'd first hit—mouth bloody, eye swollen—ducked his head inside.

I didn't think. I scooped up the Taser lying next to Rose's hand and fired. The charge hit him squarely in the chest, and he fell back into the hallway with a groan.

Above me, Addie was shouting something, but I couldn't make out the words over the shrieking in my skull. I scurried over to Rose, lying unmoving on the ground, her neck bent at a strange angle.

"Come on," I crouched next to her, took her hand. "Grandma, get up. We'll help you climb."

Simon landed next to me.

"We can carry her, right?"

"Del—"

"A fireman's carry. That's what they call it. You're strong enough." There was blood trickling from her nose and ears, and I reached to wipe it away. Her eyes—that familiar hazel color—were still open.

"I'm sorry." He wrapped his arms around me and lifted me to my feet. "We need to go now."

"Del," Addie cried, her voice strangely thick. "Listen to him!"

"We'll get her to a doctor," I said, struggling to get free.

He let go of me long enough to bend and close her eyes. "She's gone."

"But I just found her!" All those years, all this work,

everything she'd fought for. It was incomprehensible that she wouldn't live to see it through.

The fire alarm went off, filling the entire building with a bone-jarring buzz. Over it, Addie shouted, "Hurry!"

"We can't leave her," I pleaded to Simon. "Lattimer—"

"Is going to catch us if we stay." He dragged me to the ladder.

Numbly I followed him up the rungs. Addie had braced herself in the doorframe, screeching in frustration as she tried to pry the doors open, wisps of coal-black hair sticking to her wet cheeks.

I peered down at Rose's crooked, unmoving body. She looked so small. I could feel myself starting to crumple, the shock that had kept me upright disintegrating as the grief rolled in.

Simon growled as he hauled on the doors. They cracked open—no more than a half inch, but enough for Addie to dig her fingers in and help. Together they pried the doors apart. Simon held out his hand for me, and I made the leap to the parking garage, cavernous and dim, the fire alarm still blaring. A battered minivan pulled up with a squeal. Monty and Original Simon threw open the side door and jumped out.

"You got them?" Eliot shouted from the driver's seat.

Simon scooped me up in his arms and headed for the side door, his Original lurching away to avoid contact. "She's hurt."

"Where's Rose?" Monty asked. He peered around impatiently.

Addie took a step toward him, choking out a sob. "Grandpa . . ."

Sometimes horrible things aren't real until they're spoken. It's easier to tuck them away and hope their awfulness withers away, that they lose their power.

But sometimes tucking away the worst allows it to fester instead of fade. Sometimes the only way to defeat something horrible is to drag it into a cold and merciless light, so you can know what you're fighting, and know when it's done.

Simon set me on the middle row's seat, but I nudged him aside and leaned forward. "Rose is dead."

Monty rounded on me, eyes wide with disbelief. "No."

The words burned in my throat. "She went back to disrupt the elevator controls and a guard hit her. Hard."

"She fell," Addie said, coming to stand next to Monty. I couldn't hear her words over the fire alarm, but Monty's face seemed to sag and collapse, a candle that's burned for too long.

"No!" he shouted. "It's a trick, like before."

Wringing his hands together, gripping his head as if he thought it was going to burst. He shuffled toward the elevator doors and stopped again, lost.

Addie took his arm, squaring her own shoulders, smoothing back her inky hair, the familiar gesture surreal amid the chaos. "We'll talk about it when we're safe."

"We should be gone already," Eliot said. "Everybody in."

My injuries were blurring into a single enormous hurt, blocking entire swaths of the world—bits of conversation filtering in past the blaring of the fire alarm, flashes of what was happening around me appearing between blinks. My eyelids felt heavy, and

I let them close, focusing on breathing despite the stabbing pain it sent through me.

When people say the world can change in the blink of an eye, they usually mean longer than an actual blink.

Walkers know better.

I should have known better.

I blinked.

CHAPTER FORTY-SIX

T HE FIRE ALARM CUT OFF. THE SILENCE WAS SO sudden, so abrupt, it seemed to crash around us. My eyes flew open.

Lattimer stepped out from behind a car, gun in hand—not the weirdly futuristic lines of a Taser, but an actual gun, heavy-looking, with an oily black sheen.

"I suppose congratulations are in order," he said. "Breaking out of the oubliettes once was a notable accomplishment. Twice is truly impressive."

I watched through the side window as he motioned to Addie, Monty, and Original Simon to step closer, away from the van.

"Where is Rosemont?"

No one answered. "I see. Pity, really. I had such plans."

Monty jerked.

"Keep your head down," Eliot hissed at me.

"I need to see!"

"You need to hide. We're here to get you out, Del. That's the only objective." He slipped down farther in the driver's seat, contorting his lanky body to stay out of view.

"He's right," Simon said from the back of the van. "Eliot, if this gets bad, floor it."

"It's already bad," Eliot muttered.

I craned my neck, trying to for a better view.

"The fire department is on the scene, but they'll clear the building shortly." Lattimer's voice reverberated through the cavernous space. "Once they depart, the guards will escort all of you back into the oubliettes. In the meantime, we'll stay here." He cocked his head at Original Simon. "You look familiar."

"Never met you in my life," Original Simon replied.

Next to him, Addie looked at the van and cut her eyes toward the exit ramp.

Eliot nodded and put his hand on the ignition.

"Throw the keys over here, Eliot," Lattimer called. "Unless you'd like the body count of your mission to increase substantially. I'm assuming the fire alarm was your work? We could have put your talents to greater use, young man."

"I doubt it," he muttered.

"Do it," I whispered, but Eliot's hand stayed put.

"The keys." Lattimer's eyebrows lifted. "I dislike repeating myself."

"We can't leave them," I pleaded, and Eliot looked back at me. "Please. Do what he says."

"Not a chance," he said. "I came for you."

Lattimer leveled the gun at Addie.

I stumbled out of the van, leaving the laptop behind. "Don't shoot her!"

"Delancey," Lattimer said cheerfully. "You look a little worse for wear. It would have been so easy to avoid all this mess and inconvenience."

"I'm here now," I said, and limped in front of Addie.

"You are a moron," she snapped. "I didn't risk my life so you could turn yourself in. Again."

I shoved her with my good hand. "I didn't turn myself in so you could get killed. Dumbass."

"Such a disappointment you two are," Lattimer said, and gestured to Monty with the gun. "Blood will tell, I suppose. And speaking of blood . . ." He turned to Simon. "Gilman Bradley. Your father?"

Original Simon shrugged. "That's what I'm told."

"The resemblance is remarkable. Seeing all of you together is like a window to the past. You look like your grandmother, Delancey. And you have approximately the same success rate. Come here."

"Don't take a step," Monty said, fingers twitching. "Don't do anything he says."

I glanced over. His usual, conniving gleam had turned almost feral, but I obeyed.

The air shifted. One of Original Simon's knife-sharp pivots formed, as if he'd made a deliberate decision.

"You did that?" Lattimer demanded, looking startled for the first time.

Simon shrugged.

"Gil truly was a rule breaker, wasn't he? I knew the Free Walkers had recruited some Originals, but creating a half-breed?"

"I prefer hybrid," Simon said coolly. "Best of both worlds. Best of all the worlds, actually."

I forced myself not to look at the van, willing my Simon to stay out of sight.

"You can't hear it, can you?" Lattimer said. "Can't move through it."

"Where do you think I've been for the last seventeen years?" Simon said. "With the Free Walkers. Moving through Echoes, undermining you."

"The first escape," Lattimer said. "That's how you sustained a pivot inside the building. And then Delancey helped you cross. Fascinating."

"Hybrids aren't news to you," Monty said. "You've taken them before."

Lattimer barely gave Monty a glance. "Certainly. We analyze their genome, determine if they're useful, find a place for them."

"And if they're not?" I asked, rage crackling inside me.

"The point of evolution is to eliminate the weaker beings."

"You're the weak one," I said. Out of the corner of my eye, I saw Monty edge closer to Lattimer, a few inches at a time. "Simon's evolving. Don't you see? He's the solution. He can make Echoes. He can move through pivots, handle the threads, help us keep up with the multiverse. And his Echoes can too."

"Not if he's dead," Lattimer said. "Your father never once mentioned you. Odd, don't you think?"

"Don't know," Simon said. "I never met the guy."

"I'd say you were unimportant, but if that were true, I'm

not sure he would have kept you secret. You must have mattered quite a bit, if he was so desperate to keep me from finding you."

"Well, now you have." Simon lifted his chin. "Congratulations."

"Indeed. All this time, we've been hunting a weapon. And now the hunt is concluded."

I felt the wrongness of the moment before it occurred, the rest before a movement, the drop in pressure before a storm.

Lattimer raised the gun and fired, the sound ricocheting off the walls. Addie screamed as Simon staggered back, clutching his stomach.

"No!" I raced for him, but he was already sliding to the ground, teeth clenched, breath too fast. "Simon, hold on!"

I knelt on the concrete, frantic. Not another death, not another death, not another sacrifice, it was too much, it wasn't fair, it was *wrong*. I pulled away the layers of his coat to find the gray T-shirt underneath dark and sticky, the blood spreading into a single, horrible stain. My hands came away red and wet.

"Some weapon," Lattimer said. "Now—"

"Enough!" roared Monty. The rage made him unrecognizable. In the dank air of the garage he seemed to grow stronger and broader, closing the gap between him and Lattimer before any of us could react. I braced myself for Lattimer to fire, but he merely pointed the barrel at Monty, almost nonchalant. Monty halted inches away, barely moving, eyes narrowed and arms hanging stiffly at his side.

Lattimer snorted. "This is only the beginning, Montrose.

Whatever you thought your weapon could do, he won't be doing it. Whatever revolution you thought Rose was going to lead died with her."

Monty closed his eyes, singing to himself, but I tore my gaze away to focus on Simon, pale and sweating and trembling on the ground. "It'll be okay. I'll call nine-one-one. We'll get you to the hospital."

He shook his head. "Sorry about Rose."

I shushed him. "Try not to move."

"Look at them, Montrose," Lattimer said. "The lives you've ruined. Your granddaughters. Your wife. The child of your dear friend. Every one dead or destroyed because of you."

"Not me," Monty said finally. He opened his eyes, but his tone was oddly distant, as if he was only half-paying attention. "All I did was love. Loved Rose, loved Del. Recognized the way Gil loved his boy, because it's as much as I loved my Winnie. You wouldn't know anything about it, because all you've ever loved is power, and the more you got, the greater you hungered. You destroyed entire worlds, Randolph, because it made you feel powerful. It wasn't enough to touch the multiverse and listen; you had to control the strings."

"And I do."

"You forgot something," Monty said. "Or maybe you never learned it."

"What's that?" Lattimer smiled, indulging him.

"We're stewards, not gods. We don't control the strings. They control us." And with that, Monty's hands curled and spasmed.

398

Some kind of attack, I thought, until Lattimer fell to his knees, gasping.

"Turns out the boy *is* a weapon, Randolph. If it weren't for his Echoes, I never would have figured it out."

"Figured *what* out?" Addie asked.

"Grandpa?" I said.

"You can cleave a single life as easily as you can a world," Monty said. "All you have to do is find the right string, and—"

"Montrose—" Lattimer wheezed, his own hands scrabbling helplessly in the air.

Monty twisted his wrist sharply. "—snap."

Lattimer fell, face-first, into the concrete. He didn't move again.

"Grandpa!" Addie said. "What did you do?"

"What needed to be done," he said grimly. "How is he, Del?"

Blood pooled thickly around Original Simon and me. "We need a doctor. Addie, help me get him up."

I slipped my good arm around his shoulder, but his face contorted and he slumped back.

"Hurts more'n I thought," he panted.

"They'll fix it," I said. "Just hang on."

"Can't fix this." He lifted a hand, shaking and ice cold, and touched my cheek.

I covered his fingers with my own, willing warmth into him. Willing life into him, even as the blood leaked everywhere. "It'll be okay."

"Del." The words were soft now, slurred. I bent close, tears dripping, trying to hear him. "Rose . . . warned me."

"Warned you about what?"

"If they didn't believe . . . this was the only way."

"But—"

"I didn't mind. Not until I came here. Saw you. Saw my mom." His lips brushed my cheek.

"I don't understand! Simon, please. *Please*."

"No time," he said, each word painful, each word an effort. "For either of us. Cauterize me."

"What?"

From the van there was a thud and a moan. "Del!" Eliot shouted. "We have a problem!"

"You're not going to die," I said, wishing I believed it. Wishing that words could make it true. *If wishes were horses . . .* "We're going to fix you."

"He's the proof," Simon wheezed. "An Echo without an Original. But you have to cauterize me first."

"And then you'll be okay?"

His laugh turned into a cough. "Not a chance. But they need him. It was always him."

"And you . . ."

"Wished it was me. For all sorts of reasons." He tangled his fingers in my hair. "Do it now, Del."

Addie put her hand on my shoulder, and I looked up at her through my tears. "He's unraveling. Your Simon. Go."

I touched my lips to his forehead. "Don't die." I ordered.

"I'll stay with him," Addie said. "Hurry."

I scrambled up and stumbled around the van. Simon was

sprawled on the middle row's bench seat, too tall and brawny for such a small space. I reached for him, then stopped.

"I don't hear anything."

"There's a signal," Eliot said, phone out, zooming in on Simon. "But it's super faint."

"Hey, you," Simon said weakly. "Hell of a day."

"Hell of a day," I agreed, climbing inside. "How do you feel?"

"Not awesome," he admitted. "Everything goes in and out, you know? Bad reception."

His face was as gray as his Original's, his eyes glassy and focused on something distant.

"It shouldn't be happening this fast," I said to Eliot.

He looked so sorry for me. "It's because their signals are the same. Both of them are tied to this world; they're in close proximity. It increases the rate of unraveling."

I leaned over and kissed Simon gently, despite the silence. Felt the beating of his heart against my hand, the rhythm of my own pulse, as if we'd synchronized long ago.

"Simon, listen to me. If I cauterize your Original, it should stabilize you."

He gave me a thumbs-up.

"But I haven't done it before. None of us have. It's a huge risk."

The corner of his mouth quirked. "You love risk."

"I love *you*."

"Then who better to take a chance on?" He laced his fingers with mine. "You already got my heart. Might as well put the rest in your hands too."

"But if I can't . . ."

"Then you can't. I'd rather you try than give up. Don't you ever give up on us."

You play until you hear the buzzer, he'd told me once.

I pressed my mouth against his, giving and receiving strength in equal measure.

"Bring him out of the van," Monty called. "They need to be close but not touching."

"Will it hurt his Echoes?" Eliot asked when we had Simon settled on the cement floor, his sweatshirt cushioning his head. "The cauterization?"

I looked over at Original Simon. His eyes were closed, his breathing barely visible. Addie was keeping pressure on the bleeding, but her shoulders shook with sobs.

"His Echoes will die if you don't," Monty said. "These two, their strings are tangled together. If you can cauterize the Original and weave the strings of your Simon with this world, his Echoes should survive."

Addie glanced up, cheeks wet and eyes red rimmed. Original Simon had gone silent.

I knelt beside him, pressed a kiss to his forehead. "I'm so sorry."

"Sentimental," he mouthed, with the faintest hint of a smile.

I ran my hands lightly over his shoulders, slid my fingers through the air until I made contact with the strings. "How do I do it?" I asked. "How do I tell which ones are his? They all sound the same."

With a grunt, Monty lowered himself next to me. "Some will lead directly to him."

"Which part? His head? His hand?"

"The whole of him," Monty said. "I can't explain it any better than that, Delancey. We're all part of the multiverse. It's woven into the warp and weft of who we are, and binds us together. All one, all distinct. You have to find the connection."

"The connection," I murmured, and shut my eyes, blocking out the garage and everyone in it, keeping perfectly still, letting the vibration of the threads fill me up. The Key World sang its clear, crystalline song, so familiar I often ignored it. This time I listened so closely that I could almost see the strings, resonating in tune against a field of black velvet, each with its own texture and voice. This was the only place entropy hadn't triumphed, this perfect arrangement of notes, strong and vital. But one of the strings was going silent, and I searched for it, for a sound that dropped away, an unexpected rest in the symphony.

I searched for Simon. All the Simons, through all the worlds, and it gave me a sensation of falling asleep, sinking deeply into something vast and billowing, the world expanding with every second, spinning out like the arms of a galaxy, tiny and infinite at once, and the order of the Key World gave way to the multiverse, entropy crashing around me, and still I searched for Simon.

For his silence.

I caught the string, its stillness against my finger so wrong in the middle of all the noise, and traced a finger along it. The line was slackening, and I knew what it meant. I listened to the faintness of the signal, my heart bleeding with every faltering beat.

"I've got it," I said. "Now what?"

"There are more," Monty said. His hand pressed heavily into my shoulder. "They'll be nearby. Gather them up, gently."

A life should come down to more than a few memories. A few acts. A handful of strings clutched like a child's balloon. A life should be summed up by its connections, by the way it alters the world around it, the daily choices that accrue and give it meaning, that shape the world in ways you never imagine but couldn't exist without. A life should be about the people it has touched, an infinite, ever-widening circle that expands even as its song stops. A life isn't contained in words or moments, but in the traces it leaves throughout the world.

I held Simon's life, and the lives of his Echoes, and I listened as hard as I could, so I could carry it with me, so I could make it a part of my own song.

"You have to cut the threads," Monty said, pressing a divisi into my hand. "Hold them fast, and make the cut on the side closest to the Original. I'll help you finish them properly."

"Do you promise?" Strange, in this moment, that I would trust Monty over everyone. But who better to guide me than the person who best knew this pain?

"I promise you, Delancey."

I opened my eyes, to see Original Simon's face one more time, to tell him, once more, that I was sorry. To thank him for the life he had lived, and for the life he'd given to my Simon. But it was too late. His face was gray, his eyes shut, his chest still.

404

"Now!" Monty said, and the force in his voice propelled my knife hand upward.

A turn of the wrist, jerky and rushed, and the strings fell free, brushing against my arm.

Before me, Simon exhaled, soft and slow, slow, slow, and was gone.

The sob choked me, and I struggled for air, dropping the knife.

"Pay attention," Monty said sharply. "You have to weave the strings. Once you start, they'll grow and cleave together, but you have to give them shape, then knot the ends."

I shifted, angling myself toward my Simon, clutching the remaining threads tightly.

"Let me help," Addie said, and her hands brushed mine. Carefully she separated a cluster of strings, roughly half of them, wrapping her elegant, shaking fingers around them. "I've got them, Del. Let go."

I shook my head. If we failed, Simon would vanish. All the Simons, everywhere, would fade away to nothing. He'd exist only in my heart, and in terminal Echoes, like clocks winding down. Every death would be my fault. I would kill the boy I loved, a million times over.

I tried to imagine the Echo forming from this moment. Too weak to sustain, of course, but if there was . . . my Simon was dying and I wasn't there for him. None of us were. The longer I waited to act, the longer his time there was drawn out, solitary and in flux. He was waiting for me. Every Simon in the multiverse was waiting for me, whether they knew it or not.

I looked over at him, lying on the ground. His lips were moving, silently, but I knew what they were saying. Could hear his voice in my head, even now. *Don't you ever give up on us.*

Weaving is a question of layers, of overlapping strings in a way that will make something three-dimensional out of two. Like playing counterpoint.

Like falling in love.

I met Addie's eyes. "Ready?"

"Ready."

In the background I heard Monty, singing. "Nimble fingers, open mind, hum a tune both deft and kind."

My fingers didn't feel nimble—they felt cold and clumsy, sticky with blood. I had to work without my broken finger, and the muscles in my hand cramped as I tried to compensate. Addie matched her rhythm to mine, moving the threads over and under as necessary, keeping the tension even, knotting the ends to keep them from ever unraveling again. We hummed in the Key World frequency, infusing the fabric with its strong, steady tone.

As we worked, I envisioned my love for Simon as a tangible presence, a silver-bright filament mingled with the others, strengthening the threads, reinforcement against entropy. I was his, and he was mine, and I wasn't going to let anything—the Consort or the multiverse or entropy itself—part us again.

And then I felt a string—a wisp, really, twined with another one, its song faint as memory, different from the silence that had fallen around us, a contrast to the Key World pitch.

Simon's home world. This was his anomaly, the difference that had destabilized the multiverse, that had caused him to fall in love with me the first time.

Hum a tune both deft and kind.

I could tune him. If we could cleave a person, cauterize them, certainly we could tune them. Take a single strand of their being and transform it. Would it change him? If I could tune it now, as we were reweaving his connection to the multiverse, the tuning would stay. He'd be safe, permanently, and so would the multiverse. But what if it changed some essential part of him? Would it change how he felt about me? Did I have the right? Did I have the courage?

"Almost there," Addie said. "You with me?"

"Yeah." I stroked a single finger along the errant thread, smoothing and singing it into submission. The one choice only I could make for him, and I did, even if it meant he forgot me, or no longer wanted me.

"Tie the strings off," Monty instructed. He sounded weary, like he'd been right in there with us, working and weaving and holding his breath. But maybe he was just worn down from the loss, from years of seeking Rose, only to find her and lose her again within days. "If it's worked, that will be enough."

Carefully we knotted the last of the ends together, making a seam in the fabric of the world, a thin raised line like a scar.

It's a myth that scar tissue is the strongest in the human body. But right now, when I was made entirely of wounds, scars were the best I could hope for—healing no matter how imperfect. I wanted scars that would knit together the loss and the grief and the triumph into something strong and flexible, into the person who was worth the sacrifices that had been made.

I turned to my Simon, lying on the ground. I took his hand in mine, held his palm against my cheek. "Can you hear me?"

His arm was heavy, his eyes closed. His chest rose and fell, so slowly that my own lungs seized up.

He blinked. His lips moved, silently at first, and then he said, "You were singing."

I nodded, too overwhelmed to speak.

"You were singing inside me." The corner of his mouth lifted. "You've got a good voice. Way better than mine."

"That's not saying much," I replied, clinging to the teasing like a lifeline, like it was the only thing that could pull me out of the tidal wave of emotion. "You're okay."

"Better than okay." He sat up, shaking his head gingerly. I touched my mouth to his, savoring the feel of him. The strong, steady sound of the Key World surrounded us as he kissed me back. "I knew you'd do it. Knew you'd be amazing."

"How?" I helped him to his feet.

"Because everything about you is amazing, Delancey Sullivan."

"I was amazing too," Addie pointed out.

"I'll be sure to tell Laurel," he said.

Her face lit up, then dimmed. "Amazing or not, we need to leave. The fire department's sweeping the building—and the minute they're done, the Consort will send more guards down here."

"We can't leave Simon," I protested.

"How are we going to explain two bodies, Del? They'll assume Lattimer had a heart attack or something, but a bullet wound is another story."

"We're not leaving him!" I cried, even as Addie tugged me toward the van. "I'm not abandoning him to the Consort."

"You won't," Simon assured me. "But we can't help him now. Let the fire department find him. They'll take him to the morgue. Once we're safe, we can figure out how to get him back."

I shook my head. "They don't know him! They won't take care of him the way . . ."

The way he deserved. It was cruel to leave him here.

"We'll come back for him," Simon assured me. "I swear it, Del. But right now we have to leave, or this will all have been for nothing."

I shook my head, pulling away and crossing back to kneel at Original Simon's side, taking his hand in mine.

"Would you rather go back to the oubliette?" Monty snapped. I glared at him, and he glared right back. "Say your good-bye, Delancey, and then do him proud. It's all we have left."

I smoothed his hair back, searching for the words. But nothing I could say would reverse this moment or save him, or give him the life he deserved. So I pressed a kiss to his forehead and touched the spot at the corner of his mouth, the place where his scar wasn't.

Monty's hand pressed hard on my shoulder. "It's time."

Numb and wordless, I climbed into the van. Before Simon

had pulled the door shut, Eliot was flooring the accelerator. We burst out of the shadowy garage into sunlight and freedom, but the frozen feeling remained.

Nobody spoke until we crossed the city limits. Finally, I said, "Did the Free Walkers cauterize the First Echo?"

"Doubtful," Monty said. "They won't cut it off unless their attack fails, and they're still trying to figure out how they'll get inside the building."

"How'd you manage?" I asked Addie.

"The only people allowed inside CCM were on Lattimer's short list. So we found some guards with similar features and . . . replaced them." She gave me a quick, sad smile. "Simon was right—a smaller team was better."

Eliot caught my eye in the rearview mirror, his eyes bloodshot and exhausted. "We're going to have to deal with the Consort. You're free, but they're still running everything—and we're terrorists."

"We're not the ones killing innocent people," I said.

"There's no proof," he replied.

"What about the laptop?" I asked. It had slid beneath Monty's seat, and I nudged it with my toe. "There's video of Lattimer admitting everything. If we can show it to the rest of the Walkers . . ."

"Two videos," Simon said, voice strained.

"What do you mean?" Addie asked.

"Every part of that building was under surveillance.

Including the parking garage," he said. "Which means there's a tape of Lattimer shooting me. Him."

"And of me cauterizing him," I whispered. "They won't be able to see the strings, but they'd know what they were seeing."

"They couldn't ignore that," Addie said, sitting up straight. "There's too much evidence."

"You'd be surprised what people can ignore," Monty said softly.

"Where's the footage kept?" Simon asked.

"It all feeds to the same server I hacked before," Eliot said. "I can pull it once we get somewhere with a Wi-Fi signal. But what do we do with it?"

"Get it to the Free Walkers?" Addie offered.

"Not the Free Walkers," I murmured, but only Simon heard me. He lifted his eyebrows in a silent question.

Original Simon had known he might die. Rose had warned him, and his animosity made a perfect, horrible sense. It wasn't only because my Simon had lived the life that should have been his, all those years he was on the run with the Free Walkers. It was the life my Simon was *going* to live. He'd known his death— and his Echo's survival—was the ultimate proof. He'd known the Free Walkers would sacrifice him for the greater good, and he'd gone along with it. He'd believed in it, and them, and their methods.

I wasn't sure I did.

The similarities between the Free Walkers and the Consort were too great to ignore. Their willingness to treat people like pawns, to conceal the truth for their own ends, to justify their actions in the name of a cause, to view dissent as something to be crushed rather than understood. Both were absolutely convinced of their nobility, but I wasn't. Not anymore.

"Whatever we do, it needs to be fast," said Addie. "You can bet the Major Consort's going to be all over this. Unless we can get it out quickly, they'll manage to cover it up."

"We could upload it to a public site on the Internet," Eliot said absently, checking his mirrors. "But there's no way to stop Originals from seeing it. Everyone would know."

"Maybe everyone should," I said, and leaned my head against Simon's chest. My hands were bloodstained but rock steady. "Maybe the time for secrets is over."

CHAPTER FORTY-SEVEN

ELIOT DROVE TO AN EXTENDED-STAY MOTEL near the airport. Laurel let us into the suite, so similar to the Free Walker base camp I half expected to see Rose come out of the adjoining room.

Simon must have read my mind, because he drew me inside, saying, "We didn't want to risk going anywhere the Consort might track. And we weren't sure how long we'd be here."

This was my life now: living out of motels, running from the Consort. Exactly as Addie had predicted. I stood in the middle of the room while Laurel, Addie, and Eliot conferred in the corner.

Simon helped me to a chair. "You need to rest. What can I do?"

"Coffee would be good."

"Chamomile tea," he replied. "The last thing you need is caffeine."

He caught Addie's eye, and she sat down next to me while he ducked into the tiny kitchenette.

"You're going to tag-team me, aren't you?"

"I would think you'd had enough alone time," she replied. "You look awful."

"I feel awful."

"You need a shower," she said. "Laurel brought some clothes that should fit you. We'll burn the stuff you've got on."

The appeal of being clean battled with the appeal of staying in one spot. But when I looked down at my shirt, stiff with blood—mine, Rose's, Simon's, the guard's—I couldn't argue.

Addie helped me to my feet as Simon brought in tea, steaming and fragrant. The paper cup was similar to the ones I'd stacked in the oubliette. Hands shaking, I pushed it back toward him, swallowing down bile. "No."

He took it away silently, exchanging a worried glance with Addie.

Addie led me to the adjoining room with a king-size bed and a typical, hotel-room cramped bathroom. She turned the shower on, the mirrors fogging up immediately, and left, promising clean clothes.

I was alone again, with only the rush of the water and the knocking of the pipes for company. I could hear the rest of the group down the hall, but they sounded distant, like they were miles away. Gingerly I peeled off my clothes, leaving them in a heap on the floor. I even untied the splint on my finger, hissing at the pain. We could reset it later. For now, I wanted to scrub away every trace of the day.

The spray burned, but I welcomed the distraction, letting it beat against my muscles until they began to ease. The water swirled at my feet—rusty, as the worst of the blood was washed away, then pink, and finally clear. But it couldn't carry away the memories, or my grief, no matter how many times I lathered and rinsed. Slowly I began to take inventory: the cuts and bruises purpling my skin, the broken finger, the lump at the base of my skull, the still-tender cheekbone. Even my scalp hurt, as I shampooed again and again, trying to coax the knots out.

For an instant I luxuriated in feeling clean, until I remembered where I was—in a strange shower with a line of bruises down my side and eyes gritty from tears—and I couldn't stand, not for a second longer. I crouched at the foot of the tub and wept for all we'd lost today, and how close we'd come to losing so, so much more.

And then Simon was pushing aside the curtain, turning off the water, easing me out of the tub, wrapping a cheap white towel around me.

"I'm here," he said, but I couldn't answer through my sobs.

Dimly, I heard Addie ask if she could help, but whatever he told her must have sufficed, because the door closed again, and he sank down to the floor, pulling me onto his lap. He tucked my head under his chin and stroked my hair, carrying away the grief as surely as the water had, bringing solace in exchange.

Eventually I sat back and studied him. His eyes, the dark glittering blue I'd missed so much, were quiet and worried. "Better?"

"I think so. Sorry," I said, gesturing to his soaked shirt. "I dripped all over you."

"It'll dry. Besides, if you think I'm going to complain about having a wet, naked girl on my lap, you don't know me at all."

"I'm wearing a towel," I pointed out, and smacked his shoulder.

"We need to get you bandaged up," he said, and I nodded. "You're going to be okay."

I didn't reply.

He scooped me up and carried me to Laurel's room, depositing me gently on the bed. "Sleep," he said. "I'll tuck you in."

"I keep seeing them. Rose, and Simon, and . . ." I brushed my fingers over the scar at the corner of his mouth. "He looked like you."

My breath hitched as the tears threatened again.

"Sleep," he said firmly, pointing to the stack of clothes Addie had left on the bed. "Can you get dressed on your own?" He stood at the edge of the bed, shifting from side to side.

"Yeah. Don't leave. Just . . . don't look." I didn't want him to see the bruises. Didn't want him to see the damage instead of the girl. I put on Laurel's clothes—a thin navy T-shirt and pajama pants, the cream-colored flannel sprinkled with stars.

The bedsprings squeaked as I sat on the edge of the mattress, and Simon turned around.

"Lie back," he said.

"He looked like you," I repeated. "He wasn't you, but I couldn't stop thinking . . ."

"I know the feeling," he said. "I woke up, and you were gone. All I could think about was that I knew what Lattimer had done to my dad, and I knew what he'd do to you."

"I had to," I said. "Rose, too. We bought the Free Walkers time."

"But it's not done," he said. "Let's say Eliot uploads that video, and the whole world knows about the Walkers. There's still tons of work to do."

"Then we'll do it," I said softly. "Together."

He traced my features, skimming along my hairline, over my good cheekbone, down my nose, across my lips. He kissed my eyelids and my mouth and my collarbone, featherlight and healing, the first touch that hadn't hurt since I'd crossed the threshold of CCM, days ago.

"He thought I'd stolen his life," he said. "I did, kind of."

"No. That was your father and Rose. Neither of you had a choice."

"I guess not. He didn't have to tell you about the cauterization, though. He could have died, and let the rest of us die along with him."

"He would never have done that," I said. "The Free Walkers used him, but he wasn't going to punish you for it. He was setting you free."

"We have to tell my mom," he said, bleak as midwinter.

"Tomorrow. We'll tell her tomorrow."

"What about Monty?" Simon asked.

"Let the Free Walkers handle him."

"He told you how to save me," he pointed out.

"He's the reason I lost you," I replied, and sighed. "I know. I get it now, how easy it would be to lose yourself when you look for someone. Rose lost herself too, I think, in the opposite way. She was so focused on the Free Walkers—on the mission—she lost all the people she was fighting for."

"I'm glad they got a few more days together," he said.

"What do you think he'll do now?" I asked.

"Keep going," he said. "What else can he do?"

I wasn't so certain.

The sound of a door easing open, then shut, woke me early the next morning. I slipped out of bed, and Simon reached for me. "I'll be back," I said. "Promise."

He froze, but let me go.

The suite was dark. Eliot slumped over the desk, snoring in the blue light of his monitor. Addie and Laurel curled together on the couch, fingers entwined. Monty was nowhere in sight.

I padded outside, not bothering to stop for a coat or shoes. Monty stood on the balcony, looking out at the sleepy city, the purple-blue dawn, and the winking red lights of planes landing and taking off. He wore a green parka and a plaid newsboy cap, gnarled hands gripping the railing.

"Where will you go?"

He turned, his face tired but pleased. "She's still out there."

"Grandpa," I said. Grandpa, not Monty, because it was like I had told Simon. I understood, finally. "She's gone. I saw it happen."

"Ashes to ashes, dust to dust," he said. "Think they'll hold a service?"

"I'll make sure of it."

He nodded. "I'm glad. Your mother could use some closure. Isn't that what Addison's always calling it?"

"You could stick around," I pointed out.

"Nah. That'll be her body. Her soul's what I loved. Her soul's what I've been chasing after all these years, and when she died, it left her. People aren't just atoms or cells or strings, Delancey. It's the movement within that makes a person, their music. When Rose died, the music went out of her and into the multiverse. She Walked through worlds and left a trail of that music, and I'm going to follow it."

"You'll get lost," I said. "You won't be able to find your way home."

"Sweet girl," he sighed. "How many times have I told you? Rose is my home, and she's everywhere."

"But—" *You'll never come back*, I wanted to tell him. But he already knew. I wrapped my arms around myself, shivering in the icy morning air.

"You're a better Walker than I ever was," he said looking out over the traffic.

I shook my head in protest, but he continued. "I taught you everything I knew, but it wasn't enough. I didn't have your heart, or your fight. I thought without Rose, I wasn't me, and it left me hobbled.

"You're entirely yourself, Delancey. It's why you're able to fight for that boy in there, and for Echoes you've never seen, and a future you can't imagine. You're strong in a way I'm not, and you can love in a way I couldn't. With your whole heart. It's a better way—to be complete, and love completely, instead of trying to fill a gap. And it's how I know you're going to be all right."

He shuffled over and kissed my cheek, the familiar scent of shaving cream and brown sugar wafting over me. My eyes filled, and he patted my hand. "It's all right. Nothing's lost. Nobody's ever lost, not truly. Just changed."

"Grandpa—" I paused. "Thank you. For teaching me."

"Oh, Del. My best, brightest girl. It was absolutely my pleasure."

He headed down the stairs, toward the stoplight at the corner. I dashed my hand over my eyes, and when I looked again, he had vanished, the sunrise catching on the edge of a pivot where he'd been standing a moment ago.

Inside, Simon pulled me back under the blankets, gently rubbing warmth back into my limbs.

"Monty's gone," I said.

"I figured."

"It'll kill him," I said. "He can't last out in the Echoes."

"No. But he'll be happier, for whatever time he has left."

"You don't hate him?" I asked.

"He saved my life," he said quietly. "He told us how to save you. It balances out."

And maybe it did. Maybe that was the secret of the multiverse, that tragedy was balanced out by joy—not canceled, but countered. Maybe what allowed the Echoes to keep unfolding was a delicate system of loss and growth, and we were no different. Entropy breaks the world apart, and love brings it back together.

CHAPTER FORTY-EIGHT

I SHOULD GO WITH YOU," ADDIE SAID, TWO days later. "What if they call the Consort again?"

"They won't," I said. "Not till they hear what I have to say. Once I've said it . . . I don't think they'll want to."

The news from CCM was a jumble. Lattimer's death had thrown the Consort into chaos—and the fact he'd killed an Original had given the Free Walkers' claims credibility. The Walkers were listening, and more importantly, asking questions. The Major Consort was stepping in, but even their presence couldn't gloss over the cracks in the Consort's facade.

I didn't doubt Prescott and her team were planning how best to shatter that facade completely, but we hadn't heard from them. I wondered if we would—if they still believed Simon was their weapon, or if they could start a revolution without him.

I simply wanted to say good-bye.

We were sitting in a distant Echo of my attic bedroom, on a burnt-orange velvet couch someone should have sent to the dump, and instead had stashed up here amid cobwebs and cardboard boxes.

"Do you think the Free Walkers will win?" I asked.

"I think the Consort is going to have to change," she said. "If you upload that video, there's no going back."

"That's what I'm counting on," I said. "What will you do?"

She nibbled a thumbnail, considering. "They'll have to rebuild. I could be good at that."

"You want a seat on the Consort?"

"If we even have one after this, maybe." I made a face, and she shrugged. "I'm not like you, Del. You see rules as something to be broken. I want to make better rules. I can't do that by taking off."

I bristled. "You think I'm bailing?"

"No. But we can't all be the leader of the rebel forces. I'll do what I can to help, with the Major Consort, with the fallout. But I want to do it my way."

"I wish Rose were here," I said, fingering the pendant Simon had returned to me. "I always thought I'd bring her home."

"We've got answers, at least. That's better than questions."

Was it? I couldn't help thinking that answers were an end. It was the questions—the asking and the searching—that made me feel most alive.

Addie gestured toward the pivot humming across the room. "Go on," she said. "Simon's waiting for us."

I approached the rift slowly, my good hand outstretched. My broken finger had been wrapped and splinted. We wouldn't know how much movement or sensation I'd lost until the splint came off, but this path was easy to follow.

I pushed my way into the Key World, into my quiet, dim bedroom. Light streamed through the octagonal window, highlighting the disarray the Consort had left behind after they'd searched for leads while hunting me. But there was a faint trace of dust on the music stand, and the musty smell of a closed-off room.

My entrance stirred the air, dust motes dancing in the shaft of light, my origami garlands—the few the Consort hadn't torn down—swaying gently. I went up on tiptoe to grab one, coiling the string around my hands and tucking it in my backpack.

There wasn't much I wanted to bring with me—some of my favorite sweaters and jeans, the sheet music I'd written with Simon, Rose's violin. I trailed a finger over the intricately carved music stand. Addie would take care of it. I might even come back someday, and the idea pleased me. I could come back, and I'd be different, and my place here would be different too. A song in a new key, a variation on a theme, a second movement. This was an ending, in the same way the horizon was both the end of the earth and the beginning of the sky.

Violin case in hand, I took the steep, narrow stairs to the first floor, past the music room with its jumble of silenced instruments, and down the hall to the kitchen, stopping before they saw me.

They sat at the kitchen island, the same one Addie and I had done homework at, and argued over, and rolled out cookies on for our entire lives. But it was swept clean now, empty of everything except teacups and their hands, loosely clasped. My mom dabbed at her eyes, as if pushing tears back inside, and gave a shuddering sigh. My father rubbed a thumb over her knuckles.

"They'll find her," he said softly. "They'll let us know as soon as they find her."

"I don't understand it," she said. "Where would she go? She knows how much trouble Del's in; she knows how it would look to disappear."

Addie. They were worried about Addie, which meant they thought I was still locked away at CCM.

"She's probably with Laurel," he said. "Or off on some assignment and they haven't tracked her down. At least Del's safe."

"Being in custody isn't safe, Foster. The Major Consort's not going to accept Del's apologies."

I stepped into the light. "I'm not apologizing. I haven't done anything wrong."

"Del!" The word came on a gasp. My mother flew across the room and wrapped her arms around me. "What on earth—why didn't you tell us they released you?"

My dad approached more slowly, taking in the bruises and cuts, the splint on my finger, the way I winced at my mom's embrace.

"Because they didn't," he said.

My mom's arms fell away.

I pushed my hair out of my face. "Addie's okay. She'll come by once things settle down."

"You're hurt," my dad said, and the words seemed to snap my mother out of her daze.

"Sit," she ordered, guiding me to my old chair. I let her ease me down, watched as she put on the kettle for tea. My hands rested in my lap, and my father looked at the splint, eyebrows raised.

"What happened?"

"Lattimer." The word burned as I said it, caustic in my throat.

"He promised us they only wanted to talk to you," my father said, eyes welling up. "He knew you were confused, that Monty had been manipulating you all along. He was sure that they could make you see sense. Prove to you that the Free Walkers were spouting nonsense."

"He talked to me in an oubliette. He gave me this." I held up my hand. "And this." I pulled my hair back so they could see the green-and-purple bruise of my cheekbone. "And more that you can't see."

My mom's eyes shimmered, her lips tightening, color draining from her face. "We didn't know, Del. You've always been so headstrong . . . we believed him. "

"You still do. All of you do." I shook my head. "I get it. Why you believe the Consort, why you fall in line."

"The Free Walkers," she murmured. "The boy who died . . . none of it makes any sense."

"It would, if you'd listen to me."

"It's the only way," my father said. "The Key World . . ."

"Is ours to protect. And so are the Echoes, whether you like it or not."

He drew a breath, but I held up my hand. "I'm not here to argue with you. You believe what you have to. It's going to change soon, and when it does, when the Walkers start over, maybe we can too. But that's not why I came."

My mom's fingers knotted together. I'd never noticed before that we all did it—Rose, my mom, Addie, and me. A nervous habit, fighting back the urge to reach for the strings, to reach for other people, to reach out and find comfort or strength or direction.

I covered her hands with mine. "Rose is dead. Not gone. Dead. She died helping me escape from the oubliette."

She rocked backward, taking the news like a blow, and my dad was beside her instantly. I'd always envied the bond between them, so strong that it crowded out the rest of us. Now I was grateful for it, because it meant that even after I left, they wouldn't be alone.

"Did she suffer?" my mom asked, barely a whisper.

My dad's eyes met mine. There is a limit to how strong any one person can be, and my mother had just reached hers.

Rather than break her, I bent the truth. "She was brave," I said. "She was smart and brave and fierce, right up to the moment she died."

"What about your grandfather?"

I exhaled slowly. "Without Rose, there was no reason for him to stay. He's Walking the Echoes. I don't think he'll come back."

She sank into the chair, shoulders shaking, face in her hands.

"And you?" my dad asked. "What are you going to do? Run from the Consort for the rest of your life? That's not a future. They'll find you again. Not through us, never again, but they will find you."

"They're going to have bigger problems to deal with, believe me."

"You can't leave," my mom said as I stood. "Del, please. We're sorry. We didn't know what they'd do, and if you stay, we can figure out some way to get you out of this. But you can't leave us, not now. Not after we almost lost you."

"You wanted me to choose my future," I reminded them, keeping my tone gentle. "And I have. But it's not here, and it's not among the Consort—not as it stands now."

"You're joining the Free Walkers? "

"I'm joining the rest of the world."

Addie was waiting for me on the front porch of the Echo, scowling.

So was Prescott.

"We need him back," she said. She looked painfully thin, eyes haunted behind her glasses.

"Addie," I said. "This is—"

"I know who she is," Addie replied uneasily.

Prescott held up her hands in a "hey look I'm harmless" gesture, and I realized Addie's distrust of Free Walkers wasn't entirely philosophical.

"We need Simon back," Prescott said. "We're about to go into CCM and we need proof. We've got the tape from the parking garage, but it's not enough. We need Simon, or nobody's going to believe us."

"How will he prove anything? Are you going to bring in his Echo and cauterize them, see who survives?"

"We wouldn't—"

"You'd do anything to serve your cause, same as the Consort. You would have let Simon's Original die to prove a point."

She flinched, her face going pale. "We'd hoped it wouldn't

turn out that way. We thought it might be possible for both of them to survive."

"But not probable." Addie touched my shoulder, but I shook her off. "I don't trust you and your people, Prescott. I don't like the way you lie. I don't like your dirty secrets, and the way you play God. I don't like how little you value the lives right in front of you. And do you know what I think's going to happen, if you waltz into the Consort and take them down? I think it'll be more of the same. You're so desperate to destroy them that you will become them. You want change? You want to make the Walkers better? Start by *being* better. Simon's life—and death—is more than enough."

I headed down the steps, Addie behind me.

"I grew up with him," Prescott called, and I turned to face her. "We weren't like you and Eliot—we moved around too much for that. But he was the closest thing to a friend I had, when I was a kid. And then when we were older, he was . . ." Her breath hitched.

"He was *your* Simon," I said, my anger dissipating as I realized the enormity of what she'd lost: Simon. Rose. Her mother.

"He might have been," she said, her voice thick. "This is all I have left now, Del. The mission. If we're going to destroy the Consort, we need Simon."

"I've had enough destruction," I told her. "I'd rather have a change."

CHAPTER FORTY-NINE

Simon was waiting for me at the ceme-
tery, as we'd planned. The gate protested as I shoved it open.

Instead of sitting along the stone wall, he was studying one of the
headstones, a marble angel, her features weathered to solemn grace.

"How did it go?"

I tried to shrug, but the world weighed too heavily to pull it
off. "They think I'm throwing my life away."

He brushed my hair back. "And what do you think? What
do you want your life to be?"

Snowflakes dusted his hair, and I caught one on the tip of
my finger. It melted instantly, as fleeting as the moments of quiet
Simon and I stole lately.

"I want it to matter," I said, remembering the feel of Park
World, how it disappeared at a touch, the price of my careless-
ness. "I can't make worlds, but I can change them. I want it to be
for the better."

He tucked my hand in his and led me out of the cemetery,
stopping to close the gate behind us, checking the latch. "Eliot
says we should be able to put a headstone in without too much
trouble. Laurel's handling the . . . other logistics."

The logistics of recovering Original Simon's body, he meant. I couldn't let him stay in the morgue. He deserved better, and so he'd be buried here, where Amelia could visit him. We couldn't bury him as Simon Lane, so the headstone would read, fittingly, "Gilman Bradley."

"How did she take it?" I asked.

He ran a hand over his face. "Hard. I think she was expecting it—expecting to lose one of us, anyway. She just didn't know which one of us it would be."

Grief was sneaky, impossible to guard against all the time, the way it ebbed and flowed, a tide that receded, leaving behind bits of memories as polished as glass, and then rushed back in to steal your breath.

I touched the button I kept in my pocket, turning it over in my fingers.

We stopped outside the house, the snow drifting down around us, and his eyes were serious as he spoke, halting and bewildered. "She knew, didn't she? About the swap. Why didn't she hate me?"

"People believe what they need to," I said carefully. "And sometimes, if they believe in something hard enough, it becomes true."

"What do you believe in, Delancey Sullivan?"

I reached up on tiptoe, brought his mouth to mine. "Us."

"Funny," he said. "So do I."

We entered through the back door. Addie and Laurel were there, arms around each others' waists, Addie's head on Laurel's shoulder. Eliot sat at the kitchen table, fingers flying over the

430

keyboard while Amelia, eyes swollen but face composed, sipped a cup of tea opposite him. Iggy whuffed in greeting, raced over to Simon for a rough and loving pat on the head, and returned to Amelia, who rubbed his ears between her fingers. Simon crossed the room and stood next to her, his hand on her shoulder, and she clasped his fingers tightly. I swallowed against the tears clogging my throat.

"You ready?" Eliot said.

"Yeah." I tugged off my coat and draped it over the back of the chair.

"I spliced together the footage from your interrogation and the parking garage, closed-captioned everything, and put your introduction up front. It's uploaded to four different servers already, so even if the Consort takes it down at one location, we'll be able to bring it back online without trouble."

Laurel shook her head, curls dancing. "Once it goes viral, there's nothing the Consort will be able to do."

"You're sure about this, Del? The Free Walkers aren't going to be happy. They wanted to protect the Echoes, not expose the Walkers."

The power of secrets lies in misdirection—in drawing the eye to what it wants to see, while hiding the truth away. There had been too many secrets, corroding lives and worlds in equal measure, so deeply buried that we didn't see the extent of the damage until it was nearly too late.

It was time for the truth. The light was only blinding until your eyes adjusted, and we would adjust.

I looked at Simon—half-Walker, half-Echo, woven into the Key World as strongly as his Original. The Walkers' hope and my future.

We would evolve, and be the stronger for it.

"I'm sure."

Simon left Amelia's side and stood behind me, wrapping his arms around my waist and resting his chin atop my head.

"Do it," I told Eliot, and he clicked a button.

The screen filled with a girl's face: reddish-brown hair pulled back in a messy braid, wisps falling into eyes ringed with exhaustion, cheeks hollowed with hunger, mouth tight with resolve.

Me. Not the girl of three months ago, but a new girl, rooted in the old one but grown beyond what she'd dreamed possible. A girl who had touched infinity and loved in particular and seen the fragility and resilience of the world. A girl with a purpose, and a future, and a calling all her own.

CHAPTER FIFTY

REALITY IS BIGGER THAN YOU THINK.

Every time you make a choice, the universe splits in two. You continue on, and the choice you didn't make creates an entirely new world. Every person. Every choice. It's been happening since time began, and it will never end, and there are more worlds than grains of sand in the ocean or stars in the sky or drops of rain.

There are people whose job it is to keep the worlds in harmony. We Walk between worlds, fighting off entropy. Protecting you. And you'd never know, because we've done it in secret.

I am done with secrets.

My name is Delancey Sullivan. I was born to fight entropy.

I lost.

I am not done fighting.

Neither are you.

The video rolled on, images of my interrogation. Of Simon, bleeding on the ground. Of my Simon, gasping back to life. But I didn't look at the past, at the battles we'd fought.

I looked at the counter at the bottom of the screen. At the page views, ticking steadily upward.

1

2

4

5

8

12

24

33

47

76

108

I looked at the truth, unfurling like the leaves of a tree, growing stronger every second, and our future along with it. The world we had shaped and the world we would tend, as carefully as we did each other.